The Country Gentleman

The Country Gentleman

Fiona Hill

ST. MARTIN'S PRESS

NEW YORK

THE COUNTRY GENTLEMAN. Copyright © 1987 by Ellen Pall. All rights
reserved. Printed in the United States of America. No part of this book may
be used or reproduced in any manner whatsoever without written permission
except in the case of brief quotations embodied in critical articles or reviews.
For information, address St. Martin's Press, 175 Fifth Avenue, New York,
N.Y. 10010.

Library of Congress Cataloging-in-Publication Data

Hill, Fiona.
   The country gentleman.

   I. Title.
PS3558.I3877C6   1987   813'.54   87-16312
ISBN 0-312-01016-8

First Edition

10 9 8 7 6 5 4 3 2 1

TO RICHARD
THIS BOOK IS SPECIALLY INSCRIBED
WITH ALL HER LOVE
BY THE AUTHOR

The Country Gentleman

ONE

MISS ANNE GUILFOYLE YAWNED MAGNIFICENTLY, stretched, stirred her chocolate with a silver spoon, examined the back of the spoon as if she had never seen one before, licked it, tapped it thoughtfully against her nose, stretched again, dropped the spoon into a China saucer, rubbed her cheeks, squinted at the morning sun streaming into the breakfast-room, and demanded of her companion what in the world had possessed them last night to engage to breakfast together this morning.

Maria Insel confessed that she did not know.

"Not to breakfast merely, but to breakfast at eleven o'clock," Miss Guilfoyle continued, holding the cream pitcher in the air and dreamily inspecting the glaze on its undersurface. "To meet here over food sufficient to keep us till Friday, when the truth is I cannot eat before two, and you never eat at all. We must have been mad." She traced with a long, delicate finger a small figure-eight in the condensation on the pitcher's side, then replaced it with a brief clatter on a China tray. "We must have been wildly mad; simply, frothingly, absolutely mad."

So saying, she pushed aside the empty plate before her, frankly folded her arms on the table, and dropped her head into them. She appeared to have subsided; but after a moment, "It frets the servants dreadfully," she went on from this posture, her voice slightly muffled by her jaconet muslin sleeve, "to be obliged to cook and serve at this hour—this frightful hour, when all good Christian souls lie snug in their beds. Let us pledge, Maria"—she set her chin upon the place where her arms crossed and looked over the table at Mrs. Insel—"never, ever, to meet for breakfast again."

Mrs. Insel, who did look rather as if eating was an occasion with her, smiled and gave her word. She was a narrow woman of some thirty years, dressed in a lavender which lightly suggested mourning, rather dark complected than otherwise, with a massive knot of chestnut hair weighing upon her neck and a short, modish frizzle spread across her bony forehead.

"Do not you think kippering a monstrous unkind fate for a salmon?" asked Anne, her eye happening to fall upon a plate of fish whose lot this had been. "To be plucked from the water, then kippered! Insult on the very heels of injury! I should not care even to be salted, while the mere notion of being smoked makes me positively shiver."

Maria laughed, then endeavoured to suppress a yawn.

"I saw that." Anne sat up again. "How polite you are. I

think you are even tireder than I. Did not you sleep well at Lady Seepes' last night? I had a wondrous easy chair, just behind one of the larger potted palms in the Egyptian Saloon. I dozed off about nine, I should guess, and did not stir till eleven. Most refreshing. Colonel Whiddon was telling me the story of his India days. Eat some toast, my dear." She slouched forward once more to collapse in a heap upon the table; her slurred murmur continued, "It will make Cook feel she has been useful."

Maria obligingly picked up a piece of toast, but she did not eat it. Instead she gazed, with a sisterly, almost a maternal affection, at the golden crown of her friend's cradled head. At the same time her fingers absently tore the toast to bits. It required no very shrewd observer to see in that unconscious action, or for that matter in Mrs. Insel's whole person and demeanour, a certain tendency to nerves, even some particular strain, the reason of which was not immediately apparent.

As for the other lady, nerves (she had occasionally remarked) somehow failed to interest her. Whatever pleasures spasms, swoons, and sensibility might hold for some females, they could not tempt Anne Guilfoyle. At the vigorous age of eight-and-twenty she slept soundly, ate well (though admittedly, not earlier than two o'clock), regularly took such modest exercise as could be had in the Park, and altogether enjoyed her life thoroughly. She had an open and inquisitive nature; everything—Colonel Whiddon's India days excepted—interested her; she read widely, considered closely, and was well known among the London *ton* as that rare thing, a woman of wit. Indeed, a few whispered that she was the "A." whose satiric letters to the *Times*—letters describing the fashionable exploits of the writer's friend Lord Quaffbottle—had last year obliged so many gentlemen to hide the numbers of 12 and 15 June, not to mention 2 July, from their wives. Whether these rumours sprang from truth, Miss Guilfoyle declined to say; in either case, her intelligence had won her a place in society not the less remarkable for being substantially above that to which mere birth or fortune would have entitled her.

This achievement had had its cost, however. Perhaps, more than one matchmaking mamma said with unmistakable smugness, perhaps if Miss Guilfoyle had kept a little more to her own sphere, she would no longer be Miss Guilfoyle, but Mrs. Someone, or even Lady Who. Anne, only daughter of Sir James Guilfoyle, Bart., and the well-dowried Miss Bowman that was, should have had fair prospects of finding a suitable husband. She had not been an unattractive girl; some ladies who had witnessed the event even admitted (now) that at her come-out she had been quite lovely. But that was eleven years ago, and she was a girl no more. Graceful, yes. Manners such as must please, yes. A spirit most lively, most winning, granted without argument. One might even say that—if one liked the sort of thing—her trim, rather athletic figure, her blond curls and fair complexion, her China-doll nose and jade eyes were still rather pretty. But the first bloom of youth had gone from her, the *doyennes* agreed with satisfaction, never to come again. Miss Guilfoyle she was and Miss Guilfoyle would remain, and much happiness might her celebrated wit bring her.

The object of these hearty good wishes now raised her head (a movement which appeared to require a Herculean effort), observed the pile of crumbs to which Maria had reduced her toast, blinked at it, blinked at her, and declared, "My dear, I move this breakfast be pronounced an abysmal failure and adjourned immediately. All in favour, Aye. All opposed? Motion carries." She stood. "Reconvene in the Garden Saloon in forty-five minutes." She lightly blew a kiss to her companion and staggered away.

So did the two ladies part and remove themselves to their several chambers, leaving the breakfast-room empty. It is no very common thing to find a domestic establishment composed solely of two young females (females, that is to say, who are visibly no sort of kin to one another) and the reader may wonder without impertinence how it came to be. As it happens, Anne and Maria had known each other since, indeed before, they could remember. Miss Guilfoyle, as has already been noted, was the daughter of a baronet. Sir James and Lady Guilfoyle had had two children, but the son dying of the smallpox at age three, Anne was raised very nearly as an only child. The family resided at Overton, not far from the village of Eling-on-Duckford, Northants., where Guilfoyles had lived since the reign of Henry VIII. Sir James being the local magistrate, and Overton by a good measure the finest property in the county, the importance of the family was universally acknowledged. It need hardly be added that Anne, the only surviving child and a precocious one at that, was petted, admired, and indulged with a similar universality.

Her bosom friend was Maria Pilkinton, of Halfwistle House, some eight miles distant. Maria's father was a gentleman, but idle and of small means. Only his family was large; indeed, Halfwistle House would have needed to be Twicewistle House to accommodate them all comfortably. Mrs. Pilkinton's tongue, sharp to begin with, grew sharper, for economy makes a fine whetstone. Altogether, Maria's happiest days were passed outside her own family, with that of Sir James. The girls were almost of an age, and Lady Guilfoyle being of a generous and motherly disposition, Maria became almost as familiar to her as her own daughter.

When Anne was twelve, however, and Maria thirteen, Sir James died of a sudden fever. Overton passing to his brother Frederick, who with his young family promptly came to claim it ("Showing all the politeness and restraint of a pack of ravening hyenas," Lady Guilfoyle quietly remarked to Anne), its erstwhile mistress at once determined to remove with her daughter to London. She had never cared for Frederick, still less for his pickthank wife and spoiled children, and their conduct on the occasion of Sir James' death resulted in more or less of a clean break, and a settled animosity. Happily for her, her ladyship had money on her Bowman side, and with this she engaged the house at number 3, Holles Street whose breakfast-room has just been abandoned.

Naturally the girls parted. Letters and visits prevented their total estrangement, but the differences in their backgrounds began inevitably to tell, Maria showing more and more the sobering effects of a straitened and unhappy country household, Anne the stamp of freedom and town life. For in London Anne's education decidedly broadened. She had always shown an extraordinary, a voracious intelligence. (Her governess, Miss Gully, had already confessed herself sadly outstripped by her student, and went to London more as companion to her ladyship than as any sort of teacher.) Now all manner of tutors and scholars were made available to her. When her mother—a woman of no mean understanding herself, and of a sociable temperament—came out of mourning and began to entertain, the girl was permitted, though only thirteen, to join the company, matching wits with fully developed minds.

Maria learned to expect letters from her whose rich ab-
struseness she could never aspire to equal; in her periodic
visits to Holles Street she got in the habit of saying little
when Anne was by. The conversation at Lady Guilfoyle's
dinner table, though perhaps not quite brilliant, gave the
girl plenty to sharpen her mind upon; and she profited by
this opportunity with as much enthusiasm and pleasure as
by her riding and dancing lessons.

When the girls were seven- and eighteen Lady
Guilfoyle offered to bring Maria Pilkinton out along with
Anne. Mrs. Pilkinton being only too glad to relieve the
household of a mouth, Maria was duly sent. She arrived in
London to find her girlhood friend following politics with
a keen interest, talking military strategy with men who
commanded regiments, playing the pianoforte to perfection, speaking French and reading German, composing
yards of rhymed couplets extemporaneously—arrived to
find her, in short, rather more clever (much more, some
said) than a young lady strictly needed to be.

So it was not surprising that, though her first season
brought Anne plenty of admirers, admire them she could
not.

"Jests on the topic of drinking!" she exclaimed to Maria
as they prepared for bed one April night following a dinner in particularly select company in Berkeley Square.
They had been presented at St. James' only the week before; Maria was quite entranced with the glitter and ac-
tivity of the Season already, but "Did I say jests?" Anne
went on. "Essays, novels rather! Sagas of bagged pheasant! Epics of pugilism! Whist, and wagers," she splut-
tered, seizing the brush from her abigail and savagely
dragging it through her own curls, "and—and waistcoats!
Are these the gentlemen whose good opinion we are ex-

pected to cultivate? Are these the celebrated wits of our time, of our nation?" And Maria was startled to see her burst into tears. "I am disappointed," she cried, violently wiping the tears away. "Forgive me, my dear, but I am so very disappointed."

Maria comforted her, though she could not join very deeply in her sentiments. Her own understanding was good, but not much above the common. She had found the conversation that evening perfectly acceptable, even bracing. As for Sir James' relict, too late did she perceive the miscalculation she had made in their daughter's education. "Bluestocking!" went the stern, whispered verdict round among the oracles of fashion; while meanwhile the young bluestocking sank deeper into dejection.

But then, *mirabile dictu*, one night changed all this. It was at Almack's late in May, as the Season reached its height. A tall, fair gentleman with an open, handsome countenance asked Lady Jersey to introduce him to Lady Guilfoyle. This favour granted, it soon became clear he had wished to know the mother solely in order to know the daughter, whom he had seen and (like many other gentlemen, for she was excessively pretty) hoped to ask to dance. And when his hopes had been answered and the dance accomplished, and a glass of lemonade brought to Anne by her partner, Maria and Lady Guilfoyle observed from across the room the two of them begin an extremely animated discussion—and not merely begin, but prolong and pursue it so heedlessly of their surroundings that her ladyship finally felt it best to dispatch Maria to interrupt the colloquy.

This tall, fair gentleman was soon to become familiar to the ladies as George, Lord Ensley, second son of the Marquess of Denbury. In the carriage on their way home to

Holles Street that night Anne sang his praises: Lord Ensley was so agreeable; he was amazingly intelligent; fancy his being secretary to a secretary of Henry Addington at twenty-three! They had not agreed on every thing—Anne had thought they might come to cuffs on the subject of taxation—but how well informed he was! How interested to hear her own views! Lady Guilfoyle and Maria exchanged glances and smiles while Anne chattered on: finally, a break in the gloom, a gentleman Anne could like.

In the morning Lady Guilfoyle set about her researches. A series of discreet questions dropped in the course of three or four well-chosen calls and she had her answer. It was not the one she had hoped for: every one agreed Ensley would never offer for Anne. Denbury was in no immediate need, but the estate was failing, the family fortune much reduced. The oldest son having run off to Scotland last year to wed the dowryless, rather vulgar Miss Burnham, it was clear that Ensley must marry to bolster up both the finances and the consequence of his family. Miss Guilfoyle was all very well, but Ensley needed a brilliant connexion. Thus the oracles.

Disappointed yet resigned to her duty, Lady Guilfoyle went home and told her daughter what she had learnt.

But, "Good heavens, ma'am!" answered that lady. "May not a girl enjoy a civilized conversation with a gentleman without marrying him?"

Lady Guilfoyle was tempted to reply that no, a shrewd girl might not; but she held her tongue, and so began the pattern of Anne's life. To oblige her mother, she danced with other admirers, accepted their offers to ride out in the park or to take her in to supper; but all her affection was reserved for Ensley. Now they seemed to meet him every where; and each occasion, Lady Guilfoyle knew, only strengthened the regard between him and her daughter. For ("More's the pity," her ladyship tartly observed to Maria) it was soon clear that Ensley returned Anne's partiality with equal fervour. Indeed, if the spiteful matchmaking mammas had a legitimate complaint to lay at Anne's door, it was that (without in the least benefiting by it herself!) she utterly absorbed the so eligible Lord Ensley, and prevented him from looking elsewhere.

The girls' first Season closed upon this situation. Lord Ensley went home to Denbury; the Guilfoyle ladies, with Maria, embarked upon a long chain of visits to friends in various counties. Perhaps, during this interlude, Ensley endeavoured not to think of Anne; perhaps Anne likewise set herself to forget Ensley. If so, their efforts went for nought. Maria believed that her friend had not at first credited the justice of Lady Guilfoyle's prediction. By the time she did it was too late: Anne was in love. Whatever the case, when, quite without expecting it, the Guilfoyle party discovered themselves engaged to stop through the whole of January at a house where Lord Ensley also was a guest, the two young people renewed their acquaintance with a delight and a naturalness that made Lady Guilfoyle's heart sink.

At about this time, Lady Guilfoyle began to be ill. Mother and daughter returned to London in the middle of February; Maria went back at last to Halfwistle House. The irony of her passing nearly a year in London yet remaining unattached, only to encounter her future husband the very week she went home (her older brother Frank brought him there, a very dashing Captain Insel, of Frank's own regiment), was widely, and humorously, remarked upon for many months in the neighbourhood of Eling-on-Duckford. The wedding came in April, but

Anne Guilfoyle was conspicuously absent: her mother had succumbed to a wasting fever and died in March.

The bereaved Miss Guilfoyle remained in London, spurning a half-hearted invitation from Overton to make her home there once more. With Miss Gully to chaperon her, her mother's fortune to support her, and the sedatest entertainments of the Season for diversion, she set about, deeply grieving, to make number 3, Holles Street her own establishment. How welcome, then, was the warm friendship of Lord Ensley! How comforting his attentions! Maria being gone with her new husband to Canada (her brother's battalion, unhappily, was posted elsewhere) Ensley became the solace of Anne's mourning. This new Season, and every Season after that for ten years, she owned openly to a particular friendship with him. And when her mourning was over, she went out into society not to find a husband, but to talk, and argue, and laugh. Which, as the reader has heard, she succeeded in doing extremely well, ever more gaily, and within increasingly rarefied circles.

A soberer and more nervous Maria than had left it returned to Holles Street some eight years later, just when Miss Gully's retirement could be postponed no longer. She wore black, then lavender, and spoke little of her husband, who was generally understood to have been killed accidentally during manoeuvres. Mrs. Insel's spirits gradually lightening with the passing of time, the house at Number 3 became first comfortable, then happy again; and thus do we find its occupants this July morning: Maria still in lavender but tolerably cheerful, Anne unmarried, nearly twenty-nine, hearty, merry, and looking forward (as no very great coincidence would have it) to dining at Celia Grypphon's that night in company with Ensley.

As to Ensley, Anne had come to accept that he would

someday marry. She supposed herself reconciled to the eventuality. Indeed, as he postponed it from year to year, the prospect had aged and mellowed till (she quite believed) it had lost its sting. She understood his position; had he offered for her she would have reproached him for talking nonsense; anyway, the slightly vulgar former Miss Burnham having thus far produced no heir, Ensley's wife must at the least be quite young, with a good many bearing years before her. An attribute, she needed no one to tell her, which no longer applied to Anne.

The Garden Saloon was so called on account of its being hung all over with paper that convincingly depicted an ivy-covered trellis. It was a small sitting-room at the back of the house, in which the ladies generally passed together an hour or two of the earlier part of their day. They re-met there on this day more or less punctually, Maria with a basket, Anne with a book. The weather, now they were awake enough to see it, they perceived to be perfectly awful, hot without being sunny, close and hinting at rain without raining. "Too oppressive for exercise or errands," they agreed, and throwing wide the windows to receive such paltry and fetid ventilation as was to be had from the alley, each settled to her chosen task. Anne obliged herself to read again a particularly dense passage in Kant's *Critique of Pure Reason*, which she was determined to understand if it killed her, while Maria profited by the morning light to work a bit of specially fine filagree. And so, in a silence broke by nothing louder than the turning of a page, they sat together some half hour.

Into this quiet intruded first the knock, then the venerable head, of Dolphim, Miss Guilfoyle's butler. He bowed, then presented to his mistress a letter only just arrived—a letter of business, she saw as she took it, from her solicitor, Mr. Nicodemus Dent. Guiltily relieved by the distraction, she closed a silver marker into her Kant and opened the letter at once.

Maria, who had looked up, seen Dolphim, seen the letter, and looked down at her filagree again, was startled a minute later to hear, "Good heavens!" and again, "Gracious God!" burst from her friend. She dropped her work to her lap and regarded Anne in some alarm; but as the exclamations were immediately followed by a rich peal of laughter, her emotion changed to mere curiosity. She observed Anne turn the paper over, read farther, then heard her laugh again. She was just on the point of demanding to know what was in it when, looking up and waving the paper about in amused delight, Anne addressed her: "My dear Maria, imagine it! I am the beneficiary of a will."

Mrs. Insel obligingly responded to this news with eager applications of "Whose?" and "What?"

Anne settled the page in her lap again and, referring to it now and then, informed her, "My great uncle Herbert Guilfoyle. Do you recall, we saw the notice of his death not long ago?"

"Of Cheshire, was not he?"

"The very same."

"But you said you remembered meeting him only once, in childhood—"

"I was twelve. My father had just begun to ail, and his uncle came to see him. What a queer man he was! The veriest eccentric. He refused to speak to me till I had read Jean-Jacques Rousseau. Fancy saying so to a girl of twelve!"

"Fancy!" Then, as Anne seemed to have fallen into a reverie of sorts, Mrs. Insel hinted, "It is difficult to imagine what he may have left you. Not a copy of *La Nouvelle Heloïse,* perchance?"

"Not at all. Or rather, perhaps he has, for he's left me his entire estate."

"But my dear," Maria said, wondering in this case at her friend's light tone (for she could not help thinking it would be no small thing to her to be left a home of her own), "that is very fine indeed! How peculiar, yes; but also, how fortunate, how kind."

Anne laughed again. "You have not heard all, my love; I told you he was eccentric. My great uncle leaves me—" She scanned the page, frowning lightly, for some particular word. "Here it is. 'Linfield, at Faulding Chase in Cheshire, its house, its land, and its income'—*providing I reside there ten months a year!* Having—let me see, where is it? Oh yes, here: 'Having a horror most particular and principled of a landlord who knows not the condition and character of his tenants, his lands, his etc. etc. . . .' Hm; Oh yes, here we are again. 'Having such a particular horror, the estate is left to his only surviving relation of whom he at least knows no certain evil—'" Anne paused to smile at the thought of Frederick hearing that. "'The estate is left to his great niece Anne Guilfoyle on condition she reside there—' Well, what I told you. 'In the event the above-named Miss Guilfoyle prove whether unwilling or unable to conform to this provision, either now or at any future time, the estate and all its' so on and so forth 'to pass irreversibly to—'" Anne ran a finger along the lines, searching again. "Ah, to 'Mr. Henry Highet, Gentleman, Fevermere, Faulding Chase, Cheshire—'" She folded the letter and looked up, finishing, "Whose lands apparently adjoin those of my great uncle."

Mrs. Insel, who did not appear to share her friend's hilarity, inquired, "But surely you may sell it? It is not to pass to Mr.—Mr. Highet for nothing?"

"As I read it, it is indeed."

"But how unkind of your great uncle. To offer such a gift, yet at the same time remove it by his terms."

"I am relieved to hear you say so; for a moment I half feared, from the seriousness of your countenance, that you intended to suggest I accept the bargain."

"No, indeed not. It is only that I dislike to see such a boon pass through your hands."

"Your concern is generous," Anne smiled, "but pray recollect this particular boon is, thank heaven, as unneeded by us as it was unlooked for. If we acccepted only half the invitations we receive to stop in the country we should never be in London at all; what use have we for an estate? I know nothing of farming and less of Cheshire, and the more I think of that the better I like it. Imagine passing ten months a year in the country—the deepest country! It makes one's blood run cold. Why, every thing to make life agreeable, to give it order and pleasure"— Maria knew she thought of Ensley—"is in London. And consider: it must be a two days' journey at least from here to Chester. That would leave us . . . let me see, taking July and August in town, since they are the two longest together—fifty-eight days in London annually. Good God! 'Tis not to be thought of." And she rose at once to go to a large library table. "I shall tell Mr. Dent I decline the legacy with respectful thanks," she went on, sitting down and collecting paper and pen, "and you and I, my dear, will never mention this painful, I may even say cruel, suggestion again." She dipped her pen. "'3 July, 1816,'" she read aloud as she wrote. "'My dear Mr. Dent—'"

"You don't suppose we ought at least to visit the property before you refuse it," Maria suggested timidly. "After all, the Season will shortly dwindle to nothing, and we might spare a week or two—"

"Have you forgot we are engaged to go down to Devonshire?" Anne interrupted rather sharply.

Mrs. Insel had not forgot. Lord and Lady Bambrick had invited them, and Lord Ensley was to be there too, until Parliament reconvened. At which time, Mrs. Insel had no doubt, Anne would discover some business to bring her back to town as well. Maria sighed. She would have been glad to see a little less, all in all, of Lord Ensley. She esteemed him very much; but she could not help feeling he had done her friend an ill service over the years. His constant attendance on Anne had done more than delay his own marriage: it had impeded—practically speaking, had prevented—hers. In the last weeks, moreover, Mrs. Insel had heard, not rumours exactly, but hints, intimations of the coming of an announcement she doubted very much Miss Guilfoyle was prepared for. Though perhaps she was prepared; perhaps Ensley had told her. One couldn't know with them, they were very deep and secret together. At all events, she let drop the idea of a visit to Cheshire. Really, it was an impossible offer. Mr. Herbert Guilfoyle must surely have been a quite impossible man.

Mrs. Insel was roused from these thoughts by a fresh burst of laughter from her friend, who had lifted her pen and sat gazing at her. "It has just occurred to me to wonder," she said, "what manner of person Mr. Highet, Gentleman, might be. Unless he is a saint, I cannot suppose he would have been very happy to meet his new neighbours—had we accepted, that is to say. He would very probably have done what he could to make Cheshire a living Hell for us. Careless of my great uncle not to foresee that."

"Perhaps Mr. Highet is unaware of the terms of the will," Maria suggested.

"Perhaps. I wonder. My great uncle seems to have had little doubt he would fulfill its conditions. From what Mr. Dent writes here, he made no provision for the case of his refusing."

"Indeed! That does sound rather as if they had agreed upon it," Maria remarked. "But possibly Mr. Highet is quite settled in his ways. He may be a country gentleman altogether. How old was Mr. Herbert Guilfoyle on his decease?"

"I should think at least five-and-seventy. Perhaps as old as eighty."

"Then very likely the neighbour for whom he shows so marked a partiality is elderly as well. The observed habits of a lifetime must have reassured Mr. Guilfoyle."

Anne conceded the likelihood of this explanation and was about to return to her letter when she lifted her pen again and said, "In either case, figure to yourself the pleasure my refusal must occasion. I feel positively virtuous, bringing an old man such satisfaction. I envision him rubbing his frail hands together with glee, then perhaps calling for a horse—if he is still able to ride—and venturing forth to survey his new property."

"I see him summoning his good wife, a little younger than himself it may be, and obliging her to guess what has occurred."

"Which she will never guess in a million guesses, he of course assures her—"

"But which, shrewder than he, she will divine at once. Oh yes, Anne, indeed they will be gratified."

"And let us wish them joy," Anne murmured, finally bending her head and writing in earnest.

But her pen had not scratched out three lines before Dolphim reappeared, this time bearing a card.

"Ensley," thought Maria to herself; but,

"The very thing," Anne announced, when she had read it. "Mr. Dent, in person. Pray show him in, Dolphim." She crumpled up the letter, then rose to resume the armchair she had vacated before.

Mr. Dent was a white-haired, cherub-cheeked man, benign and compact, much given to hurrying both in speech and movement. He hurried into the room now, his neat head ducking briskly by way of greeting. Anne had known him since she was ten, for he had been her father's solicitor, then her mother's, before he was her own. He acted for her in every kind of business: It was he who had first found the house in Holles Street, he who negotiated yearly with the owner for its lease, he who had explained to her the terms of her mother's will, he who oversaw its execution. Mr. Dent had had white hair and had hurried for as long as Anne could remember. She now returned his bow cordially, for she liked him; but she was surprised to see, on looking more closely into his face, that his cherub cheeks sagged, and his kind eyes were pink.

"Are you well, sir?" she asked seriously, waving him into a chair.

Mr. Dent thanked her, bowed to Mrs. Insel, and sat, immediately drawing from his pocket a large white handkerchief, with which he swabbed his damp brow. "Not well," he then gasped out, speaking as it seemed with the utmost difficulty.

Anne stood and pulled the bell. "I shall have some orgeat fetched; or do you prefer a cordial?"

Mr. Dent, looking down and again mopping his brow with his left hand, signalled no with his right.

"The heat . . ." Mrs. Insel began vaguely.

"Exactly. The heat, sir, is very great. I am afraid it must have affected you. Perfectly natural, but—"

At this moment Dolphim, an elderly man himself, appeared, gave an assessing glance to their guest, and vanished again on his commission.

But Mr. Dent repeated his negative gesture, stuffed his handkerchief away, and, with a visible effort, said, "Miss Guilfoyle, I must beg to speak with you privately."

Anne, tentatively reseating herself, smiled and replied, "Pray consider that we are private, sir, for I have no secret from Mrs. Insel. Indeed, I know what business you are come upon. We were speaking of it just now. I had begun a letter to you—"

But she fell silent, for Mr. Dent had again dropped his head into his left hand and with his right was waving frantically for her to stop.

"Not that, not that," he managed to squeak out.

Mrs. Insel and Miss Guilfoyle exchanged a glance: Mr. Dent was clearly worse, terribly agitated, perhaps about to faint. "Hartshorn," Anne mouthed silently, and Maria at once left the room to fetch it.

"Good," breathed Mr. Dent, and began, "I am not ill. I beg you will not alarm yourself—"

He was interrupted by Dolphim, who set down a tray and departed. Anne poured a glass of cool orgeat, gave it to the visitor, and forbade him to speak till he had drunk it all, silently deploring the while that social code which teaches men (even old men) to conceal their frailties. Not until Mr. Dent had handed her his empty glass would she resume her chair; and even then she wished Maria would return with the hartshorn, for Mr. Dent looked very poorly indeed.

"Miss Guilfoyle," he brought forth, after a deep, audible breath.

"Mr. Dent," she answered, meaning to beg him not to continue till Maria rejoined them; but,

"You are ruined," he at last brought forth, "and I am the cause of it."

This said, he appeared to breathe more easily; Anne did not. "I beg your pardon?" she said, but at the same time felt her heart begin to race. "I did not understand you."

"I say, you are ruined. Your fortune, your inheritance . . ." One hand fumbled for his handkerchief, the other clutched expressively the air. "Gone," he said.

"Gone?" Anne felt the colour drain from her cheeks, her forehead suddenly go moist and cold. Just then Maria entered, started to move towards Mr. Dent, caught sight of Anne and changed courses. But by the time she reached her, Anne had begun to feel her senses returning. Waving away the hartshorn, she straightened and hoarsely murmured, "Maria, Mr. Dent says—" Her throat seemed to close. She stopped, smiled dazedly, and said, "I cannot say it." She swallowed and tried again. "Mr. Dent says my fortune is gone."

Mrs. Insel turned to him questioningly, at the same time holding and chafing Anne's chilly hands.

"Miss Guilfoyle, are you certain you desire . . . ?" His voice trailed away interrogatively. He seemed stronger now that his news had been broke.

"No secret from Maria," Anne repeated feebly.

"As you wish it. Let me explain—but before that, pray allow me to say, that if I could change by any act the story

I have to tell—if even my own death could alter it a little—I would not shrink from that act for all the world.
You behold me a broken man, Miss Guilfoyle, for you
must comprehend—well, but I had best begin at the beginning."

And so he did. Gradually recovering, if not his vigour,
at least his composure, Mr. Dent recalled to Miss
Guilfoyle a certain merchant ship, the *Maidstone*, of which
he had spoke to her some seven months before. The ship
then preparing for a trading journey to the East, and Mr.
Dent having received thoroughly reliable information as to
its excellent prospects for doubling, nay perhaps trebling,
the money of those who cared to invest in it, he had taken
the opportunity to increase the wealth not only of Miss
Guilfoyle but of some half-dozen of his clients, and for
that matter, himself ("But of this I say nothing, this I pass
over, mentioning it only to demonstrate, to prove . . ."
his voice trailed away), by putting into this ship the better
part, in a few cases all, of their fortunes. He hoped Miss
Guilfoyle recalled giving her consent?

Miss Guilfoyle nodded.

Good. Now then, the *Maidstone* had indeed done well;
a report received two months ago indicated the likelihood,
even the certainty, of the voyage's fulfilling Mr. Dent's
most sanguine hopes. A month ago she was reported
speeding towards home. But— But—

Mr. Dent fortified himself with another glassful of
orgeat.

But. The ladies had surely heard of the recent savage
acts of certain Algerine pirates off the Barbary coast, in
which English vessels were attacked and sunk, their crews
murdered. To be brief, then, such had been the fate of
the *Maidstone*. This morning early came the report: the

ship lost, all hands lost, and the precious cargo . . . Alas, Mr. Dent hardly needed to say . . .

By now Anne had recovered enough to think. Indeed she knew well of the insults practised by the Algerines on English merchants. An expedition was even now preparing under Lord Exmouth to retaliate. She and Ensley had, not a se'ennight ago, discussed what effect the raid would likely have on English relations with Turkey. But how little she had dreamed, then—! All her fortune sunk!

Maria was protesting, "But was not it insured? Surely Lloyd's . . . ?"

Dent shook his head. "I assumed as you do . . . The owners assured me . . . But in fact—" He fell silent, then spoke again. "Naturally I reserved some part of your funds to meet your needs while the ship was yet at sea. Of which funds, some four— Some four—" Mr. Dent's voice caught in his throat; he coughed, drank, coughed again. "Some four hundred pounds still remain."

"Four hundred?" Anne echoed, almost inaudibly. It was a pittance, a nothing. Twenty pounds a year to live on, and Maria to keep as well, not to mention—

"If I had any money," Mr. Dent was saying, "God knows I would give it you gladly. When I think of Sir James' trust in me, when I recollect—" Mr. Dent shuddered and could not go on. Anne understood for the first time that his eyes were pink from crying. Probably this was not the first call of this nature he had made that morning. Her initial flare of anger at him softened: If she knew anything, she knew that Mr. Dent wished her nothing but good. If he had erred, he had done so from a generous wish to enrich her, nothing else. The realization of what his feelings must be eased hers a little.

"Dear sir," she said in a low tone, "I beg you will not

distress yourself. I am fully conscious of your many kind acts—"

But as Mr. Dent looked like weeping again, she stopped. "I recommend to you, Miss Guilfoyle," he said, swallowing hard, "that you remove to Northamptonshire at once and take up residence at Overton again. Your Uncle Frederick will, I am certain, gladly receive you, and I believe that if you remove at once, I can persuade the owners of this house to restore to you the balance . . ." His voice faded away again before he added, as delicately as possible, "You see, to stop here any longer would be a gross extravagance, given your—given your position." Here Mr. Dent once more produced his capacious hand-kerchief and this time buried his whole face in its folds.

Maria had never ceased to hold Anne's hand. Now she squeezed it valiantly and whispered, "Do not think of me, my dear. I shall do very well." For, as anyone could tell from the colour of Mrs. Insel's face, she lived entirely dependent of Miss Guilfoyle.

Anne straightened. "Nonsense," she said. "I had rather take up pickpocketing than live with Frederick. No doubt he would take me in—and you too," she added, with an answering squeeze to Maria, though in truth she doubted it very much, "But it is not to be thought of. Mr. Frederick Guilfoyle deeply insulted my father, my mother, and me. I will not return to Overton."

What she was really thinking as she made this proud declaration, was that she had to provide not only for herself and Maria, but for Dolphim, and her abigail, Lizzie, and Cook, and Mrs. Dolphim, who kept house, and the parlour-maid, Minna, and John Coachman, and that little Sally he had just taken to wife, and . . . The world seemed to waver before her. To think she had waked that morning with nothing on her mind save breakfast!

"If you would consider it," Mr. Dent was saying, his voice brimming with anguished shyness, "Mrs. Dent and I would be extremely honoured by your presence in our household. Both your presences," he added to Mrs. Insel, though obviously wondering at the same time he said it where on earth he would put these ladies should they accept. "It is only the most humble cottage in—"

"Bless you, Mr. Dent," Anne broke in firmly, "but we could not think of so burdening you. We will never forget your generous offer."

"But in that case," Mr. Dent objected, though ceasing to urge his most recent suggestion, "where in the world will you live?"

Anne was silent, thinking. Could they traipse about like gypsies, stopping first with one friend, then another? It might answer for the summer, but—how would she pay the servants, how cover the expense of travelling? And how long could—

"Cheshire," Maria Insel declared.

"My dear?"

"We must take your great uncle's house in Cheshire."

"Gracious God! I had completely forgot it," Anne exclaimed.

"I too. Since this morning, I have no thought but . . ." Mr. Dent subsided. The truth was, unless his son assisted him, he was destitute.

Maria, for the moment the only one of the three not in danger of dissolving into tears, inquired as calmly as she could whether Mr. Dent had ever visited Linfield.

Mr. Dent had not. Mr. Herbert Guilfoyle had been in the habit of coming up to town once every five years (the ladies heard this number with a shiver) to transact his business with Mr. Dent. In the most recent years, advancing age having made travel inadvisable, Mr. Guilfoyle had sent his steward, an excellent man by the name of Rand, if Mr. Dent's memory served him.

But did Mr. Dent know anything of the property?

Only that it was a fair one, well run from the look of the proceeds (here Mr. Dent named a good figure of income likely to be seen in a year), a dairy farm in chief, he rather thought, with some dozen or fifteen tenant houses. Mr. Guilfoyle, a younger son and a lifelong bachelor, had bought it as a youth and there resided till his decease.

But the house? Had it a park? Gardens? A view? Any amenities?

Mr. Dent confessed his ignorance, but added that, since Mr. Guilfoyle had been an admirer of Robert Owen, the house was at the least likely to be healthful in its situation, and well maintained.

But were there gentry in the neighbourhood? A manor house, a squire? How distant was it from Chester? Were there servants?

Of all these questions, Mr. Dent could answer only the last, and that vaguely: There were some servants, he did not know how many. Mr. Rand, he trusted, was still in charge, for Mr. Dent had orders to pay him from the estate.

At this point, Anne at last recovered her tongue enough to ask, "And Mr. Henry Highet, who is to be deprived by our coming—if we come—of a rich inheritance; what do you know of him?"

Mr. Dent knew nothing; a country gentleman, he speculated, shrugging his shoulders.

But what, in that case, did Mr. Highet know of Anne Guilfoyle?

Mr. Dent was equally uninformed on this point. Whether the gentleman was acquainted with the terms of the will or no, he could not say.

"We thought," Mrs. Insel hesitantly put forward, "you see, we thought that if he did know, perhaps he might not be so—so rejoiced to meet us as one hopes a new neighbour will be."

But Anne spoke before Mr. Dent could pronounce an opinion on this head. "If he prove uncivil, we shall pay him in kind," she said briskly. Maria was relieved to hear in her tone something of her wonted vigour. For the first time in half an hour, she released Anne's hand. "If civil, then we likewise. Perhaps, at all events, we shall not need to stop there very long. Perhaps"—her voice began to fluctuate—"we need not go at all. We must reflect. We must consider."

She wants to talk to Ensley, thought Maria.

Mr. Dent stood. "If you will forgive me—"

The ladies, standing also, set him at liberty to go. He went, but not without turning to Anne, taking her hand, and saying in a very low tone, "Reflect and consider indeed, dear ma'am, but remember also that each day in this house . . ."

But he could not bring himself to finish his sentence, and hurried away.

TWO

LADY CELIA GRYPPHON WAS FAMED AMONG THE London *ton* on three accounts: one, the brilliance of the conversation at her small, select dinners; two, the excellence of the sweetmeats at same; and three, the absolute thrall under which she held Charles, Lord Grypphon, her husband. Her ladyship was near forty years of age, my lord not yet twenty-nine. The former was small and pinched, the latter broad and easy. She was not pretty nor showed any sign of ever having been so (nor, in fact, had ever been so), while he, though overlarge perhaps, was possessed of a set of distinctly attractive, rough, and friendly features, and a high, pleasant colour. Her ladyship was (even her closest friends admitted it) impatient and frequently ill-tempered. Her lord repaid her, and every one, with unfailing kindness and good humour. She ignored him. He doated on her. She set him down. He smiled upon her. In short, theirs was a marriage of which every one understood the wife's share, but no one the husband's.

Yet Lady Grypphon was far from being a mere shrew. On the contrary, she often showed her friends a ready generosity with both sympathy and—when need was— money, that many who are publicly more affable would do well to emulate. Her tact was such that both men and women frequently confided in her, unburdening their souls in great secrecy and anguish. Then, confessions made, they found themselves calmed by her shrewd good sense and her apparent invulnerability to shock. More than one subsequently guided himself by her sound advice. She had won many friends in this way; and yet, even among these, all were baffled by the incomprehensible hold she kept upon the gentle Charles. They could not, it appeared, imagine he liked her for the same reason they did; and so the marriage remained a mystery.

Anne Guilfoyle liked Lady Grypphon particularly because she had been among the first in the *beau monde* to regard Anne and Ensley as an established pair. She never invited one to dine without the other. There was no trace of irony or condescension in her voice when she met Anne in the Park or at a shop and, as was her invariable habit, politely inquired how Ensley did. Moreover, her kindness to his lordship was marked: Often she had bestirred herself to whisper his name in an influential ear, or to introduce him to some person of consequence, and so further his career. There was no better means than this to ingratiate oneself with Anne. Altogether, Celia was one of her oldest and most valued friends.

And yet Anne was in no humour to see her tonight. Celia might have an excellent heart, but it took so much energy and resolve to penetrate to it (especially on such an evening as this, when the company was to be rather larger and even more brilliant than usual) through the thicket of black wit and sharp observation she threw up round it that Anne determined actually to avoid her and seek out Ensley. Dressing for the evening, she thought herself much recovered since the afternoon, though still tender and anxious and very far from understanding how she must meet her difficulties.

"How pretty you look," said Maria, standing up as Anne came into the drawing-room. "Turn round."

Miss Guilfoyle obediently turned, showing the Princess Charlotte drapery over the shoulders of her silver satin gown. Mrs. Insel was, as usual, in lavender.

"Lovely," said Maria.

"I am pale," said Anne. "Dreadfully."

"Lovely," the loyal Maria repeated, wistfully fingering the silver satin as if, after tonight, they might neither of them ever wear satin again. Anne caught her wistful look and hurried her to the waiting carriage.

Lord and Lady Grypphon occupied a large, elegant brick house in Portman Square. Her ladyship, lately avid for all things Oriental, had fitted it out in hand-painted Chinese wall-papers, and filled it with highly worked brass tables, curious scrolls, and exotic poufs. Miss Guilfoyle and Mrs. Insel stepped into the Pekin Saloon together, but Anne was at once urgently called to join a hot debate on the Alien Bill, while Maria faded quietly in the other direction. Anne entered the fray with a sense of relief, glad to think for a moment of something other than her own reverses, but even as she vigorously refuted Sylvester

Frane's contention that the Bill was poorly written, her eyes frantically scanned the swelling company for Ensley. She had sent a note round to his house already that afternoon, but he had never answered; she supposed he must have been working (he had gone from Sidmouth's office to become an Undersecretary in Lord Liverpool's, and the Prime Minister himself had recently, though subtly, suggested he might soon rise to Second Secretary). He did sometimes work straight through the evening; but Celia had said nothing of his sending his regrets, so Anne told herself he must arrive soon.

He did arrive, though not particularly soon—the company was just on the point of going to the table—and with Lady Juliana Canesford so close upon his heels that Anne almost thought they had come in together. Lady Juliana, moreover, clung so maddeningly near to him that he could not avoid taking her in to dinner. He gave Anne a discreet glance of complicity and despair as he offered the silly girl his arm. Anne was left to go in with Tom Maitland, who was certain to drink himself into helpless idiocy before the second remove.

And indeed, her dinner partner very shortly too foxed for conversation, Miss Guilfoyle found nothing better to interest her in the dining-room than a very excellent cold sole pie for which she had, alas, no appetite. Ensley was on the same side of the long table as herself, but at the other end, so that he might have been in France for all the good he did her. At last, after what seemed an eternity, the ladies withdrew. Anne was able, as she went past Ensley, to whisper into the ear Lady Juliana had finally been obliged to relinquish, "I must speak with you privately."

Ensley moved back a little from the table and smiled down upon her. He was as tall and as fair as on the night they had met at Almack's, but in other ways the years that had gone by since could be seen in his face. His pale, crinkly hair had begun to creep up his forehead, and a fine net of reddish lines showed at the corners of his blue eyes. Still, it was an intelligent face, and a handsome, amiable one, and Miss Guilfoyle could not even tonight look upon it without a thrill of pride and fondness. Now Ensley put a hand lightly on her wrist and murmured, still smiling, "Mind-reader! I must speak with you. Excuse yourself in twenty minutes and go to Charles' library. I'll be there."

Anne turned and followed the other ladies to the drawing-room. Already she felt better. Even if Ensley had no brilliant solution to suggest, it would be such a relief to tell him, to hear his kind, sympathetic murmur and rest her head against his shoulder. When her mother had died he had been consolation itself. As she counted the minutes till she could quit the drawing-room and steal upstairs, she remembered to wonder what exactly it could be that he had to tell her. It must be about rising to Second Secretary. Perhaps he had been with Liverpool that afternoon. And her spirits lifted even higher as she thought of the figure he would cut, the speeches they would write together, the fine work he could do.

She was thinking this as she crept into Grypphon's library. Ensley had reached it ahead of her. The night being hardly cooler than the day, she discovered him standing by the open windows, his back to her, trying to get a breath of air, she supposed. She walked noiselessly halfway across the room before he knew she was there and turned round.

"It's Liverpool, isn't it?" she demanded at once, glad to defer her bad news some few minutes longer. "Has he advanced you?"

But to her surprise, Ensley looked first confused, then unhappy. He had not come away from the windows but stood there with his hands behind his back—twisting and wringing them, she knew from long acquaintance with his habits. "What is it?" she asked sharply.

"It is nothing to do with government, Anne," he said at last, very gently. She did not like this gentleness, which seemed to presage something painful. She went to a settee covered in dark Morocco and abruptly sat.

"What is it, then?"

Ensley came nearer to her and brought his hands forward, where he proceeded (for a change) to squeeze and twist them in full view. "I—" He went to the door, which she had left ajar, and shut it. Then he sat down beside her and carefully took up one of her hands; his own were damp and cold. "My dear, I have been obliged to offer for Lady Juliana. I am so sorry not to have been able to tell you before, but I—"

"I beg your pardon?" asked Anne. She had heard him, but what he said seemed not quite to make sense. "You have been obliged to offer what to Lady Juliana?"

Ensley blinked and began to knead her hand. "Marriage, dear Anne. I was waiting to know whether she would ac—"

Anne gave her head a violent shake, as if to clear her brain of dust, or cobwebs. "Forgive me, sir, but—Lady Juliana who, exactly?"

"Canesford." He seemed a little taken aback. "Lady Juliana Canesford. Lord Balwarth's daughter. I thought you were aware . . ." His voice trailed away, but he reached up to Anne's cheek, cupped it lightly and turned her face towards him. An instant later he took his hand away and looked down at his fingers in mild amazement, then again at her.

To her infinite chagrin, Anne realized she had been crying. It was her tear that had amazed him. Making a tremendous effort, she resolved to govern her feelings and regained, after a moment, a certain measure of self-command. "I wish you very happy," she said, her voice low but fairly steady.

"Anne—"

"Indeed I do." Angrily, she dashed another tear away from the same troublesome eye. "You must forgive me. I was not expecting . . ." She obliged herself to smile and to look full at him. The treacherous tears dried up. "Are you satisfied with the match? Did you—" She had been going to ask about the settlement, but the words froze in her throat. She found she could not look long at Ensley's face without risking tears again, and so stood and strolled to the window. The room gave upon the Square. A crowd of carriages was rolling up opposite. "Another of Lady Mufftow's crushes," she observed, turning back a little to Ensley.

Now he rose and came near her. "My dear Anne, this changes nothing between us. You know it does not. Except that I must play the bridegroom for two or three months— But that you understand. The wedding is fixed for October. My dear girl—" He broke off, and muttered, "My father is in worse and worse straits. I could not delay—"

"But sir, no, of course not. You have done perfectly right; indeed you ought to have done it before." She did not know where the words were coming from, or how she could say them so reasonably, but was only grateful to find them coming. "We have often spoke of this; you know my thoughts. It is only— You will think me a great goose, but I had not realized it was to be Lady Juliana. She is—" Again she faltered, but soon continued, "She is very young. Does she quite understand the nature—the nature—" But here she found she could not go on.

"Lady Juliana knows this is no love match," he said, "if that is what you mean. She is young, but by no means deficient in understanding."

Miss Guilfoyle was sorry to discover that even this modest encomium infused her with a wild fury. She said nothing, but reined in her temper even more tightly.

"Indeed, she is quite a spirited little thing," Ensley was going on. "I have no doubt she will make good use of the greater freedom married life will bring her."

"You intend to leave her free?" Anne asked drily. She could not but think of all she herself had done to advance Ensley's career: Was Juliana Canesford to reap all the profit of it? She consoled herself by recalling her young ladyship's thick nose and the fat mole at the corner of her mouth.

"Naturally," Ensley promptly replied. "And so must she leave me."

"And the Denbury heir?" Anne inquired, more drily than ever.

Taken aback again, "Well, naturally she cannot . . ." He seemed to lose the other end of his sentence.

"No. Naturally not," Anne agreed presently. She turned to face him squarely and stood gazing up at him in silence for some little while. He gazed uncomfortably down. Anne was recollecting her small store of knowledge about Juliana Canesford. She would certainly bring a substantial dowry: Everyone knew Balwarth was one of the wealthiest men in the land. And hers was an excellent old family—more than one Earl of Balwarth had distinguished himself in service to his king. But about Juliana herself Anne considered Ensley was rather too sanguine. She was a silly, romantical little chit, and the more Anne thought back on it now, the more she seemed to have seen something moony and lovestruck in Juliana's eyes when she came trailing into the Pekin Saloon after him. She was not the sort to accept a marriage of convenience—her husband's convenience, that is, not particularly her own—without a struggle. Unconsciously, Anne shook her head. Ensley had miscalculated.

He interrupted her thoughts to ask what she was shaking her head at. With this he smiled hesitantly at her. He had often teased her about the way her emotions showed in her face and gestures. His smile reminded her how well they knew one another.

"Nothing that signifies," she lied briskly, and took his hand in both hers. She squeezed it, mustered a little smile in return, and told him almost laughingly, "We ought to go back to the others now, my dear. What will people think?"

She had already turned to go when he objected, "But your business? You said you had something to discuss with me."

She stopped. "Did I?" She stood looking blank with a hand to her forehead. "Did I indeed?" She frowned.

Anne Guilfoyle had not had a pleasant day. She had received two bits of unexpected news, neither even remotely welcome. She felt exhausted, bruised, and had a shattering head-ache; but she was not so far gone that she would blurt out, to a man who had just told her he was marrying someone else, the fact that she was destitute. If anything was important to her at the close of this interview with Ensley, it was to give him no reason to think of her with pity. If he must marry, let him marry. If he must play the bridegroom, let him play it. Only for God's sake keep him from thinking that she was the loser by it. Her dignity, her poor dignity—it was all that kept her sane.

"Upon my word, I do not remember. Very likely I merely wished to give you this." And she stood on her toes and pecked at his long cheek. "And now I have given it, and now good night." She smiled and, with a great effort, laughed up at him, then turned and fled the room.

When the gentlemen rejoined the ladies some half hour later they found Miss Guilfoyle exceptionally gay. Her wit was madder, her satire keener than anyone could recall. To approach her with a joke was to touch a knife to a grindstone: She sharpened it, she threw off sparks. Nothing escaped her. She carved the assembly—Lady Juliana Canesford included—as neatly as a butcher does a side of beef, and with as little trouble from them. On the contrary, they were delighted: Tales of her heights of raillery and the *bon mots* she had coined circulated from mouth to ear among the London Quality for quite a week and a half afterwards.

Number 3, Holles Street was in an uproar.

"Every dish in the house to wrap, every rug to roll, every every thing, and two days to do it!" Mrs. Dolphim exclaimed (for perhaps the fifth time) to little Sally Clemp, the coachman's wife. Not twelve hours had gone by since Anne's scene with Ensley, not twenty-four since Mr. Dent's evil visit, but already she had given her orders: Number 3 must be packed up.

"Does she think we're witches, you and I?" the housekeeper went on. "Does she think we're conjurers, that we can wave our hands and say Puff! 'Tis all done? And Dolphim sent all over town, as if he was nothing but the boots or a backstairs page or I don't know what . . . Told to fetch this, leave that, see to t'other! Thirty years in service I've been, thirty years, and never heard such a freakish whim. Cheshire! I've known Miss Anne Guilfoyle since before there was a Miss Anne Guilfoyle *to* know. I come up from Overton with her ladyship, ask Dolphim if I didn't—"

Sally, who was tediously wrapping icicle number seventy-six or so of a crystal chandelier that seemed to have several thousand pieces to it, neither doubted Mrs. Dolphim's assertion nor would have cared one whit had it turned out to be the grossest fabrication. She had been with the household a mere three months, and was only glad to be told she and John would remove along with it, since it was removing. Besides, any fool could guess it was no "freakish whim" of Miss Guilfoyle's to leave for Cheshire: Something was wrong. Could not Mrs. Dolphim see red eyes when they looked at her? Had not Mrs. Insel, the soul of gentleness on every other occasion, spoke sharp to Minna twice in two hours? And the fact that they were all under strictest orders to say nothing to anyone with regard to how they were going—not to mention to a soul that the house was being packed up, not to say they were taking every stick of furniture, but only to pretend it was a country visit, like as usual? Didn't that tell Mrs. Thirty Years Dolphim trouble was at the root of it? Besides which, every one in the household knew that Lizzie, Miss Guilfoyle's abigail, had actually heard Miss Guilfoyle absolutely sobbing! Not that Lizzie told every one herself, of course: She was much too loyal to Miss Guilfoyle to do that. She only whispered the story to Cook, who mentioned it to Minna, who never was very close with a secret. But, "No use talking to the deaf," remarked Sally to herself, detaching icicle number seventy-seven, and aloud said only, "Indeed Mrs. Dolphim, yes Mrs. Dolphim, Gracious Goodness!"

Early on the third day after Mr. Dent's announcement, Miss Guilfoyle dropped her head back against the red plush squabs of her travelling carriage and gave a long sigh of something like relief. It had been sad—very sad—to quit London; but now that the deed was done and the coach well into Buckinghamshire, a glad sense of having taken some action against her sea of troubles swept through her, lifting her spirits.

"Off to adventure," she remarked to Maria, who sat opposite to her in the comfortable carriage. Mrs. Dolphim, Lizzie, and Minna were in the curricle following close behind; Dolphim and the others would come at a slower pace, in a hack-chaise with a train of waggons to carry the furniture. How Anne knew not, but Mr. Dent had contrived not only to free her of what remained on her lease of Number 3, but even to recover the money she had laid out for August and September. This windfall paid the hire of the waggons and the hack-chaise; the four hundred pounds still left of her fortune, meanwhile, was being transmuted into food and other necessaries at an alarming rate. "How long do you suppose one can live on Cheshire cheese?" Anne asked, her thoughts having drifted (as they invariably did of late) to finances.

"Will not the income of the farm begin at once?" Mrs. Insel inquired, looking out the window at the soft, misty landscape slipping away (she had insisted on taking the backward seat) into the past.

"I hope so. Soon enough, Mr. Dent assured me—but from now on, I will believe I have money when I see it in my hand, and not before." This was said rather grimly. They drove on in silence for some while; then, her tone lightened, "Only fancy what marvellous letter-writers we shall become in our exile," Anne suggested. "Perhaps we shall learn to talk to rats, as other prisoners are said to do."

"In our case, I should think cows would be our chief interlocutors," replied the other, pleased to encourage even this mild levity.

"Indeed. And we shall scrawl our names across the walls not in blood, but milk."

A fat raindrop streaked over the glass of the window, then another.

"Rain," observed Maria, as more drops came faster and faster. Then, gloomily, "Mud," she added.

"Quite," agreed Miss Guilfoyle.

A new silence fell as each entertained the thought of poor weather and two hundred miles to cover. Drenched coachmen. Stuck wheels. Short evenings. Moonless nights. Still, there was no turning back.

"'See how the rain doth wash the flowers,'" Anne began to sing a catch she and Maria had known in childhood.

After a moment Mrs. Insel joined in, her clear soprano adding a high descant.

Not until they had arrived at the Lion in Coventry, where they were to pass the night (Mrs. Insel had suggested they stop at Overton instead, which was nearly as convenient and a good deal cheaper, but even in her extremity Miss

Guilfoyle did not care to ask her uncle for favours), could Anne find the heart to tell Maria what she nevertheless knew she must tell sooner or later. She gathered her courage up through the early removes of the very indifferent supper—mutton sausage and carrot pudding—provided to them by the inn, often looking out the small window at the dreary night, as if courage might be found there. Finally, just after the arrival of a dish of stewed pears, she forced the words to her lips. "Oh, my dear," she said, with a brave attempt at nonchalance, "did I tell you Ensley is to marry the little Canesford girl?"

Mrs. Insel, choking on a mouthful of pear, answered, "No indeed. Is he?" She thought it as well not to mention she had been hearing rumours to that effect this past month. Her dark cheeks flamed with sympathy and a kind of embarrassment for her friend, who felt herself obliged to announce news of such significance with an air of insouciance.

"Yes, in October." Miss Guilfoyle suppressed an impulse to weep—she could see the pity in Maria's countenance—and went on, "I fancy she is a good choice. The Canesfords are great breeders" (Lady Juliana was the eldest child of seven) "and Ensley tells me she's a biddable little thing. He is quite pleased about it."

"And how are you pleased?" Maria asked, at the same time advancing her thin hand across the table in case Anne should want it.

"I? Oh, la, what should it matter to me?" Her cheeks had gone very white, but otherwise she presented a tolerable façade. "So long as she knows what the marriage is for—and she does—Ensley and I shall go on as we always have. Indeed, I think it high time he took a wife. Evidently Denbury has been pressing him, too. He told me so that night at Celia Grypphon's."

Maria surveyed her friend's pale face. "Indeed? And what did he have to say to your news—the loss of your fortune, I mean?" She had been longing to ask this question, but had not dared till now. Anne could be very bristly indeed when it came to Ensley.

"Nothing," said Anne, and took a great spoonful of pear into her mouth. She chewed slowly and swallowed, seeming to enjoy Maria's stare. Then she added, "For I never told him."

"Not tell him? But—where does he suppose you have gone, then?"

"Oh, I sent round word of our new direction," the other responded airily.

"And no explanation?"

"Not particularly. Why should I? It will do him good to wonder a bit about me," Anne declared. "He takes me rather for granted, I should say. Should not you?"

"Yes," said Maria resoundingly, delighted to have an opportunity at last of criticizing Ensley to his (she thought) too devoted admirer. "But I am surprised," she went on cautiously, "that he did not come to call on you between that night and our departure."

Anne said nothing. She too had been surprised—bitterly so. Not until that very morning had she received a note from him saying he'd been suddenly obliged to go into Suffolk and pay a visit to Balwarth. Her return note (waiting for him in London; she would *not* write to him in care of his prospective father-in-law) had been as brightly elusive as she could make it. Finally she shrugged at Maria, smiled, and turned the subject. They went to bed without any further mention of Ensley passing between them.

The truth was, Anne had been extremely displeased with her own response to the news of the marriage. It should not have shocked her as it did. She thought she had been much better prepared. She blamed herself harshly for what she termed, though only privately, her babyishness. Ensley's conduct had been perfectly correct, entirely appropriate. She had been telling him he must marry for years, had not she? So he had arranged it. It would change nothing between them. He would continue himself, she (she hoped) herself. As for the tears she had shed before him, she would have lost her fortune three times over to have them back.

When she opened her eyes in the morning, the sky was so black and dismal that Anne thought at first Lizzie had been confused and waked her in the night. But a moment's observation told her this was not so: It was storming.

"Raining straight through since yesterday, ma'am," Lizzie informed her, with the satisfaction of those who bring bad news for which they cannot be held accountable. She was a tall, handsome woman a year or two younger than her mistress, with a wide, humorous mouth and clever hands. Except that Miss Anne tended to find a coiffure that suited her, then stick to it for months or even years (which deprived Lizzie of much opportunity to show what she could do), she could not have wished for a better employer. Miss Anne was a trifle high-handed at times, perhaps, but never otherwise than fair. And anyhow, it suited a lady to keep a bit high in the instep. It redounded to the credit of her servants; and indeed, many were the households where Miss Guilfoyle's employees could count on being given precedence over those even of lords and ladies.

"The roads are a perfect pig-bath, so we're told," she now went on, as she hunted in a portmanteau for Miss Anne's silver peignoir. "Two coaches what ought to have come last night drug up to the inn an hour ago, and the coachmen say they've never seen worse weather. Shall we be leaving just as planned?" she then inquired, plumping a pillow for her mistress to lean back against. A bright flash of lightning followed almost instantly by a tremendous crash of thunder punctuated her question. Anne sat up.

"Very witty," she muttered at the heavens, then raised her voice and said more clearly to Lizzie, "Yes, I am afraid we must."

"What, in the rain?" was startled out of the poor girl, who had counted on a negative. The curricle, in which she was travelling, was a ridiculous conveyance for such heavy going, and must surely give trouble before the day was out. "Begging your pardon, ma'am, but Mrs. Dolphim and Minna and I—"

"I am perfectly aware of your situation," Anne was obliged to interrupt. The fact was they simply could not afford to stop another night at the Lion. She had budgeted out the dwindling £400 very strictly, and what remained in the purse for removal had already got perilously low. A healthy sum had gone with Dolphim, to cover his travelling expenses; the rest gave no margin for such a luxury as waiting for fine weather. "If it becomes necessary, Mrs. Insel and I shall change carriages with you."

"Oh, but ma'am—"

Over the girl's heartfelt protestations she continued,

"Thank you, Lizzie. Pray go down and ask them to bring my chocolate now."

Lizzie hurried from the room convinced a bolt of lightning would fry them all before evening.

In the event, the rain was a far greater hindrance than Anne could have imagined. Curricle or carriage made little difference: One of the pair attached to the former stumbled and injured a foreleg, one of the wheels of the latter hit a rock in the deep mud and needed mending on the road. Time and again the ladies were obliged to get out and stand at the wooded roadside—under torrents of rain and once within yards of lightning striking the ground—while the men hoisted one vehicle or the other out of two feet of mud. In no time the seats and floors of the coaches were awash in squelching rainwater. The only thing that could be said in defence of the day was that it was not cold—and that was little enough, since it was so unpleasantly hot one felt one had stumbled into a Turkish bath.

They came within view of Middlewich amidst a steady downpour, at about six in the evening. The prudent thing to do would have been to stop the night at the Rose and Crown, where they ate dinner; but being prudent did not make it affordable, as Anne remarked to Maria, and so they set forth again. The last leg of their journey, the good innkeeper assured them, would keep them on the road no longer than an hour. They had only to put the town at their backs, keep a good sharp eye out for Jack Gant's farm (which they couldn't possibly miss), and then mind they took the left fork up at the big elm . . . Anne listened with half an ear to the parade of dreary landmarks which, she supposed, would soon become as familiar to her as Pall Mall and Hanover Square. "Then drive up the road a bit to a great cunning ant-hill, you'll know it the minute you see it," she murmured sarcastically to Maria, "and after that, you'll see a place where three oak leaves are turning red early . . ."

The carriages rolled back out through the narrow streets of the town, its damp walls brought oppressively together by the gloomy aspect of the darkening sky. Neither Miss Guilfoyle nor Maria Insel had ever been to Middlewich. Still they could muster but little interest in it now. They were soon out of the town again and slogging over a sodden road that ran between fields dotted with cottages and interrupted by stretches of dense, dark forest. The landscape was softened and obscured by the rain, which had slowed now to a fine mizzle. Under other circumstances (say, a day's excursion from London for a pic-nic) the ladies might have found the country quite beautiful, with its gentle swells and muted colours; but as they faced simultaneously with it the prospect of living, will they nill they, constantly surrounded by it, they viewed it with sinking rather than cheerful hearts.

Which was a shame, because as it happened they were to see a monstrous great deal of it that very evening, and later that night to travel quite up and down it, though scarcely seeing it at all. Not to put too fine a point upon it, they got horribly lost—first one carriage, then the other, then both severally, and again (coming at one another near ten o'clock, each with the joyful idea the other carried a local citizen who could point the way) together. Whether or not one could possibly miss Jack Gant's farm, as the sanguine keeper of the Rose and Crown had put it, they did; and so began one of the most uncomfortable, vexatious evenings any of the travellers could recall. For it had begun to rain again in earnest, so that even to move in the wrong direction they had often to stop and emerge from the carriages, as during the afternoon, till the wheels were unstuck. In the end Anne went and helped the men pull—it was better, she said, than standing like a clod of mud oneself, getting muddier and more cloddish by the minute.

At about ten-thirty she began to get giddy, a condition Maria at first mistook for hysteria (more what she was feeling). By eleven the whole company was somewhat madly a-giggle, all drenched, all filthy, with fine points such as who was mistress and who servant quite forgot. In more or less this state they finally turned in to what John Clemp swore simply had to be, by default if nothing else, the drive to Linfield. It was a long drive, and the exhausted voyagers had plenty of time to remember to wonder what was at the end of it—a hovel? a castle?

The night was too dark, as it developed, to see. Something large, an imposing edifice, perhaps Tudor, perhaps not—the darkness was impenetrable. No lamp had been lit to welcome the travellers, though Anne had written to warn the house they were coming.

"Of course, it is nearly midnight," Mrs. Insel suggested in defence of the household, when Anne complained of this scant hospitality. "They must naturally have imagined we were not coming, and gone to bed."

"They might still have left a lamp burning," Miss Guilfoyle objected, striving to peer through the shadows at her great uncle's bequest. The carriage slowing to a stop, the ladies wrung themselves out as best they could and poured out the door John Clemp held open. James, who had been driving the second carriage, had already loudly sounded the house bell, and stood knocking briskly. Rain continued blandly to tumble from the sky.

"It's a second Flood," Anne murmured to Maria, lean-

ing against a pillar on the wide front porch while James
hammered at the door. Her voice was hoarse (she hoped
from their madcap singing, though she feared a cold). She
had just started to mutter, "Where in the name of God are
the blasted serv—" when the huge oaken door at last
swung open, revealing a plump young lady in a mob-cap
holding a smoking candle.

Anne marched past her without a word, pulling Maria in
and, in view of the weather, gesturing the rest of the rag-
tag assembly in behind her as well. The girl, too surprised
to object, stood back a little and watched goggle-eyed as
the front hall filled with strangers. "I am Miss Guilfoyle,"
Anne finally vouchsafed, when the door had been closed
against the night. She spoke peremptorily, all the irri-
tability engendered in her by the night's drive perfectly
audible in her tone. "We are wet, and tired, and you have
given us but a dim, haphazard welcome. What is your
name?" she demanded, as the young woman gawped but
said nothing.

A tremor in her voice, "Joan, ma'am," she replied.
"Would you be—"

"Well, Joan," Anne cut her off, "I wonder if there is
someone here who can make us a pot of tea?"

Joan either did not know or would not say. Though her
mouth was open, she stood silent.

"Go on, Joan. You look a clever, capable girl. Suppose
you put some water on the hob and wake the housekeeper. We shall want her to show us our rooms. Go on,"
she added, as the girl still stood there. "No use staying to
watch us drip on the floor. It's the only trick we know and
we've already done it the best we're able."

The plump girl contrived at last to take her eyes from
Anne Guilfoyle and found tongue enough to say, "One

moment, ma'am, if you please." She turned to go, but Anne reached out and caught her apron string.

"Joan—"

"Ma'am?"

"Light a candle for us, please, before you go."

"Yes, ma'am." The girl went to a sideboard and lit two branches of a candelabra, discovering to the visitors that they had come into a large hall with a lofty, arching ceiling and a parquet floor.

"That's a girl," said Anne, as Joan scurried away. Anne turned to Maria with murder in her eyes. She drew her a little apart from the others, who were hovering in an awkward knot, uneasy at entering the house with their mistress. "Have you ever seen such a thing?" she demanded in a frantic whisper. "The most perfect imbecile I have ever encountered in my life, and we must either turn her off or find some use for her. I wonder what she knows how to do, other than open the door? She does speak English, in a sort of a way. And she seemed to know her own name. These are hopeful signs. Do you suppose she could learn—"

At this moment, Anne became aware of a man's steps coming into the hall. She wheeled and saw the ruddy, puzzled countenance of a very tall person indeed, a person of about five-and-thirty with dark, curling hair, a fine, wide brow, large, heavy-lidded eyes, and a generous, well-shaped red mouth. He was dressed in an old-fashioned striped flannel night-gown and what appeared to be a black frock-coat. A pair of unbuckled country boots, well-worn, completed his costume. Added to the look of utter confoundment on his face, it would not be too much to say that this man, whoever he was, looked ridiculous.

Anne, forgetting for a moment that she—begrimed,

drenched, sopped and soaked again, her hair a mop, her clothes draggled—likewise was not at her best, took one glance at him and laughed aloud. She had stepped forward a little ahead of the others, signalling in this wise that he had to deal with her.

The gentleman, after a moment, looked as if he might have liked to laugh (whether with or at her) as well, but did not. He merely smiled and gave a little bow, pulling the frock-coat tighter over his broad shoulders. He had a sleepy smile more than an intelligent one. He inquired, "May I know whom I have the honour of addressing?"

Anne, suddenly furious at the impertinence of this groom, or valet, or butler, or whatever he was, receiving her in his night clothes, replied in so chilling a tone that it was a wonder the rain in her dripping hair did not turn to ice, "You have the honour of addressing Miss Anne Guilfoyle. What is your name?"

"Miss Guilfoyle," the other repeated, not answering her question at once but appearing instead to muse, either from stupidity or rudeness, over this information.

When she judged full half a minute of silence had gone by, "No, *I* am Miss Guilfoyle," said that lady. "I asked you who *you* are. Butler? Boots? Coachman, perhaps?"

The fellow gave a happy laugh, as if he did not hear the contempt in her words, and bowed again, more deeply this time. "I am Mr. Henry Highet, Miss Guilfoyle," he answered finally. "You are in my house. How do you do?"

THREE

Miss Guilfoyle felt the clutch of something like panic in her chest. With a will of its own, her hand reached back for Maria, who grasped it damply but securely.

"Mr. Dent informed me—" Miss Guilfoyle brought forth, and stopped.

"I beg your pardon?"

"I had understood from Mr. Nicodemus Dent—"

Mr. Highet shrugged as once again Anne's words froze on her lips. Either he did not know the name of Mr. Dent, or he did not care about it.

"Do you think we might sit down?" Maria suddenly interposed. She dropped Anne's hand to come forward and shake Mr. Highet's. "Mrs. Insel. How do you do?"

He bowed. "And these—?" he asked, with a glance at Lizzie and the others.

"Perhaps the kitchen . . ." Maria suggested with some little embarrassment.

Mr. Highet retreated a few steps and pulled the cord of a bell; in a moment, Joan returned and was asked to show the newcomers to the kitchen, then bring tea into "the best parlour."

Joan bobbed and obeyed.

Henry Highet took up a candlestick and led the ladies through a series of turning corridors to a room at the back of the house. It was a large saloon and they could make out no more of it, by the half-dozen candles he lit there, than that it had many windows and was cosily, if unstylishly, furnished.

Mr. Highet motioned the ladies to a small sofa. They sat on its edge, for fear of drenching the cushions. He took an arm-chair across from them but immediately sprang up and drew out from under him a bristling pincushion. He held it up to display.

"My mother," he remarked, and Anne thought, "Dear God, he's already installed her here as well!"

Aloud she said, "Sir, I fear an error has been committed." As she hesitated, wondering how exactly to frame her next sentence, she wished Mr. Highet would think to excuse himself and go dress properly. She found it extremely unnerving to confront a gentleman in such deshabille; but Henry Highet seemed hardly aware of it at all. He was sitting back now with his sleepy, stupid smile upon his face, waiting to hear her for all the world as if they had both been in court dress.

"Mr. Nicodemus Dent informed me," she went on

presently, "that I am the inheritor of this house. May I ask if you have had intelligence to the contrary?"

She was not sure whether he raised an eyebrow slightly, or if it was only a trick of the candlelight. He said, very slowly—he spoke maddeningly slowly, whatever he said—"No. No specific intelligence, that is to say. But as my great grandfather built this house one hundred and thirty years ago, I must admit the information given you by—Mr. Dent, I think you said?—surprises me."

A dawning apprehension stirred in the recesses of Anne's mind. "Are we at Linfield, sir?" she asked abruptly, to have the worst of it over with at once.

"Linfield?" Mr. Henry Highet smiled, threw his head back, held the attitude some instants in silence ("While the idea sank into the marshes of his brain," Anne later said to Maria), then threw his head forward, broke into a tremendous guffaw, slapped his knee and laughed till tears came to his eyes. He wiped at these last, chuckling helplessly, then shook his head and stamped the floor lightly with both feet alternately.

Miss Guilfoyle, who hated above all things to be laughed at (unless she intended it), said, when she thought he could hear her again, in a very small, very cold voice, "I take it that we are not."

Mr. Highet calmed himself, apologizing, and shook his head again. "No, Miss Guilfoyle. You are at Fevermere. I thought some confusion might have been in the wind when I heard of your behaviour towards Joan." Here he went off again in a gale of snickers and appreciative hoots. "The poor girl— Excuse me— I knew your great uncle well—" He broke off and seemed to set himself to recover his composure. In a minute Joan came in with tea and a plate of bread-and-butter. From the way he looked up at her, Miss Guilfoyle feared he was about to explain her own (hilarious, as he seemed to find it) mistake to the girl there and then; but he did not, only thanking her for the tea and sending her back to the kitchen.

Anne turned her gaze to Maria, who smiled encouragingly and began to pour tea. But, "Mr. Highet, we have trespassed upon your hospitality long enough," Anne said, rising as she spoke and shaking out her damp skirt as well as she could. She turned again to Maria, who had naturally looked up at her from the teapot, and nodded meaningfully. Mrs. Insel (though not without a mutinous glance, for she dearly wanted her tea) replaced the pot and stood as well.

Henry Highet jumped to his feet. The frock-coat dropped open, revealing a long row of red buttons down his middle. He snatched it shut again and commenced imploringly, "But my dear ma'am, you are wet through. You cannot possibly leave without taking—"

"Thank you, Mr. Highet," Anne broke in, firmly and freezingly, "but no."

The gentleman turned to Mrs. Insel. "Intercede for me," he begged, gesturing widely with large, work-reddened hands. "Tell her—"

"We are perfectly fine, I thank you," Anne interrupted again, "and if you will be kind enough to tell my coachman how to reach Linfield, we need disturb you no longer." With this she gasped, opened her mouth, clapped a hand over it, looked horrified, and gave a thumping great sneeze. She fumbled for her reticule (which she had left in the carriage) in search of her handkerchief (which she had lost in the mud two counties back). Finally she was obliged to accept one Henry Highet had found in his frock-coat pocket, which he had been trying to give her all along. Looking away, she blew her nose, stuffed the handkerchief into her sleeve and muttered, "I shall send it back laundered to-morrow," then added very faintly indeed, "Thank you."

Mr. Highet begged she would not trouble to return it. Miss Guilfoyle insisted she must and would. Mr. Highet, turning the topic, declared his attention of accompanying the ladies' party to Linfield, with or without tea. "Though I'd much prefer it if you stopped here the night," he added earnestly, with an excess of generosity calculated, it seemed to Anne, to make her feel small. "We have plenty of rooms. I'll wake my mother—"

Miss Guilfoyle could not think of it, nor of his accompanying them to Linfield. "We have roused one inhabitant from his bed here this night," she said, striving for dignity as another sneeze threatened to overset her. "That is sufficient." And, taking up a candle, she began to walk out of the parlour and retrace, as best she could recall them, the steps they had taken from the hall to the parlour.

Mr. Highet, bowing Maria out, followed after them anxiously. "Do you mean me? I was not asleep. It don't signify at all. I was reading in bed, Miss Guilfoyle, listening to the rain. Now you must— Excuse me, dear lady." He caught up with her and gently guided her shoulders in the opposite direction to the one she had been turning. "That's the way to my library," he explained kindly. "The door—you are looking for the door you came in?— is along here . . ."

In the end, after many polite offers and many firm refusals, Maria intervened. She had had quite enough of wandering over the countryside for one night.

"I must say," she broke in, softly but deliberately, "it

seems to me the height of foolishness to set forth again without a guide. Perhaps if Mr. Highet has a groom he could send, or . . . ."

Anne cast her a dark, angry look; but Maria, content that she had both common sense and prudence on her side, received it with serene indifference. Since Anne knew she was right (and was even a little relieved by her interference) no objection was made aloud, and Mr. Highet was permitted to oblige his visitors at last.

"The very thing," he said, ushering them into the front hall, then begging to leave them for a moment. He disappeared forthwith, ostensibly to rouse a groom, but actually, as it developed, to dress himself to go out. He returned looking much less risible in riding-breeches and a country coat. "Couldn't bring myself to wake the lad," he explained, though it was clear a minute later that he had waked someone, for a saddled chestnut mare was brought round to the door. "Your horses are tired." He led the ladies out to the carriage sweep again. "I have taken the liberty of replacing them with mine—to be returned with the handkerchief," he added gravely to Miss Guilfoyle, apparently intending no humour. John and James were already mounted on their respective boxes, and a moment later Anne realized the others were inside the curricle. Mr. Highet accepted a lantern from a tiger, handed the ladies into their carriage before they had an opportunity to protest, and mounted the mare. And so the party set off into the foggy night.

With a knowledgeable guide to keep them off the poorer roads and to steer them on course, they arrived at Linfield in a matter of forty-five minutes or so. In good weather, Mr. Highet informed the ladies as he handed them out onto the wooden portico of a decidedly smaller house than Fevermere, the journey was twenty minutes to ride (across the land that joined the properties) and no more than thirty to drive. "It is a road I have often taken to visit Mr. Herbert Guilfoyle. He is gone and we regret him," he went on, with a bow to Anne by way of condolence (they were waiting at the lighted door for someone to open it), "but now that you have come, I hope I may have the honour of continuing to travel it often."

Anne skirted the question, muttering only, "You leave us much in your debt"; but Maria, a little shocked at her friend's grudging manner, answered,

"Indeed, sir, we shall hope to see you again very soon," and thanked him prettily.

She was still thanking him when the door opened at last and a very thin, very old lady looked out. Her grizzled hair was skinned back off her face and hidden in a scrap of lace at the top of her head. Seeing Mr. Highet, she curtsied, held the door open to admit them, then introduced herself as Miss Charlotte Veal.

"Franklin, run out to the coaches and show them where they must go," she directed over her shoulder at a young boy who had been hovering in the hall behind. The boy departed on his errand and the ladies identified themselves. Miss Veal stared at them curiously with great, round grey eyes.

"But Mr. Highet, how do you come to be here?" Miss Veal inquired—rather impertinently, Anne thought, for a person she presumed to be the housekeeper.

"Mr. Highet discovered us lost and was kind enough to show us our way," she interposed coldly, before he could answer. She was feeling almost light-headed with fatigue, and though she mechanically took note of her surroundings (square, wainscoted, tiled hall; plain glass lamps; wa-

tercolour landscapes, wooden staircase beyond) all she
could really think of was bed and sleep. "It was very good
of him, and we are grateful," she went on, "but my friend
and I are both extremely weary, and I hope Mr. Highet
will excuse us if I ask you to show us to our rooms. You
might summon someone else to help him to any
amenity . . ." Her words faded off as Henry Highet
begged her not to trouble about him and Miss Veal simultaneously asked if he mightn't like to stop the night at
Linfield, now he was here.

The housekeeper having extended this invitation, the
ladies had perforce to second and urge it upon him; but
the gentleman declared repeatedly that he was not the
least tired, neither the dark nor the rain distressed him,
and he would not stop. Miss Veal, who had evidently a
great liking for him, protested vigorously; but in the end
he was allowed to depart. Bowing, he vanished into the
night. Miss Veal, loudly tsk-tsking ("As if we had sent
him away by force," Anne indignantly commented to
Maria the next morning), took a candle and led the ladies
up two pairs of oaken stairs to their bed-chambers.

These were across a corridor from one another. Miss
Guilfoyle doubted from their size and their furnishings if
either was the one her great uncle had inhabited; but she
was in no mind to quarrel, so long as there was a bed to
climb into. As there was—a large four-postered one—she
meekly thanked and dismisssed Miss Veal for the night,
asked Lizzie to unbutton her dress and sent her off to
bed, wriggled out of the rest of her damp clothes and
crawled under the covers.

She slept a long time, and woke sneezing. The spiritual
mortifications of the previous night, then the fleshly ones

of the day that preceded it, flooded painfully into her memory even before she could fumble for the handkerchief (Mr. Highet's—she reminded herself to hand it to Lizzie directly she came) on the night-stand. She lay back upon the pillows and shut her eyes. Henry Highet's stupidly smiling face appeared before her. A new sneeze welled from the back of her throat. "Devil fly away with you," she muttered, whether to the face or the sneeze was not clear. She sat up, reopened her eyes, erupted explosively, then found a bell-pull over her head, rang it, and sat back.

The rain had stopped ("It would, now," she thought) and strong sunlight brightly edged the heavy brocaded curtains hung over her windows. The chamber, now she could see it, was large and rather bare, with a plain wooden floor over which a few Turkey carpets had been scattered. A huge country cupboard stood in one corner, a deal wardrobe in another, and a small vanity table (too small for the seriously vain, she considered) in a third. A blue-and-white porcelain washbasin sat upon this table, with a white ceramic pitcher. The room was scrupulously clean, and when (Lizzie duly arrived, also sneezing) the curtains were opened, sunlight poured into it through three large, diamond-paned casement windows.

"Good morning, Lizzie. I see that you also kept a souvenir of last night?" Anne observed in heavily nasal tones.

"Yes, Miss. I'm afraid so, Miss."

Exploding again, "You have my deepest commiseration," Anne told her. "Are you well armed with handkerchiefs? Take some of mine, if not. And please see that this one is laundered and returned to Mr. Highet," she finished, distastefully holding out the crumpled linen square. "I think there is a pile of fresh ones in that port-manteau, if you wouldn't mind."

Lizzie opened the portmanteau, located the needed re-inforcements, and supplied Miss Guilfoyle with them. "I've fetched your lap-desk up, ma'am," she said, disap-pearing into the corridor momentarily, then returning with the desk. She set it on the bed and stood back.

Since it was Miss Guilfoyle's habit to write three or four letters each morning from her bed, and since each morn-ing Lizzie fetched her lap-desk to her for that purpose, it seemed no strange thing that the desk should be brought to her this morning. Yet Anne lay contemplating it as if it had been a meteor dropped from the sky. "Thank you, Lizzie, you may go. Keep warm to-day. Ask for my choco-late, if you please," she added rather dreamily, her eyes still fixed and vacant.

Lizzie curtsied—she had a long-legged, loping gait and a curiously jaunty curtsy—and departed. Her mistress' gaze did not shift. She lay many moments in silence, then said at last, "Do you feel as foolish as you look, I won-der?"

It was true the desk looked foolish. It was an ebony desk elaborately inlaid with brass scrollwork. Its clasps im-itated the talons of a hawk, its hinges two fantastical birds in profile. Inside, the polished ebony writing surface was bordered with a vine of nacre, and a jade oak cluster em-bellished each corner. The compartments below, where pens and paper and ink were kept, were lined in green velvet embroidered with silken birds and flowers. It had been made to Miss Guilfoyle's specifications in happier days. In this plain, light-swept, cheerful room, it looked as ridiculous as a bishop in a donkey cart—or, thought Anne bitterly, a bluestocking at a farm.

There was a tap on the door. Maria, wearing a grey day dress, came in. Her eyes and nose were red, and in the draught made by the opening and closing of the door, both ladies sneezed mightily.

"You too?" was Anne's greeting.

Mrs. Insel took the ladder-backed chair from the vanity table and sat down. "Yes. Minna also, and Mrs. Dolphim, from what I hear."

"A flush," said Anne, who despised cards but knew the rudiments of play. She blew her nose; at the same moment came a knock on the door. A young girl with ginger hair walked in, bearing a tray.

"Your chocolate, Miss. My name is Susannah. It's a lovely day out. I feel quite cheerful after all that rain."

"No one asked your name or your opinions," thought Anne automatically, waving her to set the tray on the bed, but saying nothing. She gave a cool nod of dismissal. "What did my great uncle do, do you suppose, to encourage the servants to confide in one so?" she demanded of Maria as the door closed. "We have not been here fourteen hours, and already I know more of Miss Veal's ideas, and Miss Susannah's biography, than I feel the slightest need to know. Have you been out into the house at all?" she went on before the other could answer. "Is it this all over? Deal tables and chintz counterpanes and sunshine?"

Maria, understanding at once, gave a sorrowful, sympathetic nod. "I fear your lovely parcel-gilt suites will suit Linfield but ill. It is a comfortable house, only—"

"Painted shutters?" Anne broke in.

Maria nodded.

"Delft fireplaces? Cambric curtains?"

"I'm afraid so."

Anne shook her head. "I shall not tell you," she said, "for fear of breaking your heart, how much money exactly we spent to remove our eight Venetian chandeliers, my mother's Chippendale settees, the Aubusson carpets, and the other three waggon-loads of furnishings from London to this place; but let me assure you, my dear, that if I did tell you, we should both be here weeping till Tuesday. Still"—she straightened and poured a cup of chocolate with an air of resolve—"it is done. And what is done, as Mrs. Macbeth so pithily and incontrovertibly observed, is done. I'm sure there is some barn or other where they can be kept. Now, what shall we do today? Mowing? Sowing? Rearing? Shearing? Till? Mill? Drill—"

"I believe Miss Veal wishes to speak with you," Mrs. Insel interrupted, noticing the increasing asperity in Anne's tone. "And I know Mrs. Dolphim will like to be told what her duties are. Then there is the steward, Mr. Rand. Surely he will wish to take you over the estate. And we ought to thank—"

"Stop, stop," cried Anne, who heard Mr. Highet about to be mentioned. She gulped what remained of her chocolate in one swallow, flung off the bedclothes, and leapt up. "You persuade me: A day of adventure and obligation awaits. I shall make haste." She rang the bell for Lizzie. Mrs. Insel stood to go.

"You will not forget—" she began hesitantly, from the doorsill.

"To thank Mr. Highet again," Miss Guilfoyle finished. "No indeed. We shall send him a brace of cheeses, or a golden fleece, or whatever is best from Linfield—"

"An invitation to dine, I should have suggested."

Anne flashed her a dark look but yielded. "Or an invitation to dine." She winced, as if the idea crushed her somewhat.

Maria smiled, opened the door, and was going out when she added over her shoulder, "And his mother, of course."

Her look ever darker, "And, God bless us yes, his mother; a poor party we should make without his mother," Anne said, suppressing a sneeze. "Now do go away before we are to invite little Joan as well."

Maria went.

"Rand, Veal. Veal, Rand. Farm, household. Household, farm. Can't decide," Miss Guilfoyle muttered under her breath as, dressed and determined, she made her solitary way down the staircase some half hour later. "They both sound so utterly fascinating, that's the deuce of it—Oh!" she suddenly broke into her own remarks as she rounded a corner and nearly collided with Charlotte Veal. "Forgive me, I did not see you. I was just hoping to find you. Is there an office where we might discuss the household?"

"There is the housekeeper's room," Miss Veal replied, with more emphasis on the penultimate word than Anne could quite account for. "But—are you alone, ma'am? I did hear you speaking to someone, I think?" She squinted on this side of the corner and that, as if there might be someone only faintly visible still lingering in the air.

"Speaking, yes. To someone, no," Miss Guilfoyle said cheerfully, taking Miss Veal rather firmly by her muslin sleeve and making an inquiring gesture at random. "This way? That way? It is my lamentable habit to apostrophize myself aloud. Ah, thank you, this way after all. I cannot say, truthfully, at what epoch of my life I first fell into this custom . . . Oh, the dining-room is this?" she inquired, as they passed through a spacious, airy room furnished with a stout, well-worn oaken table suitable for, perhaps, the family of a yeoman farmer. "Very pleasant, very tidy. Thank you. I see evidence of your good management every where. I take it this is a sort of pantry, and— No, thank you, the kitchens will wait till later. Yes, very clever indeed, building the kitchens and dining-room so close to one another. A hot dish is a good dish, is not it, Miss Veal? At any rate, pray do not be alarmed by my little soliloquies. Merely the afterclap, the bilge if you like, of a somewhat overbusy mind. Which— Ah, down here? Thank you, Miss Veal." The ladies descended a half-flight into a small, panelled study furnished with a large walnut library table and little else. The windows of this chamber gave onto a small, artless flower garden, beyond which a lawn, and in the distance fields, could be glimpsed.

Miss Veal drew a chair up to the desk for Anne, then one for herself. When she had settled herself—with a brief, catlike switching of skirts—she opened, in a silence rather solemnly ceremonial, a very large, leather-covered ledger.

"These are the household accounts," she intoned. She began to turn over page after page filled with (Anne presumed) her own, neat hand in brown ink. "Every thing that is used in the house is written in here. If it comes from the farm, the value lost by not selling it is inscribed. If it comes from Outside"—Miss Veal's manner of saying Outside capitalized and made it sound quite terrifying— "the price is inscribed. Household wages are similarly noted in these pages"—her old hands, wrinkled and spotted, but with the nails still white and carefully shaped, reverently turned to a different section in the ledger—

"here. It is the method devised and prescribed to me by Mr. Herbert Guilfoyle," she said quietly, then looked sharply into the eyes of that gentleman's great niece and demanded, "I do not suppose you know a better system?"

Miss Guilfoyle, mastering an impulse to smile, meekly confessed that she did not.

"Good." Charlotte Veal returned her gaze to the ledger. Her eyes seemed to linger lovingly on a notation of one pound six pence paid as quarterly wages "to Susannah D." while she said slowly, "Mr. Guilfoyle and I examined these books every Wednesday morning between ten o'clock and eleven. I do not suppose"—again she glanced abruptly up and fixed her stern regard on Anne's face—"you know a better hour?"

"Scarcely," said Anne.

"Good." Miss Veal looked quietly down again and seemed as lost in her ledger as if it were a Psalter. Anne felt she had been forgot. She blew her nose, and when this failed to attract Miss Veal's attention asked (mostly to assert herself about some one thing at least): "Is not one pound six pence rather a high wage for a country maid?" She pointed to Susannah's name in the still open book. "I seem to recall that at my friend Lady Drayton's seat in Hereford the maids are given—"

Charlotte Veal stood. Her brow was dark, her hands clenched. "Mr. Herbert Guilfoyle set that wage," she declared, the grey locks on her neat head trembling with suppressed indignation. "Mr. Guilfoyle believed in high wages. Of course it is high. Mr. Guilfoyle believed that a labourer lives up to the value put upon him by his employer. I do not suppose . . ." She paused; Anne perceived there were tears of anger in her eyes, "I do not suppose you know a better wage?"

After a moment, "No," Anne said. "A higher or a lower one, perhaps I do know. But not a better. Pray sit down, Miss Veal."

Miss Veal obliged her.

"Now I must speak to you about Mrs. Dolphim, and my own staff," said Anne, already thinking how she would describe this comical scene in a letter to Ens— well, perhaps to Celia. "As you are surely aware by now, I have brought a whole household of my own servants—"

But Miss Veal had popped up again ("A perfect Jack-in-the-Box," Anne wrote in her imaginary letter) and was freshly a-tremble. Her frail hands clutched each other; her voice shook as much as her curls. "Miss Anne Guilfoyle," she commenced, and it was clear from her tone she thought that to be Miss Anne Guilfoyle was a pretty mixed honour, "your great uncle brought me into this house thirty-four years ago. I have prepared tea for him some twelve thousand four hundred times. Under my supervision, twenty-four thousand eight hundred breakfasts and dinners have been cooked for him. I have filled thirty-three ledgers before this one"—she smacked the open album demonstratively with a good deal more vigour than Anne would have thought was in her—"and sat across thirty-three Christmas geese from him. If you imagine he intended—"

"Miss Veal." Exasperated, Anne stood too. "For heaven's sake calm yourself. I have no intention of turning you off, if that is what you are building to, or of turning anyone in the house off who does not wish to leave." She wondered as she spoke, however, just how she could retain such a superfluity of servants—for at the wages her great uncle had fixed, surely none of the present ones would go. Still, she was not about to unhouse and impoverish an aging, obviously devoted (for all she knew, very tenderly devoted to the bachelor Mr. Guilfoyle) retainer. "I merely wish to discuss with you some means by which my own housekeeper, Mrs. Dolphim, can profitably employ herself—if there is not some means of sharing out your tasks," she extemporised, realizing that it would sow a fatal discord to suggest the sensitive Miss Veal merely assist Mrs. Dolphim, yet knowing from long acquaintance that Mrs. Dolphim (whose greatest, and justifiable, pride was the faithful service she'd given to the Guilfoyles) would equally contemn a demotion to the position of helper to Miss Veal. "This we must consider and resolve."

She sat, and suggested the other lady sit as well. It was clear to her now that the slight forwardness she already thought to detect in Miss Veal, and in Susannah as well, was no illusion. Her great uncle's servants were accustomed to be treated in a wise quite different from the ordinary. Remembering his eccentricities, she was not surprised. Reluctantly, but with a sense of having little choice, she engaged the housekeeper in an earnest colloquy whose end was to discover some equitable means of sharing the responsibilities and privileges of Housekeeper at Linfield. The discussion, which must needs touch upon such details as who was to precede whom to the servants' dining-table, who to keep the books, who to reprimand the lesser staff, who to order from the dairy, and so on, continued some hour and a half and left both participants exhausted. Miss Veal went immediately to her room to lie down. Miss Guilfoyle was not so fortunate: Quitting the housekeeper's little office she came directly upon Mr. Rand—just on his way, he declared imperiously, to find her.

Mr. Rand, she found, was a brisk, dark, sturdy man of
no great stature, well muscled, brown from the sun, and
with a very noticeable pugnacity in his bearing. Whether
this last was habitual with him, or on the contrary was
assumed for her benefit, Anne could not yet tell. That he
was suspicious of her, and (looking her over) thought her a
paltry replacement for his late master, she guessed at
once. "I shall be very much obliged," he said, after a curt,
rough bow, "if you will come with me." She could hear
the country in his accent, but also that he had had some
education. "There is a deal of going-over to be done in
the office, and then you'll be wanting to ride out with me
and see the place," he informed her.

"Perhaps you will allow me to make that decision, Mr.
Rand," Anne replied sharply. "I can meet with you in an
hour and a half, after I have had some nuncheon."

But Mr. Rand shook his head. "In an hour and a half
they'll be gone," he said. "You can't expect them to
wait."

Anne counted to ten. "Who will be gone?" she inquired.

"The people to cut the hay. They want one shilling
two pence and beer—six pence and beer for the women.
Does that sound fair?" he asked, then folded his arms and
stood back a little. He had intercepted her in the corridor
between Miss Veal's room and the pantry. Anne, worn out
by her long closeting with the housekeeper, her eyes
rheumy, her head heavy and thick, longed to sit down,
but Mr. Rand was watching her with a gaze that glittered
coldly. She knew he had no opinion of a woman running
an estate—and a London woman at that—and was only
waiting for her to say something idiotic. The knowledge
piqued her. She straightened and rallied herself.

"Since I have never hired a man to cut hay, I can have no idea," she said crisply. "Does it sound fair to you?"

"Middling fair," Mr. Rand allowed after some thought. "And how many must I hire?"

"As I have no knowledge of how many acres of hay are to be cut, I can form no very good notion of that either, Mr. Rand," she replied.

"Three hundred twenty-five," said he at once, then returned to his speculative glare.

"Good; yet since I have no information as to how many workers it generally takes to cut a single acre, I continue in the dark. Can you inform me?"

"Depends how quick you want it done," said the laconic Mr. Rand.

"How quickly need it be done?"

He shrugged. "If it will not rain, there is no hurry. They can start day after tomorrow, and four or five men might do. But if it will rain, then I should say ten or a dozen."

"But since we cannot tell whether it will rain—" Anne commenced.

"Ah, there it is!" Rand answered wisely.

Trying a new tack, "How many men did you hire last year?" she asked.

"Eight men, four women."

Starting to move down the corridor again, "Good, then, that's settled. Hire so many this year as well."

"But last year we had but two hundred acres planted to grass," he called after her, arresting her.

"Mr. Rand." She did not care to look at him angrily, for it displeased her to show he had roused any feeling in her, yet she could not help herself. "Let us hire in proportion, then," she snapped. "We have half again as many acres, hire half again as many workers. Twelve men, six women. Do you understand?"

Evidently she had handled herself a little better than he expected, for the man looked sulky as he replied, "Yes."

Pressing her advantage, "Pray find me in one hour and a half in—" She faltered, realizing she still did not know the house well enough to appoint a convenient meeting place. "In the dining-room," she finished lamely. Then she turned and walked as quickly as she could out of the corridor, lest the insolent man should attempt to precede her.

She took her nuncheon in her bed-chamber, lying down a little afterwards and even sleeping briefly. She woke from a dream in which Ensley had come to Holles Street to offer her an enormous, golden Cheshire cheese. It was painful to open her eyes on the unfamiliar windows, the white walls, the bare floor. "What time is it?" she asked the quiet room, suddenly in mortal fear lest she had missed her appointment with the intimidating Mr. Rand. She found her watch and discovered it was not so, blew her nose several times, and got up, smoothing her skirts and splashing her face with water from the blue-and-white basin. "I must get hold of some books on farming," she murmured to herself as she hurried from the room. "I wonder whether my great uncle has some in his library. I wonder if he has a library," she continued as she descended the staircase, thus startling Susannah, who had been trimming the wicks of the lamps in the hall below. "I must look over the house . . ."

But Mr. Rand had it in mind that she should look over the grounds first ("While the light holds," he argued unanswerably), and so it was. Anne invited Maria to come with her, the two ladies changed into riding dress, Mr. Rand ordered horses to be brought round for them, and they set off. Anne mounted grumblingly; but as they rode on her spirits lightened, soothed by the pale sky, the sunlight, the lush greens of midsummer. It was in a mild, quiet way a lovely property: The house stood on a gentle hill just high enough to command miles of flat, hedged (the estate had been inclosed for more than twenty years) field and meadow, and in the near distance, a substantial park. Sheep and cattle grazed in a dozen spots within easy view. The farm buildings, when they came to them, were new and solid. The dairy was clean and cleverly ventilated, run on principles laid down, Rand proudly noted, by Mr. Harley of Glasgow; and it was complemented by one of the new pig-sties, a quite well-tenanted one. The barn was of good timber, the granaries ingeniously set up to keep out vermin, the sheep yard sheltered and guttered (Mr. Rand further pointed out) to prevent the dilution of manure. Miss Guilfoyle would observe, in fact, that the whole pattern of the buildings had been carefully laid with manure in mind. Miss Guilfoyle was not shy of his mentioning manure, he hoped? She knew the saying, no doubt, "Nothing like muck"? Truer words were never spoke, in Mr. Rand's opinion. Indeed, one of Mr. Guilfoyle's last experiments had been to purchase oilcakes for the cattle. And, Mr. Rand assured her, the resultant muck had been richer than any he had known, well worth the price of the fodder in improved wheat and barley harvests. But perhaps Miss Guilfoyle would not care to keep up the experiment? Perhaps Miss Guilfoyle had some better idea as to how to improve manure?

Miss Guilfoyle, with a sidelong glance of amazement at Mrs. Insel, replied that—as of this moment at least—she had not. "What a stench," she whispered, as they finally rode away. "One is positively grateful to have a cold!"

As the afternoon stretched on, Mr. Rand escorted the ladies all over Linfield's home farm. They were informed of the crop course (turnips, barley, wheat, barley, clover for three years, peas, and turnips again) favoured by Mr. Guilfoyle—and of course asked if they knew a better one; they were introduced to sheep whose complicated lineage, Anne remarked, fairly cried out for an ovine *Debrett's* (her great uncle had been a frequent visitor to Mr. Bakewell, Mr. Ellman, and Coke of Holkham, and had taken sheep from them to cross-breed himself). They observed the clipping of the milk ewes. They learned how many pounds of wool were to be got from each, and how much more money ewes generally had fetched last year than this. Mr. Rand made some morose observations concerning plunging corn prices. He informed the ladies that several of the tenants were expecting poor crops this year—and even Linfield's were not up to the mark. Still . . . and again the steward waxed loquacious, this time on the subject of seed-drills and marling and drainage. As he spoke they all rode on, and on, and on, till at last (though it went against her pride) Anne could not help asking how much farther they had to go.

"Not much. Five or six mile—unless you care to visit the tenant farms today as well?"

"Five or— How large exactly is the home farm?"

"One thousand acres," said Rand, rolling the syllables out on his tongue with a pleasure more proprietary, Anne thought, than custodial.

"And how many tenant farms are there?" asked she.

"Twelve," replied the steward, with more of that same satisfaction. "Farmer Gough there, Haydon there, Morris . . ." He went on through the dozen, pointing east, west, and south. "North lies Fevermere, with twenty of its own—that's thirty-two families for the school."

"The school?" Miss Guilfoyle was startled into echoing.

"Certainly." Mr. Rand, who had been riding a little ahead of the ladies (for the pleasure of making them trot to keep up, Anne suspected), reined in a little and dropped back. "Didn't you know? Mr. Guilfoyle and Mr. Highet share in the keeping of a school for the children of the tenants. 'Tis an idea Mr. Guilfoyle stole of Mr. Robert Owen. Mr. Guilfoyle said the one thing a good man ought to steal is a good idea."

Anne, who was beginning to tire a little of her great uncle, was nevertheless curious to see this school. It distressed her to reflect that the enterprise tied her affairs inextricably to those of the endless Henry Highet. Still, to one for whom learning mattered so much, the school must be of interest. She asked Maria if it would tire her excessively to pay a call there. Mrs. Insel declaring herself game, Miss Guilfoyle bade Mr. Rand conduct them to the place. The steward wheeled his horse to the north. The ladies followed.

Anne thought as they rode of her old life, setting it mentally next her new one. What would have occupied her at this hour, had the Maidstone never sunk? This was Tuesday, her at-home day. The drawing-room at number 3, Holles Street must have been filled with visitors: politicians set at liberty by the prorogation of Parliament, scholars, scribblers of all sorts . . . Ensley must have come (she felt a stab of loss), unless Lady Juliana had prevented him (the metaphorical knife turned in her breast). Still, the Blue Saloon would have buzzed with talk about court and country, the events of the day, pleasant projects for the

end of the Season—not a whiff of muck in the discourse,
not a blade of barley. While instead she rode along a field
of—clover, she thought Mr. Rand had said—in his company and that of Maria, with no one to invite to tea save
the labourers who boldly and sceptically stared at her
when Mr. Rand ("They work for you. You want to know
them") introduced them.

A habit of honesty obliged her to append the names of
Henry and Mrs. Highet to the list of invitables. And in
the next week or so, no doubt, the rector, the squire, and
the families of the county would come to call and enlarge
her circle of Cheshire acquaintance. It piqued her to realize that the squire at least would do so more or less as a
matter of amiable condescension—for Miss Guilfoyle in
the country was not what she had been in town. Here she
could claim no more than her old family, and the lapsed
baronetage, to distinguish her. The brilliant society she
frequented in London signified nothing to gentlefolk
hereabouts, and her connexion to Ensley must inspire
stricture sooner than admiration. Even this bumpkin
Highet ranked ahead of her here, she supposed, for Fevermere she now perceived to be considerably larger and
finer than Linfield. She had not been accustomed to think
of herself as vain of her position—but that had been before she lost it. Easy to shrug off what falls again to one's
shoulders on its own. Here she felt stripped and exposed.

With such gloomy thoughts as these filling her mind,
Anne scarcely noticed at first the actual clouds, low and
grey, drifting into the pale sky above her. The afternoon
was well advanced and the sky quite dark by the time
they came within view of a small brick edifice Mr. Rand
identified as the schoolhouse. No chorus of young voices
floated out from it to meet them, and as Anne dis-

mounted, and took in the dreary sky, and remembered Ensley, and felt new aches from the long ride and old ones from her cold, her spirits dropped to a lower pitch almost than any time she could recall.

But they were soon to turn, and her thoughts to find a diversion; for behind the bland brick walls of the school-house sat Mr. Lawrence Mallinger: young, fair, kindly, intelligent, single, and unaware even then of the fate that had come a-riding so far to find him.

FOUR

"Mr. Rand!"

Startled, Lawrence Mallinger sprang to his feet and hastily swept his long, light hair into a semblance of order. At the same time he unsuccessfully attempted to cover the book he had been studying with another. Except for himself, the schoolroom was empty. The children had their lessons early in the day. The room was an open, pleasant one, wide and lofty, with a dozen windows and two good fireplaces ready to keep out the chill of winter. Mr. Mallinger looked open and pleasant as well, with a deepening pink blush on his pale skin and a pair of large blue eyes in his lean face. He was lean altogether, and tall. Miss Guilfoyle, curious to know what reading matter could inspire such furtiveness in him, went a few steps nearer to the desk behind which he had been sitting and was able (thanks to her long and intimate acquaintance-ship with the alphabet, even if upside-down) to identify the work of Thomas Spence.

She was not surprised. She had never read Spence herself, but she knew him for a radical—like all the other dangerous fools her great uncle had evidently admired. She and Ensley had no opinion of the sort of claptrap these rabble-rousers put about. She began to be quite grateful the late Mr. Guilfoyle had come so seldom to London.

"We have surprised you," she said now, smiling civilly and bringing Maria forward with herself. She put out her hand. "I am Miss Guilfoyle, and here is my friend Mrs. Insel. You must be Mr.—?"

Mr. Mallinger obligingly supplied his name.

"We must apologize for appearing so suddenly," Anne went on, perceiving that the schoolmaster's blush of surprise still had not ebbed. "Mr. Rand has been showing us Linfield. I expect you knew my great uncle well?"

Collecting himself with an effort—was he always so shy? Anne wondered—Mr. Mallinger replied, "Indeed. Though not nearly so long as I could have wished. My deepest condolences, ma'am. Your uncle is sadly missed by all who knew him."

"Great uncle," Anne corrected with a touch of impatience, thinking, "Good God, another devotee." But her eye happening to wander over Mr. Mallinger's desk, the direction of her thoughts changed sharply and she cried out, "Great heavens, the London paper! Bless you for a good man." She reached out greedily. "You will permit me? I have not seen one since . . ." But she had already bent her head over it and was scanning it before he could answer.

"Indeed, pray carry it away with you. Mr. Highet sends his over to me each afternoon, when he is finished with it. Very obliging of—"

He was not destined to finish his sentence. Miss Guilfoyle had looked up again and was exclaiming, in the most indignant accents, "But this is Friday's number! I saw it before I left town!" Her tone suggested some thing beyond mere disappointment—betrayal, perhaps.

Taken aback, Mr. Mallinger none the less managed to say amiably, "They are a while in getting here, unfortunately."

"A while? Say rather an age, and I agree with you." As if revolted by it, Anne tossed the paper onto his desk again and sat abruptly in one of the pupils' little chairs. Here she fell into a silence supplemented by a speaking look of dejection.

A little embarrassed by her friend's stormy words and ill-concealed moroseness, "Poor Miss Guilfoyle," Mrs. Insel explained. "Not to know the news from London vexes her dreadfully. It signifies so very much to her, you know."

Mr. Mallinger gave a sympathetic "Hm," but seemed rather nonplussed. Mr. Rand, casting a look of frank disgust at his new mistress, said he would wait outdoors with the horses and disappeared.

"You are not so much at a loss in the country, I think?" the schoolmaster smiled at Maria. There was something in his glance which made her feel uncomfortably conscious. She reached a hand up to pat the smooth coils of her hair before answering.

"No, in that wise I am more fortunate than Miss Guilfoyle. The sorry truth is, I can do very well for weeks without a word of the Cabinet, or the House of Lords, or—" she waved her small, beringed hand vaguely, "all that."

Mr. Mallinger bowed. "Still, no doubt your husband keeps you informed of—all that, as you call it?"

"My husband—" If Maria had felt conscious before, she was half undone now. In a visible flutter and with a dark blush she would not have cared to think much about, "My husband is . . . no longer with me," she said, then murmured suggestively, "A soldier . . ."

"I am very sorry to hear it," Mr. Mallinger rejoined, gazing steadily at the lids of her downcast eyes.

Anne, emerging from her brown study, thought she had never heard so unconvincing a testimony of grief. It was clear to her that Mr. Mallinger meant to flirt with Maria, and clear moreover that he had caught that lady unawares, and disconcerted her. She jumped to her feet and interrupted without warning, "But you, Mr. Mallinger—you, I trust, are not one who can ignore the state of his country long. I see you reading Spence and know you for a man of ideas."

"Indeed," said Mr. Mallinger, reddening slightly. "But not ideas you are likely to share, I fear."

"Probably not," Miss Guilfoyle agreed. "Still, it is a wide world, and though we come to different answers, at least we concern ourselves with similar questions. I dareswear you and I shall find more to say to one another than I should to—well, for example, Mr. Rand," suggested Anne, overcoming the temptation to mention Mr. Highet instead.

It was a pretty escape from conflict, and a civil one, and

Mr. Mallinger gladly followed her in it. Smiling and again raking his fingers through his blond, shining hair, "I think Mrs. Insel must also have her share of ideas," he said, "though they are not political. I see them in her eyes, do not I?" he went on, searching those orbs. "They are so full, I seem to see hundreds."

Maria, who had recovered her composure, lost it again at once. "Ideas . . ." she echoed uncertainly, turning her head towards Anne in such a way as (inadvertently) to present her small, chiselled profile to Mr. Mallinger. "I do not . . ."

"More than you or I can count," Miss Guilfoyle affirmed, as Maria's voice faded to nothing, and her face paled alarmingly. "And such funny ones too," she added rather mysteriously; but with so much obvious affection that Mr. Mallinger quite forgave her her earlier eccentricity, and even (though not quite) what he supposed was her staunch Toryism. Now, putting her arm round Maria's narrow waist, Anne went on, "I must take this mouse home, for one of her funny beliefs is that I like her to jaunt all over the country with me, never mind how fatigued she is. Good day to you, sir. I trust we shall meet again soon. Won't you wish Mr. Mallinger good day, my dear?" she asked the small figure on her arm as she turned her about and rapidly escorted her towards the door.

"Good day," came Mrs. Insel's faint voice from the doorstep.

Mr. Mallinger was left to reply, and even to bow, to her back—and to puzzle over Miss Guilfoyle's manner of taking her off, and the significance of Mrs. Insel's blushes, and a few other matters.

It was a fair ride home, even travelling directly, as Miss Guilfoyle (secretly worried for Maria, who continued withdrawn and agitated) insisted they travel. She put off all Mr. Rand's objections, saying she would see what remained of Linfield to-morrow and the next day, and even refused, once they reached the house, to sit with him and look at his records.

"They can wait," she told him firmly, dispatching Maria to her bedroom and ringing for Susannah to send some orgeat up after her.

"Crops don't wait," growled Rand in reply. "Even for fine London ladies."

"Then they can rot," said his exhausted and irritated employer. Really, the behaviour her great uncle tolerated in his people! "I have other business to attend to than turnips and bacon, though you might not think it. Kindly carry on with any pressing matter as you would have before my arrival."

And Mr. Rand turned away, grumbling something that sounded very much like, "Before—! God grant us such days again."

It was nearly six o'clock. Maria had invited the Highets *mère et fils* to arrive at eight. Anne allotted herself exactly one quarter of an hour to sit still, after which she was determined to go over the house with Miss Veal. She did her sitting still in a drawing-room Susannah (requested to fetch some lemonade there once Maria had been attended to) identified as merely that—"the Drawing-Room." Anne tried not to think, while she waited, how strongly this suggested there was only one in the house. If so—well, it was comfortable enough, at least, furnished with deep chairs and sofas covered in flowered chintz, with a set of French windows opening onto a brickwork terrace that afforded a view of the park, and a large marble fireplace. A small pianoforte kept, she soon discovered, tolerably in tune stood in one corner. In another was a clever, many-draw-ered work table, with good lamps and every kind of scissor and needle ready furnished. Anne suspected strongly that Miss Veal had sat at this table many an evening, bearing the bachelor Mr. Guilfoyle company while she darned his socks.

She had no intention, however, of attempting to verify her conjecture. "Let sleeping dogs lie," was the adage in her head when the old lady duly arrived to escort her through the rooms. The tour, mercifully for Anne's tired bones, did not take long. On the ground floor were this drawing-room, the dining- and household rooms she had already seen, a study which had been used by Mr. Guilfoyle, a snug parlour furnished, in shades of green, rather more plushly than the other apartments, and a quite large library filled with the works of every kind of radical and free-thinker, as well as scores of tomes on farming. Upstairs were eight bedrooms, of which she had already seen her own and Maria's. None of the others was at all grander or more elegant than the one she had slept in, though each, like it, was airy, scrubbed, and comfortable in a homely way. Besides these there were two small sit-ting-rooms obviously not much in use, and a large, care-fully tended conservatory at the end of one wing. Above this floor were the servants' rooms and the attics—and that was all. Saving the pianoforte, there was not a stick of fruitwood in the place, not a gilt frame (nor even a family portrait!), not an inch of inlay, not a scrap of silk on the walls.

Anne thanked Miss Veal and went at once to the desk in her great uncle's study, which she intended to make her own. She found a good supply of writing paper and some pens and ink in a tolerable state, and at once dashed off a brief but impassioned letter to Celia Grypphon begging her to come to Cheshire. To be sure, she included the anecdotes saved from this morning, with an account (as humorous as she could make it) of the afternoon with Rand; but the heart of the letter was a plea that her friend should join and comfort her here. "For a week at least— no, even for a day. I can offer you nothing but cheese and fine walking (there might be a pheasant hiding in the wood nearby, though I rather doubt it), a plain feather bed, and all the barley you like. It is little to tempt you with, but pray do come. I deserve it. I need the solace of your wit. My life is overturned, not only because of E.— whose news I guess you have heard—but for a reason even he does not know. Anyhow, if you will not come, put this letter into Charles' hands and let him persuade you to it."

She closed after asking Lady Grypphon to bring with her the latest numbers of certain journals she felt sure could not be had in Cheshire. The mere act of writing made her feel better, as if Celia invited were Celia half arrived, and she rose from the desk with a lighter step than she had had all day. She was just looking for Charlotte Veal to ask where she must leave the letter to be posted when that lady came into the front hall looking for her, carrying a letter just arrived.

The two missives were exchanged. Anne, looking at the one confided to her, felt her heart lurch with relief and could hardly repress a lunatic smile. She hurried upstairs. In the privacy of her room, with fingers that trembled idiotically, she broke the seal and read,

My dearest Anne,
    If you do not mean to return to London be-

fore next week, pray allow me to come to you. I
must see you at once. I have a thousand things
to say. Be merciful and tell me I may come.

ENSLEY

Anne rang her bell, opened the ebony lap-desk, wrote
"Come," on a clean sheet, folded, directed, and sealed it.
Susannah arrived to collect it a moment later. Then Anne
summoned Lizzie to help her bathe and dress for dinner.

Curiously, Miss Guilfoyle found herself almost looking
forward to her guests from Fevermere. When Maria
(neatly and soberly dressed as usual) went in to tell her
they had arrived, she was delighted to hear Anne actually
singing, and to see her robed in a delicate gown of celestial blue, with a bandeau to match.

"Enter, enter, my dear," trilled Anne, looking over her
shoulder while Lizzie put a finishing touch to her golden
curls. "Quite rested now, I hope? My reliance is all on
you, you know, to make this evening 'go.' Not but what,"
she added mischievously, "I am sure Mrs. Highet is a brilliant conversationalist. Like her son."

"You seem happier," observed Mrs. Insel, wisely letting this slur pass without comment.

"Who would not be happy, who has one hundred
Shropshire cows to call her own?" Anne hopped up from
her chair, sneezed, provisioned her reticule with a second
handkerchief, and tucked her arm under Maria's. "Oh,
Ensley will come to see us soon," she remarked carelessly, as they strolled to the stairs. "I have invited Celia
and Charles as well. Is there any other person you would
like to have? Some one hardy, with a sense of comedy?"

A few more light observations such as these and they
were in the snugly fitted Green Parlour, saying good eve-

ning to their guests. Henry Highet, quite correctly attired now in a blue coat, a white waistcoat, and black pantaloons, stood and bowed rather deeply. His cravat puzzled Anne a little—it appeared to have started life as a *Noeud Gordien*, yet ended with more than a hint of the *Bergami* twisted into it—but even with her disposition to find fault in him, she could not help but be favourably struck by the regularity of his strong features, the mobility of his mouth, the freshness of his high colour, and the liquidity of his sleepy-lidded eyes. His black hair, she noticed now, he wore rather long. It curled (without encouragement, she supposed) *en Cherubin*. The blue coat fitted his broad shoulders well, if not perfectly, and he was so tall as quite to tower over her when he had finished bowing. His was not, all in all, a style of handsomeness that had ever interested Anne (as she noted silently); but she had to confess it was impressive.

Now Mr. Highet gave his slow smile and introduced his mother, who had also risen when the ladies came in. Mrs. Highet was discovered to be an immensely gawky person, tall, large-boned, almost hulking. It was difficult to imagine how a woman could have gone through so much of her life—Miss Guilfoyle judged her to be above sixty years of age—yet acquired so little of gracefulness; but there she was. The strong features she had passed on to her son still survived in her wrinkled face but, as so often happens with women, what suited and enhanced him made her plain. Anne thought she caught a shrewd glimmer in the mother's eye which was not to be found in the son's. The ladies shook hands. Anne was surprised to notice her own hand was damp. Her mind began to tick. Might a cold make one's hands damp? She could hardly be worried about meeting an elderly country widow, she reflected. But then why—

Her thoughts were turned from this confusing channel by the intrusion of Mrs. Insel's voice. Maria was thanking the Highets for accepting the invitation to dine, describing to the old lady all the various, generous feats her son had performed the night before, expressing her delight in knowing them . . . Anne listened with a guilty apprehension that she herself ought to have been saying these things; only she had been so occupied with her private prejudices and strictures that she had neglected her duty. She resolved to mend her ways henceforth and set herself especially to be gracious to Mr. Highet. Maria having entered with that gentleman's mother into a discussion of needlework (for she had remembered the pincushion Mr. Highet sat upon last night) Anne was free to initiate her program of amiability at once. So she begged Mr. Highet to join her on the chintz-covered settee and gaily confided,

"Mr. Rand has been showing us over the home farm of Linfield today. I confess, he quite terrifies me. Such a brusque fellow; I wonder if he is so to everyone. I suspect he is but indifferent pleased to find himself employed by me."

Though Anne's tone had been light and cheerful, Mr. Highet listened to her very seriously, and answered with a gathered brow: "Indeed, I am sorry to hear it. Such an attitude must hamper you severely in managing the estate."

"Oh dear," said Anne, disconcerted by his solemnity, "I cannot blame him so very much after all. I dareswear he considers a town-bred lady has no business to run such a place as Linfield—and I dareswear he is not far wrong."

As she spoke she could not help but wonder again whether Mr. Highet knew who would have inherited if she had not. Perhaps Rand knew; perhaps the two of them were in a plot to make her uncomfortable at Linfield, so that she would leave. But that was preposterous. Mr. Rand was a mere common garden-variety misogynist, while Mr. Highet was a mere common country—but no, she must, she *would* learn to be tolerant of Mr. Highet. Making an effort she continued, "I have a very great deal to learn if I am to fill my benefactor's shoes. I hope I may ask you to help me now and then?"

"I shall be glad indeed to assist you in whatever way possible," Mr. Highet replied, just as gravely as before, "but I fear I do not know enough myself to teach you to be Herbert Guilfoyle. He was a gifted farmer indeed, and a sage and kindly friend. You must feel his loss keenly."

"To be quite truthful, I hardly knew him. I met him only once, when I was twelve." Out of patience with all this reverence of her eccentric relation, she added impulsively, "Actually, he refused to speak with me until I had read Rousseau."

To her annoyance, Mr. Highet seemed to find in this ridiculous incident only another rich example of the late Herbert's worthiness. To be sure, he did laugh—throwing back his head and waiting, as he had last night, quite two seconds before exploding noisily—but when he had recomposed his countenance it was only to say warmly, "How like him; what a wonderful story. A most remarkable man!"

Finding nothing to say, Miss Guilfoyle listened to this tribute in uncomfortable silence.

"But about Mr. Rand," Henry Highet at last reverted,

"you must certainly ask me whatever he fails to make clear to you."

"I am most grateful."

"How do you like the farm? It is a model, is not it?"

"If you say so, I must think it is. I have no other farm with which to compare it."

"But have you always lived in London, then?" he asked, his tone profoundly pitying, as if the mere idea distressed him terribly.

Ignoring his intonation, "Not always," she replied. "Before my father died I lived at Overton, in Northamptonshire. But then his brother inherited and my mother and I removed to town."

"What, for ever? How sad for both of you! How dreadful," continued he sympathetically, "to be obliged to quit your home." And he shook his head as if for very sorrow.

"We preferred it, in all candour," Anne coldly rejoined. If she hated to be laughed at, she fairly squirmed to be pitied. Anyway, the theme of being obliged to quit one's home struck closer to the bone than she could bear just now. How was it Mr. Highet contrived to see her as luckless and pitiable? No one else did. "We throve in London. My mother loved London," she declared. "So do I."

"You speak of your mother in the past tense," he observed quietly. "Have you lost her?"

"Many years ago," Anne snapped. What a genius this dolt had for making her look pathetic! But could he really be sincere? There was something almost womanish, she found, in his gentle, tiresome sympathy; and whatever his intention, the effect of his commiseration was certainly to torment her.

"I am so sorry," said Mr. Highet simply, with a glance

at his large, very lively mother which seemed to say, "Thank God, I have been spared that loss as well."

"Are you often in London?" Anne demanded, hoping to turn the topic (and wondering yet again if he knew the terms of her inheritance).

"Not often. Never, actually, since coming down from Oxford. Now I think of it, that means—good heavens, sixteen years ago. I have been at Fevermere sixteen years," he repeated wonderingly, then called across the room, "Mother, we have been at Fevermere sixteen years!"

"Have we?" answered that lady, much struck, and evidently not at all surprised to have her conversation interrupted by such news. "Dear me, so we have." And she turned placidly back to Maria.

"I had never stopped to count it up," Mr. Highet explained blandly, turning back also. "But about London—I am afraid I find it intolerably dirty, and noisy, and crowded. Not at all the way you think of it, I daresay. But—what do you do there all day, day after day, with no riding, nor hunting, nor—well, occupation?" And he fixed Anne with such a sleepy, earnest gaze that she felt ready to scream.

"Oh, one manages to amuse oneself," she responded tersely, not trusting herself to point out that there were museums there, and libraries, and the Court, and Parliament, and Hyde Park, and thousands of the best minds in the country, lest her tone betray the wild exasperation he provoked in her. Immeasurably frustrated by the sputtering conversation, she cast about for something that would interest this clunch, a topic he could understand and expand upon. Finally, she hit on the obvious. "But pray tell

me about Fevermere. Is your farm very different from
Linfield's?"

Yes, here was a topic Mr. Highet could like. As she sat
back and listened, Anne blamed herself for not asking the
question sooner. Easily, with palpable enjoyment, Mr.
Highet warmed to his subject. Fevermere's was a mixed
farm, like Linfield's, but it was bigger. He had had it from
his older brother, who gave it him when (their father
dying while Henry was still in school) the brother fell heir
to the family's chief estate in Staffordshire. The father
had always run the Cheshire holding through a bailiff; but
Henry devoted himself to it utterly, as Miss Guilfoyle
could guess. His brother being a married man, with a numerous family, their mother chose to reside with her
younger son, where she could continue to command her
own household. And so they had been here for sixteen
years, as he had just become aware.

And was Herbert Guilfoyle always at Linfield since Mr.
Highet came here?

Yes, indeed, Herbert had taught Mr. Highet all he
knew of farming. Why, it was Herbert who had persuaded
him to give up a fallow year in his rotation and try turnips
instead, Herbert who had induced him to practise sheep
housing during bad weather, Herbert who . . . Anne listened, suppressing sneezes and yawns, and longing to
hear of Colonel Whiddon's India days, or to watch Tom
Maitland drink himself into a stupor, anything except endure these everlasting tales of turnips and her sainted
great uncle. She was determined to learn about farming,
since she must needs run a farm; but did Mr. Highet have
to talk about it with such enthusiasm? Such passion,
rather! He was just explaining the Duke of Portland's irri-

gation scheme for the Nottinghamshire sands when Miss Veal (who acted as butler till Dolphim arrived) appeared and announced dinner.

"Oh dear," said Anne, rising. "You *must* tell me more of this later. So fascinating."

Mr. Highet nodded seriously and, without speaking, offered his arm to take her in to dinner. Anne accepted it; but because she turned round to see the others follow she chanced not to notice an expression on Henry Highet's face which must have interested her a good deal. If one had not already observed him to be in every particular a most sober and straightforward gentleman, one would almost have called the expression a smirk. One would almost have thought he was laughing, albeit silently, at Miss Anne Guilfoyle—that he knew she had been feigning interest, perhaps, and was amused. But since one has, after all, observed him to be so especially earnest and frank a country gentleman, one must instead suppose he was suppressing a cough, or had been tickled on the wrist by the deep flounce of Anne's celestial blue sleeve.

Among such a small party conversation at table must perforce be general, and Anne was spared any further tales of ditches and drainage for the moment. Mrs. Highet, who had a peculiarly loud, unmodulated voice, dominated the discourse with an informative catalogue of the local gentry. She spoke approvingly of Mr. Samuels, the rector at Faulding Chase, and of Lord and Lady Crombie, who had brought him into the county. Miss Guilfoyle and Mrs. Insel remembered to have met Baron Crombie and his wife on several occasions in town (and Miss Guilfoyle to have been highly diverted by the latter's maniacal devotion to her children). Mrs. Highet confirmed that they did indeed go up to town pretty often. She mentioned

London with none of the disapprobation her son had displayed. On the contrary, Mrs. Highet professed herself quite astonished that the ladies should chuse to remove themselves to Cheshire, when town life must have been so stimulating. She was afraid they would find it very dull hereabouts. The weather was scarcely ever fine, so that they would find themselves indoors a good deal, and the society was sadly limited. Particularly so, she went on, in the matter of eligible gentlemen—a matter (she directed her shrewd twinkle at Miss Guilfoyle) which must always interest a young single lady. In fact, there was scarcely an unattached gentleman to be seen here. "For my Henry is a confirmed bachelor, you know," she finished with a sudden access of something like vehemence, "and"—more quietly—"I do not expect Miss Guilfoyle considers Mr. Mallinger a suitable *parti.*"

Miss Guilfoyle, who had been wondering strongly where all this gloomy foreboding was tending, understood at last. Mrs. Highet was afraid lest Anne steal her son away. Anne had already perceived the wilfulness of the old lady, and her fierce attachment to "her Henry"; she could easily imagine how little Mrs. Highet would like to be supplanted in his affections, or at their board. But good God! Apart from the fact that Anne had long since ceased to regard herself as "a young lady," or to look for a husband (an odd flutter in her breast as her thoughts reached this point made her unconsciously lay a hand on her *bleu celeste* bodice, and hurry on in her meditations), Henry Highet must certainly be the last man on earth she would have been drawn to. Moreover, his shrewd mother must already have remarked there was not the least hint of gallantry or admiration in his manner to Anne. Ridicule her he had; pity her he might; but love her—? If Miss

Guilfoyle had not been drinking soup she would have laughed aloud.

Instead, "Oh, la," she said, when she could say anything, "I hope we shall not pine quite away. Surely there must be assemblies in Middlewich?" she suggested, suppressing a shudder at the thought of the sort of company which must likely be met with in such a place. "And how far distant is Chester? If none of the other families in the neighbourhood arrange dancing-parties and the like, I at least mean to. Anyhow, we are not so frightened of an evening at home as you may think, are we, Maria? I daresay we shall do very nicely, and become quite settled here," she concluded—for the Highets might as well understand, if they did not already, that she and Maria were not fly-by-nights, but intended to make Linfield their home.

Mrs. Highet received Anne's cheerful, confident speech with a darkening of the brow that confirmed the latter's suspicions of her motives. The conversation moved on to further inquiries and answers on the subject of local life, and the evening passed peacefully enough. The ladies withdrew when the meal was done to permit Mr. Highet his glass of Port; but he did not leave them alone above twenty minutes. After this the guests stopped only half an hour more; for though the clouds of the late afternoon had broke up again, and it was moonlight, the sky here was so prone to be overcast that one felt one ought to go when one could, rather than risk a dark journey. The party being small, the Linfield ladies escorted their guests to the front hall and good-byes were said there all round. The only additional circumstance of the visit worth noting (and some doubt might even attach to its worthiness: Miss Guilfoyle, for example, did not trouble to mention it later

to Maria) was that when Mr. Highet and Miss Guilfoyle
shook hands and said good night, Miss Guilfoyle felt a
shock of pleasure in the touch of Mr. Highet's warm hand
which quite astonished her. Her face actually reddened
(had anyone seen it—it is possible Mr. Highet saw it,
though doubtful, since his own expression continued mild
and bland) and she hastily thrust the guilty hand into the
grip of her other almost as if to hide it.

But that was all.

The next five days at Linfield were taken up with tours
of the tenant farms, inspection of Mr. Rand's books, the
arrival of the (quite useless) furniture from Holles Street,
and of the (quite useful) Dolphim with it. Both ladies'
colds passed off quickly; which was fortunate, for they
had several callers. Lady Crombie, notably, condescended
to pass fifteen minutes enlightening them as to the various
achievements of her progeny. The rector visited with his
wife, and Mr. and Mrs. Hartley Ware of Stade Park (a
very considerable property, Miss Veal afterwards remarked), and some few others, not one of whom seemed
to have the least interest in any affair or topic which did
not touch his own life directly. Anne's evenings were
taken up with reading about techniques of agriculture: "I
dip freely," she wrote to Lady Holland, "into my great
uncle's substantial collection of literary works on farming,
and come up (as Fortune dictates) with piggeries, or seed
drills, or muck." All of which she wrote only for the joke
of it, because in truth she found her reading very interesting, as she had always found interesting any branch of
learning or science.

On Sunday she suggested to Maria that they invite Mr.
Mallinger, who at least read something, to dine with
them; but Mrs. Insel seemed gently averse to this and

Anne gave up the idea for the moment. Instead they merely went to church—where Mr. Samuels preached a quite unexceptionable sermon on Sacrifice—and returned to dine alone. The rain held off, the haying went forward, the Highets (except for a nod in church) stayed away. As for that unaccountable rush of pleasure Anne had felt when Mr. Highet clasped her hand, she soon dismissed it with a laugh and a mental shrug. Perhaps the hall had been draughty and what she really felt was a shiver. Anyhow, it was of no consequence. She determined to forget it. Even if she had not, an event occurred to chase it from her mind: Just before noon on the Monday, Dolphim came into her study bearing George, Lord Ensley's, so familiar card.

# FIVE

ANNE WENT TO ENSLEY WITH BOTH ARMS OUT AND was immediately enfolded in his well-remembered embrace.

"My dearest," breathed he into her golden hair. "My darling!"

But strange—very strange—to say, this fond apostrophe, the low, vibrant timbre of the voice that uttered it, the faint scent of the soap the speaker's laundrywoman used on his linen, and the fragrance of the boot-polish favoured by his valet, rather disturbed than reassured Anne. She stepped back (though pretending to do so to look at him) really to get away from him.

"How do you do, Ensley?" she heard herself ask, not at all in the easy, affectionate tone she had intended to adopt. She allowed him, as they stood a little apart in the middle of the chintz-bedecked drawing-room, to retain her hands in his; but hers were cool and lifeless.

"You seem angry at me," was his answer. He scrutinized her. She turned her gaze uncomfortably aside. She had forgot how fine his blue eyes were, as well as how closely they could observe her. "Tell me why."

But, "I am not angry," Anne said, at the same time firmly removing her hands from his. "Not at all. I was delighted to receive your note, and to know you were coming. You look well. How was your journey?"

Again he ignored her question. Instead, "Delighted to know I was coming, perhaps, but now that you see me," he persisted, "not so delighted. Why is Dolphim with you? What is this Linfield?"

With a resentful sense that he had no business reading her so easily, "You mistake me," she said. "Sit down, my dear. Is there any thing you would like fetched? Wine? Have you lunched? If I am subdued"—she drew him to a sofa opposite the French doors—"it is only that I am tired. I slept poorly last night. I could never be sorry to see you; that you know." With this she stroked his hand a little, and smiled up into his eyes.

But Ensley was not the least satisfied. "Anne, why have you removed here?" he demanded bluntly. "It is my marriage, is not it? You quitted London almost as soon as I told you. I can only surmise—"

Miss Guilfoyle left off smiling and abruptly jumped to her feet. This time there was no pretending she was not angry. "You can only surmise," she repeated scornfully, rounding on him. "Exactly, my lord. You can only surmise that your life is the spring of every event in mine. It does not occur to you that I have a life independent of yours"—

this was very unfair to Ensley, who on the contrary loved her so well precisely because she did have such a life— "with its own incidents, and its own reversals. As it happens, my fortune has been lost." And she went on, a little less heatedly, to explain the sinking of the *Maidstone*, and her inheritance of Linfield.

"My poor girl." When she had done, Ensley reached up a hand. Anne allowed herself to be drawn down into the comfort of his encircling arm, and leaned her head against his shoulder. His solidity, the scent of his hair oil, the brush of his lips atop her head all began to soothe her at last, and for some moments they merely sat still, while his lordship murmured indistinct consolation.

Then, "But that blackguard, Dent!" he remarked. "What the devil did he mean staking all your money on such a risky business?"

Anne, though not enthusiastically, defended Mr. Dent, pointing out he had ruined himself as well and (more persuasively) that he would be quite unable to pay her back, should she take him to law. "He would only end in the Marshalsea," she finished listlessly. "I should not be a penny the richer for it. Anyhow," she went on, vigour returning to her voice as fear of appearing pitiable before Ensley urged her to a show of spirits, "I rather enjoy Linfield. I never realized before how exhausting endless sociability can be. The house is not quite what I like, to be sure, but I look forward to setting my imprint upon it. And you cannot imagine what a pleasure it is to be able to read and read without interruption—no tiresome callers, no foolish parties—"

"For the love of heaven, stop!" Ensley exploded at this point. This time he rose from the sofa and began to pace nervously over the room, speaking as he went. "I see your face, yet you expect me to believe you are happy here? I find you in a house of which the kindest thing that can be said is that it is clean, and you ask me to imagine your pleasure in improving it? I, who have known and loved you ten years—ten years, Anne"—he stopped to turn a stormy, serious face upon her—"am to credit that you feel relieved, refreshed, disencumbered by your removal from intelligent society? Be angry with me if you will, but at least do me the kindness to acknowledge I cannot be turned away by such gammon as that!"

Anne stood. It was painful to argue with Ensley but impossible to admit he was right. "I do not know why you should imagine," she began, "that the only intelligent society in England is to be found in London. A person may live in the country and yet pursue all manner of knowledge. A thinking life can, thank God, be lived in any—"

But he had heard all he could bear. He strode to her, seized both her hands, and begged, "Come home with me, Anne. For the love of common sense; for love of me; by all that is, and has been, and always will be between us, come home."

Anne had begun to listen raptly. She was silent for a moment, as if expecting him to say more, then tilted her lovely face up to him and asked, simply, "How?"

He had already started to smile at her again, reassured by the return of life to her hands, and the lightening of her upturned brow. "There is nothing easier in the world, nothing more natural," he said. "I shall take a house for you and you will live in it. I shall give you all you need, and you will want for nothing. Everything will go on between us just as it was, and all this"—he waved a hand at the neat, genteel parlour—"will vanish like a dream."

Miss Guilfoyle was still gazing up at him, but something had changed in her eyes. Poor Ensley could not read them fully at first, but he saw at least that his plan did not suit her. The fact was, something had gone slightly wild inside Anne Guilfoyle's orderly head. Though she knew as well as she had ever known—knew incontrovertibly and with every ounce of logic in her—that Ensley could not, must not, and would not marry her, she also knew (quite suddenly, and utterly against all sense) that she wanted him to do so, must have him do so, and would never forgive him if he did not. She had never known two things so mutually exclusive so perfectly well in her life. From the battlefield where these two ideas warred with each other, she was able to wrest for now only the following rather homely words: "Ensley, is that all you can suggest?"

He blinked at her, innocent and nonplussed. "If you can think of a better solution," he at last brought out carefully, "I shall be glad to hear it."

In the seconds before his lordship answered Anne had recovered, if not her reason, at least her sense of fairness. He had never promised to marry her, never even hinted at such a thought. On the contrary, it had always been understood between them he would not. How reprehensible in her, then, to blame him for not offering now! How peculiar; how unreasonable. She struggled for self-command and gained enough to say, in a voice tolerably calm, "No, it is not that I know a better solution, only that—" She reminded herself of his countless kindnesses to her, the two or three thousand evenings they had passed together. "Dear Ensley, you must understand I cannot like the idea of living on your bounty," she resumed. "It would not suit me at all." She strove to soften and sweeten her words by her tone, succeeding a little. "It is better for me to stay here. You will come to see me often, and I shall pass every minute of the two months allotted me in London. I daresay we shall succeed, over the year, in passing quite four or five months together. It is not ideal, but it is the best we can do."

Encouraged by her tone (though still wondering what that was he had seen in her eyes), Ensley remonstrated, "But how can you characterise such a plan as 'living on my bounty'? Is not everything I have yours? Would you not do the same for me if our situations were reversed?"

"If I did, would you accept it?" Anne inquired, with a touch of her former sharpness.

He ignored this and spoke on, "If you fear my doling money out to you, let me give it you all at once. A house, an easy competence, enough to keep Maria and all your servants—I shall give it you once for all, and you will administer it as you like."

"You cannot afford such a thing," was her first, smiling objection. Preposterous as it was, she admired the generosity of his idea.

"But indeed I can, that is just the beauty of it. Inside three months I shall be married, and whatever I had of straitened circumstances will be over," Ensley declared warmly. "It will mean nothing to me to endow you so, the merest—" But he broke off as he saw storm clouds in her face again, and asked, "What is it?"

"Can you think," Miss Guilfoyle snapped, backing away from him as if he had been Lucifer himself, "can you think I would consent to take that woman's money? Live on her money? Can you think it?"

But Ensley only pointed out, mildly and simply, "Why not? I am."

"You—" But, making an heroic push, she forced the angry words down and answered instead, "That is your choice, sir, but it will not do for me. I think, if you will excuse me, it will be better if we do not talk any more just now. Perhaps to-morrow. How long do you stop?"

"I had hoped to set out again tonight, taking you with me," Ensley muttered ruefully.

"Can you spare a night or two?"

He looked uncertain. They both knew he was thinking of his duties to Lady Juliana. But he said, *"Mais oui, pour faire plaîsir à ma Minerve."*

"Good," she said shortly. "Then I should like very much for you to go away now and come again in the morning. I had meant to put you up here, of course, but this is a small house as you see, and I need some time alone. Will you mind very much?"

"I am yours to command," he bowed.

Even this empty formula grated on her; she murmured, violently subduing an impulse to scream, "Then please do go away. I am not myself now." She put a hand to her temple. "My head aches, and I should be sorry . . . sorry to say good-bye to you in this state." Then, more naturally, she added, "Pray forgive me." She put her little hand into his and whispered, "I do not understand myself, to say truth."

Ensley, though he did not like it, was obliged to accept this arrangement for the moment. He bowed again, kissed her gently on the forehead, and walked out of the house.

He left behind him a woman who had never known such confusion. Had she blamed Ensley for taking her for granted? Very well then, witness his headlong pursuit of her into Cheshire, testimony to the reverse. Had she other complaints to lay at his door? She searched their history together. He had comforted her in her grief, rejoiced with her in her small triumphs, puzzled with her over her difficulties, petty or great, and helped her through. He had been unfailingly tender, affectionate, kind. In this business of his marriage, he had done only what they agreed he must do. And yet she was angry at him! That, at least, she could no longer deny. More than angry: She was furious, outraged, inflamed. How dare he suggest—? How dare he offer—?

But when her thoughts had reached this point she obliged herself to calm down. She climbed the stairs and shut herself into one of the small sitting-rooms there. A tolerably cosy room, she noticed. She made herself think of the furnishings in an effort to regain her tranquillity. She lifted the lid of a small mahogany box sitting on a Pembroke table and discovered a sticky cluster of long-forgotten comfits. The box made a pleasant, clopping sound as it dropped shut, and she opened and closed it a while, at the same time resisting a rising wave of frustrated tears.

"I will be calm," she said aloud. "I will be calm."

Then she recommenced her meditations, starting with What did she want from Ensley? His love? He did love her, or else why dash up here? Respect? He respected her most sincerely—or why ask her, as he often did, to write his speeches? Did she wish him to understand her? Who understood her better? Did she desire—

She desired him to marry her. That was it. Wriggle away from it as she might, this was what she came back to. She wished him to marry her. But he could not marry her. And anyhow, she had always said she did not particularly wish to be married. Wedlock seemed to her to carry very few privileges, and the loss of a great deal of liberty.

She did not want children: People under the age of six-teen could seldom hold her attention long, and it seemed rather clumsy to have a baby and wait sixteen years for it to become interesting when there were so many adults about ready-made. She would be able to live with Ensley, to be sure; but the truth was, she liked her solitary life, and viewed its theoretical disruption with dismay. Society would no longer look askance upon her connexion to his lordship—but the society she cared about already did not, and she didn't (she told herself) give two pins for the rest.

Then what tormented her so?

It was a measure of the keenness of her distress that she actually went to Maria Insel to ask for help. In whatever concerned herself and Ensley, her policy in the past had always been quite the opposite: If some thing really puzzled her in his behaviour, if a decision regarding him teased her dreadfully, she might—might—set an oblique question to the discreet Celia; but she never unburdened her heart to her, nor even permitted anyone else to see that she was in doubt. This grew, not from a lack of faith in her friends, but from a proud desire to manage her own affairs. Anyway, she knew Maria thought on principle that every woman ought to marry, and therefore could not be impartial.

But Maria was here, and Celia (who had sent to say she had another obligation but would try to come soon) was not. Therefore . . .

After luncheon, she invited Mrs. Insel to walk in the considerable park that lay between Linfield and the road. The day was warm, the sky softly grey, and Maria, who had tactfully been busying herself with a variety of house-hold tasks during the last week, was glad of an oppor-tunity to explore the grounds. So the two ladies set off at a brisk pace, following a small path into the woods and turning at random as it intersected with other paths, then carelessly following these.

With as little elaboration as possible, Anne told Maria she had something on her mind and set the trouble before her. She reminded her the issue of marriage had been discussed and decided between herself and Ensley many years before. "And yet"—she broke an unlucky leaf from an oak tree and tore it to bits—"I cannot stop being angry. I talk to myself and talk to myself, but . . ." Her voice trailed away and she flung the shredded leaf into the mild wind.

Maria Insel pressed her lips together. Anne might be baffled by her own response, but Maria was not. If she had been a man she might have called Ensley out for his conduct towards her friend. "Everything just as it was," indeed! "Take a house for her in London—" The idea! But it would not do to express outrage. That would only incline Anne to defend him. Instead, "I wonder, my dear," she said reasonably, "if you know your heart quite thoroughly when you say you do not wish, in general, to marry. Are you certain?"

"Of course," Miss Guilfoyle promptly answered. "Why should I wish to marry?"

"Most women do."

"And most are bitterly disappointed. Look at your own case," Anne added, not roughly but deliberately.

"I am convinced my case was extreme," Maria said in a quiet voice.

"Perhaps; but I should not like even a moderate dose of what you had, poor thing. I never can understand why you are such a champion of marriage."

"Perhaps 'extreme' was a poor choice of words. I should have said extraordinary—exceptional."

"Let us hope so," said Anne sceptically.

"At all events," Maria persisted, always happy to turn from the subject of her matrimonial history, "I still suspect you do not know your own feelings. One's desires may change, you know. What one did not care about at twenty, one may want at twenty-five. It would be foolish to hold oneself bound to a declaration made ten years ago when the truth behind it has changed."

"Foolish? Honourable, I think. Ensley has not changed in his feelings towards me."

"You have not married another man!" Maria objected, before she could stop herself.

"I have no need to."

"You could not! No one would dare to ask you, when your connexion to Ensley is so— Excuse me, my dear," she interrupted herself, observing tears start to Anne's eyes. "I didn't mean to distress you."

"It is only that it makes me so angry, the way you misunderstand him. Ensley loves me! If he could, he would marry me. He simply can't. If I cease to love him now that he is betrothed to Lady Juliana, *I* shall have betrayed *him*! Don't you understand? He trusted me to mean what I said. He believed me when I assured him I expected him, wanted him to marry properly. It is I who am breaking faith, I who am unable to stand by my word."

Anne had grown so agitated that Maria did not chuse to contradict her again, though she longed to. She waited until the other had been silent some while, then gently suggested, "Well, my dear, since Ensley does love you so, I am sure he cannot wish you to be unhappy. Perhaps you had best set the truth before him, and the two of you puzzle it out together." Secretly she was convinced the result of such a confession would be to annoy Ensley without making him change his plans. The two would then quarrel and Anne might break free of him at last.

However, "I could never tell Ensley a word of this," Anne protested. "I should die of shame. It is so weak of me. It is unforgivable."

Maria hesitated. Then, "I do not like to argue with you, Anne, but I cannot say I see anything the least bit unforgivable in it. On the contrary, it seems to me perfectly natural. You are accustomed to have Ensley for yourself, you feel jealous of Lady Juliana—"

"I am not jealous of that little chit," Anne broke in hotly. "What should I envy her for? Her thick nose? Her thin wit?"

"Her husband?" Maria suggested.

"Maria, you are not helping at all!" Anne declared passionately. "All you wish to do is prove Ensley unworthy of my regard, and that you cannot do, for it is not so."

"It is," the other declared, goaded into equal fervour. These thoughts had been weighing on her heart so many years that she could scarcely govern her tongue now that Anne had, at long last, turned to her for an opinion. "The bargain he struck with you is one no true gentleman could consider."

"Bargain—"

"Yes: That he would gallant you about, and keep all his freedom, and prevent your marrying, yet marry himself— and further his career at the expense of your happiness, and with the aid of your intelligence—"

"Maria!"

"Yes! And at the same time, you are to like it, and to

imagine he is your true friend, and never to complain of the terms."

"Maria, are you so much wounded by your marriage that you have no sympathy to spare for any man? You suppose it is only women who are tender, who need loyalty and affection. But I tell you Ensley loves me. He trusts—"

"No gentleman could use you so ill," Maria insisted. The ladies had ceased walking now and turned to face each other in the narrow path. "No true gentleman. I cannot believe—" She cast about in her mind for examples. "I cannot believe Lord Grypphon would do such a thing, for instance. Or Charles Stickney. Or—or even Mr. Highet," she added, though she must have known this particular example was calculated to inflame Anne the more.

"Mr. Highet?" Anne sputtered, too surprised at his name being brought up to explode straightaway. "But— Good God, Maria, if no gentleman would—strike such a bargain, as you call it, then what does that make me? Do you suggest I am no lady? I think you must. Henry Highet!" she went on immediately, the explosion coming before Mrs. Insel could answer. "You must be raving mad! Why do you mention him?"

"Because he has more feeling than Ensley. Because he has a more refined sensibility." Maria heard herself almost shouting—both ladies had unconsciously raised their voices to a pitch more likely to impede than facilitate communication—and lowered her tone. "Because, though we have known him so briefly, my every instinct tells me what I have never believed of Lord Ensley—what in fact Ensley has disproved of himself—that he would rather choke back his own feelings—conquer them, hide them if that were all he could do—than take advantage of yours. And as for what your being a party to all this makes you," she added, her voice dropping again, "it makes you fallible. That is all."

Anne, who had begun to walk once more, now stood still, as if something of what Mrs. Insel was saying had sunk into her. Then, slowly, she took Maria's arm. The two went a few steps along the path before them in silence. At last, "Where are we, do you imagine?" Miss Guilfoyle asked in a tone almost of mere curiosity.

Maria, weary of vehemence, said, "Except for in the park, I do not know."

"Nor I." A note of laughter crept into Anne's words as she went on, "I do believe we have lost our way." She turned completely round, looking for any familiar thing, but saw only oaks and elms. She laughed outright. "We have, Maria. Ah, heaven, the perfect illustration of the state of my wits: We cannot see the forest for the trees. Quite, quite lost." She began to laugh so hard she nearly sank to the ground with it. Maria, naturally, caught the contagion and laughed also. At last,

"The sun is—well, with the clouds it is hard to see, but I think it is over there, don't you?" Anne asked, pointing.

"I should have said . . ." Maria uncertainly indicated a different direction. "But I cannot be sure. If it is there, then . . ."

"As it is nearly four o'clock, that must be west—if it is the sun, of course—and so we want to walk . . . hm . . ." After a little more looking and considering, Anne turned herself and her companion round on the path they were in and set off smartly in the other direction.

But it was not so straightforward a task as that, for the park had been laid with a veritable maze of paths, set at any one of a score of angles, and they had made their way in (so engrossed in talk were they) without the least thought for how to come out. "Blast those blasted romantic writers!" Anne was saying frankly by the time they had hurried a mile or more without coming any closer (so far as they could tell) to house or road. "Blast them for their blasted nuisances of romantic forests; and blast my great uncle for reading them!"

"Anne!"

"Well, as you like then. Do not blast him. But blast everyone else. Chateaubriand!" She began to stride ahead more quickly, spitting out the names as she went. "Rousseau! Byron! Rows of plane trees were not good enough for them, I suppose! Neat alleys and wide lanes made them sad, I expect. They needed nice dark vines and tangles to cheer them, doubtless," she muttered, while Maria, straggling behind her, began to giggle at the ridiculousness of this diatribe. "Nothing like a clump of gloomy pines to brighten a person's day! The taller the better— no sense letting the sun shine— Oh! Excuse me," she suddenly broke off, for she had been talking so loudly and moving so fast that she actually collided with another walker before she saw him. They had both lost their balance a little. Dusting her skirts off, "Mr. Mallinger!" Anne exclaimed, while Maria came up even with them. "God sent you to us. Where are we?"

"Miss Guilfoyle. Mrs. Insel." Lawrence Mallinger bowed his compliments while he absently brushed off his hat. "Have you lost your bearings?"

"Our bearings, our wits, our mittens," Anne told him cheerfully, "all."

"Then I am doubly glad to happen upon you, for I shall

have the pleasure of escorting you home. You were going home?"

The ladies nodded.

Mr. Mallinger turned them round and offered an arm for each of them to lean on; but as the path was really not sufficiently wide too permit such an arrangement, and as Miss Guilfoyle particularly disliked leaning while she walked, "I shall go behind you, if you do not mind," she said.

Maria glanced meaningly at her friend. Surely Anne recalled the schoolmaster's marked behaviour to her when first they met? Did she not guess Maria would rather have remained lost than risk a reprise of his flattering attentions? But she saw in Anne's green gaze a look which seemed to say, "Best confront him now, my dear; I cannot always be with you." And since Maria was obliged to admit the truth of this, she made an inward resolution. Aloud, she merely murmured politely to Miss Guilfoyle, "If you are certain you would not prefer . . ."

"Perfectly certain," said that lady firmly, relinquishing with a gesture her claim upon the gentleman's arm. "Walk ahead. I am quite content to splash in your wake." And she kicked up a little cloud of brown pine needles demonstratively.

Maria laid a light hand on Mr. Mallinger's sleeve and began to walk on. Perhaps he would not, after all, resume his earlier manner towards her. Perhaps she would be spared any confrontation. But in fact the schoolmaster very soon fell into the tone of his first remarks to her. He repeated, in an undervoice which, though it did not attempt to exclude Anne, did not strive to reach her either, that he was delighted by this chance meeting. He asked Mrs. Insel how she had been occupying herself, then how she liked the country. When she replied that she liked it very well, Mr. Mallinger assured her that it must like her in return, for she was looking blooming. Maria (who moreover doubted this was true) saw her opportunity and took it.

"Sir," she began, "forgive me if I refine too much—too foolishly—in what I am about to say, but I must tell you your . . . your kind compliments to me, today and when we met, only make me uneasy. In short, I wish you will not— I must ask you not to—" She broke off in confusion, colouring deeply.

"I understand you," Mr. Mallinger took up, directly he saw she had lost the struggle for words. With a sincerity so natural she knew it was neither forced nor assumed, "Pray allow me to apologize for causing you discomfort," he went on. "It is the last thing I desire." And as he contrived to speak even these last words in a tone so civil, so restrained, that no hint of flattery was in them, Maria believed him and began to relax.

"Tell me about your school," she begged, hitting upon this topic to set him at his ease again. "How many students have you?"

Mr. Mallinger saw her stratagem and did not resist it. He supplied her with the number of his students and went on with a rough outline of the sort of lessons they learnt, the hopes he had for them, the pleasures and travails of teaching them. He informed her that he had come to Cheshire at the late Mr. Guilfoyle's behest some three years earlier, when the school was just being established, that before that he had been at Jesus College, Cambridge, and before that at a Mr. Harkwood's Academy (both places on a scholarship), and before that with his family in Suffolk, who were there still. He agreed that Cheshire must be quite different to Suffolk. He repeated his praise of Herbert Guilfoyle, regretting that Mrs. Insel could never know him, and confirmed her tentative opinion of Mr. Highet with his own—to wit, that he was as kind, as industrious, as thorough-going a gentleman as he ever hoped to meet. But as he spoke, an hundred questions occurred to him which he dared not set her, as for example: How long had her husband been dead? Had she loved him very much? Was it the freshness of her grief that made her dislike Mr. Mallinger's erstwhile attentions? If so, why did she no longer wear black? If not, was it an objection to Mr. Mallinger himself? If that, was it something he could alter? Could she imagine how long it had been since a woman of her demeanour—simple, gentle, tactful, quiet (though nervous: he had noticed that, and longed to soothe it away)—had come into his neighbourhood? Had stood before him with her glossy masses of hair, her dark, downturned gaze, and made him feel he must seize and protect her or die? Under that gleaming, chestnut crown, between those narrow temples, hid the answers to all these questions, he knew—and the knowledge made him ache to stop her polite, chattering inquiries, turn and take her face in his hand, and demand she tell him.

But of course he did nothing remotely like this. With only the gentle (too gentle!) pressure of her arm on his to recompense him, he talked on about Linfield and Fevermere, sun and snow, asked her any number of civil questions whose answers did not interest him, and dutifully guided the party (though he would have preferred to lead them round and round just to be longer with Mrs. Insel) through the intricate twists and turns that would take them back to their abode.

He had almost forgot Miss Guilfoyle (who struck him as too 'cute by half, and somehow volatile) for she lagged quite ten feet behind them during the chief of this colloquy; but as they made a peculiarly sharp turn out of a clump of firs, "Huzzah!" she cried out, "I know where we are!"

She came up even with them and asked, "It is that way, is not it? And then through a stand of birches, then left, and left again, and home." She fairly danced with exultation—an extravagant response, Mr. Mallinger thought, but the truth was, Anne really detested not knowing a thing she ought to know, whether the way home, or the former post of some minor statesman, or how to prove a geometrical theorem. But even the schoolmaster was shortly to bless her, for, "Maria dear, I think we must reward our Virgil," she declared. "If he had not led us from the dark woods we might have been lost for ever, and would perhaps have had to live on nuts and berries the rest of our days, and combed our hair with pine cones. Do you think dinner a sufficient prize? I do not," she faced him, "but I fear it is all we can offer. Will you do us the honour to come? Not tonight, for I fear we should make but dishevelled, exhausted company—but to-morrow?"

Mr. Mallinger was looking uncertainly towards Maria Insel. It was hard, but if she did not like him to come, he was resolved to decline.

But, "Pray do," she endorsed, not fervently or with any tremor of enthusiasm (alas) but evidently without distaste either, and quite sincerely. "We shall like to have you."

"Then I accept with thanks."

"Good. It is decided." Anne put out her hand to shake his. "We shall make a little party of it, perhaps—invite a friend of mine who is visiting Cheshire, and the Hartley Wares, and—" She remembered a question about the clipping of ewes which she did not like to put to Mr. Rand (who regarded all such questions as admissions of her unfitness to direct Linfield) and added, "—the Highets, *mère et fils.*" She thanked Mr. Mallinger for rescuing them. Maria followed suit, and in a moment they had parted.

"And how did you fare with Mr. Mallinger?" asked Anne rather gaily, as the two ladies crossed the wide lawn to the waiting house. In the grey, horizontal light of afternoon it beckoned pleasantly from atop its gentle hill. "Did he renew his compliments? Were you obliged to set him down?"

"I hope I did not do that," said Maria. "But I did make it clear to him he must not think of me so."

"And did he take it well?"

"Very well, it seemed to me. He strikes me as a very courteous gentleman, and most intelligent."

"Good! Now you may enjoy his acquaintance in tranquillity. Merciful heavens, but my feet feel ready to fall off! Don't yours?" She went on without giving Maria time to answer, "Though I must confess, once I felt sure of emerging from them alive, I rather liked the woods. They are pretty, and somehow soothing. Do you know, I realized as I went what had happened to me—about Ensley, I mean. It is merely that the news of his marriage startled me. He did not care to tell me of it before it was settled, lest it should come to nothing; and so when he did, announcing it as a *fait accompli* . . . Well, that would startle any one, I expect. But once I have had some time to think of it, to get accustomed to the reality, I am sure I shall approve it as heartily in its actual mode as I did in its theoretical. Lady Juliana is a pleasant-enough girl, I think.

We shall all deal famously with one another, no doubt."
And before Maria could find a polite way to tell her friend
this whole line of thought sounded like fustian to her,
Anne had gone on, "Thank you, dear, for listening to me
babble before. I was rather confused." She laughed, but
the purpose of her words was plain: She was withdrawing
her earlier invitation to Maria to speak her mind about
Ensley. "I must send a note to him at once," she finished,
shaking her head at her own brief folly. "The poor man
no doubt suspects all this country air has quite unseated
my reason!"

Miss Guilfoyle was at her merriest when she greeted her
guests the following evening. She had added the rector,
Mr. Samuels, and his stout, comfortable wife, to her invitation list, so that the party made an even ten. Ensley
arrived, by special permission, a little ahead of the others;
and Anne discovered herself (to her relief) fairly easy with
him now.

She waved him into a plush arm-chair in the drawing-
room, seating herself in its twin nearby. "I fear the company is not just what you have been used to see," she
warned him teasingly (her apology and his glad acceptance
of it having been sent by messenger, both felt the subject
of her behaviour to him on the previous afternoon to be
closed). "But you will know how to enjoy yourself, I am
sure." And she went on to give him several deft, not entirely respectful portraits of the people he was about to
meet. When she came to Mr. Mallinger's reading Thomas
Spence,

"Good God," Ensley exclaimed, quizzing her, "and
does he teach his students they have a right to own the

land they farm? What a queer nabs your great uncle must have been to engage him!"

"Queer indeed! I assure you, I have fallen into a very hotbed of radical ideas. The library here fairly flames with nonsense of that sort—and I collect Mr. Henry Highet, whom you will soon know, has a mind very much of that stamp as well."

"Ah, this is the neighbour you mentioned, I think? What manner of man is he?" And Ensley dropped his quizzing glass and settled back with a half smile on his lips, ready to be entertained by another of Anne's pithy, acid sketches.

But Anne found herself unaccountably incapable of obliging him. "Oh, well, the first—" she began lightly, then stopped all at once. She had been going to describe her first meeting with Highet, when he received her in flannel and unbuckled boots. But even as she framed the quick sentences in her head, the thought came to her that this would be an ill-natured act indeed when, after all, it was she who had waked him, he who had been so kind as to come out into a beastly night to escort her home.

Her nimble mind, still searching for fun, leapt to look at Mr. Highet from another angle. She could say he was dull, could not she? The sort who considered the design of a plough good conversation, and irrigation scintillating . . . "He is—" she recommenced; but this too was rather unfair. After all, farming was his life's work; and what did Ensley talk about (if one let him) except his work? True enough, Ensley's career was far more interesting to Anne than Mr. Henry Highet's. But that did not change the principle of the thing.

Anyhow, she discovered herself curiously reluctant to prejudice Ensley's mind against Mr. Highet. She could not have explained why; but in the end all she said of the latter to the former was, "The truth is, I scarcely know him. He seems a good, plain gentleman, I guess—steady, careful with his tenants, happy experimenting with potatoes and the like. Rather tedious, of course, but affable. He is a bachelor—" To her horrified amazement, Miss Guilfoyle felt herself begin to colour with these words. She hastened on, "—and lives with his mother." She plunged into an excoriating, and quite accurate, portrait of that lady, till her blush subsided. She was glad when Ensley laughed and seemed not to have remarked the brief flaming in her cheeks.

But half an hour later, when Mr. Highet and his formidable progenitrix actually arrived, Anne was sure not only Ensley but Maria and Mr. Mallinger and even the Hartley Wares could not have failed to notice the quickening of her breath and pulses, the blood again creeping heavenwards from her neck, the mist of perspiration on her brow at the sight of the master of Fevermere. Useless to will these manifestations away: While Mr. Highet bowed to her, and beamed down about her, and asked how she did, they intensified relentlessly. Not even the strident booming of Mrs. Highet's voice while (apparently as surprised to see them as if their families had lived on separate stars) she greeted the Wares could break the spell, and give Anne surcease. She was finally obliged to pretend the sudden recollection of an overlooked detail, and to hurry abruptly from the drawing-room. Outside, encountering Dolphim, she turned her red face away from his solicitous gaze and pretended to be coughing. Then she scurried round a turning in the corridor, where he could not see her, and, holding her hand above her heart, commanded it to behave.

In a minute she could go in again, laughing at the ab-sent-mindedness which had made her think she forgot to tell Dolphim Mr. Samuels and his wife were expected— when in fact she *had* told him that afternoon, as she now remembered perfectly to have done; but inside she was still baffled by her own response. She was like a girl who broke out in spots the moment she ate strawberries: Mr. Highet reacted upon her.

Once recovered from the initial encounter, though, she had no trouble meeting Mr. Highet's glance. On the con-trary, she found him if anything more sober-sided, senten-tious, and deadly dull than ever. He seemed to outdo himself in the bringing of sheep breeds and butter prices into the conversation; and when she overheard him ex-plaining the action of a new sort of winnowing fan to En-sley, she almost suspected him of seeming thick-witted on purpose.

But that was ridiculous. Mr. Henry Highet had no need to dissemble to seem dull. It came to him as naturally as grapes to the vine, poor thing; and she was quite surprised when, towards the end of the evening, Ensley confided to her that he and Highet had had rather a dust-up over their Port, when the ladies were withdrawn from the table.

"For a moment I thought we should come to cuffs," Ensley whispered. They had gone a few steps outside the open French doors to stand together on the terrace. The sweet-scented air of the open fields drifted to them through the warm night. "What an obstinate, opinionated clown the man is." And he smiled down at Anne and laughed so as not to appear, even from behind, to be talk-ing about what he was in fact talking about.

"You astonish me," whispered Anne in her turn. "What on earth did you find to take issue about with him? You did not, I hope, deprecate the usefulness of marling Cheshire soil? That is one of Mr. Highet's firmest convic—"

"Nothing so pleasant," Ensley broke in almost grimly. "It was the Corn Law—which, I troubled to point out to him, was formulated exactly to benefit people like himself. But your Mr. Highet—"

"He is hardly my Mr. Highet—" Anne broke in, but Ensley kept on,

"Your Mr. Highet is not satisfied with that. He is worried about the poor. He maintains the Corn Law is pushing the common work man over the edge of starvation. I don't know what the fellow would have! If there had been no Corn Law—and as you know, that was a very good piece of legislation I put no small amount of work into myself—he would I am sure have been complaining that farmers all over were going under. And so indeed they would have been. Why, it is preposterous! To be quite frank, I myself brought the topic up, for I thought it must be one thing, at least, we could discuss intelligently. If I had guessed—"

Anne at last succeeded in interrupting his indignant tirade at this point. It came as news indeed to her that Mr. Highet could discuss the Corn Law at all, let alone argumentatively. "And what did he suggest as a remedy?" she inquired, her sceptical tone masking (she hoped) a very lively curiosity.

"Oh, you know the sort of thing—a minimum wage tied to the price of a loaf. The usual starry-eyed claptrap."

Anne recognised the very word she had used to characterise the ideas rife around Fevermere, and sighed. She had almost been hoping Mr. Highet would prove himself unexpectedly astute.

"I can't explain it," Ensley was going on, sounding a little calmer, "but I do not like that fellow. Not at all. Something about him . . . It is a shame you are neighbours. But that"— Ensley's voice took on a different tone, and he drew Anne a little away from the pool of light that spilled out the French doors—"that I hope will not long be the case. You did not say as much in your note, exactly, but I hope you have changed your mind and mean to come home with me after all? It is unfortunate this Highet person should be the one to benefit by it, but this is a case of noses and faces—can't spite the one without t'other."

Anne laughed abruptly, and to Ensley's inquiring glance explained, "Have you ever noticed how Tom Maitland always says he won't bite his nose off to spite his face? He is a dear man, really. I think he mixes it up with biting off more than one can chew."

"You have not answered my question," Ensley observed.

Suddenly serious, "But yes, I have," Anne replied. "I told you yesterday, I cannot possibly accept your—" Recalling Maria's use of the word "bargain," her tone sharpened involuntarily as she amended, "—live on your bounty. That's flat. I will not discuss it. However, you will always be welcome here, and I shall expect to see you often. As to my visiting London, I begin to think a month at the height of the Season and another during the Little Season will be best after all. For the rest we must trust to the post—and to chance. Who knows, perhaps the *Maidstone* will be recovered, her cargo of teas and exotic woods miraculously unspoiled—"

"Anne—"

"—or perhaps another great uncle I have forgot will die

and leave me a more convenient farm, in Hampstead. Or—"

Ensley, however, was in no humour for joking. "This is your final answer?" he cut in.

"Yes."

He was silent a moment; then, "In that case, I must trust to time as my ally. Please recall that my offer stands whenever you chuse to take it up."

But Anne, misliking the word "offer," said lightly, "I think we must go inside now, or my guests will imagine a dreadful fate has overtaken us."

"And so it has," Ensley gloomily replied; but he followed her obediently enough, and engaged Mrs. Hartley Ware in what soon became an animated discussion of Princess Mary's impending marriage.

SIX

MR. LAWRENCE MALLINGER, MEANWHILE, HAD BEEN passing a rather uncomfortable evening at Linfield (which he would by no means, however, have exchanged for any other elsewhere, be it never so easy) endeavouring on the one hand to impress Mrs. Insel with his intelligence, his discretion, his trustworthiness, while on the other not discomfiting her with any special attention or distinction. This was a fine line to walk, and required a good deal of watching her from the corner of one eye (turning deliberately away if she happened to come near him) and directing loud remarks intended to interest her to other people. He had developed a theory (sitting up half of last night for the purpose) that what Mrs. Insel objected to in him was his age. Mr. Mallinger was seven-and-twenty, Mrs. Insel (he guessed) nearly thirty. It was no great gap, of course; but perhaps she reckoned him younger than his years. His first order of business, therefore, was to correct any such miscalculation. To which end he contrived to mention, in the course of the evening, his exact birthdate (to Mrs. Highet), the precise dates of his sojourn at Cambridge (to Mr. Ware), the number of years before he would reach the midpoint of man's three score and ten (to Mr. Samuels), and the age of his sister Augusta (to Miss Guilfoyle) together with the information that she was four years his senior.

But he also feared that, even if Mrs. Insel knew his right age, she would still imagine him not sufficiently mature to make a match for her. In this case he must impress her with his maturity—a more difficult matter. Still, he set about it methodically. He brought into the general conversation (lest she consider him not well-travelled enough to know the world) the walking tour he had made in Scotland with his brother two summers ago—when, as he noted, he had been twenty-five. He gravely discussed with Mr. Samuels the moral welfare of a student of his, a boy of eleven years of age (sixteen younger than himself) whose mother regularly drank to excess. And in case Mrs. Insel should imagine he did not know his own mind, he described to Anne in stunning detail the manner in which he had insisted on becoming a schoolmaster, clinging to that purpose though his parents strongly urged him to apply as secretary to a great man.

How much of this effort was wasted and how much to the point not even Mrs. Insel (who did not know what she had missed) could have said. What is certain is that she heard him advert to Scotland; for she engaged him in a long conversation on that head, coming to him after dinner (he noted with delight) specially to do so. Mr. Mallinger obliged her with a very rich account of his travels, bringing in many quaint details and amusing anecdotes; but he took care not to smile too much at her while he did so. Nor did he allow the pleasure being with her gave him to show in his eyes. Without being formal, he was restrained; without being cold, civil. And he succeeded in his object to such a degree that he had the gratification of seeing Mrs. Insel behave, before the evening was out, perfectly warmly and amiably towards himself, quite as if all her early wariness had been forgot.

Across the room, during Mr. Mallinger's Scottish monologue, Miss Guilfoyle and Mr. Highet might have been seen in close colloquy. Coming in from the terrace, Miss Guilfoyle had found her moment to pounce on her agricultural informant, and had skilfully removed him from the conversational grip of his mother and Mrs. Samuels to draw him aside to a sofa.

"Now I have you to myself," she began, unconsciously dimpling at him in a smile that had pried any number of secrets from unsuspecting Members of Parliament, "I hope you will forgive my asking you a question?" Mr. Highet had somehow failed, so far at least, to make Anne feel pitiable this evening, though his manner towards her continued as sober and bare of compliment as before. She was willing to endure his solemnity, but determined to give him no opportunity for commiseration, and so added quickly, "Of course, if it bores you, I can ask Rand. He is quite obliging now," she finished, lying.

She seemed to see a flicker of something—intelligence?

interest? indigestion?—deep in Mr. Highet's dark, sleepy gaze before he answered, "Ask any thing at all."

"I fear it is not a very intriguing matter. Only—why does one clip some ewes in June, and others in July?"

For the first time, except when he had laughed at her, Mr. Highet smiled at her broadly. "But that is quite an intriguing question, Miss Guilfoyle; or rather, an intriguing tale hangs from it." And he launched into a long explanation of the growth cycle of sheep, the times and ways they and their wool may be sold, and allied lore. Anne listened closely, for he gave a more complete and coherent account than any of her great uncle's books—or at least, he phrased his in a way more understandable to her. To be sure, when he came to talk of tupping, her gaze dropped to the floor and stayed there; and when he spoke rather too vividly—perhaps it was only scientifically?—of gelding, she grew visibly pale, and hurried him on with a question on another topic. Still, it was a pleasure to be able to call upon his encyclopaedic knowledge at will; and so she told him.

"But I see you have been studying the matter yourself," he answered approvingly. "Do you find it tedious?"

"On the contrary. There is a special challenge, isn't there, in working with nature to make the best of things? To be frank, I had not expected to care for agriculture as a study. When you were last here and we spoke of it a little, I admit I could not follow your remarks, or understand the significance of new developments. But now I have done some reading, and explored Linfield a bit, I find farming very interesting indeed."

Mr. Highet's brow furrowed seriously, and he almost scrutinized her before saying, "Do you really?"

Disconcerted by his gravity, "Yes, I do," she replied. Mr. Highet seemed to have gone into some sort of trance, he was staring at her and frowning so hard. Finally,

"You have a wide spirit, Miss Guilfoyle," he said. "I like that."

Anne felt herself draw back a little from his concentrated gaze; but on the whole she discovered (to her surprise, for how could she have imagined she would ever have cared for his opinion one way or the other?) she was rather gratified to have pleased Mr. Highet. A smile found its way to her lips quite without her directing it to go there, and she bowed very slightly, still looking into his eyes.

It was at this point that Ensley recalled he had a message for Anne, excused himself to Mrs. Ware, leapt to his feet, and materialised at Miss Guilfoyle's elbow. "Celia Grypphon," he announced. He smiled smoothly at Highet, said, "Pardon me, old man," and repeated to Anne, "I have a message from Celia Grypphon. Forgive me, my dear; I don't know how I contrived to forget it. She is coming up here next week. You can expect a letter from her with details soon."

Though she had initially been more startled than delighted by Ensley's sudden appearance beside her, this was enough to divert Anne from her musings about Henry Highet. "Ensley, you beast!" she cried while, had she but noticed, Mr. Highet went on looking very closely from her face to his lordship's. "How can you have failed to tell me till now? But this is famous! This is heaven! To have Celia in this forsaken— Excuse me," she glanced at Mr. Highet, "to have Celia here! How long will she stop? Is Grypphon to accompany her? Ensley, for goodness' sake, tell me all."

Lord Ensley did not know how long her ladyship meant to stop. He believed her husband would be with her.

"But can you stay till they arrive?" Anne asked, looking up appealingly from the sofa. It had not been discussed between them yet how long Ensley would remain in Cheshire.

"I am afraid—" Ensley did not finish, but shook his fair head regretfully. Anne thought immediately of Lady Juliana.

"I am sorry," she said, in a tone suddenly icy and certainly very far from melancholy. She turned to Mr. Highet again and heard herself go on, "Lord Charles and Lady Celia Grypphon are two of my dearest friends in London. Oh, there is no one like Celia! I hope you will meet her when she comes? You are sure to enjoy her—though she is rather prickly at first."

"I shall look forward to it as an honour—prickles and all."

"There's a brave man!" cried Anne, before Mrs. Highet, breaking free after many attempts from Mrs. Samuels' inexhaustible smalltalk, stood up and shouted to her son that they must be going, for the sky appeared to be clouding over again.

Mrs. Samuels rose to look out the French doors, saw nothing alarming in the face of the heavens, and said so; but the party began to break up anyhow. Mr. Mallinger, determined to display his polite indifference to the question of spending ten minutes more or less in Mrs. Insel's vicinity, stood also and announced his intention to depart. The Wares were too well-bred not to follow, and since the Samuelses could hardly linger by themselves, every one drifted to the door. Ensley, out of a very proper regard for Anne's comfort in the neighbourhood, left with Mr. Mallinger, though he did not like to. He whispered in her ear that he would visit her again in the morning. If he expected her to beg him not to leave he was disappointed, for she nodded equably and bade him an almost cool good night. Her farewell to Mr. Mallinger was more cordial; and when the Highets' carriage came at last round the sweep, her parting from Mr. Highet might have been observed—was observed, by that gentleman's mother—to be nearly affectionate. Fearful of a renewal of her bizarre palpitations, Anne deliberately did not offer him her hand; but she thanked him with warm sincerity for coming, and for bearing patiently with her neophyte's questions. Hearing this, Mrs. Highet broke in with,

"Oh, my dear! Henry don't expect you to know farming! Not the thing for a lady at all. You can never be comfortable here: You belong in town. Why, we know you will only stay with us a short time, don't we, Henry? Not but what we're sorry! Thank you for the evening. Most enjoyable!"

And though Anne could not know this, Mrs. Highet continued talking of her half the way home, pointing out to her son all the various signs she had observed of a quiet understanding subsisting between Miss Guilfoyle and "that Ensley fellow."

"They'll tie the knot before Easter, mark my words—though the dear only knows what he sees in her! Sharp, ain't she? Mighty sharp. Ah but we're comfortable at Fevermere, aren't we, love?" And she gave her younger son's strong whip arm a playful squeeze.

Since his mother habitually defamed the character of every spinster in the parish between the ages of fifteen and forty, and since, for good measure, she invented from

thin air matches every one of them was sure to make before six months had passed, Henry Highet did not trouble
himself to listen too closely to his respected relative as
they rolled along. Yet the subject of her discourse was not
so far removed as it ordinarily was from the matter of his
private thoughts. Actually, he was thinking of Anne
Guilfoyle, and to a lesser extent of Ensley. Indeed, he sat
up unusually late that night, with a glass of brandy, mull-
ing and musing precisely about them.

Some six or seven days later, "Oh, my darlings!" Anne
crowed involuntarily, unable to keep from running out the
door of Linfield to fling her arms round Lord and Lady
Grypphon the moment they emerged from their carriage.
"Thank heaven you have come! Only look where you find
me—did you ever think to see such a sight?" And she
ruefully waved at the house behind her, whose plain
oaken door still stood open.

"Don't be a goose, dear. It is charming, in a—er, rustic
way," protested Celia absently. She turned to give orders
to a footman (the Grypphons had arrived with two carriages in train), then turned back to Anne. "We shall put
the horses up at that little how-do-you-call-it in Faulding
Chase—"

"It's an inn, dear. The Red Lion," said Charles mildly.

"Yes, of course, if you like to call it that," said Celia,
who would rather have termed it a hovel. "Any how, do
not trouble your stable about them—"

"We have plenty of room—"

"Do not be absurd, pray. No one has room for three
carriages, or grooms to fuss with them. Anyway—" And

she turned back again to charge her own groom with some further orders.

Anne gave over arguing and profited by Celia's distraction to give her husband a hearty embrace. "You cannot imagine what it means to be here," she informed him, clinging to his arm. "One goes to bed and wakes up and goes to bed and wakes up and unless one is a seed or a ripening cheese it is all absolutely the same. It rained every afternoon but one this past week, till Maria and I thought we should scream. The last paper we saw—we do have the *Times* sent from Middlewich every afternoon, thank God, though naturally it's days old—any how, the last one we saw—because of the rain—was dated 17 July. So you must tell us every thing! What a place! When we are at absolute *point non plus* from boredom, we drive into Faulding Chase and buy ribbon in the shop there—I say shop, not shops, for a reason. But I am frightening you, poor dear, when you were so noble as to come all this way. Walk in!"

Lady Grypphon finally joined them. Anne put her other arm through hers. "Walk in, my angels. Fill my aching ears with *on-dits*. Are you tired? Let me call Maria down." So chattering, Anne brought her guests inside and made them comfortable.

She found herself even gladder to see them than she had expected. The mere sight of them awakened keen longings in her which the last three weeks had, without her quite realizing it, dulled. Like a girl in the schoolroom whose mother has been to a ball, she was full of envious queries—only Anne, of course, sought to learn the latest intrigues from Melbourne House, not the depths of flounces and the lengths of sleeves.

"Perfectly dead," Celia assured her, coming into the Green Parlour with a quick look about her, and sitting down. "Half the *monde* is gone out of town, and the other is too stupid with heat to do more than nibble and drowse. Anne, you must not live in this cottage much longer. You will go mad. Who bought the furnishings, Little Bo-Peep? Come home with us. What's happened to you?"

All of this having been spoke with Lady Grypphon's habitual mixture of harsh candour and warm affection, Anne took no offence but only seated herself (begging Charles to follow suit) and once more explained Herbert Guilfoyle's will and the loss of the *Maidstone*. In the midst of the account Mrs. Insel entered. Maria had never fully shared Anne's partiality to Lady Grypphon, but she had a real affection for his lordship. Anyhow, both their familiar faces were most welcome after so many weeks among strangers. She greeted them warmly and sat down, urging Anne to resume the narrative her entrance had interrupted.

Anne did so. When she finished,

"But how absolutely ghastly!" Celia exclaimed. "You poor little fish. Why did you not tell us before leaving London? But you were too proud, I suppose. We guessed something was up when we heard of your quitting Holles Street, but we never imagined anything like this. It's too awful, is it not, Grypphon? What must we do?"

Charles added his bluff, sympathetic tsking and clucking to his wife's, then said, "Of course you will come back with us. Come to Highglade," he went on, naming his family's county seat in Surrey. "Such a damned big place, we'll never notice you." He stood. "That's settled.

Where's the bell-pull? I'll have the carriages brought round again.''

Anne laughed and told him to sit. "We cannot simply leave, you good, silly man," she continued. "I have a whole houseful of servants—two houses full, more accurately—and any how, we could not possibly accept such a daft—"

"Don't go on, pray," Celia broke in. "You'll offend Charles. But I quite see it is no solution for you to stay with us indefinitely. Strictly *entre nous*, I sometimes think of running away myself. Still, you must not remain here for ever either. What does Ensley say to all this—or mustn't I mention his name?"

"Oh, you may mention him," Miss Guilfoyle obliged herself to respond promptly, with no sign of disconcertment. "He was here just a se'ennight ago—as I guess you know. We parted best of friends." (If this was not true, at least Anne had done her utmost to make Ensley believe it was. When he had returned the morning after the dinner party, it was to stop an hour, then say good-bye. Anne pressed him to return as soon as he might—and when he answered that, because of his wedding, he probably could not before September, she exerted all her powers of dissembling to appear to receive this with mild regret only, and to remain affectionate.) "He would do anything he could, of course—but what can he?"

Lady Grypphon thought a moment, then said, "Yes, I see." Maria Insel might be so soft-headed as to imagine Ensley could marry Anne, but Celia Grypphon was not. Moreover, she knew without asking (and quite proper of her too) that Anne would never take money from him. "I don't suppose Overton would suit you?" she presently inquired.

Anne shook her head. "Not but what I have thought of it—more and more, as the dreary round here plods ahead—but even if I could keep Dolphim and the others with me—which I could not—the truth is, we should be nearly as much in exile there as here. For though Overton is closer to town, we should have no money at all to go there. And if there is any less attractive prospect than being buried alive in Cheshire, I think Maria will agree with me it is the prospect of being buried alive in Northamptonshire with our families to bear us company!"

Maria, reluctant to endorse Anne's vivid way of putting this, nevertheless murmured, "I do think we are better here. I am, at all events."

"What, are you out of charity with your family too?" asked Celia, always interested in gossip and never shy of seeking it out.

"Rather the reverse," Anne replied, a note of grimness in her voice.

"Not out of charity?" suggested Celia.

"*They* are out of charity with *her*," Anne corrected, and this time there was no mistaking the disapprobation in her tone; but she hurried on, "But that is neither here nor there. The fact is, Linfield is the best we can do for ourselves just now. Let me have Miss Veal show you your rooms," she went on, rising to go to the bell-pull. "You will see most of the house on your way there, I am afraid."

"Miss Veal is—"

"The housekeeper."

"And Mrs. Dolphim?" asked Celia, sounding shocked.

"Also the housekeeper. Do not seek to understand this arrangement, I warn you: The distinctions and divisions between the two of them will make your head ache. They do mine; and I am afraid they are turning poor Mrs. Dolphim's hair grey. But I cannot turn my great uncle's people out—particularly not with what the end of the war economy has done to the gentry hereabouts. They could never find situations. Even staying on, Miss Veal suffers. I suspect my great uncle included her in all his little parties, for on the few occasions when we have given modest entertainments here, she has gone about looking quite martyred. God knows what his death meant to her—but here she comes," Anne interrupted herself. "Go upstairs and rest. We dine early, naturally—at seven, if you can bear it." And she kissed them both impulsively and gave Miss Veal orders to make them comfortable.

The plain fact was, though, that no orders, however faithfully executed, could have made Lord and Lady Grypphon comfortable at Linfield. Their rooms, though the best in the house, were cramped and bare compared to what they were used to. The servants were too many, and too familiar; the rain stoutly refused, the next day, to vanish, but was with them constantly; the house was so small that, even with only a party of four in it, there was no getting away by oneself—except to the abovementioned cramped and underfurnished rooms. Had she been mad for pigs and hay (which she emphatically was not) the rain must anyway have kept Lady Grypphon indoors; and though he had been a fanatical angler (a proposition equally far from the truth) her husband could not have been fanatical enough to stand in a stream in this weather. Their hostess endeavoured to get up a dinner party (which would have been dull enough, heaven knows, but at least must have made a change) by inviting Lord and Lady Crombie and some few others—not the inmates of Fevermere, though, lest Henry Highet renew his remarks on irrigation and drive the Grypphons screaming from the house; but the messenger could scarcely deliver the invitations, so bad had the roads become, and the idea of driving a carriage on them that night kept every one away.

So the four unwilling inmates of Linfield resigned themselves to their own company. They played whist and Emulation, told one another's fortunes with cards, ate rather more than they were wont to do, remarked on the storm (which now became noisily electrical), and generally had an excellent opportunity of showing off the good manners which were all that kept them civil. By ten Lady Grypphon was yawning. Two minutes later her husband had caught the hint and was seconding her. At five past the hour Maria Insel involuntarily joined them; and the whole party must have broke up before ten-fifteen if Dolphim had not entered rather abruptly to announce that a gentleman was in the hall who begged Miss Guilfoyle to spare him a minute there.

The lady so applied to started up in surprise. The first thought in her head (for she was, despite herself, as prone as anyone to the eternal springing of hope) was that it might be Ensley, changing his mind at last and returning to offer for her. But how would Ensley have come here, if no carriage could travel safely? When Celia asked, "Who can it be?" Anne said,

"I have not the least notion. Dolphim, do you know him?"

"I do, only"—the good man paused, and his grey brows drew together in a look half quizzical, half perturbed—"only not liking to disrupt your evening, the gentleman asked me particularly not to announce him."

An especially ear-splitting thunderclap coming almost simultaneously with a bolt of lightning appeared to punctuate this sentence.

"How mysterious. If you will excuse me . . ." Anne hurried from the parlour, Dolphim behind her, leaving the others to listen to the storm's roar, watch the flicker of lightning over the walls, and wonder among themselves.

Anne met her visitor, for once, with neither flush nor quickening of the pulse. She was, instead, all surprise; and Mr. Henry Highet was all apology. Soaked through, in a blue coat and buckskin breeches which clung to him like a second, wrinkled skin, his top-boots thick with mud, rain dripping from his dark curls, he beseeched Miss Guilfoyle to forgive his uninvited presence.

"Gracious heavens," Anne interrupted him. She remembered with quick embarrassment her scant hospitality to him the first night she had come into Cheshire and wondered whether he really thought she would begrudge him shelter. "You are drenched. Come in to the parlour. I shall have Sally lay a fire. What happened to you? Have you been out all the day? But don't answer, only come with me—"

But though she had taken his wet arm and was tuggging at it, he did not budge. "I asked Dolphim not to give my name because I know you have London visitors. Your Susannah told my Joan, you see, who told our Trigg, who told his wife, who told my mother. Who told me."

Anne blushed, wondering if he knew he had been specifically excluded from to-night's failed party. If so, he would not mention it. He went on,

"I detest an unbidden guest. I should never have stopped except for—" A roll of thunder interrupted him,

and he had only to wave his hand. "At all events," he
went on, at his most earnest despite the loss of dignity a
good soaking will bring to any one, "pray do not visit me
upon them. I am sure—"

"Oh, in the name of all that is sensible," Anne finally
burst out impatiently, "will you stop? Believe me, if we
had gone on our knees, my friends and myself could not
have been more fervently praying for some one, some
thing, to come and save us from each other. Besides, you
will not deny me the opportunity to do for you what you
did for me. This storm is bound to keep up for hours, if
not all night." She summoned Dolphim, who had only
gone discreetly round a corner. "Dolphim, Mr. Highet
will stop the night with us. Please show him to a room
where he can dry off. Have Susannah fetch him some hot
water, and tell Sally she must lay a fire there. And Cook
must send up a tray of dinner. I shall ask Lord Grypphon
to have his valet send in clothes for Mr. Highet. They are
much of a size, I think. And you—" She put out a cau-
tionary hand to the master of Fevermere. "You be quiet. I
find I quite like fussing over you. You must not deny me
my pleasures."

So saying, she bustled off to the parlour, to acquaint the
others with this turn of events, and to exact her favour
from Charles.

When Lady Grypphon heard the identity of the mysterious caller, "Good God," she cried, "the tedious gentleman who must inherit Linfield if you quit it! How
interesting! How providential! What would happen to the
estate—heavens, I feel just like Lady Macbeth—if the
inconvenient Mr. Highet were accidentally somehow to
die in the night? Could you keep it without living here?"

Anne had fresh misgivings about introducing Mr. Highet to her old friend. True, she had warned him Celia was prickly—but she had said nothing of her being lethal. How would the stolid, slow Mr. Highet fend her off? She had never succeeded, in the past, in persuading Celia to hold her wit in check. Still, she must try.

"I fear I might have his mother to deal with, and that would be much the worse," she began carefully. "They are both complete country sorts, you know—and that reminds me, none of your swift arrrows at Mr. Highet, Celia. He is a barn door to your wit: too wide a mark by half to make fair sport."

"Is he indeed? Do you mean he is dull, or thick-witted, or both?"

"Dull, mostly. Or—well, perhaps a little of both," she amended.

"Anne!" Maria objected, "I do not find Mr. Highet either of those things. He is a very gentlemanly, amiable man, and though his interests are different than ours, perhaps, he seems perfectly well-informed about them."

"Controversy!" cried Lady Grypphon, delighted. "More, more! Anne, refute her."

But Anne, desperate as she was for entertainment, found she could no more put her heart into this game than she had been able to draw a wicked sketch of Highet for Ensley. "There is wit and wit," was all she would say. "Mother-wit and rapier-wit, for example; and the one against the other may be a stick against a sword. So do, please, Celia, sharpen your weapon on someone else—me, if necessary—but spare him." And feeling that the object of her dubious solicitude might soon be dressed and with them, she turned the topic to the recently uncovered scandal among the London patrole.

Mr. Highet joined them while this discussion was still underway. When he had been introduced and (looking a trifle conscious about it, on account of Grypphon's breeches being rather smaller than his own) seated well away from the windows, Miss Guilfoyle reverted to the topic of the scandal by saying, "I dareswear you have read of these scoundrels in the *Times?* But you must find it all very much of a piece with your idea of town life. Mr. Highet has no opinion of London," she explained, with a smile, to the Grypphons.

"Perfectly right," Celia pronounced swiftly, while Anne breathed a sigh of relief. Lady Grypphon was looking at Mr. Highet with a great deal of curiosity, or speculation, as one might look at a Persian bear or an Indian elephant; but at least there was nothing cutting in her tone. "Filthy place; shocking morals. And how do you like it in the country, sir? Can you appprove it better?"

"Much better," he smiled. "For at least the muck here serves a purpose."

Anne cringed, but Lady Grypphon only laughed appreciatively. "And the morals?" she asked.

Mr. Highet took on the sober, earnest look Miss Guilfoyle knew so well. "Dear God, do not let him provoke Celia," she prayed inwardly. "Do not let him prose at her; she will never stand it." But when Mr. Highet spoke, it was to say:

"To be frank, Lady Grypphon, I have grave fears for the morals of country folk. Since the Speenhamland System has put every man on the dole whether he works or no, drunkenness and ignorance have become the rule more than the exception in some of our parishes. The people have no land to farm. They eat nothing but bread and cheese six days in the week. Poverty is rampant, and whatever the Bible may say about the blessedness of the poor in spirit, I can assure you that the poor in Cheshire are half sunk into infirmity, sloth, and viciousness." He shook his head. "I am no enemy to inclosure, ma'am, for good farming could not go forward without it; but what Parliament thinks of when it grants the right to enclose a district without allotting so much as an acre to each working man—that, I confess, baffles me. You may be sure no one at Fevermere goes without his little plot—nor Linfield either."

Lady Grypphon's eyebrows had been climbing higher and higher during this speech, and when it ended she cast a speaking glance at Anne in which amusement, puzzlement, and surprise mingled equally. Miss Guilfoyle read it pretty accurately, though she hoped no one else—Mr. Highet particularly—could decipher it. It said, "Why did you tell me this man was dull? He is perfectly intelligent—and extremely pleasant to look at besides." Aloud she said, "Mr. Highet, you ought to come to Parliament yourself and say as much. I am sure your eloquence would persuade them. Do not you think so, Grypphon?"

His lordship affably concurred, adding, "But then Mr. Highet would be obliged to come to town, which we know he detests."

"If I thought anyone would listen to me, I would come," Highet answered. "But I am no one particular there—only a farmer, with no knowledge except of my own little spot."

Celia looked meaningfully to her husband. "I daresay we could arrange . . ." she began.

But Henry Highet cut her off. "I should feel a perfect imbecile," he affirmed. "I keep after the parish officials to urge them to do their duty; and I speak to the Lord-Lieu-tenant when I can. But here my crusading ends." He laughed, and flashed a queer glance at his hostess. "I know my limits," he said. "The rest I leave to William Cobbett."

At the mention of this dangerous radical's name a silence fell on the Green Parlour which even Celia Gryphon was too shocked to break. Finally,

"Tell us about your misadventure to-night," Maria Insel invited Mr. Highet. "Poor man—how did you happen to find yourself out in the storm so late?"

And on this safe subject (which had to do with the difficult birthing of a calf from a prized cow Mr. Highet had bought from Colling of Ketton himself) the conversation turned for some while. Except for the fact that Mr. Highet pronounced the name of the great breeder Colling with as much reverence as if he had been an archbishop—whereupon Celia naturally cried out, "Who?"—the tale was told without untoward incident, and the talk wandered naturally on, first to horseflesh, then to cookery, last to the lateness of the hour and bed. The party thus broke up before Henry Highet had much opportunity either to scandalize or (as Anne feared much more) to bore the company.

Miss Guilfoyle woke late and did not see her unexpected guest before he departed. But Lord Grypphon, who was an early riser, had encountered him at the breakfast table, and later conveyed a message of thanks from him to Anne.

"I daresay you know more than I do about it," his lordship went on, "for of course I don't pretend to have half the wits of any of you females"—this was spoke in the dining-room at about noon, when the remainder of the party had assembled for a nuncheon—"but he seemed a quite sensible fellow to me, your Mr. Highet, and most amiable. Not a sound thinker, mind you, or he couldn't be taken in by that fool Cobbett—but intelligent enough. Didn't you think, my dear?" he appealed to his wife.

Lady Grypphon thoughtfully chewed and swallowed a bite of cold capon. "Actually, I have been asking myself that question half the morning. I find myself rather inclined to agree with Maria than Anne about him. A bit prosy, but no dullard. Misguided, as you say. Still, quite amiable, and perfectly satisfactory as to manners. Anne, I wonder you were so afraid I'd sink my claws into him. He certainly showed no signs of wishing to bore us to death, as you hinted."

Miss Guilfoyle, finding herself in the uncomfortable position of having made apologies for a person everyone else enjoyed, bristled and countered rather lamely, "Well, you were not obliged to listen to him on the subject of ditches. I promise you, if you had been, you would feel very differently. He bored the life out of me the first time we spoke at any length; and any how, he can be extremely rude. On the night I made his acquaintance, he absolutely laughed at me—"

"Oh, dear!" Celia interrupted, knowing her friend could never tolerate this. "I am surprised you have him in the house. Surely you will never forgive him."

"Now you are laughing at me too," Anne charged, "though you are sly about it. It is very bad of you. And as for Mr. Highet—" But she found she did not know how to end her sentence; for her feelings about that gentleman were in a state of confusion quite unlike any she was accustomed to maintain in her forceful, orderly mind. In the beginning, of course, she had positively disliked him. He made her feel foolish, and pitiable, and nearly drove her wild with his turnips and sows—which was boorish in him at the least. His ideas, such as they were, were frightful, the worst sort of radical drivel. And yet, in the last weeks . . . She could no longer ignore his many kindnesses, nor the fact that his presence sometimes called forth such curious symptoms in her. Was it a crime to be tedious?

"Oh, hang Mr. Highet!" she finally exclaimed, seizing a pitcher of almond sauce and violently upending it over her dish of pudding. "Whatever he is, I am sure *he* is not sitting at a nuncheon table meditating upon *us*! Now, where do you go from here, my lucky Grypphons? Tell me your winter plans."

SEVEN

LORD AND LADY GRYPPHON STOPPED A BARE FOUR days before, as Lady Grypphon frankly owned, they could "stick it no longer," and departed bag and baggage. It was nothing to do with Anne, of course: She and Maria were always welcome at Highglade, or in Portman Square when they were in town, for as long as they liked. It was only— well, after all, Anne herself confessed she could scarcely keep her wits in Cheshire. That was the whole problem, was not it? Then she would certainly understand . . .

She did understand; though she also, curiously, felt a faint resentment against the friends who had come so far to see her. Like it or not, Linfield was her home—for the moment, at least. It was as if Celia had criticized her gown, when that was the only gown she had. Moreover,

the Grypphons' departure made her feel abandoned, more
so than if they had not come. Though she secretly acknowledged both these unpleasant emotions, she branded
them irrational (how could the Grypphons like Linfield
better than she did? Ought they to stop there for ever because she was obliged to?) and vigorously suppressed
them while her friends were still there. But she cried as
she watched their carriages drive away, and was obliged to
lie in bed all that day with a sick head-ache.

Their visit extinguished such faint ideas as Anne had
had of inviting other friends to Cheshire. Lady Grypphon
might be more candid than the rest of their circle, but she
was no more accustomed to comfort and good society than
they. "The fact is," as Anne put it to Maria a few days
later at dinner, "the people I like in London know how to
think, and read, and write, and talk—and that is all they
know. Oh, they may ride an hour a day. If you set a
pheasant before Lord Bambrick, he may shoot it. And naturally we can all sit up in an Opera box with our eyes
open—for an act or two, any how. But we are lost without
one another to talk to. In a way it is rather monstrous.
Surely God did not give us arms only to hold books to our
noses, nor legs only to stroll from drawing- to dining-
room!"

Mrs. Insel (who, though her daily occupations were
quite as sedate as those Anne mentioned, was nevertheless innocent of living only to talk) agreed that this was
not likely to have been the Divine Intention. Though she
did not regret London to anything like the degree Anne
did—their life in society there was for her largely a matter
of following Miss Guilfoyle where she liked to go, and
keeping quiet—she knew its loss must chafe her friend
sorely, and added from sympathy, "It is dreadful to be

sentenced to exile from all one cares about! To have one's news arrive cold and stale, when one has been in the habit of making it oneself; to be unable to judge the pulse of thought in the metropolis, when one has been accustomed to set it; dreadful!"

Miss Guilfoyle, glancing up in some surprise, said, "I never guessed it fretted you so badly. Poor dear!"

About to say, "No, not me—I only worry for you," Maria thought again and checked herself. Far better to let Anne believe she had company in her misery than to seem to pity her. Since the day of their talk in the park about Ensley she thought Anne had held a little aloof from her. Maria would do nothing to drive her farther away. Instead, "I daresay I shall go on better when we have been here longer," she suggested mildly. "When once one has lived in Canada, you know, one learns to take root any where." She then turned the topic (since Dolphim had left them alone at table) to the simmering rivalry between that gentleman's wife and Miss Charlotte Veal.

In time, the lives of the inmates of Linfield began, as lives are wont to do, to settle into a pattern. Most afternoons between two and four Miss Guilfoyle made it her habit either to walk or to ride (according to the weather and her fancy) into the park. Each Monday she visited the farms of some of her tenants. Each Tuesday, accompanied by Mr. Rand, she rode over part of the home farm. Wednesday mornings between ten and eleven she naturally went over Miss Veal's housekeeping books with her; Wednesday afternoons she continued the momentum by sitting with Mr. Rand over his. On Fridays she and Maria drove to Faulding Chase, where they patronized such commercial establishments as were to be found there, and paid a call on the rector and his wife. Sunday morning found them at church, Sunday afternoon (a signal honour, here) at dinner with Lord and Lady Crombie.

Thursdays Anne devoted to a very particular correspondence with London: With the utmost discretion, she had resumed her letters to the *Times*. Under the name of "A." she faithfully reported the further adventures of Lord Quaffbottle as, driven out of town by duns, he rusticated in an unnamed corner of the country. It was a matter of some satisfaction to her to be able to turn Stade Park, Fevermere, and Faulding Chase into grist for her small but elegant mill. She said nothing of it to anyone and trusted to human vanity to prevent those of her neighbours who read the pieces from recognising themselves, even if, improbably, they guessed Lord Quaffbottle was in their midst.

Meanwhile she heard regularly from Ensley. His letters were kindly conceived and minutely executed, containing exact records of discussions behind Government doors, or of lively conversations at Holland or Melbourne House. His lordship had a keen eye, and he did not hesitate to include, as part of a Chancellor's communication, a quick twitch of one corner of his sly mouth, or a slow change in the angle of his left eyebrow. Besides these informative and entertaining passages, his lordship never failed to devote at least a paragraph, often more, to his feelings for Anne: how he wanted her, regretted her, dreamed of her, admired her. At the risk (he noted) of re-igniting her wrath, he begged her to keep in mind his project of bringing her back to London, and to remember she could call upon him to enact it at any time. Nor was he so craven as to censor the wedding plans which, she knew, must make up a good deal of his life now. He referred to them briefly but forthrightly. And though it did pain her, Anne liked him for this. It was as she had told Maria: Ensley's confidence, his affection, were still hers. It was she who had wavered.

But with so much distance between them, and receiving such loyal, vivid, and loving letters, Anne was finding it easier to care for Ensley again. The hurt and confusion of the past few months were nothing compared to the ten years of happy, mutual esteem they had enjoyed. For the first time since that terrible hour in Charles Grypphon's library, Anne felt things coming right in herself again, and rejoiced. Her replies to Ensley lost their forced, wary accents, growing tender and trustful once more. With relief, she resumed her habit of thinking of him as her dear, constant friend.

At the same time, she began to consider it rather fortunate than otherwise that events had conspired to take her out of his way just when they had. Trustful or no, mere common sense informed her it could never have been pleasant for her to be near him while his marriage to another woman went forward. She revised her plan of taking one of her two months in London during the Little Season, when the wedding events would be at their height, and postponed the journey till November instead. Since Ensley was due back in Cheshire in September, she still need not go more than six weeks without at least seeing him. She advised Maria and Celia Grypphon (in whose town house she meant to stay) accordingly, and set herself the double task of feeling completely at peace about Ensley's marriage by then, and amusing herself meanwhile.

Aiding her in this latter object more than she ever expected were two frequent visitors to Linfield, to wit, Mr. Mallinger and Mr. Highet.

Mr. Mallinger got in the way of calling upon the ladies every Wednesday afternoon about five, staying an hour or so on each occasion. His first visit had the ostensible purpose of bringing to Mrs. Insel a book on Scotland he had mentioned during their previous meeting, at the dinner party. His next visit had the object of collecting this book. His third had the aim of fetching to Miss Guilfoyle a volume he mentioned during his second—Colonel Kirkpatrick's 1793 *Account of the Kingdom of Nepaul*, and— By his fourth, this pretence of a very obliging lending library could be dropped in favour of a mere sociable visit by a gentleman to a pair of ladies he esteemed.

If Mr. Mallinger noticed that, Wednesday being the afternoon Miss Guilfoyle did the estate books with Mr. Rand, he had chosen a poor day on which to make his habitual visits to her and her companion—for Anne was often engaged with her steward until as late as five-thirty or even six o'clock—he neither remarked nor acted upon the circumstance. On the contrary, he seemed always rather surprised that she should be so engaged just when he happened to call. Still, he sat pretty happily with Mrs. Insel to wait for her. Mrs. Insel, modest to a fault, accepted this piece of recurrent forgetfulness without drawing special conclusions therefrom. She had been struck, since the night of the dinner, by the complete effacement from Mr. Mallinger's manner of any hint or suggestion of flattery to herself. So far from renewing his addresses, he had come to behave towards herself exactly as if he were a friend of long standing, the sort of stable, unexceptionable friend one might make through a family connexion. Relieved of the need to hold him at arm's length, she had come to like him very much indeed, for he was on all occasions genial, attentive, mild, and sympathetic. Anne, she knew, mistrusted his ideas; but the way he explained them to her, they seemed to Maria to make a great deal of sense. Education, for example: An infant was only an infant, after all. Why should not the child of a labourer grow up to be as clever as that of a lord, so long as their educations were the same? And she thought Mr. Mallinger spoke very feelingly of the plight of the poor around Faulding Chase, and was right to deplore it. If that made him a radical, perhaps Maria was a radical as well. However, she did not say so to Anne.

Anne, for her part, came rather to look forward to Mr. Mallinger's visits as well. She tweaked him about his reading, and they crossed swords in a friendly way. Later, as he started to tell the ladies some details of the lives of his students, she began to think well of his dedication, and to admire the subtle, playful ingenuity with which he administered his lessons.

As to the other visitor, Mr. Highet, he was at Linfield even more often than Mr. Mallinger. Sometimes Miss Guilfoyle sent for him, as when a farmer on one of her tenant farms died, and she needed to know how to let it again, and what to do for the widow; sometimes he came on business that touched both his estate and hers. Anne did not know quite how it was, but he rendered her so many good services and kind favours that she felt herself obliged nearly every Saturday to ask him and his revered mother to dine. He seemed to be at Linfield almost daily. Even when the weather was foul, and Miss Guilfoyle had settled down to a long day of reading and writing indoors, she might often look up to hear Dolphim announce Henry

Highet. Going in to the drawing-room, she would find he
had by error received twice the number of oilcakes he
needed, and wished to know if she could use the surplus;
or he was going to order a weighing machine, and wondered if she would like him to order one for Linfield as
well. That much of this intercourse might have been carried on by note did not escape Miss Guilfoyle. But a farm,
she was learning, was a lonely place, and if a neighbour
rode over instead of writing, it could not but make a welcome interruption.

His manner to her on these occasions was civil and
friendly, no more, no less. Anne imagined the visits were,
for him, a natural extension of those he had made to the
house in Herbert Guilfoyle's time. The only change was she
could not, as a single lady, return them. So he came twice as
often. In no other respect, however, did he seem to notice
the difference in their sexes. Certainly he never flattered
her. In his sleepy gaze she discerned no interest at all in how
she looked, or moved, or gazed back at him. Except to ask
how she did, he confined his remarks to estate matters. (He
was a little wider in his topics, though not much, when they
dined in company.) Occasionally he made a joke, always
very broad, which he then enjoyed with much knee-slap-
ping and head-tossing. Anne, a wooden half-smile on her
lips, would wait quietly for him to subside. But he did not
laugh at her. Indeed, he seemed increasingly to accord her
the respect he would give to any conscientious, thoughtful
fellow landlord.

Treated in such a steady, friendly, undramatic manner,
Anne could not help but begin to relax with him, and respond in kind. She ceased to compare him to town beaux
and town wits, to statesmen and Corinthians, and started
to look for in him what he had in abundance: experience

in farming, knowledge of the land, a shrewd sense of his neighbours. Gradually her tendency to blush in his presence abated. She might feel it rising once in a while, as on the occasion when Mr. Highet caught up her hand and thrust it with his own into the thick fleece on the back of a ewe, that she might feel how it differed from another bred not for wool but mutton. But such episodes were brief. In the main she spoke to Mr. Highet with neither more nor less interest than she felt when conferring with Mr. Rand (whom she had succeeded, by dint of hard study and management, in subduing if not winning over). So mild, indeed, did her feelings towards Henry Highet become, that he quite ceased to appear among Lord Quaffbottle's adventures—where he had initially cut a very noticeable, clumsy, and rather ridiculous figure. Mrs. Highet, it might be noted, remained.

Meanwhile summer drew on towards its close. In the fields the corn ripened and turned gold. The harvest at Linfield (which its mistress could never have accomplished properly without the advice of her neighbour at Fevermere) was a good one—not excellent, by any means, but not at all the disastrous failure so widespread in England that year. The days became slowly shorter; the air turned and crisped. Miss Guilfoyle rode into the park less for exercise now than for pleasure in its beauty. Often she dismounted and walked for the mere enjoyment of feeling the brown earth beneath her feet. There was a difference between wandering here and wandering through the parks of London, or even the parks of the numerous estates at which she had hitherto made one of the party. There was something invigorating in the solitude, in knowing the land was her own. After the harvest, she felt a certain pride, even a love, for the earth that had been worked under her direction, and that had brought forth fruit. She liked to watch the threshing and winnowing of the grain, to see it carted to the mill and brought back flour. When, one late August afternoon (after she had been visiting the threshing floor) she read in the *Times* that Parliament was again in session, the news had an alien and artificial look to her, and she wondered with a smile by what cycle of nature Parliament knew itself ready to recommence.

Mr. Highet advised her to marl certain fields of hers before the ploughing and cultivating began. Mr. Rand, in accordance with old Cheshire notions, advised against. Anne decided to trust Mr. Highet, so great was her faith in him now. She had long since concluded he could not possibly know the full terms of Herbert Guilfoyle's will. If he had, he would not have befriended her so.

Into this tranquil, steady flow of days erupted an evening of event. It was the second Wednesday in September. The men had just begun to harrow. Anne had passed a lengthier afternoon than usual with Mr. Rand, for the time to sell the wether lambs had come and a number of decisions were necessary. She emerged from her office just before six to learn from Dolphim that a letter from London had arrived, and that Mr. Mallinger and Mrs. Insel were waiting for her in the Green Parlour.

"Who is the letter from, can you tell?"

"I believe Lord Ensley, ma'am," said he, in a tone whose practised indifference expertly concealed a hearty mistrust of this particular correspondent.

"Oh, then I must look at it before I join the others. Where is it?"

Dolphim fetched it while his mistress retired again into her now empty office. She had just had a letter from En-

sley the day before, so this one was an agreeable surprise.
The butler returned with it at last and Anne broke the
seal as he discreetly bowed himself out the door.

But her eagerness soon turned to disappointment. The
words were few and to the point. Anne would remember
the legislation Ensley had spoke of in his to her dated
August 30? Well then, Liverpool being determined to
press on with it before . . . Her eyes skipped to the bot-
tom of the page. It was as she feared: Ensley was obliged
to cancel his visit to Linfield. He was chagrined, he deplored it—et cetera, et cetera—but it could not be
helped.

Anne knew when Ensley wrote cancel rather than postpone he meant he would not come till after she had seen
him in London. Dully she returned her gaze to the top of
the page and read the full text. She did not doubt but that
it was true. If Lady Juliana or her family had been what
kept him in town, he would have said it bluntly.

With a deep sigh, she rose from her desk, folding the
letter into a drawer. She would write a reply later; for the
moment she wanted only to lie down. Passing Dolphim in
the front hall,

"Would you tell Mr. Mallinger and Mrs. Insel I am not
feeling quite the thing?" she asked him. "I shall take my
dinner in my room." And she ascended the staircase leaning heavily on the bannister.

Dolphim, though far too well-trained to show it, observed his mistress' manner closely before going to carry
out his errand. Unseen, he shook his head disapprovingly.
He could not like Lord Ensley, for all his valet reported
he was a good, kind man. It wasn't natural, the way he
kept after Miss Anne. In fact, none of Miss Guilfoyle's

household favoured Lord Ensley's suit, or friendship, or whatever it was.

"Miss Guilfoyle regrets to say she is slightly ill and will not come in," he announced, putting his head into the Green Parlour. He wondered briefly whether Mrs. Insel ought properly to stay alone with her guest, and not even a pretext of a chaperon on the way; but it was not for him to judge. He returned to the hall. Miss Charlotte Veal, no doubt, would be happy to plant her dry stick of a self in the Parlour and so lend the meeting respectability; but Mr. Dolphim was not about to contribute new fuel to Miss Veal's already inflamed idea of her own consequence, and that was that.

The correct, conscientious Mr. Dolphim might have changed his mind if he could have heard what was said in the Parlour after he vanished. But he could not hear, which was just the point. Mr. Mallinger, seeing his moment at last, could no longer restrain himself. Interrupting what had been a rather arid but certainly correct discourse on the subject of higher mathematics, he stood, walked up the room and down it, then begged Mrs. Insel's leave to address her on a matter of some importance to him.

Startled, Maria nevertheless told him, "If it is important, I am honoured you should wish to consult me on it. Pray, go on."

Mr. Mallinger thanked her, walked up and down the room again, turned resolutely to face her, turned away, walked again into the long stretch of late sunlight by the fireplace, and back to the sofa on which Mrs. Insel sat, where he burst out, "Dear ma'am! You charged me soon after we met to make no remark touching your personal— er, that is," he amended, "to restrict my remarks to you to such as might be made by any civil gentleman to any lady. I am sure you recall that request?"

Maria, whose dark complexion at once went whiter, nodded.

Mr. Mallinger paced restlessly again while he continued, "I hope you agree I have carried out that charge about as thoroughly as a man could?" He stopped pacing to turn and look down upon her again.

Mrs. Insel, whiter still, nodded once more.

"I have said nothing to vex you? I have neither in my words, nor in the tone in which they were uttered, nor even in my look, betrayed any particular admiration for you? I have not?"

Maria, hands trembling, small head a little bowed as if under the heavy burden of her massive knot of chestnut hair, managed to peep, "No. Nothing."

The schoolmaster stopped his perambulations and stood facing her from some ten feet away. He ran his fingers through his untidy blond hair, tugged the knot of his neck cloth away from his long throat, and said, "I am gratified to know I achieved my goal. But Mrs. Insel, to-day I must beg permission to throw off these restraints and speak to you from my heart. To-day I must tell you how I cherish your shy confidence, your womanly timidity, your quiet beauty. I must tell you how I long to protect you. I must plead with you to allow me to soothe—"

"Mr. Mallinger." Maria's voice wavered and was pitched so low even she could scarcely hear it.

"Mrs. Insel, if you would do me the honour to be my wife; if you would even think of me, promise to think of me in that way, accept me as your suitor; if you would consent to share my humble—"

"Mr. Mallinger!" Shaking, Maria stood and made an

awkward, violent gesture to him to stop. Her admirer did
so, though with some amazement at the state of excited
emotion in which he seemed to see her. For a moment
neither of them felt able to speak. Then, recovering herself after several deliberate, deep breaths, "Pray be
seated," Maria said, indicating a chair. She sat herself in
an opposite chair several feet distant and gestured again,
this time to let her think before she talked. Finally,
speaking with great effort,

"Dear sir," she said, "I blame myself for failing to
make my full meaning clear to you. That day in the
park . . . I intended to say you must never think of me
other than as an agreeable friend. That you do find me
agreeable—" Again she held up a hand to silence him, for
he was about to break in, "I must own, flatters and
pleases me. It is rare for me to find a friend I esteem, and
who esteems me. Miss Guilfoyle—" She looked down at
the tips of her shoes, which peeked from under her hem.
"You must not misunderstand me, for Miss Guilfoyle is
every thing that is kind and generous to me; but though
she does not realize it, she is . . ." Mrs. Insel thought a
while, then smiled wistfully. "She is a rather brighter bird
than I, if you understand me. The people we meet are
chiefly attracted to her. But you— Pray be silent," she
forestalled him. "You seek me out, which gratifies me extremely. In every way you are gentle towards me, and respectful, and perfectly kind." Her thin hands clutched
together in her lap, she raised her dark eyes again to Mr.
Mallinger and went on, "I must be very spoiled, or very
stupid, not to be pleased by that." She smiled and her
voice lost some of its edge as she said, "I consider you an
industrious, intelligent, admirable gentleman. Indeed I
do, Mr. Mallinger. Please believe that. But—" And here

her voice again grew strained; she stood abruptly but would not allow him to stand. "But you must never, never, address me in this way again. Pray do not ask me to explain." Her cheeks suddenly ashen, "I cannot explain," she continued. "It is nothing to do with you. Never think of me in this way. Only misery can come of it. You know I am no coquette. You think me—I hope—no fool. So you must trust what I say—"

"Is it my age?" Mr. Mallinger finally burst out in a wail, unable to keep quiet any longer. He reached his hands out to her in an involuntary gesture of supplication, and she seized them in hers before she replied,

"Dear God, no! Nothing so simple as that. For the love of kindness, desist in this. Forgive me for letting you come here at all. Do not—" She shut her eyes as if summoning all her inner strength before tearing her hands from his and concluding, "Do not come again. Goodbye." And with this she ran from the room before her would-be lover could catch her.

The news that neither of the ladies of the house would come down to dinner that evening provoked a good deal of consternation in the kitchen, and not a little conjecture. "Grippe," Miss Veal diagnosed with a firm, satisfied snap of her old jaws. "It is hardly to be wondered at, the way Miss Guilfoyle will gallivant about."

"If it were grippe she would not eat dinner at all," Mrs. Dolphim countered, determined to refute any calumny Miss Veal might invent, while Mr. Dolphim merely stared, as if struck dumb by her impertinence.

"Female troubles," pronounced Susannah, who was standing at a sideboard polishing a pair of brass candle snuffers.

"Female troubles!" echoed Sally Clemp, scathing fire
in her tone. She'd found herself a bit queasy suddenly,
and had come down to the kitchen for a rusk and a cup of
tea. "As if they could catch such a complaint from each
other! You're a sharp one, Miss Susannah. And how do
you dare to be talking of the mistress so any how, I'd like
to know? Or even thinking of her so! For shame!"

Susannah, utterly cowed, begged pardon, but muttered
sulkily (and scarcely audibly), "A person still has the right
to think, I hope," into the bell end of a snuffer.

Lizzie entering at this time, all conversation ceased;
for no one—not even Miss Veal—dared discuss Miss
Guilfoyle when her loyal abigail was there to hear it.

Some while later, when Mr. and Mrs. Dolphim were in
their room for the night, the former described to the latter
the effect of the letter from Lord Ensley, Mrs. Insel's
headlong flight up the stairs, and Mr. Mallinger's defeated
departure.

"Never saw the like," he told her. "Walked in a confident, spry young fellow; walked out an old man. It was
like she took the heart out of him. Pitiful, he looked."

Mrs. Dolphim clucked her tongue. "Poor thing," said
she, sympathy inflaming her imagination. "In love with
her, I don't doubt, and she holding herself too high for
him. But fancy that Susannah setting the trouble down to
female complaints! I never heard such a thing!"

"Our Sally put her in her place, though," answered her
husband. "Who would have guessed she could talk so
fierce?"

"Oh, she's a good girl enough." In London Mrs. Dol-
phim had called Sally flighty, and even advised John
Coachman against marrying her; but since the move to
Cheshire the London people had closed ranks against the

common enemy. "I think"—she set her brush down and turned to wink at her husband—"I think she may be in the family way."

The conversation thereupon turning to babies, confinements, and other matters of no immediate concern to us, we may perhaps leave these two to their privacy and walk down one pair of stairs to the first floor of the house. Here, at this moment, Mrs. Insel was tapping at the door to Miss Guilfoyle's bed-chamber. Anne, who had finally opened her ebony desk and settled down to write a tempered reply to Ensley, looked up and called to her to enter.

"But my poor dear, whatever is the matter?" she demanded the moment Maria came in. She jumped from her desk and hastened to put an arm round her friend, whose red eyes and pink nose told volumes already. "Come and sit down," she said, bringing her to the bed and fixing her among the cushions. "I shall fetch you a cool cloth. Poor dove! What happened? You have not had a letter from Halfwistle House, have you? Those beasts! How dare they reproach—"

But Maria interrupted her, saying, "Nothing like that. I wish it were!" And she began to cry again, hiding her face in her hands.

Tenderly, Anne raised her head and obliged her to lie back among the pillows. She went for a moment to the white pitcher on the vanity, then returned to press a dampened cloth against Maria's brow. Stroking her hair she murmured gently, "Now, whatever it is, we shall see to it. Are you unhappy here? Do you miss London?"

Making an effort to regain her self-command, "Mr. Mallinger," Maria answered at last. "He— This evening he asked me to marry him."

Hearing this Anne ceased her clucking and soothing

and sat, rather abruptly, on the foot of the bed. Her face
lost its look of motherly solicitude and took on a darker
expression. She was silent a moment, then asked, "What
did you answer?"

"Only that he must never think of me in such a way."

"I thought you had told him that long ago? Did you not
say—? That day, after we had been lost in the
woods . . ."

"Indeed. But he either did not believe me, or did not
understand me, for he has been thinking of me so all the
time. What an idiot I have been not to guess! But I so
enjoyed his friendship." She seemed about to cry again
but controlled herself and resumed, "I told him not to call
any more, but I am bound to see him. Only yesterday we
met by accident, at the dairy. And remember? You and I
came across him in the village last week. Besides which,
there is church every Sunday. Oh Anne, what must I do?"

After some hesitation Anne replied slowly, "If you gen-
uinely feel him to be your friend, my dear, perhaps you
ought to tell him the truth?"

Maria's tearful eyes widened. She sat up a little. "Tell
him I am married already?" she demanded. "When I have
deliberately allowed him, and every one, to believe me a
widow?" Her cheeks flushed with anger and shame. "I
could not. Anne, what would he think of me?"

"I am sure he would be astonished at first. But if you
explained to him the reason of the deception . . ."

"Explain to him! How, for example? 'Dear Mr. Mallinger! You see, my husband drank and beat me. More
tea, Mr. Mallinger? A biscuit? But as I was saying, sir,
Captain Insel also consorted with other—'" Mrs. Insel
could not bring herself to finish her sentence, but fell silent, a storm of humiliated fury on her face.

"My dear Maria, there is no shame to you in the monstrous behaviour of your husband!" Anne protested, as she had more than once before. "The shame is all his—"

"And would you have me tell Mr. Mallinger my own family will not receive me, but insist my place is with my husband?" Maria broke in. "That they are so unnatural as to turn away their flesh and blood? Put yourself in my place, Anne, and say whether you would tell a gentleman whose esteem you valued such horrors? But perhaps you cannot imagine it. Nothing but honour attaches to your history—no straitened means, no sordid connexion—" Again Maria could not finish; indeed, she already regretted having expressed resentment to Anne. Remorsefully, "I am sorry," she said, imagining she saw surprise and hurt in her friend's eyes. "Pray forgive me. It is not true. You are the most sympathetic and generous of friends. If you had not taken me in after I ran away from John, I do not know how I should have gone on. I suppose I must have returned to Canada—"

"Please, no more!" Anne had never quite realized before what it meant to the other to live dependent of her, what humiliation it must necessarily entail, what daily trials, what small, painful inequities. Naturally Maria must compare their lots, and feel the injustice of her own the more keenly. Anne's heart ached for her friend. She could not bear to hear another word of gratitude, and put a hand up to silence her. "I told you then and I tell you now: It is you who did me a kindness. Miss Gully's retirement could not have been delayed another twelvemonth. After that I should have been obliged— Indeed, I do not know what I should have done. Gone back to Overton"—she shuddered—"or hired a companion. Anyhow, I like to have you with me. If Miss Gully had been twenty, I should still have wished you to stay. What would my life be without you?" She moved to put her arm round Maria's shoulders again and laughed to cheer her up. "A sad charade, a lonely comedy. Especially"—she looked round the sparsely furnished room (now brightened a little by some few of her belongings)—"here!"

Maria seemed comforted, if not persuaded, by this reasoning. She smiled and was quiet a while, then sat up. "But help me think what I can do for Mr. Mallinger," she entreated. "I feel so guilty for having encouraged him; and I fear—well, without being vain, I do fear he will not give me up so easily as that."

Anne thought for a moment, then said slowly, "If he does not forget you, and will not forget you, I think we must take you out of his way for a while; for we cannot expect Mr. Mallinger to give up his post."

Maria objected immediately, "But you cannot stay here without me; and you must not take any of your precious time away when London is de—"

"What a drama! Before we trouble ourselves about such eventualities, let us see whether they arise. In all earnestness, Mr. Mallinger seems a very sensible man to me. He will make an effort to govern his feelings and in time he will succeed. Oh, for a week or two no doubt he will pine and mope. After all, he has been obliged to give up my Miss Dove . . . But he is no tragic hero. I am sure a month will see him right as a trivet again. Now you must have some sleep, poor thing." Fondly, she brushed a hand along Mrs. Insel's thin cheek, then helped her to rise and escorted her, arm round her waist, to the door. "Good night."

Maria smiled, thanked her for her good sense, and turned to leave.

"Oh, one moment," Anne called out brightly, as Maria was almost gone. "I nearly forgot to tell you. I had a little letter from Ensley to-day. Nothing of note, only he will be unable to come . . ."

EIGHT

WHETHER MISS GUILFOYLE HERSELF BELIEVED THE comforting prognostications she made to Maria regarding Mr. Mallinger's return to spirits was not clear. What became all too clear, as the weeks wore on, was that she had been wrong. Adjured to stay away, the schoolmaster did. But as Mrs. Insel had foreseen, nothing short of complete sequestration—his or hers—could have prevented their running into one another. Not two days after the dreadful evening when Maria had banished him from her sight, Mr. Mallinger was spied by the ladies from their carriage, walking away from Faulding Chase as they drove towards it. Another two days and they saw him in church. Sickened at heart by his wretched look, his extreme pallor and haggardness, Maria resolved after this to keep indoors all

week, and immured herself in Linfield. But the following
Saturday, unable to bear it any longer, she wrapped herself in a cloak and crept into the park for a walk—and
walked directly into Mr. Mallinger. On this occasion, as
on the others, they nodded and made a show of civility.
Maria could see her admirer did all his possible to conceal
his misery—only it went too deep for a bow and a determined display of manners to cover it up. What she could
not know was how perfectly her own wan face mirrored
the unhappiness in his. But Mr. Mallinger saw it, and was
less inclined than ever to forget her.

Meanwhile, Anne continued to counsel her to let time
do its work. She herself was busy, for (at Mr. Highet's
suggestion) she had decided to make certain improve-
ments on some of her tenant farms before winter set in;
but she saw as well as the schoolmaster how Maria suffered. If it did not pass off within another fortnight she
must persuade her to go away . . . though where precisely
to send her was another question, not to mention how
Anne could find a suitable companion to keep her household respectable. That Captain Insel! It made Anne simply furious to think of him abusing Maria, then going on
his merry, brawling, drinking way after she fled. He had
never—well, perhaps one ought merely to be grateful for
this, but it *was* unnatural—he had never made a single
attempt to communicate with his wife in England. Anne
had once asked Ensley if he couldn't at least be dis-
charged from the Army for his conduct—he ought to be
punished some how. But Ensley said the Army did not
interfere in such private matters; and in any case, was it
not better for Mrs. Insel that her husband remain in Canada?

She supposed it was; yet the injustice of it rankled her.

For Maria, besides having endured the pain and mortification he had dealt her, was prevented by his continued per-
nicious existence from having a proper life of her own.
Anne could not be sure how deep her affection for Mr.
Mallinger ran, but surely Maria must long to establish herself properly with some one. At Linfield, no matter what
either lady said, she depended for her bread entirely on
Anne's whim, or charity, or liking. No wonder she had
spoke so bitterly the other night. And this was the best
she could do, since those selfish, cold, sanctimonious—
But Anne would not allow herself to think of the Pilkintons: It only fanned the flames of her indignation.

It occurred to her more than once that she would have
liked to share these reflections with Henry Highet. He
had observed Mr. Mallinger's dejection and mentioned it
to the assembled company one Saturday at dinner. Maria
had gone white, while Mrs. Highet launched into a loud,
and lengthy, disquisition on inflammations of the stom-
ach, and their tendency to weaken the blood. Anne
longed to take Mr. Highet aside and pour the whole story
into his ear, that he might agree in his solemn, ponderous
way how really unjust it was. Naturally, however, she did
no such thing. In all the world only herself and Ensley
knew, besides the Insels and the Pilkintons.

For her part, Maria also suffered for lack of a confidant.
She realized that, ironically, she might well have turned to
Mr. Mallinger himself for support, had the matter been a
different one. Of course she had Anne; but she did not
like to vex her with repeated lamentations. And she had a
special reason for keeping silent with her friend too,
which she would not confess to her: The example of Lord
Ensley (whose constant presence near Anne had, Maria
believed, prevented that lady from forming an eligible and

satisfying connexion of her own) weighed heavily on her, making her feel it all the more imperative that she remove herself from Mr. Mallinger, since he could not remove from her. With an aching heart, and after much inward debate, Mrs. Insel formed a plan and resolved to carry it out if Mr. Mallinger did not look much improved by the middle of October. And since, on Sunday the thirteenth, she perceived him in church to be pale and exhausted, with hollow cheeks and a dull look in his sunken eyes, the next day she took advantage of Anne's absorption in the affairs of her tenants and drove into Faulding Chase herself.

Here, in the coffee-room of the Red Lion, she bespoke pen and ink and wrote (albeit slowly, and blotting more than one tear from the paper under her hand) an advertisement offering herself as hired companion to any suitable reader of the *Times*. At the same time, she wrote a second notice advertising that a young lady of good family in Cheshire was in need of a companion. Interested correspondents were requested to reply to Mrs. John, in care of the Red Lion, Faulding Chase.

Then she drove home.

The wedding of George, Lord Ensley, to Lady Juliana Canesford was, as any reader of the London papers must know, fixed for three P.M. on 28 October, at St. George's Church, Hanover Square. It was a date, oddly, which kept going in and out of the usually orderly mind of Anne Guilfoyle. In fact, all the latter part of October seemed to squirm and wriggle from her mental grasp, so that she was constantly asking herself whether this was Wednesday or Thursday, the sixteenth or the seventeenth, and consulting calendars. When she was busy—and she busied herself a good deal more with estate matters than Mr. Rand, for one, could like—she kept in tolerable spirits. But on her rides into the park, for example, the falling leaves, the air ever more crisp and cold, the ground harder under the horse's hooves, the earlier dark seemed to her infinitely sad, almost frightening, in their promise of winter. In the evenings, sitting alone in a pool of lamplight, she often caught herself reading the same paragraph twice or thrice without comprehending it at all; instead her mind had wandered off into a nest of small anxieties about the home farm, the tenants, the household; and when she had worried at these ideas some while, she had perforce to admit a deeper one underlay them. With his creator's mind in such a turmoil, Lord Quaffbottle found his debts conveniently paid by an unexpected windfall, and went back to London and obscurity.

Invaded by such an accumulating gloom, it might be supposed Miss Guilfoyle became quieter, soberer, in company; but this was not her way. On the contrary, her tendency to joke grew more pronounced than ever. She talked to herself non-stop, and quite shocked Miss Veal by singing "God Rest Ye Merry, Gentlemen" under her breath all the while they studied the household books. Mrs. Samuels was astonished to be asked by her whether Mr. Samuels "gave it a rest" or sermonized right through the night. She told Mrs. Highet (who never left off hinting that the ladies of Linfield must surely long for London) that she had given her house there to an organ-grinder and his monkey, the latter being a particular friend of her Uncle Frederick's. And she informed Lady Crombie that she did quite right to let her offspring run all over the house screaming however they liked—that in fact she had recently read a monograph by a German scholar,

Herr Doktor Hanswurst von Hanswurst, maintaining that any restraint whatever, even smocks and aprons, could permanently injure a child's spirit, and make him melancholy for life. Ensley's letters meanwhile continued to arrive with perfect regularity, and professed an attachment to her equally perfect. Once or twice he mentioned, without irony, that his improved acquaintance with Lady Juliana had only served to encourage his early conviction that she was a sensible girl and a tactful one. Anne rightly supposed him to imply by this that she and he had every reason to be cheerful concerning their future undisturbed relations. Somehow, though, she was not quite cheerful.

On the twenty-seventh she found she did not care to go to church, nor in fact to go any where at all; she passed the entire day in the drawing-room, scowling at a succession of unlucky books. On the twenty-eighth itself she woke to discover she could not get out of bed. After much persuasion, Maria (who had refused on the previous day to venture out alone) consented to visit a few of the tenant farms in her stead. Meanwhile, Anne lay still with a head that throbbed like a threshing floor under a thousand flails. She told herself it would all be over by evening, that it was the anticipation that was the worst, that as soon as she received an affectionate letter from Ensley dated 29 October she would be herself again. Meantime it was all she could do to drink a cup of tea and fall back among the pillows. Lizzie brought her calomel and she took it obediently, but her head continued to pound. At one o'clock Maria came home with a conscientious report on the fence-mending going forward at Farmer Haydon's. She offered to bathe Anne's forehead in rosewater; but Anne declined. Mrs. Insel being somewhat afflicted herself (in her case by having caught sight of Mr. Mallinger in the road, looking more wan and woebegone than ever) did not insist.

At three-thirty in the afternoon Lizzie came in, rather timidly, and told Miss Guilfoyle Mr. Henry Highet was downstairs and begging her most particularly to receive him privately. He knew she was indisposed—Lizzie had told him so herself, forcefully—but the matter on which he wished to address her was of such a distinctive nature, and weighed on him so profoundly, that he would consider it a great kindness if she would come down.

Miss Guilfoyle sat up in bed and gently held her hands to her temples, which felt as if they might fly away in opposite directions. She had been going mentally through the words of the marriage ceremony, which she recalled only too clearly from weddings she had attended. "I George take thee Juliana to my wedded Wife, to have and to hold . . ." recited Ensley's low, sonorous voice; and it was answered by Lady Juliana's thick, husky tones: "I Juliana take thee George . . ."

"You did tell him I was ill?" Anne asked Lizzie, tenderly massaging her brow.

"Twice, ma'am. I'll tell him again if you like."

"No. Give me my desk."

While Lizzie did so, Anne composed her note. She did not make much of Mr. Highet's asking to see her privately, for once or twice before some confidential business about a tenant of hers—whose son had been caught poaching at Fevermere, for example, or whose daughter was unmarried and with child—had brought Mr. Highet to Linfield requesting a meeting alone with Anne. Consequently she merely wrote, "Is it any thing that can wait? I have a sick head-ache, but will come down if you say it is urgent." She felt a little improved once Lizzie had departed with the message and almost hoped Mr. Highet would insist. Any thing was better—even poachers—than lying in bed hearing those ghostly vows!

Very shortly Lizzie returned, with the following written on the back of the note Anne had sent down: "Yes, the matter can wait, only I had hoped to put it before you to-day. It will require some thought on your part. If you are really ill, I shall try to ride over Wednesday. To-morrow I go to Chester, to market."

Paradoxically—such were the mild perversities of her nature—this answer piqued Anne's curiosity far more than would have any claim of real urgency, and resolved her to go down after all. Cursing the man for having "the timing of a stopped clock," she nevertheless dispatched Lizzie to tell him to wait, then crawled out of bed and splashed herself thoroughly with cold water. Lizzie returned to dress her, and (gamely rising to the challenge) to arrange her yellow curls into a semblance of order, and some half an hour later Miss Guilfoyle descended to her caller.

She found him standing in the drawing-room, in a blue coat and pantaloons—which rather surprised her, for normally he rode over, and she saw him only in boots and buckskin breeches, sometimes even in the smock-frock he wore to go out into the fields. She gave him her hand (which he shook without causing her undue perturbation) and begged him to sit down, asking, "Well? What did our good rector give us yesterday—Sacrifice again? Faith? Charity? Not Hope, I hope! I hope I did not miss Hope."

Mr. Highet received this mild pleasantry with the friendly but unsmiling gravity she had come to expect when she tried to make him laugh and answered, seating himself on the other end of a chintz-covered settee, "Tolerance, Miss Guilfoyle."

"Did he? I never heard Mr. Samuels speak of Tolerance before. I daresay you are making it up, and it was not that at all. You only say it because you believe intolerance my besetting sin. Confess it. Is it not so?"

"If it is your sin, it is for you to confess," Mr. Highet returned. Anne thought the reply rather witty (for Mr. Highet, at least) but was not certain he had intended it to be so, and therefore only smiled. "I hope you will forgive my importunity this afternoon," he went on presently. "I see you are not at your best."

Since Anne's complexion was grey, her small mouth crumpled, and her eyes heavily ringed, she did not bother to demur, but only waited for him to go on. She had been unable so far to guess from his countenance what sort of matter had brought him to her to-day. He did not look particularly solemn or troubled.

"Miss Guilfoyle, what I am about to suggest," he resumed after a moment, speaking with a slowness and deliberation unusual even in him, and gazing mostly (it appeared) across the room at a watercolour of a horse clearing a hedge, with only a glance now and then at her, "will surprise you, I think, a good deal. I ask you, therefore, to give no answer at all to-day, but only to hear me out and then to think about it as long as you wish. It is a suggestion, believe me, which I make after long thought. I cannot say how you will like it; you may even dislike it very much, in which case I can only implore you to remember that it is made in the light of the sincere admiration and respect—particularly for your perseverance in learning to manage Linfield—which I have come to feel towards you."

"Good God," Miss Guilfoyle exclaimed rather weakly.

Her head had begun to throb again, and she felt giddy. "You terrify me. Pray go on."

Mr. Highet briefly cast his sleepy, careful glance at her, then resumed his study of the jumping horse. The days had long been cold enough to require good fires in every room, and the firelight here now spread a leaping, variable glow on the gentleman's rosy cheeks and wide forehead which began quite to fascinate his auditor. As he did not look at her, she could look at him. To her dizzy, dreamy consciousness, he seemed remarkably handsome.

"Well then. You know, of course, that the lands of Fevermere and Linfield march on each other along a considerable portion of their perimeters."

Miss Guilfoyle nodded, feeling almost mesmerised by her caller's low, sleepy voice and resolute manner.

"In many small matters we manage our estates as one—the school, for example, and the sharing of forge and tools—which is a mode of operation I entered into in your great uncle's time, and which benefits us both."

Anne, half dazed, agreed.

"I know that when Herbert Guilfoyle left you his estate, he did so on certain conditions—on the condition, specifically, that you live on it ten months of the year."

"You know that?" Anne demanded, amazed, and wondered straightway whether, in that case, he knew the rest of the terms.

"Indeed. We discussed it when he set out to draw up his will. He was afraid—and so was I—that his beneficiary would take as much out and put as little into Linfield as possible, and that the place would fall to ruin. We agreed this condition was a good guard—"

Anne was on the point of asking him if he knew he himself was named in the will, but Highet continued,

"Of course, what I could not know when I so agreed was how painful the tenure would be to you. To be frank, I have been a little surprised at your chusing to stay at all. My mother . . ."

Anne waited breathlessly to hear what observation this devoted son would make about his mother.

"My mother is an excellent woman, but she is rather silly in some matters. Yet I cannot help thinking she is correct when she says, as she so often says," he added with the faintest smile, "that you must regret your old life. I remark here that I do not quite believe your story of the organ-grinder's monkey. Yet since you do not go back to town, but instead live here more and more retired, I can only guess that some circumstance actually prevents your return, and that Mr. Guilfoyle's bequest came as a godsend more than as a mere boon."

Such was the trance Anne was in, and so much had she come to trust Mr. Highet even when not enthralled, that she told him simply, "That is quite true. A ship sank, and with it all I had."

Mr. Highet received this in silence, but his face changed, and he gave her a swift glance in which inquiry, esteem, and sympathy mingled. "In that case," he at last went on, "my proposal may be of even greater interest to you than I expected."

"Mr. Highet, what is your proposal?" Anne asked in a sharpened tone, afraid even in her misty confusion lest he revert to his old habit of pitying her.

He hesitated a moment, as a man does who is about to sign a document though he has already read it, then declared, "It is that we bring our estates into even a closer alliance than any Herbert Guilfoyle and I could contrive. In brief, Miss Guilfoyle (and repeating that I admire and respect you personally very much), I suggest we marry and join the estates together."

"I beg your pardon?" was Miss Guilfoyle's flabbergasted answer.

"I knew I should surprise you. Forgive me if I could have prepared you better," said Mr. Highet (though, curiously, he seemed all the while he made this apology to be resisting a smile). "The purpose of this alliance, you see, would be, on my side, to extend my property substantially—an arithmetical extension which ought to have geometrical benefits in increased production. Whereas on your side, you will be free to return to a life you left, I am persuaded, only reluctantly. You would continue to receive the income from Linfield—which ought, as I say, to increase considerably—without being obliged to remain here. I am the more in favour of this plan, as I think it does not at all thwart your great uncle's wishes, but on the contrary furthers them. Without immodesty, I hope I may say Mr. Guilfoyle had an excellent opinion of my management."

Anne could only reply, rather vacantly, "No doubt. But this alliance—"

"Oh, I need hardly add, the marriage would be a legal matter purely. My mother has no wish to be supplanted as mistress of Fevermere, you may be sure—" On this, Mr. Highet put his head back and gave one of the hearty laughs Anne so disliked. "Any more, I trust, than you have ambitions to supplant her. No indeed, our relations—yours and mine—would remain quite as they are. Except that I dareswear I should see a good deal less of you. I should like—though you need not—I should like it if you came up now and then. Say once or twice a year, to see how the estates go on. But as for—well, how can I say it?" A fresh smile pulled at Mr. Highet's generous mouth, and he went on, "As for any *intimacies*, you may assure yourself— Oh, no! That, I will hardly require of you!" And again he flung his head back and this time laughed so heartily that Anne, her head newly aswirl, longed to skewer him with the fireplace poker. When he finally managed to recover himself, he continued, "I am sure I have mentioned once or twice the circumstance of my having six nephews by my older brother. Thoughtful of him, wasn't it, to relieve me of any necessity to produce an heir? One of the boys looks rather like being a farmer to me, when he grows up, though he might dispute it now. George, he's called. Now that's a coincidence— George is the name of your friend Lord Ensley, isn't it? What do you hear from him these days?"

As this question was asked in a tone indicative of mere polite interest, and with a smile perfectly bland, Anne could not suspect Mr. Highet of knowing it had any particular meaning to her. She turned, if possible, a shade whiter, but obliged herself to say, "He is well, I think." Her voice had a tremor in it which she hoped Mr. Highet did not hear. He was looking at her very closely, or so it seemed to her—perhaps it was only because she especially wished he would not just now. She could bring herself to say nothing more of Ensley—certainly not that he had now been married some hour and a half—but instead observed coldly, "When a country has had three kings named George, one must expect to find Georges sprinkled about. It is hardly a coincidence worth noting, I should say."

Mr. Highet appeared to take no offence from the condescension in her tone but on the contrary looked peculiarly cheered. "I expect you are right," he agreed, bowing. "At all events, you now have my proposition before you. Reflect upon it at your leisure, I beg—"

As he appeared to be about to rise, Anne involuntarily stretched out a hand to stop him, lightly touching his arm for the purpose. Ridiculously (she considered) she got another of those shocks—this one from his sleeve, for heaven's sake! But at least it brought her colour back a little. Breathing more rapidly, "Pray stop another moment," she interrupted, "I have something to tell you—though I have sometimes thought," she added suspiciously, "that you already know it. You are rather deeper than you look, Mr. Highet, are not you?"

"Am I?" He seemed surprised. "As I do not know how deep I look, I suppose I cannot say."

"You look a plain country gentleman," she told him, a little impatiently. "No more and no less."

"But that is just what I am." He gazed with unusual directness into her eyes and repeated, seriously, "I am a country gentleman, make no mistake. Neither more nor less, as you say; and I pretend to nothing else."

But he seemed, all the same, to imply by this speech that Miss Guilfoyle had perhaps never quite understood exactly how much the status he admitted to implied. She heard him in silence. At length,

"But you were about to tell me something?" he suggested.

She nodded. "Mr. Highet, I do not know whether you were privy to all the provisions of my great uncle's will; but in case you were not, I must inform you—"

"That I would inherit if you failed to keep its terms?" he broke in.

"You do know!"

"Certainly. What of it?"

"Have you always known? Since before I came?"

"Of course. Why do you seem so startled?" Mr. Highet gave his friendly, stupid smile.

"Because— Don't you understand? If I had been unable . . ."

"I understand perfectly."

"But— But you have been so kind! In every detail, you have assisted me so willingly! If I had had to depend on Rand, I must have given up by now." Mr. Highet continuing to look blankly back at her, "But do not you consider your own conduct to have been rather extraordinary?" she demanded. "It went quite against your own self-interest. You have absolutely done yourself out of three thousand a year!"

"Oh, more than that," was his tranquil answer. "As I told you just now, the joining of the two properties could increase production overall by a factor of two, or even three in time. But you see, dear Miss Guilfoyle, I have no wish to profit by your loss. If you had proved a silly woman, if you had shown no wish to learn your task here, perhaps I might have been less forward. If I had seen the tenants likely to suffer . . . But believe me enough of a Christian, I beg—even with all my 'radical' ideas," he smiled, "which I know you deplore—pray believe me still Christian enough not to wish active harm to my neighbour."

Miss Guilfoyle sat staring at him full half a minute, her crumpled mouth hanging ever so slightly open. It was hardly an expression calculated to please: For the moment, though, she had no thought for her appearance. "But you need not have married me," she finally pointed out. "Don't you see? If you had simply let me be—not hindered me, but merely kept silent—you could have had

Linfield. Who knows how long I should have stuck it out, but without your help . . . Don't you see, if only you had waited—?"

Perhaps the glow of the firelight deceived her, but Miss Guilfoyle thought Mr. Highet's ruddy glow heightened a little. He hesitated a long while. Was it possible he really had not thought of this? And did he now regret his offer? After a great pause he answered merely, "Miss Guilfoyle, I should not have cared to do that. Would you in my place?"

Anne thought. Curiously, she had never considered the question from this point of view. It took some time, especially with her head still swimming, to imagine herself in his position; but when at last she had done it, "No, of course not," she replied.

"Then why do you expect so much less of me?" he inquired. His sleepy gaze suggested no teasing or sermonizing: He simply asked.

As simply, "I do not know," she responded. "Perhaps conceit is my besetting sin after all."

Mr. Highet said nothing but only checked to be sure the watercolour horse was still flying over the hedge.

"About your being a Christian," Anne presently took up. "Does not your . . . proposition strike you as being rather sacrilegious?"

Earnestly, "I am glad you mention that," he told her, leaning forward and shifting his gaze to (as best Anne could reckon) the keys of the pianoforte. "I fancied that might trouble you. In some particulars, I suppose, what I suggest will not be a proper marriage. You will not truly undertake to obey and serve me, for example, though when you are asked 'Will you,' you must answer 'I will.' For my part, though I shall honour you as charged—indeed I shall—I expect I shall have but little opportunity, say, to comfort you. As for forsaking all others . . ." Mr. Highet's voice faded and he looked distinctly uneasy. He gave her a queer glance before he resumed, "That scarcely enters into it. But Miss Guilfoyle, I need hardly point out to you, who have lived so long in town, that hardly a marriage does get made there more sincere than this one. The estate of matrimony is daily entered into by persons with no motive at all save the increase of wealth or station, with only the barest acquaintance, if that, between the parties—"

"Hear, hear," Anne muttered bitterly, while he went on as if he had not heard:

"Whereas our alliance at least would be made in—I hope—mutual esteem and genuine good will. On my side, in any case."

Anne bowed. It did not occur to her then that Mr. Highet might be hoping for her assurance that such esteem and good will existed on her side also. She asked, "Does your mother favour this—suggestion?"

"Oh, very much." He put back his head and roared before going on, "It is the answer to all her prayers. She has lived in fear these fifteen years and more of my taking a wife—a wife who would then insist on mending my stockings and pouring my tea and performing all those other useful offices my mother so much relishes performing herself. To have me married at last, yet to retain her position—what a blessing she must think it." He added, very belatedly, "Naturally she has also a high regard for you."

"Oh, naturally." Miss Guilfoyle laughed as merrily as she expected to that day.

"But I do not wish to persuade or urge you to accept.

Not at all. I should like you to think it over and discuss it with me again. Perhaps you see a flaw I have over-looked—it would not surprise me. Consult your friends; consult your inclinations . . . For the moment, I am content that you do not, at least, resent the very notion. At least—you do not?" He looked at her searchingly.

Her head throbbed; her pulses throbbed. In all her life she had never had a day so strange. She considered Mr. Highet's question. He had taken her by surprise, that was certain; but, "No, I do not resent it," she heard herself saying. "Quite the opposite. I am honoured that you should think well enough of me, should trust me suffi-ciently, to be willing to suggest what could, after all, become a rather vexed proposition. I shall think of it, as you ask. And now perhaps—"

She stood. Mr. Highet caught her meaning and stood as well. A little awkwardly—for after all, the circumstances were awkward—they took their leave of one another, Mr. Highet bowing, Anne putting out her hand, Mr. Highet going to take her hand, Anne retracting it before he could. Mr. Highet drove away. Miss Guilfoyle returned to her bed-chamber to ponder now, not only Lord Ensley's mar-riage, but perhaps her own.

NINE

"WHAT AN EXTRAORDINARY IDEA," WAS MRS. INSEL'S first comment when, some twenty-four hours after Mr. Highet's visit, Anne explained that gentleman's proposition to her. Then, "Do you think he quite means what he says?"

"Means what he says? When a man pretends love, perhaps he wants money; but what Mr. Highet says is so preposterous, I can hardly imagine a more bizarre design hidden behind it. Can you?"

Maria had actually been thinking of a design less, not more, bizarre; but she decided on second thoughts to keep this possibility to herself and merely answered, vaguely, "Perhaps not. But what did you say to him?"

"I promised to consider it."

"Indeed?"

"Why? Do you think I ought to have rejected it out of hand?" They were talking in the modestly cosy upstairs sitting-room Anne had adopted as her own. Now she distractedly lifted the cover of the mahogany box on the Pembroke table, only to find the same sticky comfits she had forgot to mention to Miss Veal. Mrs. Insel was curled up on a couch opposite, her tiny feet tucked beneath her.

She answered, "No; but I am surprised. How would it seem to Ensley?"

"Do you mean, would he be jealous? Don't be daft, Maria. On the contrary, I think the point is, if I really love him, I must accept. How else can I ever be with him? This way I will have the means and the freedom. It makes our situations symmetrical. You may be sure that is how he will see it."

Mrs. Insel considered this line of reasoning rather baroque, but then she had never quite understood Anne's attachment to Ensley anyhow. She could not help but feel inclined, as Anne looked to her for a further response, to encourage the match—for at least this way Anne would be married to a kind, correct gentleman. Moreover, she was not so blind to her own advantage as to fail to realize such an alliance would resolve her own troubles—for if Anne could leave Cheshire, so could she. Still, she would not urge so grave a step on such narrow principles as these.

"How do you feel?" she asked at length. "Can you imagine yourself Mrs. Henry Highet?"

Anne actually shivered. "What a way to put it!" she exclaimed. "I suppose I would be." She shrugged. "Anyhow, I am glad you are not horrified. I thought perhaps you would consider this another 'bargain,' as you called it, and take me to task for not slapping him on the face. Oh, but I was forgetting: Mr. Highet is the very gentleman you cited as being incapable of proposing such a thing!" And she laughed affectionately at the consternation on Maria's features.

But, "This is quite a different business," Maria protested, rather stiffly. "The opposite, in fact. Mr. Highet offers you marriage."

"Without love," Anne added. "Which is quite acceptable. Whereas love without marriage," she laughed, "is unthinkable. Oh, quite."

"Laugh if you like—"

"I am laughing!"

"—but there is an important distinction. You will find society on my side."

"Goose!" Anne rose and went to drop a kiss on Maria's brow. "I am only chaffing you because you are such fun to chaff. Don't frown. I shall do nothing for the moment. Mr. Highet is gone to market at Chester and will not be here again till to-morrow at the soonest."

"You will not answer him to-morrow!" Maria cried, aghast. "You must take at least six months to consider such a proposal as this. Tell him you will know by—" She paused to count. "By May."

"May! Good God, and bury myself here all winter, when I might be free? By heaven, I'll ride to Chester and tell him at once."

"Then you mean to accept him?"

Struck, "I do not know," Anne replied. "Perhaps I do. Only . . ." The only, as Maria could very well guess, was that she had not yet heard from Ensley. "Only I shall wait at least till Sunday. Will that answer? Now come, little dove," she went on before Maria could reply. Rising and leading her to the door, "I know a dove who needs an airing," she said, "and I must take her into the woods."

But for once Maria resisted her. "Anne dear," she began as they stood in the doorway, "before we go down, I must beg you at least to make no decision for my sake. You know I feel I ought to remove myself from Mr. Mallinger's neighbourhood. You have seen him, I am sure, still dismal, though it is weeks since . . . since that day. But I wish you to know— Well, in short—"

She fumbled in her reticule. In truth, Anne had already considered the advantage the proposed marriage would create for Maria, and she did indeed weigh it into her deliberations. Nor was it only on account of Mr. Mallinger that she placed Mrs. Insel on the Yes side of the balance: Anne also ascribed to her the same longings she herself felt for London and society.

At last Maria brought forth two small slips of paper— her published advertisements clipped from the *Times*. "I have taken some action for myself," she said, handing them to Anne, "and am well on the way to a solution. I have had several answers to each of them," she added, as Miss Guilfoyle bent her head over the clippings.

But when Anne looked up tears stood in her eyes. "Maria! Do you really wish to leave me? If you do, I shall not argue; but if you do not—" Her voice broke and she could only finish, "I should regret you very much."

Overcome with dismay, Maria threw her arms round her. She had not thought she was so important to Anne, whose apparent self-sufficiency sometimes deceived even her. "Of course I do not wish to go," she protested. "I simply— I cannot bear the idea of your using up your precious days of freedom only so that I may quit the neighbourhood. Promise me you will not do so; promise me you will let me go alone, that you will find another companion. Temporarily!" she added, squeezing Anne's hand.

"Promised," agreed Anne, blinking away the sudden tears. "And promise me you will write to all your correspondents and tell them they have answered too late, that you have accepted a post and that the lady of family has her companion. Will you?"

"Promised," Maria said gladly.

Anne seized her hand and finally led her out the door. "I think we are both in need of an airing now," she exclaimed, then, "'Mrs. John!' Indeed!"

Ensley's marriage having taken place on a Monday, his first post-nuptial letter to Anne had been written on the Tuesday, and arrived in Cheshire Thursday, the last day of October. If anything, it was more affectionate than its predecessors. The writer reported his wedding to have gone off well; but he hinted that he could not help feeling pained, and even angry, that the face behind the bridal veil did not belong to . . . well, someone he thought of very tenderly as he stood before the altar. The new-married couple had taken a house in Cavendish Square, and Ensley devoted a paragraph or two to a description of it, and the way it was being furnished, ending, "But you will soon see it yourself, for November begins in four days, and that is the month you promised to come. Tell me the day exactly in your next to me, I beseech, that I may begin counting the hours. How I need you! Yours faithfully—" And so on.

Anne read and reread the letter, folded it, and made an inward resolve. The more she reflected, the more she believed what she had said to Maria: If she had been in earnest all these years of her friendship with Ensley, she must not fail now to avail herself of an opportunity unlikely ever to come again. Marriage to Henry Highet would not only restore her fortune to her but would grant her even a greater degree of freedom than she had had as a single lady. She had gone over and over what she knew of Mr. Highet without finding any thing to make him ineligible, or to persuade her an alliance with him was ill-advised. And she could not help but be swayed by the prospect of escape from captivity at Linfield. Even a palace is a prison to one constrained to stay there. On Friday she sent a letter to Fevermere to ask Mr. Highet to wait upon her the following morning.

He obeyed, arriving full of news regarding the livestock he had sold at Chester. If he felt conscious or awkward with Miss Guilfoyle, he did not show it. For her part, Anne had anticipated the meeting with some considerable nervousness; but Mr. Highet's tales of heifers and sows, his report on the price of butter, his easy manner, even his rough, mud-flecked boots reassured her. She had only a few questions for him, chiefly how she could insure he would not, in a fit of Spencean generosity perhaps, give her land away or (more plausibly) sell it; how—with all deference to his excellent character—she could be certain he would forward to her a proper share of the income from the proposed joint estate; and the like. Mr. Highet received her questions without offence. He intended, he said, to have the exact terms of their agreement drawn into a marriage contract—as was not uncommon, after all—and politely begged her to have her own man of business in London look it over before she accepted it.

"But have you no other concern?" he inquired, after they had established this much. They had gone out together to walk on the lawn, for it was a fine day and a shame, as he had said, to be indoors. Though the leaves were fallen, the dark branches against the bright blue sky had a simple beauty of their own. There had been a frost the night before, and the ground still crunched under their feet. "You see no other flaw in the idea itself?"

She said, "Not as yet. Though I shall, of course, consult Mr. Dent as you suggest."

"Ah, Mr. Dent," he took up, smiling. "Nicodemus, is it not? 'Mr. Dent informed me—' 'I had understood from Mr. Dent—'" He paused to give one of what Miss Guilfoyle thought of now as his horse laughs and went on, chuckling, "The look on your face! If only you could have seen it."

This reference to the night they met did little, naturally, to endear Mr. Highet to Anne. "You were a trifle distrait yourself," she reminded him tartly.

Mr. Highet wiped an hilarious tear from his eye, then went on, mimicking the voice of a condescending lady and gesturing grandly, "Run along, Joan! Fetch some tea! Come here, Joan, and light this candle before you—"

"Thank you, I quite recollect it now," said Anne repressively. At the same time, as if to make him be quiet, she caught at one of his broadly gesturing arms, striving to bring it down to his side. She stopped him in mid-movement, in consequence whereof her hand slipped along his sleeve to his hand—which, most unexpectedly, closed over hers in a grip almost convulsive. He released her in an instant, but the momentary touch had already brought them both up short, sobering him and making her suddenly eager to close the interview. Her hands now folded tightly together at her waist (Mr. Highet's hands had somehow dived into his pockets), Anne told him, "If it does not disturb you, I should like to think on this another

night before I give my answer. I shall see you in church
to-morrow, no doubt. Perhaps you will be so good as to
ride over here at four or five o'clock?"

"I shall be happy to do so. But pray do not imagine it
disturbs me to wait. This is a decision of consequence for
both of us."

"Thank you, but I am not one to debate a decision
overlong," Anne answered truthfully. They had begun to
walk up to the house together, where he would take his
leave of her. "If it seems to me sound at first, it generally
does so at the last as well. Still, I should like another
night."

Mr. Highet declared himself her servant. They had arrived at the terrace behind the drawing-room, and Miss
Guilfoyle was about to walk in through the French doors
when he stopped her, saying, "I nearly forgot. There is
another matter I wished to discuss with you." Lowering
his voice though they were still outside and alone, "It
concerns Mr. Mallinger. Does he seem to you in some
wise afflicted?"

On her guard at once, for she felt Mr. Mallinger's secret
was not hers to give away, "I have thought him more subdued of late, yes," she agreed.

"Subdued! I half fear consumption; but he insists he is
healthy enough. Nor can I think he would expose his
pupils to any ailment knowingly. Yet . . . I asked him if
his family were well, and he maintains they are."

He paused, but Anne kept silent.

"At all events, I wondered if you would be amenable to
increasing his salary. No man is happy who reckons himself undervalued." And Mr. Highet named a figure by
which he proposed to improve the schoolmaster's income.

Miss Guilfoyle, though well aware it could do little to

raise Mr. Mallinger's spirits, willingly agreed to her share
in the increase. After this, lady and gentleman went indoors, shook hands, and parted.

They re-met the following morning in church; but no
one seeing them could guess any private question hung
over them. Their brief conversation there, had anyone
overheard it, chiefly celebrated the facts that both had
slept soundly the night before and that the weather continued fine. Mr. Samuels then preached on Temptation,
which made Mrs. Insel excessively uneasy (for she judged
herself one to Mr. Mallinger) and bored everyone else.
Afterwards Anne politely declined Lady Crombie's punc-
tual invitation to dine. She sent Maria alone in the carriage to Linfield, electing to walk, though it was a full five
miles.

It was a day like its predecessor: crisp, cool, the sky
brilliantly blue. The stillness was broke only by birds, or
the occasional rush and thump of a hare startled in the dry
bracken. As she had foreseen on her first night in Cheshire, this road was now as familiar to Anne—every bend,
every stile, every prospect—as had been Bond Street or
Berkeley Square. But she had lost her sullen resentment
of it, and begun to see its beauty. She was curious to
know how the flat fields would appear when, as must happen in two months or three, snow shrouded and muffled
the sleeping earth. She liked the leafless quiet of to-day,
in which she could hear the crunch of the ground under
her own light feet; she liked the sharp air, and the wide
sky. After nearly twenty years, her childhood at Overton
started to return to her. She remembered the slow revolu-
tions of the seasons in the country, long walks she had
taken in company with her father among bare branches, or
budding leaves. The sights and smells of the Cheshire

fields and woods stirred and finally waked her memory of the scenes of her childhood, and with them hungry, poignant vignettes from a time when both her parents still lived. In short, she remembered Nature, and felt its claim on her with almost the strength Artifice, calling from London, opposed to it.

It was after two when she reached Linfield. She had only time to dine hastily and refresh her toilette before Mr. Highet arrived. When he did, she went down to him in the drawing-room at once and (her heart beating rather violently for all she struggled to appear calm and dispassionate) with scant preamble accepted his suit.

Mr. Highet declared himself pleased. A short speech such as might have been made at the joining of two commercial houses followed, delivered by Mr. Highet in his slow baritone, and with his friendly, phlegmatic smile. The happy couple then turned their attention to the calendar, Miss Guilfoyle noting it would need some weeks for her man of affairs to read and return the marriage contract once Mr. Highet's man had drawn it up. Mr. Highet, after some counting upon his fingers, suggested the twenty-fifth of November as a convenient wedding date, for, as he gravely noted, it would "leave him free to see to the tupping of the sheep on the twenty-eighth." Mr. Highet would also see, if Miss Guilfoyle liked, to the publication of the banns.

With a queer dreaminess similar to her sensation when Mr. Highet had first proposed his suit, Anne heard herself reply, "If it is not too much trouble, yes, I thank you."

"I think a quiet ceremony best, do not you?" asked her betrothed. "At the rectory, perhaps." He sat some way apart from her on the chintz settee—a good vantage point, no doubt, from which to assure himself the horse sailing over the hedge in the watercolour showed no signs of sinking.

"Oh, excellent." Miss Guilfoyle either verified the presence or inspected the cleanliness (it was not clear which) of her ten fingernails before adding, "I hope we shall not be too much discommoded with bride visits and that sort of thing. Although—" She looked up in confusion, and there was upon her face an expression of almost shyness which Mr. Highet (though it is doubtful whether Miss Guilfoyle knew this, for she was looking not at him but out the French doors) observed with visible satisfaction, "I wonder where, exactly, such a visit might be paid?" she finished dubiously.

"If you mean, here or at Fevermere, the question has crossed my mind as well. I have no wish to uproot you, but as you will no doubt be returning to London to set up an establishment of your own very shortly, it seems to me foolish for you to keep up Linfield as well." Speaking haltingly at first he continued, "If it would not discomfit you too much, there is quite a wing of Fevermere my mother and I can spare to you and Mrs. Insel. Some few of the Linfield servants, perhaps, will come with you. For the others, I happen to know that Mrs. Ware's brother—recently widowed, alas—is looking for a house to let in the neighbourhood of his sister, for himself and his children. He would be only too glad, I think, to take Linfield—and as he has no wife, perhaps the estimable Miss Veal . . ."

He paused suggestively, and Anne took up, "Oh indeed, it would mean a new life to her!" She had not failed to notice his generous, unprompted inclusion of Maria in her plans, and her gratitude made it a little harder to say what she nevertheless felt she must: "Mr. Highet," she commenced, standing and (in spite of her recent long walk) restlessly moving across the room, her back towards him, "there is one aspect of my life I must make clear to you. If you lived more in London you would know it yourself, for it is well understood among the *ton;* but as you do not . . ." Her restlessness drove her quite to the French doors, where she stared out at the terrace and the dark woods beyond. A new note of resolution, almost of ruthlessness, sounded in her voice as she presently went on, "I have a friend there with whom I am on, and have for ten years been on, extremely close and particular terms. This gentleman, whom you have met—"

She was quite startled—almost frightened—to hear his voice suddenly interrupt, "Ensley, you mean." There was sternness in his tone, she thought. He went on, coldly and as if the matter slightly disgusted him, "I am quite aware of your special bond to him. It neither concerns me nor touches our agreement."

She expected him to say more, but he did not. She had kept her back towards him while he spoke. When at length she turned, she found him poised at the door. She partly crossed the room to him, saying in a low voice, "I felt I should mention it."

Mr. Highet bowed in silence. In his face she saw that same quality she had heard in his voice—sternness, she called it to herself—and it surprised her a little. She felt she had displeased him, which was not her wish. She gave what she hoped was a conciliatory smile.

"Should you like me to go with you to your mother, to tell her our news?" she asked, to turn the topic.

"That will not be necessary." Frowning, his features taut, Mr. Highet presented almost a new countenance to her. She had never imagined him to have so much—what? Pride? Anger?

She essayed another smile. "You are very kind to offer to take Maria in as well as myself."

He said only, "Not at all"; but his scowl softened a little.

"She holds you in the highest esteem," Anne went on, still smiling. "I know she will be glad to hear of our—our alliance. You have not yet had an opportunity, I suppose," she added, through a chain of thought invisible to Mr. Highet, "to speak to Mr. Mallinger?"

"Not yet. I shall go to him, perhaps, when I leave here." His expression relaxing yet more, "I doubt money is at the root of it, however. It exasperates me, for I fear he will leave us. I should hate to lose him."

"Oh, I do not think he will leave," Anne replied a little mysteriously. "I expect by Christmas, say, he will be right again."

Mr. Highet appeared to have heard this with only half an ear. His scowl at last quite gone, he told her in much warmer tones, "You know, I hope, that we shall always be glad to see you at Fevermere, Miss Guilfoyle. Even so soon as Christmas, you may wish to return. Or if not, whenever you do like to come, you must stay as short or as long as you please, and bring any party you care to. Only give the house a little warning, and—" His brow darkened again as he went on, "I do think it would be inadvisable to bring Lord Ensley here again. In fact, that is my condition. I will ask you to observe it."

Anne murmured, "Willingly, sir," and set herself to regain, through charm and smiles, the ground she had somehow lost again; but this time Mr. Highet's scowl vanished more readily. A few more pleasantries, Mr. Highet's assurance he would ride to Chester to-morrow to see his man of business about the contract, and the gentleman took his leave. This time Miss Guilfoyle bowed while Mr. Highet put out his hand. But they smiled at their awkwardness, and Mr. Highet did not take his hand away as she had done upon that earlier occasion. Instead he put the other out as well, took both hers (though very briefly), smiled, released her, and was gone.

The wedding of Mr. Henry Highet and Miss Anne Guilfoyle took place in the rectory of the Reverend Septimus Samuels, at two-thirty P.M, on 25 November, Year of our Lord 1816. In attendance were Mrs. John Insel, Mrs. Archibald Highet (the bridegroom's mother), and Mrs. Samuels. The bride's Uncle Frederick had sent, to represent him, a letter congratulating his niece on having found "a way out of her difficulties" (her first intimation that he knew she had been in them) and, a week later, a silver bowl Anne recognised as having once belonged to her mother for a wedding gift. From Celia Grypphon— who of course knew her situation rather more intimately— came a letter equally congratulatory and a good deal warmer. Anne having written to her exactly the terms upon which she entered matrimony, Celia agreed the offer was a godsend, and only urged her to return to London as soon as ever she could. Lady Grypphon meanwhile would scout for a house to let. As for Ensley, Celia reported him looking much more cheerful since this news had come. Ensley reporting the same to Anne directly, it appeared they were all of one opinion.

How then to account for the weak knees, the racing heart, the damp brow with which Miss Guilfoyle faced

Mr. Samuels? Sentiment—sentiment and superstition were the culprits the bride scornfully put them down to herself. She urged herself to think of Ensley, but the thought did not steady her. "Clunchery! Sheer shatter-headedness!" ran her inward apostrophe, while she listened to Mr. Samuels' caution that the estate of matrimony was not to be entered into unadvisedly or lightly; but reverently, discreetly, advisedly, soberly, and in the fear of God.

She glanced at the man beside her. Well, he looked sober enough. Indeed she could not read his face at all: Handsome, heavy, impassive, his features were composed into the same sleepy mask she had seen an hundred times. When he said, "I will," when he took his vows, his voice was deep and calm. His hand, enfolding hers, was warm; hers, taking his, cold and moist. Mr. Highet could hardly hold Anne's finger still enough to slip the ring upon it, so much did it tremble. She was relieved to be licenced to take his hand again, a moment later, and hold it through the rest of the ceremony—for she felt giddy and faint, and his large paw reassured her. At the conclusion of the ceremony they looked into one another's eyes for the first time. Anne felt dimly that she had done some thing, some momentous thing, she could hardly say what. Then Mr. Highet leaned down and drily kissed her dewy forehead. He led her out of the rectory into the fresh air, which she eagerly gulped. His mother, following, cried a little; Maria appeared at the rectory door a moment later and begged the elder Mrs. Highet to come in.

Left alone, the new-married pair smiled at one another. Anne, much restored by the fresh, cold air, raised an eyebrow and said, with an almost childish glance of mischief, "Well, it's done!"

"Done indeed. And now—" He leaned down, looming dizzily over her. His breath fell warm on her ear. "Off to London with you whenever you like! You may go tonight, if you care to; I'll brave the neighbours' noises."

Whether it was the chill of the day penetrating her numbed limbs at last or some deeper coldness, Anne, curiously, heard him with a shiver, and a sensation of ice in her veins. Almost chattering, "I should like a cup of tea first," she told him, "if it's all the same to you."

"Oh, indeed! Dear ma'am, you must be frozen out here, without so much as a shawl." He bundled her solicitously back indoors, saying, "I did not mean to hurry you, you know. Only to make you easy. Stop as long as you like," invited her husband, concluding generously, "Stop a week! It is all the same to me."

TEN

IN THE EVENT, THE NEW MRS. HIGHET PASSED NEAR A fortnight more in Cheshire before journeying to town. She had her remove from Linfield to conduct, she said, and her installation at Fevermere. Moreover, Celia had found and was preparing for her a house in London, which also needed time. Besides, she did not like to expose Mr. Highet to the gossip and pity a parish must shower upon a husband so soon deserted by his wife. Mr. Highet iterated his willingness to endure it for her sake; but Anne insisted and stopped on.

As she had foreseen, Charlotte Veal had been far from sorry to hear of the change in Linfield's tenantry. Mr. Rand was wild with relief and delight at the prospect of serving a gentleman again. In fact, dry eyes were general throughout the house. The London servants were over-joyed to know they would soon return to their old haunts and friends. Nor did Anne and Maria quit the place with any excess of sorrow. The house had been too small and plain. Anne never even unpacked the vast majority of her Holles Street things—which was fortunate since, though they had been transported a long way to little effect, at least they did not need packing up again.

Fevermere, the ladies had found upon being invited to explore it, was far more substantial. Three or even four times the size of Linfield, it was fitted out with plenty of plush carpets and brocaded draperies; its walls were hung with papers and silks; its furniture was—though scarcely elegant or modish—pleasant, abundant, and not vulgar. Mr. Highet had not exaggerated when he said an entire wing might be made over to them. Their part of Fever-mere was by itself nearly as large as Linfield. They could be quite as private (even lonesome!) there as they liked, meeting Mr. Highet and his devoted progenitrix only at meals—or, if they wished, not even then, for the kitchen was happy to send whatever they desired to their suite.

As for Mrs. Highet the elder, she was a long way from making the newcomers feel they were rude to keep out of sight. On the contrary, she was full of thoughtful sugges-tions as to how they could make their wing discrete. She pointed out that one of their larger sitting-rooms might well be changed into a drawing-room for the reception of guests, and promised to undertake the alteration herself while they were gone. She even proposed the conversion of a parlour near it to a dining-saloon, so that (save for kitchens and stables) they might be quite independent. Her concern in all this was naturally, as she often re-marked, for them. She knew her daughter-in-law had lived solitary many years and easily conceived how little a change in habits must appeal to her now. The two Mrs. Highets had neither of them cared to discuss explicitly the oddities of the recent marriage, but Anne knew the other was in full possession of the facts, and so bore her clumsy shifts and thin solicitude with amused tolerance.

Mr. Highet continued quite the same towards Anne as ever. She saw him at dinner, but not often at any other time, for (she having entrusted to him the management of both estates) he had no longer to consult her on decisions, nor to lend nor to borrow of her. Their intercourse, curiously, was rather more than less public after their marriage, for the reason that it all took place at Fevermere, where the senior Mrs. Highet constantly dogged her son. Once or twice Maria Insel contrived, on a narrow pretext, to detach that venerable lady from the other two after dinner. But Maria would have been disappointed to know her efforts had no observable effect on Mr. Highet. He remained towards his wife as friendly, serious, and ever so slightly obtuse as ever.

Only once, just before she at last took her leave for London, did he seek her out privately. One morning he sent a note up with her chocolate requesting an interview in her sitting-room at a given hour. She came to him with a head full of trunks and boxes, coaches and inns, for she had been directing the preparations for her journey. She found him thoughtful and even slower of speech than usual. He apologized for taking her from her tasks, then,

"Madam, I am come to ask before you go, whether you are content with the—" he faltered, "the step we have taken together; or if, on the contrary, you have come to doubt its wisdom. I pray you speak frankly, for I don't know when I shall see you again."

Anne, surprised, thought a moment. It was a question she had already considered, of course, but she did not wish to answer hastily. Presently, "I have no regret," she said, "though I am sometimes amazed to realize my situation. But six months ago, I was single and independent. Since then I . . ." Her thoughts having turned to Ensley, and how his marriage in some ways precipitated hers, she fell silent. At length, "Much has happened. But doubts—no, I have none. It gratifies me to watch you administer the joining of the estates. You demonstrate such zeal, enjoyment, and ready ability, as is a delight to see. For myself, I confess I anticipate my return to London with the keenest pleasure." She hesitated almost imperceptibly but did not add that, at the same time, it rather saddened her to think of quitting Fevermere. It was an emotion she did not fully understand, and as such seemed wiser to keep to herself. "But you, sir. Since you are kind enough to pose it, permit me to return the question, and urge upon you the same candour."

Gravely, immediately, "I have no regret," he said.

She waited but (as he said nothing more) finally smiled, stood, and remarked, "I shall write to you, if I may, to tell you how I go on in London."

"I hope you will. I shall answer." Following her lead, he rose, smiled, and was about to leave when he turned of a sudden to ask lightly, "You have no cause, I hope, to complain of my manner towards you since we are married? I am as you like me to be? Not too familiar? Not too formal? You see I still avail myself of the candour with which you charged me to speak."

Unaccountably, Anne's cheeks crimsoned and burned while she answered, looking down, "Quite, quite. No cause, as Cordelia said. Pray be easy on that head." She wished, but could not bring herself, to reverse this question too. Instead, still looking down, she thanked him for his concern and hurried him out of the room.

Dolphim and the waggons set off on the first of December. The ladies followed a few days later, venturing forth under a leaden, overcast sky early on the morning of the fourth. Mrs. Highet the elder had arranged a small party for the previous night, at which the Crombies, the Wares, and so on, were meant to bid good-bye to Mrs. Highet the younger. But clouds and a cold, spitting rain had prevented it.

Mother and son turned out, naturally, to wish the travellers a safe journey. Mrs. Archibald Highet bade them God-speed ("and good riddance," speculated Anne silently) with admirable fortitude, then watched as her son handed first Maria, then Anne, into the carriage. No opportunity for tenderness, had they wished to display any, was granted to husband and wife. But Anne (who for her part felt an heavy, strange reluctance to go away—which she set down to mere timidity and force of habit) believed she detected a particular fervour in the press of his hand on hers, and heard a huskiness (or so it seemed) in his last words, "Come back as soon as you like."

She thought, "I shall regret him!" but at once heard another part of her mind answer, as if a spring had released it, "Anne, you *are* a gudgeon!"

Then Mr. Highet shut the door and the ladies were on their way. No torrential rain or other freak disturbing them, they made a quiet journey enough and were in Portman Square in time for dinner Friday night. The Grypphons were gone down to Surrey till Sunday, but the house expected them and they were soon comfortably installed.

On Saturday, not without some trepidation, Anne sent a note to Ensley. Since his marriage she had always directed her letters to the desk he occupied as Undersecretary in Lord Liverpool's office. But he had repeatedly assured her this discretion, as he called it, was unnecessary, that Lady Ensley perfectly understood he was in private communication with her, and would in no way be disturbed by evidence of it. Eager to see him, she made bold to give the Grypphons' man his house number in Cavendish Square, and hoped for the best. In an hour he had answered her; in two he had come.

She received him, on a perverse whim, in that same library which had been the scene of their last interview in London. Again the soft carpet, the well-oiled hinges of the door, allowed her to enter before he perceived her, and to observe him briefly. This time he sat in a chair by the window, frowning at a copy of the *Gazette*. He wore a dark frac, a shirt with a very high collar, and white pantaloons which must, she thought mechanically, show disastrously even the smallest spot of mud. Since she had seen him he had grown *favoris:* Blond and slightly curly, they made his long face look even longer. He seemed pale to her, and thin. When at last she said his name, he looked up, jumped to his feet, and raised his quizzing glass to his eye with a heavily be-ringed hand.

"Let me look at you," he breathed, not coming towards her but standing, the *Gazette* fallen to his feet, and from this vantage scrutinizing her. "Athena," he finally pronounced, "as always. Strong, beautiful, wise." He dropped the quizzing glass and advanced with hands outstretched.

She met them with her own. What a fop he looked! How unwholesome, how . . . meagre. "Athena," indeed!

And sure enough, his next words were from Homer: "All men have need of the gods," he murmured. "Or goddesses, in my case. You are mine."

She smiled; but good heavens, had Ensley always spouted Greek? Used a quizzing glass? Tied his cravat with such precious care? Had he changed, or did she only see him differently?

"You look pale, my dear," she said at last, uncertainly. "Are you well?"

Surprised, "Quite well," he assured her. "But you! Cheshire has done something for you after all. You look blooming, vigorous, charming! Mine eyes drink you with the thirst of a man dying in a desert. How I have waited for this hour, Anne. Come sit by me."

He dropped her hands and drew her to that same settee covered in Morocco on which they had sat one night five months before. But even as she sat by him, "Dying in a desert?" Anne was thinking. "He means it half in jest no doubt—yet is this the man for whose sake I bound myself to a loveless marriage? He lisps his R's, forsooth! 'Mine eyes dwink you . . .' Saints defend us!"

"How was your journey?" the gentleman who, all unawares, inspired these thoughts asked comfortably. "Not difficult, I hope? Tell me all. Do you trust Mr. Highet? Does he conduct himself as he should? If he has taken advantage of you, by God I'll— But tell me."

Anne answered him naturally enough, assuring him Mr. Highet had been perfectly pretty-behaved, that the journey was easily accomplished, and asking him how he did in turn; but all the while she spoke her brain was busily arguing, "Make no hasty judgement. You have grown accustomed to Mr. Highet's blunt country ways, that is all. Ensley is not thin; Mr. Highet is broad. Nor pale; Mr.

Highet is ruddy. In an hour all this will have passed. You
will remember yourself *and* Ensley. Patience, my girl!"

"I have seen the house Celia selected for you," his
lordship was saying now. "Quite the thing, in my opinion.
Mount Street, *tout près du Parc*. You will like that. Rather
empty at the moment, naturally, but I believe your furnishings will suit it to perfection."

"And your own new house? Do you like it?"

"Oh yes," he said carelessly, "quite pleasant."

"And Lady George?" Mrs. Highet inquired. "How
does she?"

Lady George's husband smiled. "Very well, by the look
of her," he answered. "Trots up and downstairs all day
long, happily ordering the servants about and playing
hostess to callers. I never saw a girl so taken with the business of commanding her own establishment. Her father's
given us Wiltwood, you know—little place of his in
Kent—and now Juliana's wild to assemble a party there
for February. You will be one of our guests, naturally."

"Will I? Does Lady George invite me herself?"

"Does she—? Oh, I see. Anne dear, do please try not
to fret on her account. I tell you over and over she regards
our friendship with the utmost indifference. She's a spirited girl, with plenty of interests. She doesn't feel what
you would. I'm more than twice her age, for heaven's
sake. She isn't attached to me!"

Anne said nothing, but her scepticism was written on
her face.

"Very well, when you come to Cavendish Square you'll
see for yourself. In fact we are giving a party Tuesday
night, a musical evening. Juliana's idea, of course. You
will come, won't you?"

Lord Ensley turned to her on the settee and took her

hand in his, patting it gently. Whether he guessed Anne was of a strong mind to take it away she did not know. She only left it with him by dint of considerable effort. It seemed to her extremely wrong to let him hold it now. The rings on both their fingers glinted fiercely in the morning sunshine. "If you like, certainly I shall come," she obliged herself to respond. Rallying still more, "Now Ensley, a serious matter, if you don't mind. It is—your whiskers!" she finished, laughing up at him. "Really! *Favoris?* Whatever possessed you?"

"Don't you like them?" He raised his hand to pat his cheeks with a good-humoured air of hurt. "My valet suggested them. I thought they suited me."

"They do. They make you look exactly like a middle-aged sheep. Now pray, in the name of all that's sensible, shave them off to-night, or I shan't be able to look at you without smiling."

"I like you to smile," he pointed out. But the effect of this mild gallantry was so evident that he went on at once, "For God's sake, don't withdraw from me, Anne. I see you cringe at every advance, and it tears my heart. Juliana is nothing to me, nor I to her. Believe that!"

It was the directness she had always liked in him, his habit of naming a trouble the moment he saw it, and meeting it head on. "Give me time," she muttered in a low voice, suppressing an objection that his feelings and Juliana's were not the only ones pertinent here. In a moment she turned the conversation to Lord Liverpool and the new legislation, eagerly pumped him for *on-dits*, and reviewed with him the state of his own career.

She came away from her hour with him confused and troubled. True, even in that short span his mannerisms had ceased to strike and grate on her so. He seemed less

. . . well, ridiculous. Nevertheless, why did he need a
valet at all, let alone one with such poor judgement? Mr.
Highet had no valet, and he seemed to manage. And why
did Ensley fuss at his cuffs so much? She had twice caught
him rearranging them, as if such a detail possibly mattered. And when they had spoke of politics, he very distinctly struck a pose—back straight, eyes fixed on the
middle distance, chin lifted, chest swelled—intended to
impress her as statesmanlike and forceful. Studying his at-
titudes! Indeed!

Besides all that, some of the things he said— When she
asked him about the bread riots, he answered he did not
think they would "come to much," that a little firmness
would put them down. But what of the people actually
starving? she asked. Piffle! No one need starve. They had
poor relief; anyhow, there was always work if one looked
for it. What concerned him was Spa Fields, or the riot
they had had this past Monday in London.

Anne having left Cheshire before news of that event
could reach her, and since then being on the road, had
heard nothing of it. Ensley assured her it had been frightful, quite threatening, quite intolerable. A mob in the
Royal Exchange! The Government would be better prepared next time, he assured her, his brow stern. They
would make an example of one or two of these radicals,
who put ideas into the heads of simple people. Habeas
corpus was to be suspended, he confided to her, sedition
quenched at all costs. That was what came of the abuse of
liberty.

Anne had shivered. Not that she approved of riots, or
sedition, of course; but because Ensley had seemed so fe-
rociously resolved. Surely the riots could not all be the
result of the treacherous thunderings of a few? Surely

happy people, no matter how simple, did not riot? She had read some of the books and pamphlets by the rabble-rousers Ensley deplored (the better to fence with Mr. Mallinger during his Wednesday visits of old) and had found in them, among much to scoff at, a number of worthwhile points. And she had seen more of humble folk in Cheshire than ever before in her life. Ensley must either be ignorant or hard-hearted. Yet he was so emphatical.

Well, she would talk to him. She, after all, had been equally ignorant before her sojourn at Linfield. They had always dealt wonderfully well together. In a se'ennight or so, when she had grown accustomed to London again, and seen Celia, and established herself a little in Mount Street, all would come right. So she informed herself. And with this comforting certitude to sustain her, she went upstairs to change into a new, dark violet walking-dress, then out with Mrs. Insel to call upon some friends.

By the time they returned, late in the afternoon, they had been invited to join a theatre party that evening, to attend a ridotto, and to sup at the board of a Prussian crowned head. All this at a time when even the Little Season had distinctly closed. "Ah, Maria, London!" Anne exclaimed as she flung off her *gros de Berlin* cloak and velvet bonnet. Mrs. Insel followed her into a parlour where both ladies rather wearily collapsed into a pair of low chairs covered in Chinese silk. A fire blazed pleasantly in the grate; a maidservant arrived with tea. "There is nowhere like it. Don't you feel twice as alive as you did five days ago?"

Maria, pouring tea and handing her a cup, answered doubtfully, "I suppose so. Only . . . I expect one must get accustomed all over again to the noise and the dirt. I thought we should be killed a dozen times today in the crush of carriages on the streets; and I hardly slept an hour last night!"

Anne, who had fared little better in these respects, laughed and gaily remonstrated, "You sound like Mr. Highet. Never mind. We shall get in the way of it again." And she turned the topic to Mount Street, which they had visited and strongly approved.

Lady Grypphon, when she and her lord returned in due course to the metropolis, was gratified to learn her selection of a house had met with approbation. "I made sure you would like it, my dear," she told Anne, pouring into her ears a profusion of ideas about curtains, hangings, carpets, and the best use for each room. "But tell me how you enjoy being married!" she interrupted herself at length. The ladies had settled themselves in a small sitting-room adjacent to Celia's bed-chamber. "Did you feel very queer taking your vows? Has Mr. Highet behaved himself? You have seen Ensley by now, I trust? What very odd lives you lead!" And she settled in for a comfortable chat, her bright eyes fixed on Anne.

The new Mrs. Highet had been looking forward to this meeting with her old friend as part of the programme that was to make all "come right" again. But she found herself rather squirming under her ladyship's bold, inquisitive gaze. Her life *was* odd; even Celia had said it. She gave a remarkably disjointed account of the past few weeks of it, and turned the conversation back to Celia again as soon as she could, begging to know how the weather was in Surrey, and if Grypphon had enjoyed the shooting there.

The unease Anne felt as she pondered her situation during that interview with Celia was to increase tenfold before the week was out. A card inviting both Mrs. Highet and Mrs. Insel, as well as the Grypphons, to a musical evening at the home of Lord and Lady Ensley had duly arrived in Portman Square, and had been seconded in person by the prospective host. Overcoming a vivid sensation of awkwardness, Anne determined to attend. Perhaps Ensley was right and Juliana did not mind her. She ought at least to find out.

That Tuesday night, therefore, though hanging a little behind her friends, Anne Highet, dressed in a gown of French grey satin richly trimmed with blond lace, tripped up the steps of the house in Cavendish Square. Her golden hair, banded and wound round her head, was fastened with an ivory bodkin; and she surrendered to a liveried footman a plush swansdown tippet.

"Courage, courage," she rallied herself as they mounted the stairs to Lady Ensley's music room, inadvertently muttering aloud.

Charles Grypphon turned on the steps and inquired politely, "What was that, my dear?"

"Oh dear, I didn't mean— Porridge, I said, porridge. I rather like porridge," she added, hoping Maria (who was just behind her) was not listening. "I got in the habit of eating it in Cheshire."

"Did you?" answered his lordship mildly. He gave her arm a kind, bracing squeeze before continuing, "Never fancied it myself, I must say. We'll have Cook send some up to you to-morrow."

Very likely it was the happy prospect of this treat that made Mrs. Highet smile so especially radiantly when, a minute later, she bowed to her hostess and exchanged with her congratulations on their respective recent marriages. Ensley was at the other end of the room, worse luck, the occasion being quite informal. His wife wore a dress of white satin with a vandyked slip of rose mull muslin over it. Her auburn hair, dressed *à l'antique*, fell in ringlets upon her temples, and was ornamented with a tiara of pearl. Tiny rose satin slippers peeped from under her flounced hem. Altogether, her toilette did much (Anne could not help but notice) to mitigate the effect of her thick nose, and that unfortunate mole. In fact she was looking charmingly.

"Delightful of you to invite us," Anne murmured, searching the other's eyes. She saw in them youth and shyness, chiefly, but also—or did she imagine it?—something of constraint.

"So kind of you to come," Lady Ensley replied, and Anne knew from her tone she was correct. She began to fancy Ensley had commanded his wife to welcome Anne particularly, and made up her mind to question him when she might. For now she could only bow again and move off into the room, greeting friends she had not seen since June, and rather avoiding her host.

Her pleasure in the evening was moderate at best. Miss Merry, who had made her debut while Anne was in the country, sang well, in a voice that combined science with much feeling. She performed first two arias from Dr. Arne's *Artaxerxes*, then a light piece from *Is He Jealous?* which was (Celia informed Anne) what its authors called an "operetta." It was a pleasure to Anne, after her months in Cheshire, to hear such artistry. But the room, crowded as it was, seemed to her monstrously hot and stuffy. She was aware of a degree of formality, or archness, in the company which she rather suspected had always been present in such assemblies, only without her noticing it. Moreover, she observed a species of almost forced gaiety in her own manner. In vain did she endeavour to shake this off; and when Ensley or his lady wife came near her, her uncomfortable, double consciousness only increased.

But the worst moment of the evening came when (though both ladies would have done much to avoid it) she and Lady Ensley found themselves suddenly *tête-à-tête*. Only a moment before each had been sitting—albeit in the same corner of the drawing-room—engaged in an animated conversation with another person, Anne with Lord Bambrick, Juliana with Amabel Frane. Then all at once Lord Bambrick dashed off to the supper-room, insisting on fetching a glass of lemonade to Mrs. Highet (who had confessed herself hot); while Miss Frane, abruptly noticing the very late arrival of her older sister Dorothea, jumped up quite rudely to run to her. Dismayed, Anne nevertheless steeled herself, turned politely to the younger woman, and complimented her on the modish elegance of her new home.

Juliana thanked her. "I understand you also have a new home, in Mount Street?" she said shyly.

"Indeed. I only hope to be settled in before Christmas! How difficult it is, is not it, to arrange every thing as one wishes! But you have managed excellently."

Juliana asked, "Do you think so? I do so wish Ensley to be proud of me!" But as she said these last words she blushed and looked away from Anne. Confusedly she stammered, "That is, I wish— I mean, one likes to please one's . . . Is your husband coming to London?" she finally brought out, blushing deeper than ever.

Anne, watching this performance in growing distress, answered, "No, I fear not," continuing softly, "But I am sure Ensley is proud of you, very proud indeed. I know he is."

Juliana, crimson to the roots of her hair, stared at her shoes. "Do you? Did he—has he told you so?"

Anne made an impulsive decision. "My dear Lady George," she said, speaking swiftly and praying Lord Bambrick would not return before this colloquy could be finished, "I wonder if I may be frank with you?" Overcoming a mild reluctance, she took the girl's hand as she spoke on (Lady Ensley all the while scrutinizing her satin slippers), saying, "You know of course that your husband and I have been friends since—well, almost since before you were in the schoolroom. I hope—I do hope that you and I may be friends as well!"

There was a silence. Then, "Oh, yes," mumbled Juliana, her cheeks still ablaze. As she did not raise her eyes, Anne resumed, "I am sorry, but I cannot believe you mean that, since you will not even look at me. Pray be candid; I beg you will."

But when the girl had raised her eyes, Anne could only wish she had not. They were heavy with tears, and her thick nose had gone pink. "Indeed, ma'am, I am sure we will be friends," she said, and was very obviously on the verge of a whole-hearted fit of crying when her husband (who had observed the two ladies in talk some minutes before, but—being the host—had been unable to work his way across the room without saying hello to half a dozen inconvenient guests) at last came up by her side and took her arm, exclaiming smilingly,

"Dear me, what have you ladies been at? How alarming you look, Juliana!" He bent briefly to her ear, murmured something which made her resolutely straighten and compose her features, then went on brightly, "Shall we ask Miss Merry to sing again from her comic opera? I do think people enjoyed it. Did you, Mrs. Highet?"

Anne was not slow to follow his lead, of course, the less so as Lord Bambrick returned directly with the hard-won lemonade. But she found herself distinctly vexed with Ensley. Perversely, it was his very cool-headedness, his discretion and diplomacy, that piqued her. It might be admirable, but was it quite right that a man so deeply involved in an awkward situation could yet lightly resolve it—could, with a few words, conjure it away? She thought she would have preferred him to be tongue-tied himself. And what, she wondered, could he have said to that poor silly girl to make her straighten so? That was a question she fully intended to ask him.

She had her opportunity the following day. Ensley came very early to call at Portman Square and apologize, the moment they were alone, for his young wife's "appalling misconduct" on the previous evening.

Anne, her nerves frayed after a restless night, hesitated only the briefest moment before firing her opening salvo: "Appalling? Does it appal you that a chit barely out of the schoolroom should wish to please her handsome, powerful, grown-up, newly acquired husband? Perhaps it does! Yes, having seen your cow-handed, high-handed, brutish behaviour towards her last night, I suppose it would!"

"Madam?" was all Lord Ensley replied, but in a freezing voice.

"Nor am I surprised to hear her perfectly natural actions branded by you 'misconduct,'" Anne went on, having stopped only to draw breath. "I suppose to a tyrannical, astonishingly unobservant boor like yourself, it would seem 'misconduct.'"

"Anne, Juliana repeated to me every word she said to you," Ensley broke in here, speaking more guardedly but no less intensely than his interlocutor. "And informed me of her every sniff and blush. I demanded she should do so. If, as you say, it was her intention to please me, I can tell you she is very far from doing so—"

But Anne jumped up from the settee on which she had been seated and gave an inarticulate groan of frustration and anger. "Dear God, when I think how I let you flim-flam me into believing every thing would be the same between us, Ensley, I could scream!"

His lordship received this in silence, then echoed very drily, "Flim-flam?"

She sat again. "Oh dear, I am sorry. That was wrong. We both flim-flammed ourselves—or one another, I don't know." Her lips twisted and compressed, and she clenched her hands. "At all events, we were both perfectly mistaken. Far from being exactly the same, relations between us are inexorably, irrevocably different since your marriage. And mine," she appended in an afterthought.

"I feel no difference," Ensley replied, rather stiffly.

"You ought," she shot back.

Now it was Ensley's turn to rise to his feet in agitation. "But why? I do not understand you." He walked up and down the room, his hands writhing behind his back. "I am still as much your friend as ever. I can never feel differently towards you. Do you imagine Juliana can take your place in my heart? Why, she is nothing, a little girl, with no more understanding of—"

"Pray do not disparage your wife to me," Anne interrupted.

"I do not—"

"However you may feel towards her, any fool can read *her* devotion to *you* in her face," she continued determinedly. "You deceived yourself in her character from the start. I always knew it. You take her for a cool hand, but she is not. Tell me she doesn't worship you and I shall not believe you. You instructed her to be civil to me last night, did not you? I could see it in her eyes."

Still pacing, "Naturally I encouraged her to show you the respect I would ask her to show any friend of mine," he answered. "The way you say it, one would imagine I took a whip to her. I must insist," he went on, coming to her again, "that you do not understand Juliana. You fancy you do, but you ascribe to her not her own feelings, but the ones you would have in her place. You suppose—"

Wearily, Anne put a hand on his sleeve and broke in, "Forgive me, but I will not discuss this any further now. We must both reflect a while—you as well as myself," she put in pointedly, "and then consider how we are to go on. I hope to be quite installed in Mount Street by the middle of next week. Suppose you come to dine there on Monday? I mean to make up a largish party, but we can find a moment alone."

"But I do not wish to see you in company! Anyhow, why must I wait till—"

"Please." She put up a warning hand, then passed it so exhaustedly over her pale brow and cheek that he was persuaded to desist. Even so, after she had stood and put out her hand to him,

"Anne," he said, taking the little hand and enfolding it between both of his, "can it be that your altered sentiments have more to do with your marriage than with mine?" He earnestly scanned her face while he continued, "Has your Mr. Highet changed more about you than your name?"

She looked into his pleading, well-remembered blue

eyes and found it impossible not to smile and ask gently, "Now, how could he have done that? You *are* a silly man!" And as he still gazed anxiously at her, "How much longer must I look at these preposterous *favoris*?" she demanded, giving his hands a playful squeeze before extracting hers. "A fine thing, when you trust the opinion of your valet over mine!" And with a few other such rallying remarks, to which he tenderly responded, she soothed the anxious look from his eyes, and dismissed him in tolerable spirits.

ELEVEN

ANNE WAS NOT SORRY TO FIND HERSELF, DURING THIS first week in London, very much occupied with settling in at Mount Street. Difficulties seemed to spring up like mushrooms, and confusion to flourish like the vine. A whole chest full of china and crystal was overturned by a clumsy carter; little Sally Clemp was sent off to her mother's in Dorset for her accouchement the day before it was remembered she was the only one who knew which icicles went to which chandelier; Mrs. Dolphim got the plans mixed up and had Maria's sitting-room suite installed in the breakfast parlour. Maria did what she could to be helpful; but the delegation of authority had never been one of Anne's strong points, and most of the burden either fell upon her shoulders, or was impatiently required (by her) to be placed there.

Still, she enjoyed building a new nest in London. It was a pleasure to see once again the heavily framed portraits, delicate furniture, and beloved books which had been stored away in a disused cartlodge at Linfield. Maria (though she was looking distinctly more nervous and frail than ever—Anne almost asked half a dozen times whether she was pining for Mr. Mallinger, but disliked even to bring it up) declared herself enchanted by her bed- and sitting-room. On Wednesday night, Anne had the gratification of sleeping once more within the familiar blue damask curtains of her old bed.

From this pleasant, housewifely hum (during which she often contrived if not to forget, at least to set aside, her troubled relations with Ensley) she was rudely roused on the Thursday by a visit from an unexpected caller. She was walking from chair to chair in her sitting-room, trying to decide whether a certain oval mirror which had been her mother's ought to be hung above the mahogany secretaire (where it would look well but reflect a very indifferent view onto the alley) or over the mantelpiece (where it had been hung in Holles Street) when Dolphim knocked and presented her with the card of Lady Ensley.

She must have shown her surprise, for Dolphim said blandly, "Shall I tell her ladyship that madam is not at home?"

Shaking herself a little, "No. Say I shall be with her directly," answered Anne. She lingered a moment after Dolphim went away, trying to imagine what errand could possibly have brought Juliana to her, but soon gave it up and went down to learn the answer from the lady herself.

Juliana was robed in a morning dress of the finest mulberry lustre, finished at the cuffs and hem with worked muslin, and complemented by a white velvet spencer ornamented with silk trimming. Anne did not remember her to have dressed so elegantly before her marriage, and had little doubt her new costumes were part of a campaign to appeal to Ensley. She, in a plain round gown with her hair barely coiffed, felt herself at a considerable disadvantage, but strove instinctively to overcome this by adopting an especially assured manner. Smiling cordially, gesturing smoothly, she begged her visitor (who had risen when she entered the drawing-room) to be comfortable. A closer look at Juliana persuaded her that, coiffed or not, she had the advantage over the younger woman in composure, and perhaps even in happiness. The girl's knuckles were white, her thick nose was pink, and her eyes darted furtively over the room. When she spoke—to say good morning and to refuse a glass of negus—her voice was strained. Anne, who had lately been thinking of her ladyship chiefly as a vexatious impediment, experienced a swell of almost maternal solicitude for her. Dropping her cool, assured manner,

"How amiable of you to wait upon me," she said kindly. "But I think you have a special purpose in coming? You are troubled, my dear?"

Juliana protested, "Not troubled, indeed, ma'am," but her eyes filled with tears. She drew a very deep breath, blinked vigorously several times, and went on, "Though I have come for a purpose. It is simply—" Another deep breath, and she went on all in a rush: "I should like to make plain to you, ma'am, that your friendship with my husband is in no wise a source of concern or displeasure to me!" Very obviously speaking by rote and without lifting her eyes to Anne's, she went on, "My husband was afraid you might have come away from our—our last interview with a misimpression. So I beg you will believe, nothing could be further from my desire than to dictate to Ensley his choice of friends, or to deprive him of one whose society has brought and continues to bring him so much pleasure. I hope we shall often see you in Cavendish Square," she concluded, her voice as singsong as one reciting Latin declensions. "Oh, and I almost forgot—though I am young, I am not a schoolroom miss. I had a perfectly clear understanding of the sort of marriage I was making when Ensley offered for me." Still looking down, "I think that's all," she murmured. "Yes, that's all." She made as if to rise, but Anne impulsively touched a hand to her shoulder to stop her.

"One moment, if you please," she asked, wrinkling her brow and (forgetting propriety) scratching her head. Now it was her turn to look down, in the attitude she often struck when puzzling over a problem. Soon, as was also her wont, she began to mutter aloud. "Ensley sends you to me," she brought forth, then was silent a while. "I am expected to pretend . . . Here are three—no, four people who . . ." At length she looked up, fixed Juliana's eyes, and said, "My dear, you must forgive me my candour once more, for I am about to ask you whether you love your husband."

Juliana, who had been looking merely drained, sat up, gasped, and stared.

"Pardon me," Mrs. Highet went on, her sympathy for her ladyship slightly attenuated by her mislike of the girl's pop-eyed gaze, "but shall I take that gasp for a yes?"

"I beg your pardon?" Juliana blushed so deeply that she almost matched her gown.

"I say, am I to take it that you do love Ensley? I think

you do. He says you do not. Yours will be the deciding vote," she added, provoked by Juliana's goggle-eyed expression and stubborn missishness into this mild levity, "should you care to cast it."

Burning furiously, "You put me in such a curious— such a curious position," Juliana finally declared. "I do not know what to say!"

"I don't suppose I could persuade you to say the simple truth?" Anne suggested. "Or has your husband forbidden you that?"

Her colour dropping, "Oh, dear ma'am, Ensley would never forbid me anything. He is not that sort of person at all!" her ladyship said with breathless ardour. "Our marriage is founded on principles of liberty. He—"

"Did he or did he not send you here to make that speech to me?" Anne broke in.

"Speech?"

"Did he, or did he not, dictate to you even the exact wording you were to use?"

"Dictate?"

Purely exasperated, Anne jumped up and exclaimed, "Good God, are you so afraid of the man that you will not even own he told you to say what you just said? I beseech you, be honest with me, Lady George, or we shall never understand each other. If I promise not to tell him, will you indeed confess he sent you here?"

She waited. She had been rather thundering at Juliana, which she did not like (for it was as much bullying as anything she suspected of Ensley). But there seemed to be no other way to reach her—and reach her she was determined to do. After a rather lengthy interval, during which Anne had an opportunity to compose her features a little,

Juliana answered in a small voice, "Well, if you promise not to repeat it— Yes, he did send me."

"Ah." Schooling herself to patience, "And did he also tell you what to tell me when you came here? I will not say a word," she coaxed.

Juliana looked very much distressed. She twisted the silken cord of her reticule, then answered, slowly and softly, "Well— Yes, he did." Her eyes again filled with tears. One dropped onto the mulberry reticule. "But he did not instruct me to, nor order me to," she defended fervently. "I am completely free—"

Feeling rather like a barrister on cross-examination, "You wish very much for Lord Ensley's approval, do not you?" Anne broke in.

Another tear, and a nod.

"You feel instinctively, I think, that I am in the way of your getting that?"

Juliana objected at once, "Oh no!" looking up and shaking her head; but the gaze she met from Anne's jade green eyes made her check and amend, "Yes."

"The sort of regard he shows to me, you would like him to show you?" Anne went on, feeling now more like a surgeon obliged to remove even the last bit of shot from a wound, no matter how much pain it occasioned, lest misplaced mercy prevent it from healing.

The patient nodded, staring unhappily at her lap.

Anne nodded also. "You have done right to tell me," she said presently. "I shall never mention it to Ensley. Have no fears on that head." And perceiving the girl was about to thank her (which would, she felt, have made her scream), she adroitly forestalled her with a question about Wiltwood and so gently eased the way to the close of the interview. Just before her ladyship left, "I do not know whether Lord Ensley mentioned it to you," she said, "but I mean to have a party to dine on Monday. I hope you will come."

Face full of uncertainty, Juliana mumbled, "If you . . . Do you think Ensley will like me to—?" Her words trailed off and she appeared to turn her attention to the silken fringe on her spencer.

"Whether he likes it or no, pray be sure to come." Drawing herself up very erect, she went on, "I shall no longer be receiving Lord Ensley, except in company. I shall tell him as much on Monday. You must forgive me if I take him aside one last time for the purpose."

But if she had expected these words to gratify her ladyship, she was disappointed. Eyes round with horror, "But he will be furious!" she exclaimed. "Dear ma'am, no, you mustn't! He will know, he will guess at once some thing I said today—" Too distressed to go on, Juliana lapsed into open-mouthed silence.

"Leave it to me," Anne replied firmly, propelling her guest towards the drawing-room door with something less than complete civility. "I know how to deal with Ensley."

And with that rather grim assurance Juliana was obliged to content herself, for Anne would say no more.

Mrs. Highet gave her household to understand she was not feeling quite well and went to bed. There, in the shelter of the blue damask curtains, she was free to cry, to beat her pillow with an angry fist, to reflect, and to calm herself. She took her dinner in her room; but by the following morning she felt quite strong and tranquil enough to pursue her ordinary activities. The truth was, Lady Ensley's visit gave her an excuse to do what both her conscience and even (to some extent at least) her inclination had been prompting her to do: to sever every intimate tie to Ensley. Circumstances had overtaken them at last—as they ought perhaps to have done, she reluctantly admitted to herself, ten years before.

She would have liked to send a note to him at once, to have it over with; but such a course must indeed persuade him Juliana was to blame. Anne was determined not to allow him to suppose that. Besides discomfiting Juliana, it would give him the inaccurate idea that Anne's own sentiments were not committed to a break. She knew well his tenacity, that in such a case he would never accept her decision but rather hound her until (as he expected) she changed her mind. But she would not change her mind. She was as certain of that as of any thing.

No, the best plan would be to wait until Monday, as they had agreed, then tell him briefly and bluntly during a five minutes' private interview. She knew herself and him: The necessity of appearing in company immediately afterwards would dissuade them both from the sort of wrenching scene they might otherwise give in to. Till then, she must busy herself as best she could.

As it developed, this last object was not difficult to achieve. A little after noon on the day following Lady Ensley's visit, an even more unexpected caller appeared at the door of the house in Mount Street. With a head full of blank conjecture, Mrs. Highet read the card of her wedded husband.

She hurried down to find him standing on a crimson carpet in the middle of her drawing-room, looking twice as large and three times as vigorous as any London gentleman. Dressed in a blue coat with brass buttons which Anne had never seen before, a buff waistcoat, buckskin breeches, and a massive pair of gleaming Hessians, there was nothing in his appearance to betray his habitual haunts except the bright rosiness of his cheeks, the clarity of his sleepy-lidded eyes, and the whole-heartedness of his smile. His neckcloth was neatly (if not elegantly) tied, his hair a fashionable spill of dark curls: Altogether, Anne had rarely seen a handsomer, better turned-out man. Moreover, there was in the frank smile on his generous lips so much sincere pleasure in seeing her, in his friendly gaze so much genuine interest, that she found herself going to him quite naturally with both hands out, and wringing his with delight.

"How good to see you! You come with all the freshness of a wind over the fields—look at you!" Anne exclaimed, drawing him to a long settee covered in satin brocade. "How do you do? To what do we owe such a happy surprise as your turning up in London? I protest, I feel as if violets had sprung up from under the snow—or tulips, rather, for you look positively *à la mode*."

Mr. Highet smilingly informed her he did tolerably well, inquired after her health and spirits, refused refreshments, and finally revealed, "I am afraid I come on what may prove to be a sad errand indeed. I asked Dolphim to send my card up to you, for I naturally wished to see you; but my visit is actually to Mrs. Insel. Is she in?"

"Maria?" queried Anne wonderingly. "I fancy she is not. No, indeed, I know she is not, for she came to me half an hour ago to ask if I wanted any books. She was on her way to Lackington, Allen. But what on earth—?" She paused in confusion, then asked, "Is it a private matter? May I know what it concerns?"

Mr. Highet hesitated only a moment before drawing a letter from his pocket-book. "I suppose, since you must have seen it had you been at Fevermere, I may show you this." And he passed into her hands a black-edged envelope with a military seal. It had been directed to Mrs. Insel first at Halfwistle House, then sent on, unopened, to Linfield. "Miss Veal delivered it to me," said Highet, taking it from her and folding it into his leather case again. "I almost sent it on here by post; but the more I thought of it, the less I cared to. Clearly it concerns some important matter, and as the farm is quiet at this season—well, in any case, I came up with it. I'm sorry for not warning you. I came as quickly as a message could have done."

"I am sure Maria will thank you for doing so," said Anne, mad to know what was in the letter but of course too well-bred to say so. "How vexing she should not be in to open it at once. But she must return within the hour. Stay and have a nuncheon. Indeed— Where is your baggage, sir?" she asked suspiciously. "You have not put up at an hotel, have you? Where are your things? Oh, sir, this is too bad of you!"

Mr. Highet admitted he had taken a room at the Hummums.

"But this is impossible! Send to them at once." Indignant, Anne jumped up and rang for Dolphim. "Have Mr. Highet's bags fetched from the Hummums," she commanded; then, after the butler departed on his commission, turned to scold her visitor: "If not as my husband, at least as my friend, you must stay here. Why, I've only just had the drapes hung in the perfect chamber for you. How happy I will be to have you as my first guest! I insist you will stay." And she argued so noisy and prolonged a case that Mr. Highet at last agreed.

Mrs. Insel, laden with books, arrived about half past one. At the sight of Henry Highet her narrow face, lately more pinched and strained than ever, broke into a broad smile. She dropped the parcel she had been meaning to give Anne and ran to shake his hand. He and Anne having just finished their nuncheon, the party adjourned again to the drawing-room.

Here it soon took on a more sombre tone. Mr. Highet once more withdrew from his pocket-book the ominous, black-edged letter. Receiving it, Maria's small face paled.

"Perhaps we must leave you alone?" suggested Anne, while Mr. Highet added tactfully,

"I must at all events."

Mrs. Insel waved a trembling hand and begged them both, on the contrary, to stay. Her eyes glued to the fascinating letter, she lowered herself slowly into a chair, rubbed a finger along the black border of the missive before daring to break the seal, then finally, silently, opened and read it. The Henry Highets watched her glittering eyes darting over the words in like silence. At last, dropping the letter in her lap, "He is dead," Maria pronounced. Her voice shook. Anne sprang up and pulled the bell-cord, demanding ratafia.

Then, "Captain Insel?" she gently enquired, drawing a chair up to be able to sit by Maria's side.

"Yes."

Anne glanced at Mr. Highet. Curiosity showed in his features, but no astonishment. Giving him a look that promised explanation, Anne returned her attention to Maria. "Poor dear," she murmured, "poor dear. Should you like a vinaigrette? Do you feel faint?"

Mrs. Insel felt in no need of a vinaigrette, but she was glad enough to drink the ratafia when it came. The cordial seemed to compose her a little, for she looked up from it and smiled (albeit rather weakly) at Mr. Highet. "You will think all this very odd," she said.

"Never mind what I think."

"I must— You see, my husband has not been quite so dead, until recently, as I have led you to suppose."

"So I gather." Feeling himself very much in the way, "Pray," he added, "I wish you will let me leave you in peace. You can surely feel no need of company at such a moment."

But Maria gestured to him to stay. "I do not look upon you as company, but as a friend," she explained, after another sip of the reviving cordial. "I am glad no longer to be obliged to masquerade before you." Then, squeezing Mrs. Highet's hand, "Oh Anne," she cried, "it is over at last!"

"Yes, but how? Will you tell me, or shall I read it?"

"In a brawl, I am sure. Major Adams does not say so, but then he would not. He was always kind. Look—" She handed the open letter to Anne. "John had lost his rank. Major Adams speaks of him as lieutenant!"

Anne said, "Small wonder. The miracle is he was allowed to stay in the Army at all." Then she bent her head, frowning, over the letter. While she read,

"You see, Mr. Highet, when I met John I was only nineteen years old," Maria explained. "I had been living in London with Anne and Lady Guilfoyle, then travelling with them. Then Lady Guilfoyle fell ill, and I was sent home. You cannot imagine my distress—my family was a large and quarrelsome one, and my parents ill-suited to one another. There was never quite enough money, and certainly not sufficient room for us all. My mother particularly was deeply disappointed to find me home after a whole year in society, with no suitor nor any hope of one. And I . . . I am afraid you will think me a very unnatural daughter, but I was aghast at the prospect of living again amidst so much discord, so much bitterness and

want . . ." Her voice trailed away, and she seemed to see
before her eyes the cramped rooms of Halfwistle House,
more cramped than ever in the dead of winter, and to hear
in an inner ear the harsh voices and angry words of her
parents. "At all events, when my brother Frank soon after
came home on leave with Captain Insel— Well, he was
young, and handsome, and laughing, and seemed to me
very romantic. He paid me a deal of attention. My father
made no secret of it that he thought I should accept him,
if he offered for me, for I would get no better—as my
fruitless year in London showed. When he did offer for
me, then— God help me, I said yes. I cannot blame myself, really, for I was young, and I thought I loved him.
Anyhow, I have been amply punished."

Anne, looking up from the letter, begged Maria to spare
herself the rest of her story. "I daresay Mr. Highet has
heard it before. Captain Insel bore Maria away to Canada.
There his true colours began to show: He drank deep,
beat her, frequented"—her cheeks darkened momentarily—"unsavoury women," she made herself go on,
"and made her life such a hell that—"

"She fled to England," Mr. Highet finished for her,
grimly nodding his comprehension. "Where her family refused to take her in, and where she has consequently
been obliged, for appearance's sake, to live quietly, and
pass herself off as a widow. Yes, I have heard the story
before. All too often, I fear. Mrs. Insel, indeed you must
not blame yourself. And how does this Major Adams account for Insel's passing?"

"He says he died 'in private combat,'" Anne replied,
reading, "'not on the field of battle.' I'll wager it was not!
One of his doxies probably pulled a knife on him—and
God bless her! The filthy blackguard. The least he could

have done was to die decently, and left you a pension you could live on. This"—she waved the letter—"this is barely enough to keep a hen in feed." Disgustedly, she tossed the letter onto a pedestal table.

"It is more than I have ever had," Maria quietly pointed out. If Anne's energetic invective had shocked her, she did not show it. Nor did Mr. Highet appear scandalized: Indeed, he sat gazing at Mrs. Insel with a very mild, slightly speculative look. A number of matters which had not made sense to him in the past had now suddenly fallen into place. After a moment Maria took up, "If I live very cheap, I expect I can make do on this much quite well."

"Oh dear!" said Anne. "I had not thought of that. I suppose you will wish to form your own establishment. But what a sad change for me! Perhaps you will not remove quite out of reach, my love? I hope not."

Maria smiled and patted Anne's hand. "Indeed, I should be sorry to do that. How kind you have been!" She turned to Mr. Highet. "And how kind you have been as well. Imagine travelling so far to deliver this—and when we all know how you dread London!"

But Mr. Highet would hear none of this. He stood, said he still felt a little weary from his journey, and trusted the ladies would excuse him if he went up to his room. As the door closed behind his back,

"I must write to John's parents," Maria said, "in case Major Adams has not. They may wish his body to be sent home. I confess I do not. To think it should all come to this!"

Anne patted her arm. "Little sparrow, you must be very tired," she said briskly. "Let us pack you off to bed for the afternoon. You need rest and sleep, and time to think—and then, it seems to me, you must write to Mr. Mallinger! He is one person, I trust, who will not be sorry to hear of the lieutenant's timely demise."

"Anne, if you ever breathe a word to Mr. Mallinger—!" Maria was too appalled to finish her sentence. "He does not even know I was not a widow! I told you what it would mean to me to let him hear my story. Oh, the shame! Swear you will never, ever say anything to him."

"But you let Mr. Highet know," Anne objected, sincerely confused. "What a curious sparrow it is! I thought you had decided to cast off secrecy."

"Not at all," the other replied firmly. "I trust Mr. Highet. I know he will never give me away—indeed, if you think he did not perfectly understand I spoke in confidence, I shall tell him so specifically. But I am persuaded he does understand. Only *you* could imagine rushing off to Mr. Mallinger and—" She seemed to shiver at the very notion. "What would you have said to him? That I am free now, and he ought to ask me to marry him again? Good heavens! The indelicacy of it! I must go into mourning, besides everything else—real mourning, deep mourning."

"For that snake?" demanded Anne, outraged. "You mean to put on weeds—again, I might add—for that—" She broke off abruptly. "But never mind. We need not settle all this now. You are tired, and have had a shock." She stood and shepherded Mrs. Insel out of the drawing-room and up two pairs of stairs to her bed-chamber. Here she tucked her in very tenderly, refusing to discuss any longer the question of Mr. Mallinger, but promising likewise to take no action Maria did not approve.

Mr. Highet, having made a long journey, declared it his intention (if it did not discommode the household at

Mount Street) to stay on a few days in London. Anne pronounced herself prepared to make him comfortable for as long as he liked to remain; at the same time she wondered a little how to entertain him. But she soon found she needed to have no fears on that head. Mr. Highet was off the next morning before she came downstairs, and never returned till past five. She learned (to her amazement) over tea that he had been to view an exhibition of pictures at Somerset Place, then to Tattersall's to look at some horses, after which he visited two inventors whose names he had read in various journals over the past year or two, one of whom was developing a new sort of engine bound to improve many lives very materially. He closed his round of calls with one to a dispensary at an hospital, where he had learned of several helpful medicaments to take home with him to the apothecary at Faulding Chase. He was considering, moreover, asking a London doctor to come to Fevermere for a month or two, that he might visit the farms of his tenants with an eye to inspecting sanitary conditions and so preventing disease. London itself he declared a deal less objectionable now—in winter, and out of any fashionable season—than he found it in spring or summer. The noise was less, the press of traffic somewhat lighter, and the cold weather prevented some of the fouler odours from flourishing. He was planning a visit to Covent Garden tonight, to see Mr. Kemble's *Lodoiska*, and hoped Mrs. Highet at least would join him—since he quite understood Mrs. Insel might not feel it proper for her to do so.

Maria, robed in black, thanked him for his understanding and declined; but Anne, who had made no plans for the evening save a long consultation with Cook regarding the bill of fare for to-morrow night, readily accepted.

"Now how shall we round out the party?" she asked, then caught herself, coloured prettily, and exclaimed, "Dear me, I quite forgot!"

At the same time Mr. Highet threw his head back, held the pose a moment, then exploded into the guffaw of laughter she detested so much. "Damme, I like that!" he brought out, between gasps of laughter. Anne was distressed to observe him slap his knee, lean forward as if helplessly doubled over with merriment, then plunge into another gale of hilarity. "Forgot! Forgot we were married! Wanted a cha—a cha—a chaperon!" he sputtered, till Anne could bear it no longer and icily remarked,

"Yes, we all know what I forgot. I admitted it myself. Now for heaven's sake, pray get hold of yourself!"

Wiping tears from his eyes, Mr. Highet made an effort and contrived to quiet down. "Forgive me, please," he asked. "I intended no offence, I assure you. Only when you said— It was so— Forgive me, but—" A sinister chuckle seemed to well up irrepressibly in him. "It was so— So— FUNNY!" And he roared again at such a volume that Anne simply got up and left the room.

They did, however, attend the theatre together that night. Spurred by mortification to appear to the best possible advantage, Anne came down the stairs at seven dressed in her newest and most elaborate full dress. It was sea green, carried out in a most beautiful English gauze. It suited her to perfection, as she knew; and the satin Austrian cap that went with it, trimmed with white fox-tail feathers, raised her height just the inch or two that her dignity required. A jade necklace she had had from her mother exactly matched the green of the dress, and brought out the blond of her hair, the colour and sparkle

of her eyes. She had the satisfaction of glimpsing in Mr.
Highet's face, when she walked into the drawing-room so
attired, the first admiring look she had ever seen there.
He suppressed it at once, but she knew, almost exul-
tantly, that her appearance had surprised it out of him.
Why she should have wished to provoke such a look from
a man she marrried quite as a matter of business she could
not have said. Fortunately, no one asked her.

Certainly Mr. Highet (mildly resplendent himself in a
close-fitting Polish coat liberally striped with cord and tas-
sels) did not ask. On the contrary, he was if anything less
easy and forthcoming with her than he had been in the
country. Not that he was uncivil, or even formal. Only she
was more aware than usual of a certain reserve in him. She
guessed that he felt he was trespassing, as it were, on her
life in London. He wore the mask of an interested observer, a spectator both of the play and of the audience.
When various of Anne's acquaintances visited their box,
Mr. Highet played his role of new husband judiciously,
neither too proprietary nor too remote; but when they
were alone she felt him exerting himself to keep his distance. His discretion (if that was what it was) inspired
mixed feelings in her. On the one hand, she was grateful
he made no undue claim on her; on the other, perversely,
she rather wished he would.

They both enjoyed *Lodoiska* (though Anne opined there
were more horses on stage than the plot strictly demanded). They came and went from the theatre in a
closed carriage. Anne had never sat in one alone with a
gentleman before, and it gave her a sensation of intimacy
that both disconcerted and pleased her. She wondered if
Mr. Highet felt it. He showed no sign of doing so; but she
was beginning to suspect he was not, as she had pre-

viously imagined, the sort of person whose thoughts appeared on his face. His conduct towards Maria, for example: He must have known the Army would communicate with her so only to announce the death of a husband. Yet he had come to London and handed her the letter with an expression of bland ignorance. And that flattering glance at herself she had caught to-night: A feminine instinct told her it wasn't, after all, the first time he had admired her looks. Yet she had never seen any trace of admiration in him before. What manner of man was he, exactly? She had suddenly, for the first time, an uneasy suspicion that Mr. Highet knew more of her than she did of him.

At all events, his behaviour once they regained Mount Street was everything that was correct. He shook her hand, thanked her for the evening, and vanished into his room. It was left to Anne to feel rather flat and let down while her abigail undressed her. She slipped into bed more inclined, oddly, to speculate on the nature of Henry Highet than to anticipate, with the anxiety it merited, the supremely difficult interview with George, Lord Ensley, awaiting her the next day.

TWELVE

THE DRAWING-ROOM AT NUMBER 14, MOUNT STREET was more, that Monday evening, than a large, well-proportioned saloon elaborately hung with rich silks and heavy brocades, and fitted with handsome furniture. To the properly adjusted ear, it presented a piquant symphony of voices. Conversation hummed like strings: The laughter of the ladies fluted above it, that of the gentlemen boomed, drumlike, below. Now and then a solo might be heard, as when Lady Bambrick contrived to secure half the company's attention with the story of how the portrait artist she had hired to paint a likeness of her lord had managed to keep the business a secret by pretending (at her suggestion) to be an architect; and how her husband had consequently purchased several thousand bricks he would never need for an annex to their dairy. Colonel Whiddon brassily trumpeted his opinion of the Royal Pavilion at Brighton, now under construction; Mr. Humphrey Bleyte, in rounded tones much like those of a French horn, countered with his opposing one. The strings (a chorus of feminine observations on the handsomeness of the newly decorated room) swelled generally to cover them; and so the music continued. Anne Highet, conductress for the evening, listened satisfied. This was her first soirée in Mount Street, and she wished it to be a success. Collecting so interesting and luminous a company in mid-December in London was no mean feat, but she had done it: a reflection that increased her tendency to congratulate herself.

Moreover, the evening was only just beginning. Conversation now politely confined to mild anecdotes and observations would, she trusted, grow more pointed as the night wore on. Some few of her guests—Lord and Lady Ensley, most notably—had not yet even arrived. Others were hardly acquainted with more than one or two people in the room. Mr. Highet fell into this category, of course. His hostess had been worried about him on this account, particularly because Maria—still insisting upon her mourning—had asked Anne to give out that she was ill, and had not come down.

But Mr. Highet seemed to be taking care of himself very nicely. He had found Charles and Celia Grypphon among the crowd, and Anne noticed the three of them talking animatedly during some quarter of an hour. Celia must have introduced him to some people afterwards, for each time Anne looked conscientiously round for him, ready to rescue him from a lonely corner, she found him in colloquy with some one else: Sir John Firebrace, or

Warrington Weld, or (for quite ten minutes, too!) the rather needlessly pretty Arabella Lemon. He was looking quite amazingly handsome to-night, in daring Wellington trousers she was sure he could not have had made in Cheshire, and a black stock tied carefully round his throat. That black brought out the black of his hair, and the darkness of his sleepy eyes, and set off the ruddy bloom in his cheeks. When she considered this was the same man she had often seen in a none too tidy labourer's smock-frock and boots thick with mud she could scarcely credit it.

Ensley arrived rather late. The terrified look in his wife's eyes, the pinkness of her nose, and the hastiness of her usually meticulous toilette suggested to Anne that they had quarrelled about her coming. Perhaps that was the cause of their lateness. Whatever the case, Anne had perforce to postpone her private interview with his lordship, for dinner was nearly due to be served. She could only greet them (Ensley levelled his quizzing glass at her, unwittingly strengthening her resolve) and draw them into the buzzing room. She took Juliana's damp right hand firmly in her left, took Ensley's left arm with her right, and was guiding them towards Charles Grypphon when, most unluckily, Mr. Highet bumbled directly into them.

Anne could see at once this was a meeting he desired no more than she. His heavy brows drew together and he looked down from his six inches' advantage on Ensley with no very friendly eye. What had they argued about at Linfield, the Corn Law? Dear, dear! Events (at least in Anne's opinion) seemed to be proving Ensley wrong since then. He would not like that. Nervously, she watched him pull his lips back into the semblance of a smile and extend a hand to Highet.

"What are you doing in town?" he demanded, before remembering to add, "Understand congratulations are in order," in a voice more suspicious than celebratory.

For his part, Mr. Highet did not even pretend a smile. Putting his hand out slowly, "A little personal business. And the same to you," he said, at his most sober. "I wish you extremely happy." He looked gravely at Juliana, whom Anne introduced, murmured politely his pleasure at knowing her, then fixed his attention chiefly on Anne.

"We went to see *Lodoiska* last night," chirped that lady brightly, and immediately wished she had not. She'd selected it for a neutral topic, but saw at once from the spark in Ensley's eyes that he did not consider an excursion to the theatre with Mr. Highet in that light. He had already been unpleasantly surprised to find Mr. Highet here at all (for of course Anne had done nothing to warn him); in addition, Highet's explanation of "personal business" for his presence had scarcely calmed him. Anne noticed the wording too, and thought it unnecessarily provocative (would not "business" have done as well?) but could spare little thought for that with Ensley glowering so, and Mr. Highet stern as a vicar on Sunday. She obliged herself to prattle on bravely, "Have you seen it? Mr. Kemble wrote it, you know, as well as appearing. It's quite good, really. Plenty of horses. Though they have no lines, of course, save 'Nay, nay.' "

Lady Ensley was the only one to laugh at this feeble sally, and that clearly from excess of nerves.

"What a shame to come up to town just at this season," Ensley remarked, trying for a smooth recover. He had reminded himself he must deal comfortably with Highet or risk proving to Anne the truth of her own objections. "So little to see, I mean. There was a marvelous *King Henry IV* at the Drury Lane just last month. Mr. Bengough played Henry. Excellent."

Mr. Highet (who after all had no corresponding motive to propitiate Ensley) said nothing.

"Of course, you may not care for Shakespeare. Lady George does not—do you, my dear?"

As Ensley had put this in only to demonstrate to both Mr. and Mrs. Highet the cordiality of relations between himself and his wife, and as Anne guessed this immediately, she did not come to his rescue when her ladyship merely answered, "No," and fell mute again.

A fine dew sprung up on Ensley's high forehead. For all his sang-froid, he unconsciously joined his hands behind his back and began to wring them energetically. This was going very badly indeed. He could see in Anne's eyes that she had had no good news in store for him in the first place (though he did not divine the finality of her actual decision) and a certain pique on that account, perhaps, made him venture a remark he might better have left unsaid: "Well, Mr. Highet! Still letting your schoolmaster teach Spence, are you, now that you've seen the Spencean Philanthropists at work at Spa Fields? Ha! That was an education for Parliament, I can tell you."

"Mr. Mallinger does not teach Spence. He has read him, as have I. Like Milton, I 'cannot praise a fugitive and cloistered virtue.' I dislike censorship," Mr. Highet returned, miraculously (Anne considered) declining to rise to Ensley's bait either in word or tone. Still, she silently cursed Dolphim for a doddering snail. Where was he? Where was dinner? Would he never announce it?

"How is Mr. Mallinger?" she now asked, assuming an air of gay interest. She hoped at least to steer the topic

from politics. She explained to Juliana, "Mr. Mallinger
teaches the children at Fevermere and Linfield."

"Children?" Juliana echoed, puzzled. Looking blankly
from Anne to Mr. Highet, "But I thought— Have you
children?" she asked bluntly.

"The children of the tenant farmers," Mr. Highet explained at once, while Anne blushed and Lord Ensley
glanced furiously at his wife. Kindly, Mr. Highet hurried
the talk away from the *faux pas*: "I fear he is still in indifferent spirits. My mother and I have often had him to
dine in recent weeks, but we can't seem to cheer him
up."

"What a pity," Ensley said vaguely.

"And yet, you know," Mr. Highet added, glancing curiously at Anne, "quite lately I fancy I know how to do so.
I must see if I can contrive it."

Anne, endeavouring to steal a look at a clock on the
mantel beyond him, hardly heard this, and said nothing.

"And how does your mother?" Lord Ensley, regretting
his lapse of policy and determined to be pleasant again,
inquired. "An estimable woman."

Mr. Highet contrived to look both sceptical and dour
at once, and was about to answer when Dolphim ("At
last!" thought Anne thankfully) appeared, throwing open
the drawing-room doors. The intricacies of proceeding
to the dining-room in the proper order of precedence
spared the unwilling quartet from continuing their conversation; and the table ("Thank God," breathed Anne) sep-
arated the key participants. Anne herself had a very
interesting assistant to the Foreign Secretary on her left,
and a Major recently home from France on her right. Her
only regret (a quite absurd one, really) was that Mr.

Highet had somehow ended up next to Arabella Lemon, and across from the perenially fetching Baroness Courtham.

Dinner itself passed cheerfully enough. The hostess regretted the fricaseed Windsor beans, for Cook invariably made the white sauce too watery and quite spoiled them; but the parslied tench and the veal olives were excellent, and the wine roll delicious. Of course, Anne did not taste one quarter of the dishes served: She was too much occupied by quizzing Major Lewis as to the state of affairs in Paris, and by teasing out of the interesting assistant Castlereagh's next projects. She had had no opportunity to appoint an assignation with Ensley before dinner, nor could she approach him now. On the contrary, she was soon obliged to lead the withdrawal of the ladies to the drawing-room and to leave Ensley and Mr. Highet to one another's dubious mercies.

This hour alone with the ladies was one Anne had always particularly enjoyed, for she was far from the only witty female in her set, and tongues seemed often set at happy liberty by the absence of gentlemen. Tonight was no exception. A circle of the duller, and generally younger, spirits sat apart, talking among themselves; while Anne and Celia and Amy Firebrace and some dozen others heatedly argued and chaffed one another on a wide variety of topics. Yet even here, among her own sex and in her own drawing-room, Anne was aware of a degree of artificiality in the proceedings which she had never, before her sojourn in Cheshire, noticed. There was almost a ritual aspect to the debate, as topics they had discussed an hundred times before (the role of women in Politics, the progress of the Arts . . .) were gone over yet again, with all the same complaints brought out, and all the same retorts answered to them. She was not sorry when, at length, Celia drew her aside and whispered,

"So, Mrs. Sly-boots Highet! Telling us what a tedious sow's ear your Mr. Highet was, when all the time you knew perfectly well you meant to make a silk purse of him."

"I beg your pardon?"

"I say, your husband. Who would ever have guessed he would dress up so nicely, eh? Who but you," Celia laughed.

Anne asked, rather seriously, "Do you think him well-looking?"

"Well-looking? Spectacular! Now don't tell me you don't see it yourself!" Celia rallied her. "Nor that you aren't aware how *he* looks at *you*!"

"How he— What do you mean, exactly?"

"Good heavens, Anne, you know me a sight too well, I hope, to play coy with me. Aren't you really aware your husband is in love with you?"

Anne felt suddenly dizzy. "Celia, no, I am sure you are mistaken. Why, he has never said a word of such a thing! Quite the opposite, he has been very explicit . . ." Her words faded briefly, then recommenced, "Our marriage— why, I've told you all this. Our marriage was purely for business purposes," Anne whispered rapidly.

"Yes, perhaps, but— If he is not in love with you, he is mightily infatuated. Not that I wonder at it," she added, fondly brushing a hand across Anne's delicate cheek. "Only— Surely I saw Ensley fuming at him, and vice versa? You don't deny that?"

Anne thought. She recalled Mr. Highet's "condition," the single visitor he had warned her he would not make welcome at Fevermere. But that was a question of simple dignity, she was certain. Celia must be wrong. Perhaps Mr. Highet found her pretty—in fact, she knew he had last night—but that was all.

"Ah, you don't," Celia took up again, before Anne could speak. "You don't deny either, I hope, that he is not one quarter so dull as you have made him out to be? He gave Charles and me a very good account of the exhibition at Somerset Place just now, besides apprising us of some new techniques in midwifery that quite—well, quite took my breath away. I don't say, mind you, that he will ever be Lord High Fol-de-rol; but neither, if you come to it, will Charles. And I for one should not care to live with Lord High Fol-de-rol any how."

At this juncture Amy Firebrace pounced on them, demanding to know what Celia thought of the Elgin Marbles; and as the gentlemen joined them while this discussion was still going forward, the subject of Henry Highet was let drop. Anne had no time to think of Mr. Highet anyway, for she was acutely aware that the evening was slipping by without her having spoke alone to Ensley. The prospect weighed upon her more and more uncomfortably, yet it was devilishly trickly to arrange an assignation in a house Ensley scarcely knew, and under the very nose (a nose she particularly wished not to distress with any whiff of a rendez-vous) of her husband. She had forgot the former and, naturally, failed to anticipate the latter complication when she promised the tryst to Ensley. Now how to contrive it?

Ensley himself solved the difficulty, coming up beside her as she bent to move a firescreen and murmuring, "How much longer must I wait for you? Follow me to the dining-room in five minutes!"

"No," she whispered, setting the screen down where it

would more effectively protect the elderly Lady Sandys from the heat of the fire. She smiled at the old marchioness, then mumbled into her fan, "The servants will be there. Any how, I cannot follow you out. Mr. Highet will notice."

"And is it any business of his?" Ensley queried angrily, though still keeping his voice low, and erasing any emotion from his countenance. He began to stroll slowly towards a corner in which a small marble statue of Demeter perched on a pedestal. Anne strolled with him, fanning herself.

"I think it is his business, yes," she answered in a low voice. "I do not care to hurt him, you see, and I know such behaviour must."

"You seem to oppose your nicety of conduct to mine," Ensley returned. They had now arrived at the statue and he gestured at it as he spoke.

Anne nodded, unaware that Mr. Highet had observed her situation and was now keeping a discreet eye on her unnaturally rigid back and Ensley's studied gestures. "Perhaps," she said. "Would we not do better to renew this subject later, when he is gone back to Cheshire? I expect him to leave in a day or two."

"I do not care to wait a day or two," Ensley muttered, though still nodding genially. For a change, Anne was grateful for his practised gestures, his ability to control his expression. "You have something to say to me. I see it in your eyes. If you will not quit the room with me, say it here and now."

"I cannot—" she faltered; but,

"Say it!" he hissed so harshly that, without further reflection, she burst into speech.

"I will not receive you alone any longer. I will not write

to you nor receive letters of you. I regret it; but our lives have changed and our relations must change too. Pray forgive me. Pray—" She felt tears coming to her eyes and urgently blinked them away, "Pray believe I shall always remember our friendship with the greatest affection, and think of you with tenderness," she went on, in a softened voice. Almost pleadingly she added, "As I hope you will me!" before turning away abruptly, and plunging with such energy into conversation with Arabella Lemon (who happened to be the closest person to her) that Ensley had no hope of recapturing her attention.

Out of the corner of her eye Anne saw, as she chattered to Miss Lemon of her enchanting tiara, Henry Highet watching her. The thought that it might be Miss Lemon and not herself he was observing passed through her mind; but a few minutes later, when Arabella had moved off to sit with her mother, she caught his eyes on herself again and knew she had not been wrong. She could not read his expression. Had he seen her speaking with Ensley? Seen him turn away from her? What did her own countenance show? If she had been pressed to read the look on Mr. Highet's, she would have called it kindness, or sympathy. But perhaps she merely fancied that.

Not many minutes afterwards, Ensley came to bid her good night. Juliana was on his arm, her expression as timid and tentative as ever. Ensley was unmistakably stricken. Stiffly, and in such evident pain that Anne could scarcely regard him without bursting into tears, he thanked her for the evening, made his bow, and departed. She watched him go, torn between relief and a miserable feeling that half her life was walking out the door with him. When Mr. Highet appeared at her side a moment later, and took her arm, and bracingly asked her what on

earth had gone into those delicious veal olives, she knew
for certain it had been kindness in his face after all, and
that he was aware—at least in part—of what had passed.

"Oh, eye of newt and toe of frog," she replied, grate-
fully slipping a hand into the arm he offered. Though her
voice had a tell-tale quaver in it, his very presence—warm
and solid—reassured her and helped her to find this light
answer.

"Wool of bat and tongue of inquisitive gentleman?" he
suggested.

"Dear me, no. At least, I do not think so. You had best
ask Cook. It is her secret."

"I dare not go near her until I know for certain," he
replied, laughing a little. They began to stroll towards an
open window at one end of the room. "I mean to return to
Somerset Place," he went on presently. "There is a painting there I wish to buy for Fevermere. If it is not too
much trouble, I should very much like your opinion first.
Will you go with me to look at it to-morrow?"

Surprised, "Certainly, since you ask me. Only I had
best warn you, I am no judge of art. You ought really to
take Celia," she said.

"With all deference to her ladyship," he answered in a
low tone, "I prefer your company. Any how, you are more
likely to see it again than she, so your self-interest is involved. I know you have a high opinion of self-interest,"
he added, smiling.

Anne caught the reference to the astonishment she had
voiced, the day he offered for her, at his neighbourly assistance when she first went into Cheshire. She coloured a
little, thinking of herself and Lady Juliana. "My opinion
of self-interest has come down a little since those days,"
she murmured.

"Has it!" he exclaimed. He laid his hand over the little one tucked into his arm, then patted it awkwardly. "Well, well! And here I had been thinking town wits did not change their own opinions, but only those of other people."

"On the contrary, they change them more often than anyone else—as town tulips do their linen. Come help me talk to Lady Sandys, won't you? No one has in quite half an hour, I fear, and if she falls asleep—as I see she is about to—she is the very devil to wake up!"

In the event, Mr. Highet not only helped his wife talk to the old marchioness, he kept by Anne's side through the end of the party, though it went on past two and she knew he must be dropping with sleep. She accepted this support with silent gratitude and felt a deep twinge of guilt on learning, when she stumbled downstairs the next morning at half past eleven, that he had been unable to sleep later than six, the hour at which he habitually rose. Still, he seemed cheerful and rested enough. Meeting her in the front hall, he informed her he had already gone for a gallop through Hyde Park, stopped in at Clarendon's to talk to a German baron he had met (in England to buy sheep and interested in Mr. Highet's) and made a hearty breakfast with him.

"I suppose you wish to rush off to Somerset Place at once, lest someone else snatch away your painting?" Anne hazarded, suppressing a yawn and wearily rubbing at her forehead. The memory that she had broke with Ensley definitively last night lay in her heart like a lump of ice; but, as was usual with her, the pain only sharpened her humour. She dropped into an elbow chair whose gilded arms were carved into serpents, ran her fingers idly over the hooded eyes and hissing tongue of one of these, then bent to it and asked solicitously, "You are sleepy too, aren't you, poor thing? Yes, we all are."

"Dear ma'am, if you are so tired as that—" Mr. Highet began; but Anne interrupted, staggering to her feet,

"No, no! Never let it be said I was afraid to martyr myself for Art. Go we must and go we shall. What is that bright light?" she demanded, affrightedly clapping an arm over her eyes after glancing out the long window beside the front door. Face buried, she muttered into the crook of her arm, "Dolphim, would you ask Lizzie to fetch down my green velvet pelisse? The one with the satin epaulets—she will know. And my black chip bonnet."

"We call that light the sun," Mr. Highet informed her while the butler went on his errand. Gently he took her arm and coaxed it from her face. "It will not harm you, if you let it alone."

"Like a bee," she mused, blinking at the window. "But what is it doing up at this hour? And what of ourselves? I do not wish to offend you, sir," she continued, changing her tack slightly and collapsing again into the chair, "but your extreme cheerfulness at such a moment is not at all the thing. In fact, it shows an appalling lack of taste." She nipped what would have been a vast yawn in the bud, then continued, "Here in town a man of breeding leaves the hours between six and ten A.M. to his servants. I can't explain it. He just does. It's something he knows to do. Perhaps he's born with the instinct— Oh, thank you, Dolphim," she interrupted herself, languidly standing, raising her arms, and shrugging herself into the pelisse the butler held for her. "It is true, what I've been saying to Mr. Highet, is not it? You are not acquainted with any respectable butlers who buttle before, say, nine-thirty or so, are you?"

With admirable aplomb, Mr. Dolphim replied smoothly, "It is certainly true that madam never rises before that hour without ill result." He proferred her her bonnet.

"There, you see?" Placing the bonnet on her head and fumbling at the ribands she went on, "Of course, you are not to blame for being ignorant of these things. On the contrary, since you have scarcely lived in town—"

"Don't you want some breakfast before we leave?" Mr. Highet broke in as Dolphim moved to open the door to them. She thought, as she looked sidewards at him, that she saw on his countenance an expression more explicitly amused than the bland, friendly one with which he usually met her pleasantries.

"Breakfast?" she echoed hollowly. "Do you mean that sitting-down thing at the table? With eggs in it and things?" She watched him carefully. His smile broadened. She had finally succeeded in amusing him, after all this time! "No, actually. I seem to recall having tried that once. It ended badly, I think. Any how, I am sure a few mouthfuls of brisk morning air will suffice to sustain me. Thank you, Dolphim," she murmured, as that gentleman opened the door and bowed her through it. She gave a little shriek as she gained the front steps, averted her eyes, and shrinkingly descended to the waiting carriage. Mr. Highet handed her in. "Oh, yes," she said weakly. She took a deep breath and gagged. "I feel much better already."

Mr. Highet closed the door, shutting her in. Actually, it was a rather pleasant day, cold but dry, and with a blue, open sky. It was almost a shame to be inside a closed carriage. Mr. Highet gave his orders to the groom, then climbed in next to Anne. As they crossed Mayfair he told her where he meant to hang the picture they were going to see, and explained what had drawn him to it. "It shows a harbour. At, if you will excuse my mentioning it, dawn. An artist named Turner."

"Yes, I remember a picture of his from last year, of a brook I think. Aqueous sort of fellow."

"Did you like it? You must be frank," he warned. "If you do not care for this one, say so. Don't spare my feelings."

"I shall be brutal," she promised. "I shall make you wish you never confessed to admiring it at all. You will squirm under the crushing heel of my—"

"Yes, thank you. Simple candour will answer nicely," he cut her off. But he smiled at the same time, in that lively way she had not seen before, and she smiled back.

Inside the gallery, whose high walls were covered nearly from floor to ceiling with paintings, he offered her his arm and began to lead her through the thin crowd of viewers to the picture that interested him. But they had gone no more than a few steps before a small, very portly, extremely well-dressed young gentleman spotted them and strolled over.

"Bless me if it isn't the brown top-boots!" he exclaimed, holding a hand out to shake Mr. Highet's. "Cut very high, if I recall, and particularly thick in the sole? And with Miss Guilfoyle, too," he went on, turning to Anne and bowing. "How d'ye do? Your friend and I last met among the lasts at Hoby's—and now we brush together midst the brushstrokes!"

"Lord Alvanley," Anne bowed, smiling, even as she wondered frantically how on earth it had happened that

Henry Highet struck up an acquaintance with the sharpest and most celebrated wit in London. And at Hoby's! What freak had tempted the plain-living master of Fevermere into that Temple of Dandyism? "But I am no longer Miss Guilfoyle," she told him. "You must call me Mrs. Highet. And this gentleman is my husband, as well as my friend."

"Indeed?" Alvanley passed his keen glance over them both, nodded incisively, and said, "Smart fellow. Interesting match. Seen these?" He waved a plump hand vaguely at the scores of pictures round them. "One or two good things. The rest—" He shook his head in a melancholy fashion. "Pity to think of all the useful gaiters and sails and breeches that could have been made from the canvas."

"You are too severe," Mr. Highet reproved him.

"Ah! Now I see your game. Last time we met, you told me my cuffs were too long." (Here Anne stole a look at his cuffs, which indeed reached nearly past his knuckles.) "Now you say I am too severe. You are the sort of person who goes about town telling people how they are excessive. Ha! If you want to see real excess, stop by my house about nine to-night. A whole expendable crowd of us will gather to eat a superfluous dinner, after which we shall have some nice, immoderate play." He winked, then apologized to Anne for being unable to invite her too. "Not that sort of evening. Well, don't want to stay talking too long! Perish the thought! Twelve Bruton Street," he called over his shoulder and walked off without waiting for an answer.

He left in his wake a woman who merely gaped, for some moments, at her husband.

"Friendly fellow," that gentleman observed pleasantly, when the friendly fellow had gone out of earshot.

"Friendly?" Anne gasped. "Lord Alvanley is at the centre of one of the most exclusive sets in London! He's cut more people than the guillotine. What did you say to him at Hoby's?" she demanded. "And what made you go into Hoby's any how?"

"I wanted boots," he said simply.

"But Hoby's?"

He shrugged. "Perhaps my visit to town is turning my head. I am sure they will be good boots, at all events, as well as stylish. You don't object?" he asked as an afterthought.

"Certainly not! It is none of my affair any how. Order some coats at Weston's, why don't you? I am sure Lord Alvanley will be happy to put you up for membership at Brook's or Crockford's. Gamble Fevermere away! It is nothing to me."

Seriously, "You are not anxious about money, I hope?" he asked, pitching his voice low. "The estate is doing extremely well."

"Of course I am not," Anne broke in impatiently. "Only if I have to watch you turned into a—a fashionable fribble by those—those fops—!" She sputtered to a halt. The truth was, the mere idea of Mr. Highet becoming a coxcomb, concerned with the height of his boots and the folds of his cravat and the stripes on his waistcoat, made her half ill. But,

"Did you suppose—? Do you really think—?" he commenced, then flung his head forward and back. To her horror, Anne realized he was going to give one of his horse laughs at her right here, in the middle of Somerset Place.

"Sir!" She tugged at his coat-sleeve as unobtrusively as she could, hissing again, "Sir!"

Too late. He held his silent pose as usual, then burst into the noisy explosion she knew so well, and hated so much. Only this time she was more embarrassed by his public display than piqued by his laughing at her. "You imagine I will become a dandy!" he at last brought out, wheezing with hilarity. "I! A dandy! Oh, rich, rich!" He wiped tears from his eyes while she implored in a frantic whisper,

"Dear Mr. Highet, laugh at me later, can't you? People are staring!"

He shook his head, wiped away more helpless tears, apologized, and tried vainly to recover himself. Anne bowed with as much dignity as she could muster to a viscountess she remembered to have met at Lady Bambrick's, put her arm through Mr. Highet's, and dragged him forcefully into the nearest corner. Here she apparently scrutinized the buckle of a shoe on a foot of a personage painted by Raeburn.

When some minutes had passed, "Can you govern yourself now?" she asked fiercely. "I feel as if I shall see this buckle in my dreams if I look at it much longer."

He nodded, gulped, nodded again, and replied in a slightly breathless voice, "Yes, quite. I am so extremely sorry. I don't know how it was, only the very notion of your . . . It seemed so . . . It suddenly struck me as terribly—"

"Yes, I *know* what it struck you as, only for God's sake don't say it! You'll be off all over again," she scolded him. Sternly, she adjusted his collar, which had come askew during his fit, and gave a smoothing pat to his stock. "Just calm yourself. Think of seed drills, or harrows, or something, and take me to the picture you like at once."

Mr. Highet at last succeeding in regaining a tolerable measure of composure, the two accomplished their errand. Anne whole-heartedly approved the Turner, and indeed was much impressed with her husband's taste. They managed to quit the gallery without any further contretemps.

THIRTEEN

MR. DOLPHIM BOWED, ACCEPTED MR. HIGHET'S CAPE and top-hat, and Mrs. Highet's bonnet and pelisse, then blandly announced, "Lord Ensley is waiting for you in the drawing-room, ma'am, with Mrs. Insel. There is also a letter for you from him which arrived just after you went out this morning."

He indicated a note in a silver tray on a beaufet behind him. Anne glanced at it, recognised Ensley's familiar hand, thought of him not ten yards from her, and changed colour. Her cheeks, which had been pink with fresh air and good humour, went white. Her eyes hardened till they were as stony as the jade they resembled in hue. "I am not at home to Lord Ensley," she said quietly. "Pray

tell him so." She was acutely aware of Mr. Highet standing a few steps behind her. "And return his letter to him
when he goes," she added deliberately.

Impassively, Dolphim bowed again, took the letter, and
went up the stairs. Anne turned to Mr. Highet.. Her
cheeks were still very pale, and she held herself extremely
straight. "I think I shall go up to my room, sir," she said.
"I shall order a collation set out for you if you like."

"Thank you, no." Henry Highet watched her atten-
tively as he went on, "I am not hungry."

Anne nodded and was about to turn away when he
asked impulsively,

"You are not denying him because I am here?"

She shook her head. Without looking at him, and in a
very low tone indeed, "As you may have guessed, my
friendship with Lord Ensley is finished," she said. "Not
in any rancour"—she did not wish him to think Ensley
had cast her aside or insulted her—"but finished." Still
without looking up, "If you will excuse me . . ." she murmured, and hurried away lest she linger too long and run
into Ensley in his way out.

She was glad she had told Mr. Highet. It was an aspect
of her life that had disturbed him and she liked him too
well to wish him distress. Of course their marriage would
not be affected by the change in any material way.

For his part, Mr. Highet felt as if a yoke of iron had
been lifted from his shoulders. He was surprised he did
not float to the ceiling, but merely stood looking after his
wife's hastening back with an expression of mingled speculation and joy.

Some minutes later, descending in Dolphim's business-
like wake, Lord Ensley discovered Highet still standing in

the hall. In accents of sheer loathing, "Highet," he muttered, nodding curtly.

Mr. Highet returned the greeting.

A silence set in. Then, while Dolphim went to fetch his
coat and stick, "You poor fool," Ensley suddenly spat out.
"Do you imagine you can make her happy?"

"Have you?" Mr. Highet pleasantly countered.

Dolphim returning, this civil colloquy was perforce cut
unnaturally short. Lord Ensley stalked angrily out to the
street, Mr. Highet floated to his room, and Dolphim hurried down to the kitchen to tell his wife the gladsome
news. Maria (who had heard Anne's message to Ensley)
knocked on her door some minutes later to offer comfort if
comfort was needed. She discovered Anne swallowing lavender drops, a little pale, but showing no other signs of
discomfiture. She invited Maria in, sat her down in a comfortable arm-chair, and said very stiffly indeed,

"You will be relieved to know I have finished things
with Ensley."

"Oh, Anne! I am sure you have done very right! Ensley
was never—"

"Pray do not tell me your opinion of him," Anne broke
in. "I know it already. In truth, I cannot bear just now to
speak of him further. I don't want to. I mean to lie down
now; but will you drive out with me this afternoon? I
should be grateful for your company."

Not for the first time, Mrs. Insel silently deplored the
deep, proud reserve that prevented Anne from opening
her heart when she was hurt and taking real comfort from
her friends. But what was that, compared to the news that
Ensley was out of her life? Her heart strangely light for
one dressed in the deepest mourning, Maria obligingly de-

clared herself ready for any excursion and removed herself from the room.

She had been working some filagree while she waited with Ensley and now returned to the drawing-room to fetch it, intending to take it away and work for an hour in her sitting-room. But she found there Mr. Highet, who sat frowning at a newspaper in a deep chair by a long window. He looked up upon her entrance, his brow clearing, and begged her to stay and talk with him for a moment or two.

Mrs. Insel stayed. Though she had kept very much to herself in the last few days, the news of her husband's death had come to her almost as the breaking of a spell. After the initial shock, she was gradually starting to feel at ease again for the first time almost since her marriage. The change had already begun to show in her spare frame, which seemed less severe and narrow than formerly. Her face too was losing its habitual tension, and her actions their nervousness. The alteration did not escape Mr. Highet's attention. He thought of it now, as he gazed quietly at her for some moments before speaking.

Presently, "I feel as if I have scarcely talked with you since my coming here," he took up, smiling gently. "I hope you are recovering from the effects of the letter I brought?"

"Indeed, very swiftly."

"I am glad to hear it. You know," he went on carefully, "we are sorry to do without you in Cheshire since you left. Mrs. Samuels asked after you the other day, and Mrs. Ross, Farmer Ross' wife, tells me now you were often used to come by and teach her fancy stitching. She wishes you to come back and finish her lessons. Speaking of lessons," he kept a steady watch on her face, "Mr. Mallinger regrets you too, I know."

He paused. Surely her dark eyes had widened a little at the mention of Mallinger? But she said nothing.

"I worry for Mr. Mallinger," he finally went on, still carefully studying her reactions. "He has not been happy in recent months, it seems to me. Yet he will not tell me why."

He paused again, but Maria still kept silent. Her expression clearly showed concern, though, at this report of the schoolmaster. Mr. Highet continued his experiment.

Gloomily, "I am afraid we shall lose him altogether, if things go on at this rate," he declared.

To his satisfaction, Mrs. Insel started and gave a small gasp.

Smiling faintly, "I mean, that he will quit his post," he explained, "not that he will die of melancholy."

She laughed at herself a little and settled back in her chair. Had Mr. Highet merely wished to pass the time of day with her? She had fancied, when he asked her to stay and talk, that he had something particular on his mind. She felt very grateful to him—not only for coming all the way to London to bring her letter, but also for whatever part he had played in extricating Anne from Ensley's grip. So if he did merely wish to chat (for that was all he had done so far—he could not know Mr. Mallinger meant more to her than Mrs. Samuels), she would willingly do so till the sun set.

"Please tell Mrs. Ross I shall be happy to continue teaching her fancy-work when I visit Fevermere," she remarked. "I know she hopes to earn some money by it."

"Ah, you bring me to the reason of my asking you to sit

down," he answered, confirming her early suspicion. "I wonder . . . I know you are only just returned to London, yet I somehow have a notion Mrs. Highet could use another change of scene. I should very much like you both to come to Fevermere for Christmas. We should be obliged to leave soon, I fear. But— Would it be good for her, do you think? I ask you as a friend who knows her much longer and better than I."

Maria considered. She had never believed from the beginning in Mr. Highet's "business proposal." If he did not love Anne, he was very fond of her. Either way, she thought—hoped—he had guessed long ago that she herself would do all she could to help them understand one another—that she held herself a friend not only to Anne, but to both of them together. But could Mr. Highet know already of Anne's break with Ensley? They had been out together this morning. He might have heard her instructions to Dolphim. If so, Maria thought his desire to remove her from London very shrewd. "I am sure it would be," she told him finally. "And if you put it to her as you have to me—as something that would please you—I imagine she will go very readily."

"Oh," he objected, "but I am particularly reluctant to urge her on such grounds. However, if I only suggest it, may I depend upon you to say you favour the idea? That is . . . Will you like to come?"

"Oh! If it is for Anne's sake," Maria replied, as he expected she would. "Only you know, it is no longer at all necessary that I accompany her. Why, you are married! And I shall shortly be receiving a pension." Shyly, she went on, "I have been thinking it is time for me to find a lodging somewhere on my own."

"And Mrs. Ross?" he asked humorously; then more soberly, "No, no, this will not answer. Mrs. Highet will never leave you to spend Christmas alone."

A little reluctantly, Maria admitted the justice of this. "If she asks me, I shall strongly endorse the idea," she promised at last.

Mr. Highet thanked her, silently congratulated himself on a job of work well done, and closed the interview. He had only one more fence to jump and he decided a headlong assault upon it would be best. He gave his wife the day to rest and recreate herself, then, just before dinner, sent a note up to her room requesting ten minutes alone with her.

She met him in the library, a smallish room (it was the single fault she had to find with the house) whose shelves would never accommodate more than half her books. At the moment, even those shelves were empty: She had been concentrating on other rooms and meant to make this her project during the coming week. But its very unreadiness made it private and therefore convenient for this meeting.

She came downstairs in a round dress of jaconet muslin with a dark blue *gros de Naples* spencer. To her surprise, Mr. Highet was not dressed to go out, but showed every sign of intending to dine in Mount Street that evening.

"And Lord Alvanley?" she quizzed him, sitting down upon a small settee. "Is he to ask for Mr. Highet's company in vain?"

Mr. Highet solemnly bowed, then joined her on the settee. "Lord Alvanley has hobbled along in life so far now without me that I rather suspect he can dispense with me altogether," he said drily. "If it does not too much discompose you, I should prefer to dine with you. I am the more eager to do so," he added, "as I expect to depart for Cheshire the day after to-morrow."

If the genuine disappointment he saw in her face gratified him, he did not manifest his pleasure in any way. On the contrary, he wore his most sombre look while she replied,

"Must you go indeed? It seems as if you have only just come. I thought you were rather enjoying London!"

Seriously, "More than I ever have before," he said. "Still, I should be very sorry to pass Christmas here, apart from my people. You will excuse me if I say that London seems to me a very sad place to spend the holydays."

A little ruffled (for she still felt he laid all the failings of the Metropolis at her door) she answered, "I suppose it depends upon what one has been used to. I myself have passed several Christmases in town without, I think, suffering any ill effects. Nothing fatal, anyhow. Yet I will agree with you so far as to say that a country Christmas has much to offer. Indeed, Maria and I had thought to join a party at Lord Bambrick's seat, in Devonshire. However"— she did not falter, but her tone was considerably sharper as she finished—"there are others in the party I particularly wish to avoid."

"But then—this suits my purpose admirably," Mr. Highet rejoined, "for I wished to suggest to you that it might greatly benefit Mrs. Insel, in this time of her bereavement, to pass Christmas at Fevermere." With a hint of something she could only call slyness in his tone, he went on, "I have the oddest idea a visit there is just what would suit her. Don't ask me to explain it"—here he gave her a look that was positively arch! Mr. Highet!—"I just fancy that it would. What do you think?"

Could he have learned Mr. Mallinger's secret? She dimly remembered him to have said something odd about the schoolmaster's spirits on the night of her dinner party—only she had been so distracted by Ensley and Juliana that she hardly heard it. It was possible, of course, that Mallinger himself had confided in him. Anne longed to ask, but felt she could not without betraying Maria. At all events, the notion of taking her up to Cheshire was an excellent one. After a moment she said so.

"Then it is decided," he answered, standing. "You will come with me. That is— Will *you* mind coming? We shan't have much of a house party, though my brother and his family will be there, and a few old friends."

Embarrassed by the degree to which the prospect actually relieved her—for how on earth would she and Maria spend Christmas, if not with Ensley and their friends?— she replied carelessly, "Oh, since it is for Maria's sake, I am happy to do it." Hearing the ungraciousness of this, she added with downcast eyes and an awkwardness as unusual in her as Mr. Highet's slyness had been in him, "That is, I shall like it very much. Only— You will not mind it yourself?"

"You know when you left I told you I should always be happy to see you back. I believe I mentioned Christmas particularly." He spoke gently, standing before her while she still sat. When she looked up to thank him he seemed quite to tower over her. She saw a sort of mildness in his sleepy-lidded eyes, and a softness in his features which at first she took for affection. But then he added, more gently than ever, "Perhaps the change of air will do you good as well," and she thought:

"He pities me! Again! He knows I have lost Ensley and feels sorry for me." More miserable than angry, she jumped abruptly to her feet and said indifferently, "Perhaps. At all events, I have a great deal to do if we are to leave with you. For one thing, I must persuade Maria." She moved past him briskly, turned to give a cool bow, noted they would dine at eight, and (before he could say anything) quitted the room.

"*What* a pleasure, *what* a surprise!" After she had quite done encasing her son in her prodigious embrace, Mrs. Archibald Highet turned to her daughter-in-law. Her strong nose and wrinkled cheeks pink with cold—for she had come out of the house to meet the carriage—she shook Anne's hand heartily, booming, "Here for Christmas, quite as if you was really family! Such a treat—! Step inside!"

She hurried the little party out of the chilly darkness (they had arrived an hour or two past sundown) and up to the great oaken doors, where Trigg—a stout, amiable man, with a face as round and red as a radish, who had served as butler at Fevermere more than a dozen years—bobbed energetically to the ladies, and beamed to see the master safe at home. Mrs. Highet the elder waited impatiently while solicitous inquiries were made all round as to the respective healths of the travellers, the estimable Mrs. Trigg (plagued, alas, by rheumatism), and Trigg himself, and while the last-named collected the coats and hats of the first. When finally all this had been accomplished, Mrs. Archibald dropped an heavy paw round Maria's shoulders and, leading the party into the wide front hall, trumpeted, "Now Mrs. Insel, I'll wager I owe this visit to you. When Henry wrote that you were all coming, I said to myself at once, it's that sweet Mrs. Insel contrived it, thinking we would be lonely up here. But we'd have been snug enough! When we don't go to Staffordshire, Staffordshire comes to us. You had no need to do it." She gave Maria's arm a playfully reproving squeeze and, ushering them all through the front hall, concluded, "Still, all's well that ends well, isn't it? I'll have tea sent up to your rooms, shall I? And your dinner sent up there too?" With more urgency than tact, she instructed a footman to carry the ladies' baggage to their wing, at the same time physically prodding Maria in that direction.

Anne looked uncertainly to her husband. Despite the inauspicious scene in the little library, the three of them had had quite a merry journey together. They had sung Christmas carols till their harmonies were perfect, set one another conundrums, dozed companionably or sat in a friendly silence. On the first of the two nights they had passed on the road they had all been tired and gone quickly to bed. But on the second, only Maria went upstairs early: Anne and Mr. Highet sat up quite late, alone in a private dining-room, arguing over a bottle of wine about Mr. Knight's project to reclaim the forest at Exmoor. What pleasant company he had proved! And— particularly over the wine and the flickering, smoky candles—how very well-looking he was. He was not the best-informed man she had ever argued with, nor the most acute. But he held his own. What was it Celia had said, that one would not wish to live with Lord High Fol-de-rol any how? And Celia had thought . . . But no. Anne kept a careful eye on Mr. Highet throughout the journey. Though it was true she often found his warm gaze fixed on her—even, perhaps, admiringly—what else had he to look at? As to the warmth, surely he also looked so on Maria? In truth, he was simply a warm, affectionate man. Consider, for example, how much trouble he was taking for Maria's sake. She must not misinterpret these elements of his nature as particular signs of his regard for her. Though he did respect her. He had said so when he offered for her. And like her, she rather thought. But—

Her mind ran restlessly over and over what little she knew of his feelings for her. For—and this was the more true the farther they came from London—she was increasingly aware of how very much she liked him. Perhaps it was only loneliness since letting go of Ensley (this was the first time in ten years she had quitted town without informing him). But she did not think so. The more she considered it, the more she believed there were plenty of reasons to like Mr. Highet for his own sake. He was generous (witness his aid to her when she first came to Linfield), kind (his coming to London with Maria's letter), scrupulous (his conduct towards her since they married), and even—after his own fashion—intelligent and humorous. Besides all that, she began to remember (and indeed, once or twice in the coach as he brushed her by chance, to experience again) the odd sensations his presence, his touch had produced in her early on. Why, he was handsome! In the rocking carriage she had watched him sleeping across from her and felt a distinct attraction to him, open mouth and all.

With all this in her thoughts, she was more conscious than ever of the humiliating possibility that his principal feeling towards her now was pity. She had felt, as they approached Fevermere, almost as if she were coming home. But it was not in her to insist on dining at the family table when Mrs. Highet so plainly suggested she ought to remove to her rooms. So she hesitated, and was profoundly relieved when Mr. Highet placed a hand on his mother's arm and said coaxingly to herself and Maria,

"Surely old travelling companions must not be parted so soon? Refresh yourselves a little and come dine with us."

Politely, after a glance at Anne, "If it will not disturb Mrs. Highet—" Maria answered.

With all eyes upon her, "Bless you, my dear!" Mrs. Archibald trumpeted. "I should be delighted, delighted! I only thought you might be tired, that's all. That's the all and end of it," she added, laughing as if she had made a very good joke. "Four for dinner! Off I go to tell Cook. Now you scamper up and wash the dust off you, my chickens, and—" She turned, arm outstretched. "Henry, dear, would you come with me?"

Mrs. Highet's elder son arrived at Fevermere with his wife and their extremely considerable brood about three the next afternoon. Acquaintance with them gave Anne a much clearer idea why Mrs. Archibald had fled into Cheshire with her younger son, for Mrs. Thaddeus Highet was as managing a female as Anne had ever laid eyes on. Not that she wondered at it—with seven children, six of them boys, she supposed one would be obliged to be managing—but the household at Foxleigh (this was the name of the Highets' estate in Staffordshire) could not have been comfortable for the old lady.

Anne herself got on with Selina well enough: Conversation with her was chiefly a matter of nodding and smiling while Selina interrupted herself to call to one child or another—as for example, "My dear Anne—I hope I may call you— Excuse me! William, put Charles down at once and come to me! —may call you Anne, since we are really sisters— Oh, pardon me! Arthur, I told you to leave that infernal noise-making thingummy at home, and now how does it come to be here? Put it away at once! Give it to Nurse, if you can't leave it alone. —What was I saying? Oh yes, we are sisters, really! But I started to say, I am so terribly sorry I have been unable to do more than— Charles! At your age! I expect a big boy like you to have better sense than to dangle out a window like that. Come down this moment! I am so sorry, Anne, it is really their father's fault. He will wind them up so, with his jokes and his teasing, and then of course he goes off where it's quiet and leaves them to me. But as I was saying, I feel absolutely ashamed we have not met sooner. That is my fault, I admit, for— Stay here, Anne!" She jumped up suddenly and ran to the other end of the room exclaiming continuously, "Oh dear dear dear dear dear!" till she reached the window and snatched the persistent Charles from the jaws of death.

Anne found it easier to converse with her brother-in-law, who had some of Henry's traits, though in many ways they differed. In fact, the two together made an interesting study for her. Equally large as his brother but rougher-featured and (Anne thought) much less hand-some, Thaddeus had a bluff good-humour and heartiness which, though apparent in Henry, were refined in the lat-ter (Anne considered) by his more thoughtful character and an innate gentleness the older man lacked. Thaddeus had inherited his mother's loquacity. He had not what Anne now recognised as his brother's habit of close, quiet

observation: Altogether he was more voluble, more con-
vivial than Henry. He had a natural taste for clowning
which he frequently indulged among his children. In time
Anne came to consider Selina's complaint well-founded,
that her husband "wound the boys up," then left her to
deal with the consequences. Mr. Thaddeus Highet bore
his wife's complaints with cheerful indifference.

Towards herself he showed a degree of polite interest
and friendly curiosity that made it easy for her to talk with
him, and soon to feel she knew him. If any of the
Staffordshire Highets wondered at her living in a different
wing of the house than her husband, none mentioned it to
her. All accepted Maria easily, Thaddeus chaffing her
about her constant work (she was never without a bit of
embroidery or filagree), Selina adroitly putting her to good
use as a sort of auxiliary governess-nurse.

In this last Maria willingly complied. She liked children; and anyhow, being within a few miles of Mr. Mallinger made her anxious to such a degree that any
diversion was welcome. Having arrived on a Saturday evening, the London party had slept late Sunday and forgone
church, so that she had not seen him there. But see him
she would: if not by chance on some earlier occasion, then
on Christmas Eve, when he and Miss Veal and Rand and
some half-dozen others were to come to a family supper.
The very idea of it made her tremble and gather her grey
shawl more closely about her. She had at first wanted to
excuse herself from all such festivities on the grounds of
her mourning; but to do this, Mr. Highet had pointed out,
would be to have the whole story of her earlier deception
out. This being so, Maria could only thank him for making her realize it, and think to herself what a very good
friend Mr. Highet was.

In light of the fact that it was Maria's welfare which had brought Anne into Cheshire again, by the way, it was remarkable how little attention she paid to that lady. Mrs. Archibald Highet having happened to mention that Mr. Mallinger was expected to join them on Christmas Eve, Anne vaguely considered that the matter would thenceforward take care of itself—that Mr. Mallinger, given the opportunity to renew his acquaintance with Mrs. Insel, would somehow also renew his suit, and this time succeed in it. The real subject of her reflections in these days was Mr. Highet. How patiently he played with the children! Amazed, she watched him crouch down and submit to be blindfolded in the centre of the room, then tapped and teased in a game of Hot Cockles. He pretended to wonder where on earth that slipper could have got to while the children passed it round and round, every moment giving away its position by their squeals and chortles. The Highet brood had been joined on Monday by three girls belonging to a couple named Framouth who (Mr. Framouth having been at Oxford with Thaddeus Highet) had come to swell the Christmas party. Accustomed to houses in which the nursery held children in an exile sterner than Bonaparte's, Anne looked on in astonished horror as Fevermere fell under the thrall of a pack of screeching urchins. But when she herself was asked to join a game of Forfeits and (under stringent urging from Mr. Highet himself) consented, she soon found herself pointing and laughing every bit as loud as the children, and even submitted to stand up and sing "Mary Had a Little Lamb" to win back her reticule.

She was aided in this undignified performance not only by the example of Mr. Highet (who had had to hop up and down while whistling "Hot Cross Buns" in order to regain his watch fob) but by his obvious delight in her participation. A dozen times she caught his eyes warmly fastened upon her, a smile in them and on his generous lips, while she thought up forfeits and challenges for the children. Under such a friendly gaze, she could not but unbend and enjoy herself—though she wondered now and then what clever Miss Anne Guilfoyle would have thought (a year ago) of the giggling lady now rolling upon Mrs. Highet's drawing-room floor. But she shrugged such questions off, taught the children how to play Backgammon and Speculation, and was soon as much a favourite with the Framouth girls and little Augusta Highet as their Uncle Henry was with the boys.

In the evening the older children were permitted to sit up and dine with the adults. The Wares came to dinner also, and Mrs. Ware's brother (who had indeed been glad to take Linfield and was living there very comfortably) with his older offspring, so that they sat down quite twenty to table. Afterwards, Miss Ware proposed dancing. So much acclaim greeted this suggestion that the carpet was promptly rolled back and all the music in the house that might serve eagerly ferreted out. Miss Sophia Ware, most conveniently, played proficiently but was too bashful to care to dance. She willingly seated herself at the pianoforte at nine and never rose till past eleven. Anne danced a quadrille with George Highet (the favourite nephew of his uncle), a minuet with Thaddeus Highet, a country-dance with Mr. Ware, and a rather wild gigue with his son. But her most memorable turns upon the floor were a pair of waltzes she danced with her husband, who proved to possess a surprisingly light and elegant foot for a man so large. After the first, Selina Highet took her aside and (emboldened by the punch? inspired by the figure Anne and Henry had cut upon the dance floor?) asked "if by any chance the Henry Highets expected a happy event?"

Anne's immediate instinct was to glance down, alarmed lest her slender waist should have thickened without her noticing it. But,

"Oh, no, my dear!" murmured Selina, laughing. "You are as slim as a girl, I'm sure! I only wondered." And she gave Anne a rather coy glance from behind her fan—a glance which seemed to say, "You and I know every woman longs for a baby! Come, tell me!"

Anne shook her head, looking down again. Though her natural reserve disliked the forwardness of the question, it did touch upon a matter which had been on her mind in the last day or two. It was a strange thing, but she could no longer remember how she had come to be so sure she did not wish to have children. Perhaps she had only caught the Nursery Madness which seemed to hold Fevermere in its grip; perhaps it had more to do with seeing how delightedly Mr. Highet received his nephews; in any case, she found herself nearer to liking the idea than she had ever been before. And she was not so very old! She had turned nine-and-twenty in September; but many women bore children long after that. Still looking away, "No," she answered Selina, in a tone which did not invite her to ask again. But her eyes sought out Mr. Highet a moment later and she coloured consciously when, seeming to feel her gaze, he looked round at her.

The second waltz ended the evening. Mr. Highet presented himself to claim it from Anne with a humorously deep bow, grandly swept her onto the floor, clasped her lightly in his arms, and whirled her so relentlessly that she felt quite giddy. She kept her eyes on him to ward off even a worse vertigo, and all the time they turned she felt his warm hand on her waist, and thought of Selina's question.

Then it was over. A light snow, the first of the year, was found to have fallen while they were at dinner. The wheels of the visitors' departing carriages pressed a delicate lattice into it as they went. With the informality of the season, the house party crowded at the open hall door to wave them off. Anne walked out a moment with Henry and young Arthur Highet, to taste the crispness of the air and marvel at the thin white layer on the branches of the trees and every twig of every bush. Then, shivering, all went in, and climbed to their several beds.

FOURTEEN

M<small>R</small>. M<small>ALLINGER'S</small> <small>HEART</small> <small>THUMPED</small>. T<small>HE</small> <small>BLOOD</small> roared in his ears so loudly he could hardly hear what Trigg was saying to him. From his expression, he guessed the man had wished him a happy Christmas; from his gesture, he supposed he was waiting for his coat. Accordingly, he wished Trigg a happy Christmas in return and surrendered the desired garment. Yet the man still stood, pointing, pointing, and saying something about a hat. Ah, his hat! Mr. Mallinger plucked it off, shook from its brim a fair dusting of the snow which had been falling since noon, and walked inside towards the drawing-room.

It seemed a long walk. Every step brought him closer to Mrs. Insel (whose arrival he had known of even before it happened, for the second parlour-maid at Fevermere had told the boy from the dairy, who had mentioned it to the girl who tidied up the schoolhouse). In the last two months he had almost stopped hoping such a day would ever come again. Yet here it was! Nor could he blame himself for going where he knew he was sure to meet her: On the contrary, he had most earnestly endeavoured to refuse Mr. Highet's invitation to Christmas supper. But all in vain. Mr. Highet had been adamant. When friendly urging had failed, indeed, Highet had straitly adjured him to come, even going so far as to hint the security of his position as schoolmaster rested upon it! What then could Mr. Mallinger do but bow to fate? Now his only fear was that, hearing he was expected, Mrs. Insel had elected to absent herself from the evening.

A moment, another moment would tell him. Behind that door, amid that hum of voices, did he hear hers? He sent a quick prayer to heaven. Though she had told him not to hope, though to see her and not to have her might be exquisite torment, how he longed for that torment! Screwing up such courage as the long anxiety of the past two days had left to him, he entered the room.

She was there! His little dove, all in dove grey and— could it be?—rather more rosy and round than when he had last set eyes on her. Had her weeks in London suited her, then, so well? A stab of pain that it should be so— that a separation which had stripped his life of all interest, all happiness, should have calmed and nourished her— shot through him. But he must make his bows to the company, thank his hosts, meet the Framouths, renew his acquaintance with the Staffordshire family, pay his courtesies to Miss Veal, say hello to Rand (for this family supper was the one night in the year at Fevermere when man and master sat together). At last it came time to face

Mrs. Insel. Mr. Highet led—one would almost have said pulled—him to the corner of the room where she sat, quiet and demure, upon a little sofa.

"You know Mrs. Insel," was all Highet said, with a jovial flourish of the hand.

Mr. Mallinger bowed deeply as the rest of the room seemed to fade. There was only himself and—oh, fetching, taking little thing! Instantly he forgave her her healthy bloom. How could he begrudge it when it suited her so well? "Madam," he said, rising from his bow to search her face in a quick glance. Was she angry at him for coming?

No!

Sorry to see him?

No again!

Half incredulous, Mr. Mallinger read on her sweet countenance nothing but shy pleasure in his presence. True, she did not beg him to sit down beside her. Though she asked (with what divine timidity!) how he did, she did not set any of an hundred questions which must have kept him there talking to her. But she smiled upon him! Smiled.

Mr. Mallinger was ecstatic.

The reader will perhaps be content to leave him in ecstasy for a little while—goodness knows he has been there infrequently enough of late, and he is quite safe there so long as such a numerous party surrounds him—and turn his attention to how the others passed Christmas Eve. They sat down about nine o'clock to a long table decorated with holly and drank deeply from a steaming bowl of wassail replenished, as needed, by a footman who between times took his place at the board. Mrs. Highet the eldest led the company in a rousing chorus of "Deck the

Halls"; Anne, Mr. Highet, and Maria performed their practised versions of "The First Nowell" and "Good Christian Men, Rejoice"; young William Highet, who professed to know all the verses to "The Twelve Days of Christmas," shepherded the others through that complicated carol with the liberal assistance and correction of Miss Veal; and Augusta Highet, at the tender age of six, sang "God Rest You Merry, Gentlemen" all by herself. About ten they were interrupted by a troupe of mummers from Faulding Chase, who enacted the story of St. George and the Turkish Knight most ably, and afterwards ate goose and mince-pie with equal competency. These departing, the children engaged in a game of blindman's-buff, dragging their Uncle Henry and their willing father into it. Then all played snap-dragon, Arthur Highet contriving to singe not only his fingers but his tongue with his quick and fearless style. Mr. Rand told a ghost story perfectly likely to deprive a boy of fifteen of a week's sleep, let alone a girl of six. While Augusta ran shrieking to her mother's arms, her father suddenly noticed a bough of mistletoe which had mysteriously got fastened up to the ceiling before the fireplace (where, of course, a vast yule log blazed merrily).

This mistletoe perhaps reminds some readers that we left Mr. Mallinger, some hours ago, in a state of ecstasy. But other readers, I think, will readily agree that no smile, no dove-like sweetness displayed by Mrs. Insel to the schoolmaster, could sufficiently embolden him—I might say madden him—to make him attempt to kiss her. No, the most that can be said of Mr. Mallinger and the mistletoe, is that he gave Mrs. Insel (who unluckily had been seated—by Mrs. Archibald Highet—at the other end of the table from him) a hasty, embarrassed glance when its presence was first pointed out, and intercepted just such a hasty glance from Mrs. Insel.

But in view of the history of these two, such a glance is perhaps a great deal!

Maria and Mr. Mallinger aside, however, the mistletoe caused plenty of havoc. Mr. Rand seized and roughly kissed Anne's abigail, Lizzie; Mr. Thaddeus Highet jocosely bussed a stunned Miss Veal; Masters Arthur and George Highet kissed Evaline Framouth, and tickled but refused to kiss their sister Augusta; after which Anne found herself being dragged by these same hooligans to the magic spot, her husband at the same time under forcible conveyance there by Masters Tad, William, and Charles.

"A kiss, a kiss!" the cry went up, as the new-married couple found themselves under the cursed sprig. Anne went crimson. Her husband, clumsy with embarrassment, stood foolishly still for a moment, as if dazed, then bent and chastely saluted her on the cheek.

"A proper kiss, a proper kiss!" the audience (nephews chief among them) roared, quite unsatisfied by this feeble performance. Masters Arthur and George made a human ring around Anne, preventing her from running away, while Master William positively shoved his uncle at her. The ring broke away, Henry received a second, mighty push, and amid general pandemonium his arms went round her and his mouth (somehow, for Anne doubted very much he intended it, or could have steered himself right even if he had) met hers. A dizzy moment and it was over. Exploding with laughter, the boys went back to the table to fetch their parents and repeat the performance.

Three shades of scarlet, Anne stumbled back to her place and hid her face in a napkin. But when some min-

utes later a boar's head duly decked with bays and rose-
mary was brought in, and a new bowl of wassail, and a
huge shoulder of venison, Anne looked up and caught her
husband's eye with a smile in her own, and only a little
embarrassment.

They sat till midnight, when the bells of the church,
clear over the snowy fields, tolled to tell them it was
Christmas Day. Then each man kisssed his neighbour, or
shook his hand, and a vast tray of plum-pudding was
brought out. The thimble was found first, appearing (ap-
propriately and, we hope, painlessly) in the portion given
to Miss Veal, then the button in the pudding of Master
Arthur (who loudly celebrated this omen that he need
never marry) and finally the wedding ring by Mrs. Insel.
(The reader will perhaps accuse the author of planting it
there, a clumsy and worn device; in which case the author
begs the reader please to direct his attention to the curiously smug look on the face of Mr. Henry Highet, who
served the pudding out. The defence rests.) If Mr. Mallinger lacked the courage, or vulgarity, to attempt to kiss
Mrs. Insel under the mistletoe, Mrs. Insel was equally be-
reft of the fortitude, or coarseness, a look at Mr. Mallinger
upon finding the ring would have required. She merely
noted its discovery very quietly to her neighbour—who
happened to be Augusta Highet—and gave it to her to
wear. It was Miss Augusta, of course, who made its appearance generally known. Hearing of it, Mr. Mallinger
felt the lure of superstition for perhaps the first time in his
life.

He quitted Fevermere just before one and made the
long walk across the quiet fields to his rooms behind the
schoolhouse with a lighter heart than had been in his
breast in many days. Whether Mrs. Insel's smiling face

had been only an island of Christmas amnesty in a cold sea of exile; or whether her smile invited him back to friendship, but still denied him love; nevertheless she had smiled—and, moreover, would see him again in church on the morrow, and perhaps smile again. For the moment, he was content with this. Content? Euphoric.

The party at Fevermere marked Christmas Day with a very large breakfast (from which Mrs. Henry Highet, predictably and wisely, absented herself), a visit to church (where the Reverend Septimus Samuels preached his annual sermon on "The M in Miracle"—Mary, Mercy, Motherhood and so on), and a long afternoon of skating on a small pond near the old border between Fevermere and Linfield. The children skated vigorously, Selina and Mrs. Framouth decorously, the gentlemen with that undertone of competition that so often plagues the masculine component of even a small assembly. Maria cried off, but Anne (who could not remember to have stood on skates since before her father died) gamely allowed herself to be persuaded—mostly by George Highet—to try them again. Leaning heavily on her husband's willing arm, she first tottered, then crept, then glided across the ice. At last, proud veteran of two or three successful circuits, she declared herself ready to skate alone.

"You are certain?"

Cheeks flushed with cold and exertion, eyes bright and a little watery in the December wind, "Indeed," she impatiently replied.

Still Mr. Highet lingered, holding his wife's gloved hand against his steadying arm, and regarding her booted ankles dubiously. "Perhaps one more turn—?"

At the same moment, "Mr. Highet, I am perfectly capable—" she began, wrenching her hand out from under his with a twitch of irritation. She turned smartly, set off gliding away from him on her right foot, tried to bring the left foot up for its turn, but instead caught her toe in the ice and promptly tumbled down, landing with a thud.

"Dear ma'am!" Mr. Highet was beside her in an instant, hovering over her, offering his hand. But she had buried her head in her arms. Her back shook under her fur-trimmed mantle, and a series of little choking sounds came from her. "Mrs. Highet?" he nervously inquired, while one by one the other skaters observed her situation and turned to look. Mr. Highet leaned down farther and gently touched her trembling back. "My dear?"

At last she looked up. One glance at his solemn, anxious face and she exploded into whoops. "I am not crying, sir!" she laughed up at him. She sat on the ice and laughed till she did cry, till Mr. Highet laughed with her, then Masters Arthur and George, then everyone. She never stopped till, a small, sharp noise causing her abruptly to look down, "Oh, dear heavens!" she shrieked, and attempted to scramble to her feet. "Mr. Highet!" She stretched an arm out to him, suddenly urgent—for the ice beneath her had begun to crack and a tiny rivulet of frigid water had seeped to the surface and soaked through her glove. For the next minute she seemed all knees and elbows, flashing blades, flying ermine, and awkwardly flailing limbs. Mr. Highet endeavoured to pull her up, but she could not keep her balance. She fell once more, causing another ominous crack. Then,

"Stay still!" Mr. Highet commanded her, for fear her flapping and scrambling would sink her altogether. "Remove your skates," he bade her, while he lay down full length upon the ice and stretched an arm to her. By dint of these simple shifts, he soon succeeded in removing her to safety—where, if he had hoped to receive her heartfelt gratitude for having rescued her, he must have been deeply disappointed; for she only broke (once she had recovered her breath) into howls of laughter again, not merely at the thought of his solemn countenance when she fell, but also, helplessly, at the idea of her own ridiculous performance.

Boxing Day came and went, and with it the Framouths. The holly hung so gaily on Christmas Eve soon began to dry and turn brown, and had to be taken down. But for the nightly appearance of a plum-pudding at the table (one of these was traditionally eaten at Fevermere each night between Christmas Eve and Twelfth Night, for luck in the next twelve months) the festiveness of the season might almost have been forgot. On the third day after Christmas the Staffordshire Highets left for home. Anne saw them go with some regret, for besides having got to like the children, their departure reminded her she and Maria ought perhaps to be leaving also.

Only . . . So little had passed, as yet, between Maria and Mr. Mallinger. Distracted as she was by her own concerns, Anne had not failed to observe the former's smiling behaviour towards the latter on Christmas Eve. Indeed, if Maria had been too refined to glance at the schoolmaster when she found the ring in the pudding, Anne had not. She had been gratified to see in his face a start of suppressed excitement. But at church the next day, he and Mrs. Insel had both seemed conscious and awkward. After the service, when all around them were shaking hands or kissing, Anne had watched the two merely bow to each other. She saw from their faces that neither (silly babies!) had the courage to do anything else. Still, short of going to Mr. Mallinger and telling him to be bold, Anne could not think how to help the two of them out of their mutual embarrassment. She tried inviting Mr. Mallinger to tea one day shortly after Christmas, and the effort was mildly successful—he came, he drank tea in the same room as Maria, he was civil to every one—but they parted as distantly as ever, so that Anne thought at this rate they would need till Midsummer Day to clear up matters between them. And she could not stay in Cheshire until Midsummer Day. Aside from everything else, how would it look to Mr. Highet?

She was rather surprised, late on the evening of the twenty-ninth, when Maria peeped into her sitting-room and announced her intention of travelling to Northwich alone on the following day. "I shan't be long," she went on. "The coach passes through Faulding Chase early in the morning and returns me there before five. Well, good night, dear. I only wished to let you know."

"But why are you going?" asked Anne, sitting up. She had been stretched out rather luxuriously on a chaise-longue reading Pope.

Airily, "Oh, merely a little business," Maria told her, and again started to close the door.

"Come in here properly," Anne instructed, straightening fully and setting her book down on a small cherrywood table. "What business have you, little sparrow?" she demanded suspiciously.

Maria darkened and waved a vague hand. "Some affairs to do with the Army," she feebly murmured. Reluctantly, she edged in from the doorway, still leaving the door ajar behind her.

"Indeed? I shall go with you," Anne declared.

"No, no! That is— You would not like it. I shall need

to wake up at seven to be ready. That would not suit you."

"Hm. That's true enough. But what is this talk of 'business'? You are not looking at lodgings to let, I hope? Northwich would be much too far away."

Maria raised her right hand. "I swear I will never take lodgings in Northwich," she said.

"Solemnly?"

"Very solemnly."

Anne considered. "Well then," she replied, relenting, "if you really feel you must go . . ."

"I do."

"Then be off with you. But mind you be careful. And—what do you mean by travelling alone? Take Lizzie with you, at least."

Mrs. Insel laughed. "I am hardly 'travelling'!" she exclaimed, smiling. "Only to Northwich and home." She backed out of the door, still smiling. "Next you will send a footman with me when I drive over to see Mrs. Ross. Good night." Gently and firmly she shut the door.

Early the next morning—not quite so early as she had led Anne to believe, but still early—Mr. Highet drove Mrs. Insel to Faulding Chase and handed her into a coach standing before the Red Lion.

"You are quite sure you don't mind going?" he asked her scrupulously, for perhaps the fourth time.

"Not at all," said Mrs. Insel, who would have been very happy (in view of his kindness to her) to undertake any thing Mr. Highet wanted, but was particularly so since he had asked her to carry out such a cheerful mission as this.

"Never mind about the cost," he told her.

"I understand."

"Anything you think— Well, you know," he finished; and this was certainly true, since he had given her his instructions some half-dozen times already.

Maria smiled and suggested he go home, since the coach would not leave for some twenty minutes and he could be of no use to her here.

"If you don't mind," he answered with unexpected alacrity, "I believe I will. One of my cows . . ."

He did not complete the sentence but rather, apologetically but hastily, backed away and climbed up into his curricle, thanking her all the while and wishing her luck. His uncharacteristic abruptness startled Maria. It made her wonder whether the drive into Faulding Chase had inconvenienced him after all, though he had sworn it would not. She speculated idly upon this mildly interesting idea, and others, for some minutes, while she was joined in the coach by a man she believed to be Lord Crombie's estate steward, and while the wife of one of Mr. Highet's farmers climbed up to ride on the roof. But she quite forgot the matter a few moments later, for a blond head and a pair of thin shoulders thrust themselves into the coach. The last passenger had appeared to claim his seat.

That passenger was Mr. Mallinger.

Like a trapped hare, Maria shrank back as far as the worn squabs of the carriage would allow. What must be Mr. Mallinger's opinion of a woman who first forbade him to come near her, then showered smiles upon him? This was the question that made her long to disappear, to bolt from the carriage through the opposite door, or sink through the floorboards. The schoolmaster too checked the instant he caught sight of her, and was (she thought) on the point of withdrawing when the stout coachman came suddenly up behind him to collect his shillings and sent Mr. Mallinger tumbling to the seat opposite her own. The coins produced, the man noisily shut the doors. An instant later the carriage swayed as the man sprang to his box; a moment more and they were on their way.

The late arrival nodded tremblingly to the gentleman seated next him, wished him a good morning, and asked how my Lord Crombie did. He was wished a civil good morning in his turn and informed that his lordship did pretty well before he had the courage to look again at Mrs. Insel. When he did, it would be hard to imagine a more nerve-ridden good morning than the one he received for his pains. Chagrined even in his extremity at the thought that he—he!—should cause her uneasinesss, he returned an equally shaken salutation and waited many minutes before he dared ask what her destination was today.

"Northwich," she replied, greatly relieved to be asked, for it meant she could inquire in her turn, "And you, sir?"

"Northwich also," said he, and went a little pale.

This paltry interchange—barely a conversation at all, by most standards—was all these two well-educated people could manage before the coach stopped in Tedding Minor. Here, to their several horrors, Lord Crombie's steward Mr. Booth made his adieux and descended. This unlucky turn of events was followed by one even more appalling: No one else got in. Maria, realizing this, was on the point of suggesting they invite the farmer's wife on the roof to join them inside when the coach again lurched forward and it was too late.

Alone in a coach with Mr. Mallinger! What must she do? Northwich was two hours off if not more, and there were no other stops before it. Finally,

"Would you like me to rap for the driver, Mrs. Insel?" Mr. Mallinger offered. "I can travel outside, or perhaps even upon the box."

"No, no!" What an idea—Mr. Mallinger out in the cold for her sake!

"It is nothing to me," he pursued. "Indeed, I generally do travel outside. It is only because I am on an errand for Mr. Highet that I have a seat within."

To his surprise, "On an errand for Mr. Highet?" she echoed. "How curious. I also am on such a commission."

"For Mr. Highet, do you mean?"

"Exactly."

"Goodness me!"

Much struck, both parties sat back in the jolting carriage and contemplated this coincidence in silence some while. Then,

"May I ask—" Mrs. Insel commenced, and stopped. She resumed presently, "Has your errand any thing to do with jewellery, I wonder?"

"Not at all. I am to inspect the books in a certain shop there, with an eye to getting hold of several new ones Mr. Highet hopes to buy."

"Indeed? I wonder— That is, it does seem odd he did not buy them himself, since he was so lately in London. Does not it?"

"Rather odd. And also that he did not mention . . . ." Mr. Mallinger paused musingly before going on, "But I dareswear he did not know exactly which day you would be going?"

"To Northwich, do you mean? On the contrary, he bought my ticket."

"He bought mine!" Mr. Mallinger exclaimed.

"Then it does seem very curious indeed—"

"One would certainly imagine he would have mentioned—"

Neither found it necessary to complete these sentences. Mr. Highet was not a garrulous man, but the circumstance of his having asked two different people to perform two different errands for him on the same day in Northwich, and bought their tickets for the purpose—yet never mentioned to either that the other would be on the coach— certainly had a highly suspicious appearance. Presently,

"I gather from your question that your business does have to do with jewellery?" Mr. Mallinger suggested, then hastened to add, "Of course, if it is confidential—"

"No, not at all. I am sure you can keep a secret from Mrs. Highet. I am to buy her a pair of ear-drops, the nicest pair I see. It is a New Year's gift."

"Indeed? When you say Mrs. Highet, you mean Mrs. Highet—"

"The younger. Anne Highet."

Mr. Mallinger nodded. His intelligent blue eyes, at first barely flickering over her, dared to rest on his beloved longer and longer as this discussion progressed. Now he looked at her quite steadily and asked, "I wonder, then, when he formed this intention? For unless it is of a very recent date, one would have thought that purchase, too, could have been better made in London."

"Yes." Slowly, "To be frank," Maria said, "I thought about that when he asked me. Only—he has been so extremely kind to me, in—in many ways." She hurried on, for though it was easy—so easy—to confide in Mr. Mallinger, he must never know of Mr. Highet's principal act of kindness to her. And yet, what a pleasure it was, how natural, to share with him even these few words. "Had he asked me a much more peculiar favour, I would still not have questioned him," she finished.

"He is a kind man."

"Oh, very! I do think Anne—Mrs. Highet—is so fortunate in her husband."

"Yes, very," Mr. Mallinger agreed, rather wistfully, and fell silent. He had wished—he had hoped—he would gladly have made Mrs. Insel just as fortunate, perhaps . . . He fell into a brown study.

Mrs. Insel meanwhile plunged into a fury of swift, strenuous thought. It was clear to her by now that Mr. Highet had deliberately contrived for her to meet Mr. Mallinger in this coach. Why should he have done this? Because he guessed—who knew how?—an attachment existed between them. Because he knew (she blushed even to think it) John Insel had impeded that attachment—and John Insel was no more. Tacitly, then, Mr. Highet countenanced a *rapprochement* between herself and Mr. Mallinger! Encouraged, even arranged it!

Maria drew a deep breath. If the honourable, admirable Mr. Highet saw no shame in it, surely there was none? And surely (even the modest Mrs. Insel could see this) Mr. Mallinger's wishes had not changed? Yet . . . after all she had said to him, how could she let him know hers had?

She would need to be very bold indeed. Reminding herself her happiness—their happiness—hung in the balance, Mrs. Insel plucked up all her courage (not so inconsiderable, as witness her flight alone from Canada) and squeaked, barely audibly,

"Mr. Mallinger?"

Mr. Mallinger looked up. A painful shyness showed in

the little face opposite to his, and a great effort sounded in her voice as she said, almost unbelievably,

"If you mean to lunch in Northwich . . . That is, I hope to visit the jeweller and conclude my business fairly quickly." "Bold, bold, bold!" Maria reminded herself, swallowing hard. She went on, "Then I shall take a nuncheon at the posting house before coming home. If you care to join me . . ." Her temerity exhausted, she left the sentence as it was and devoted her energies to clenching her hands in her lap.

Scarcely able to credit his ears, "I should be delighted," the schoolmaster answered, his long cheeks going pink with pleasure. "Extremely."

She smiled up at him, then turned at once to stare intently out the window (thinking jubilantly, "I did it!") while Mr. Mallinger studied her chiselled profile and wondered how long he could bear to wait before asking her to marry him again.

As it happened, the answer was about four hours. He soon interrupted her scrutiny of the landscape to initiate some easy conversation. By the time they reached Northwich, relations between the two were so cordial as to be almost what they were before he offered for her the first time. He could hardly bear to part with her long enough to visit the book-seller (and even as it was did such a hasty job there that he returned with a book called *Some Principles of Hydrophobia* instead of the desired *Principles of Hydrostatics*). The moment he could, he returned to the posting house, where he ordered wine and orgeat and an extraordinarily lavish collation to be set out. When Mrs. Insel returned, the two of them applied themselves to it; but with so little real interest and to so little effect that it later furnished the boots and the two upstairs maids with one of the nicest dinners they could remember. After this he admired the chosen ear-drops (the books were tied in a parcel and so could not be examined) and commended her upon her elegant taste.

"Indeed," he went on (they were alone in the coffee-room), "if Mrs. Highet is fortunate in her husband, she is at least so much so in her friend."

Mrs. Insel blushed and looked down.

"But you already know my opinion on that head," he continued, with a heart that beat like the tail of a happy spaniel.

Mrs. Insel glanced up and away in just such a manner as to suggest that, while it was perhaps true that she already knew his opinion, she was not averse to hearing it again.

"To me—" Mr. Mallinger paused and fortified himself with a sip of wine. "To me you far outshine the other members of your gender," he managed to declare.

She did not interrupt him.

"To me—" Another pause, another swallow of the strengthening liquor. "To me, a person who can count you his friend—or hers—is the most fortunate mortal on earth."

Still no interruption! Then it was true, her feelings had changed? Spurring himself with the last ounce in the glass, Mr. Mallinger set out to know for certain.

"Mrs. Insel, some time ago you strictly adjured me . . ." His voice failed. He wet his lips, ran his long fingers through his lank blond hair and began again. "Some months ago you flatly forbade me to think—to visit—to renew—" He floundered and was saved from his helpless sputtering only by her suddenly coming to life (for she had been frozen in an attitude half terrified, half hopeful) with the words, uttered very low,

"Dear sir, I beg you will forget what I said that day." Her pulses pounded, but she reminded herself that if she ever wished to be happy, she must profit by this moment. "You will think me mad, I fear, but at least . . . I had a reason then; and yet . . . Pray believe I was mad then, not now." She relapsed into trembling silence, once more at the end of her courage.

This speech, this unlooked for balm, this—virtual— promise had the effect of driving Mr. Mallinger even further into sputtering confusion. Still, after he had brought forth a certain number of "Then I may hope—?"'s and "Do I understand you to say—?"'s, he did succeed (inelegantly but coherently) in asking her once more for her hand in marriage.

The door opened. The waiter came in. He was a big man, a fair trencherman himself, and he had quite enjoyed taking Mr. Mallinger's generous order. Now, regarding the scarcely touched board with real dismay, "Nothing wrong, sir?" he anxiously inquired of that gentleman. "Ham not too salt, I hope? Nor the beef tough? I had a slice of it myself this morning, sir, and it seemed tender enough to me. But if it don't suit you"—the man's rough countenance gleamed with good will and earnestness—"say so, sir, and I'll be off with it. I'm not one to—"

Mr. Mallinger, in agony, was rude probably for the first time since childhood. Without preamble, in a voice thick with emotion, "Get out," he said, casting a desperate glance at Mrs. Insel, whose expression he could not read. Then, "Please, get out."

"But sir . . ." Puzzled, the man waved an imploring

hand at the laden table and asked, "With the beef, sir, or without it?"

"Out, out!" was all poor Mallinger could say. "I'll give you a shilling! I'll give you a guinea, by God. Only get out now!"

His terms were still ambiguous, but at least his meaning was clear. The waiter took the hint, bowed, and scurried from the room without another word, closing the door discreetly behind him.

Then Mrs. Insel said yes.

FIFTEEN

IT WAS THE CUSTOM OF THE INMATES OF FEVERMERE, and most of the county gentry, to dine on the last day of each year with Lord and Lady Crombie. His lordship, a hospitable man, traditionally set forth upon his table four or five removes, consisting usually of boiled turkeys in celery sauce, roast woodcocks, fricandeau, saddle of mutton, tongue, Hunter's Pudding, carrot pudding, stewed cabbage, fricassee of parsnips, and a great many dishes besides. Burgundy flowed, and champagne both white and rosy. The dessert, naturally, included plum-pudding (of which the party from Fevermere, at least, were beginning to tire a little) as well as all manner of fruits, among them hot buttered oranges and baked pears. It was at this festive repast, just before the ladies withdrew, that Mr. Mallinger (whom the Crombies in their generosity included annually in their invitation to the Highets) and Mrs. Insel announced their betrothal. Only Mrs. Samuels was sorry to hear it—and she but briefly, because she had had a private scheme going to marry the schoolmaster to a protegée of her own. For the rest, cries of genuine pleasure went up all round, and it was thought rather a shame that the two had to separate afterwards—though they would be reunited in an hour, when the gentlemen had had their Port.

Anne, as may be imagined, fairly attacked Maria the moment they gained the drawing-room, kissing her and demanding to be told how it had happened and when. Maria obligingly recounted the story, though omitting many details till they could speak alone—for here quite half a dozen other ladies naturally listened also. It was agreed by all to have been a quite dashing and romantic proposal (inasmuch as it was made in a coffee-room), and further agreed that only a very remarkable coincidence, which many of the ladies thought looked more like Destiny, could account for the pair having both journeyed to Northwich on the same day. Anne, remembering suddenly Maria's recalcitrance when she offered to go with her, caught her alone some few minutes later and demanded to be told whether by any chance she had actually known Mr. Mallinger would be in the coach. But the idea only made Maria blush, and she stammered,

"My dear, no—it was only . . . The coach left so very early!"

Unconvinced (though equally unpersuaded by the idea of the demure Maria deliberately meeting Mr. Mallinger under such circumstances), Anne let the subject drop and returned to the more interesting question of when and where exactly the wedding was to take place.

The party broke up about ten-thirty amid a hail of good wishes for the coming year. The Highets and Maria, driving home through a cold, clear night, heard the muffled churchbell strike eleven as they passed. All stayed awake by a bright fire (in the back sitting-room where Henry had led the ladies on their first night in Cheshire) till the mad peal of bells at midnight rang the new year in. Kisses were exchanged; then Maria announced she was for bed, and quitted the room. Mrs. Archibald Highet, though yawning furiously, disliked—Anne thought—to leave before her daughter-in-law. But presently Henry rose, took his mother by the arm, and led her to the door. Anne, who had thought a little further about Maria's story in the carriage home, and had since then been waiting impatiently to be private with her husband, hesitated only till he had resumed his arm-chair before demanding,

"Sir, did you send Maria and Mr. Mallinger to Northwich on purpose?"

Mr. Highet regarded her speculatively, as if wondering whether he might trust her with a secret. "I did," he finally said.

Anne stared. "And did you do so, then, because you knew they were—" She faltered. Knew they were what? "Because you divined—" Again she failed to frame her question, and relapsed into silence.

"Because I guessed they had a particular attachment for each other?" Mr. Highet asked, his heavy-lidded brown eyes gleaming a little. "Yes. Or at least, I felt if I had guessed wrong, no ill would come of it. Whereas, having guessed right . . ." This time it was he who let his words trail off. He smiled his sleepy smile.

"By heaven, that was 'cute of you!" she exclaimed admiringly. For besides not having been privileged, as she was, to hear the story of Mr. Mallinger's first proposal poured out by Maria, Mr. Highet had not been present at Mallinger's early visits to Linfield. He could scarcely have seen them together half a dozen times. Yet he had seen the truth. And having seen it, taken action. Her admiration swelled.

He gave a modest shrug. His sleepy smile faded slowly.

"You seem unhappy," she suggested tentatively, watching him.

"No. Not precisely unhappy. Only— I have been thinking all night of Herbert Guilfoyle. Every year at this hour for the last dozen years, he and I sat in this room together and drank a bottle of claret. I miss him," he concluded simply; for the first time, Anne understood that her great uncle and Mr. Highet, despite the disparity in their ages, had really been friends. Also for the first time, she regretted not having known the old gentleman herself.

Rather timidly, "If you think I would be an adequate substitute—" she began. "That is, I am sure I am nothing like Mr. Guilfoyle, but if you cared to open a bottle of claret, I should be very happy to share it."

Mr. Highet brightened at once, rang for the bottle, told Trigg (after it came) to go to bed, and said, pouring the first two glasses, "Actually, you are rather like Herbert Guilfoyle." He handed her a glass, raised his to it, and toasted the new year. Sitting down across from her, "You are extremely intelligent, as he was," he went on, "extremely sure you are right—rather stubborn in all things, in fact—and very good at heart. You are both proud, both reclusive—yes, for all your apparent sociability, I would say you are reclusive, in the ways that signify the most," he continued before she could protest. "And, though it may surprise you to hear it of your great uncle, he, like you, had a keen sense of humour. And," he added, smiling, still before she could interrupt, "I like you both very much."

Anne had been going to object to being characterised as stubborn and proud, but she felt tears spring to her eyes when he said this and was silenced. Now, why should this mixed (at best) assessment of her make her cry? Because he knew her! Those drowsy eyes had seen her, that slow mind turned her over and over till it knew her thoroughly. Even Ensley had never understood what Mr. Highet called her reclusiveness; yet how much a part of her it was, how very near the core—and how lonely did she feel this very moment! Only the fact that she had promised to sit up in her great uncle's place prevented her from fleeing upstairs, where at least she could feel alone by herself.

Instead, rallying all her spirit, she tilted her golden head and replied, "I am sure Mr. Guilfoyle returned the sentiment; as do I." She smiled, and drank rather deep. Could she have rendered so precise an account of Mr. Highet's character? She thought not.

The next day, catching Anne alone at her desk, Mr. Highet rather carelessly handed her a small box. "A token of friendship," he explained, while she opened it. "I hope you will accept them."

Anne stared at the ear-drops, intricate twists of gold in which two opals nestled. Quite forgetting the year-end entry she had been making in her diary, "Lovely!" she breathed, glancing up. "Perfectly lovely."

Mr. Highet looked embarrassed. "Oh, a trifle," he muttered. Anne did not recall her having seen him embarrassed before. It seemed unlike him. "Anyhow, if you admire them," he went on, "thank Mrs. Insel. She selected them. That was the little errand I sent her on to Northwich."

"Was it indeed? How clever of you! Naturally, with such a commission, she would not allow me to come." Anne removed the little turquois ear-drops she had on and deftly fastened the new ones in their place. "I might have ruined everything. What do you think?" she asked, shaking her head to make the drops move. She glanced into a long mirror hung above a sofa, smiled, and turned again to face him. "I think they look beautiful. Do not you?"

More and more abashed, "Very nice," he agreed, fidgeting like a boy who wishes to be excused. She noticed his discomfort but could not understand it.

"Thank you so very much," she said, beginning to catch his awkwardness, as one might a fit of yawning. "I feel quite dreadful to have nothing to offer you."

He shook his head vigorously. "Not at all, not at all. Only a friendly token," he repeated. "I am glad you like them. That is enough." He fumbled at his watch pocket, drew out his watch, looked at the back of it, and exclaimed, "Oh, the devil! I must— I quite forgot— Will you excuse me?"

And without waiting to find out whether she would, he was gone.

The next day Parliament resumed. Anne thought of Ensley. He had written to her at Fevermere twice, but she'd returned the letters unopened and no more arrived. Till today she'd feared he would come after her in person; but with Parliament in session this anxiety was at an end.

Indeed, for the moment, she had neither plans nor cares. The days went by, bringing with them their small, quiet satisfactions: a long walk over snowy fields under an unexpectedly warm sun, the discovery on Mr. Highet's shelves of the works of a Russian philosopher she had never heard of, among whose pages she wandered delightedly during several long evenings, the appearance in a kitchen cupboard of one of the dairy cats and seven tiny, mewing kittens. Maria, receiving her first payment from the Army a few days after the New Year, one evening hesitantly asked the rest of the house party if she might keep a room at Fevermere and live there—as a paying lodger, she insisted upon that!—until she married. This plan being accepted (gladly by Mr. Highet, resignedly by his wife, and rather against her will by his mother, who feared Encroachments), Maria had only to set the date of that happy occasion to have her future settled.

"And what date will that be?" asked Mrs. Archibald at the conclusion of these deliberations, with a smile not entirely convincing. "Soon, I think?" Slyly, she wagged a long finger and ducked her large head in a gesture intended to be arch. "I know what love is, though you might not think it of an old lady. You'll never sleep a peaceful night till those vows are said. Never delay a wedding, my dear! Ask Anne! She knows. It only gives them time to change their minds."

But Maria merely looked uncomfortable and said that indeed, she and Mr. Mallinger had not yet fixed a day. Her discomfiture was so obvious that (Mrs. Archibald being suddenly taken with the head-ache, and for once climbing up to bed ahead of the others) Anne reverted to the topic the moment the three of them were alone.

Her small face clouding over again at once, "I am afraid that is the subject of some little controversy," Maria answered. "Mr. Mallinger—" In spite of her troubled look, she could not help but smile a little on saying his name— "Mr. Mallinger presses me to set an early date. But I do not feel . . . I simply cannot marry so soon after John's actual death. I have told him I wish to wait till November, which will make a proper year. But he does not understand why. I am afraid he is rather hurt. He thinks I am uncertain of my attachment to him." She made a helpless gesture with her hands. "I cannot blame him. After all, what else should he think?"

"Good gracious," Anne exclaimed, "must you really wait a whole year? You've been in virtual mourning for that scoundrel more than three already. Does that count for nothing with you? What a high stickler she is!" And she looked for confirmation to Mr. Highet.

But Mr. Highet raised one heavy eyebrow and remarked, "No, to be truthful, I understand Mrs. Insel's scruples. They are a little excessive perhaps, but—for better or for worse—there are no rules dictating a long mourning for a kindly spouse, a short one for a rascal. No, I understand her. But Mrs. Insel—" He sat forward a little in his deep arm-chair, in order to face Maria roundly. "Mrs. Insel, do not you consider you owe Mr. Mallinger the full story of your first marriage? Would not you wish him to tell you if he had endured such a painful episode?"

Maria looked at the floor. "Or perpetrated such a shameful deception?" she suggested in a low tone.

"Oh, Maria—!" Anne began, bursting out on a note of

exasperation; but Mr. Highet signalled to her to let him go on, and she reluctantly subsided.

"I see nothing shameful to you in your story," he went on, carefully watching the widow's face in the leaping firelight. "Whereas not to tell it does seem to me a real lapse of—well, candour, if nothing else."

Maria continued to inspect the floor, but both her companions could see this appeal to conscience had hit home. Mr. Highet added gently,

"Lawrence Mallinger will never blame you for it, that I know."

"If anything, he will be relieved to learn his first offer to you was refused through no fault of his own," Anne put in, then immediately realized Mr. Highet had never heard of this proposal. Covering her mouth with her hand, "Oh, my pet! I am sorry! I should not have—"

But Maria looked up with a little smile and said, shaking her head, "It is of no significance now, dear. Mr. Highet might as well know every thing—and Mr. Mallinger ought to know." Looking at Highet, "You are quite right, sir. Thank you for making me see it. Only . . ."

"If you are frightened, pray let me be with you when you tell him," Highet offered. "Invite him here to-morrow and we shall all three sit together and have it out. I warrant you he'll make nothing of it, but— Will that relieve you?"

"Oh, yes!" Eyes brimming, Maria looked thankfully at him, then turned to Anne. "Only I wonder if . . . Would you, Anne, also . . . Since you know me so long, and understand how it was, and why . . ."

"But gladly! Nothing can be easier," Anne agreed.

"You'll see. We'll all be laughing before it's over, I promise you!"

In the event, this did not turn out to be quite true, though indeed Lawrence Mallinger readily understood how and why Mrs. Insel's innocent deception had been practised upon him, and how it had tripped him up. Far from blaming his bride-to-be, he was deeply moved, and dismayed, to learn of her former sufferings. With all the facts in the open it was easy, at the end of the interview, to settle on a wedding date. The ninth of November was chosen, but the banns (in deference to Mr. Mallinger's eager feelings) were to be read within the month.

With all this decided, and duly announced, Anne found herself curiously at loose ends at Fevermere. Now even Maria did not need her. She must, some time, begin a life without either her or Ensley. Yet she found herself strongly disinclined to make a move.

Mrs. Archibald Highet, however, put an end to that. "Well, Fevermere must be dreadful dull to you now!" remarked that lady one evening, only a day or two after Maria's confession to Mallinger. The newly betrothed couple had gone out for a moonlit walk in the snow while the other members of the house party sat quietly by the fire. "No, nothing to stay for now!" the amiable lady went on, energetically plunging her needle into the pillowcover she was embroidering. "Lady Crombie's footman Starkey told our Claypoole all their Christmas guests went home more than a week ago, and Stade Park, I know, is quite empty but for the Wares. Yes, the happy season has come and gone! Nothing left here but winter. The farm as quiet as a church at midnight—not even the sheep to think about at this time of year, God bless them—and the earth as cold and hard as a stone. There's the rub in farm life, after all," she cheerfully continued, snapping her embroidery out of its hoop, then spreading it over her considerable knees to line it up in a new place. "I've heard of whole families run mad in February. Nothing to do, nowhere to go . . . But that's not true for you, my dear!" she pointed out merrily. "You've all of London, and I can't guess how many private parties to join at the great houses besides. We'll be losing you soon, I reckon—more's the pity!" she added conscientiously, catching a warning glance from her son. She snapped the frame neatly together again, looking serenely down.

But though Mr. Highet's glance had quelled his loquacious mother, he himself said nothing. Since his awkward presentation to Anne of the ear-drops, he had been more than ordinarily formal with her. She felt his silence was, perhaps, an endorsement of at least the idea that she would soon feel dull here, and ought to make plans to depart. Consequently, she hurriedly replied (speaking almost at random),

"It is true that, now Maria is settled, I shall be on my way again. My friends Lord and Lady Grypphon are going to Paris in February. I have agreed to go with them." (Though Celia and Charles were indeed going to Paris, Anne had not in fact consented to join them. In fact, they had not invited her. Still, she knew they would welcome her company.) Smiling, "I hope you will not mind my desertion," she added.

"Lord bless you, no!" Mrs. Archibald promptly assured her.

She received another quelling glance from her son; but since he still held his tongue, Anne was the more persuaded that he too—in spite of his protestations of affectionate friendship—felt she ought not to stay on indefinitely. She therefore made sure, the next day, to write to Celia and ask to accompany her friends to France. Celia's answer that it would please them of all things arrived a week later.

Anne's chief diversion until her departure (set for the twentieth of January, the Monday after the engaged couple's first banns were to be read) was assisting Maria in starting to sew a modest trousseau, and helping her plan how to eke out the sparse furnishings of the bachelor's rooms Mr. Mallinger kept. Her relations with Mr. Highet consisted mainly in civilities. Mrs. Archibald Highet's opinion of the tedium of winter farm life notwithstanding, Mr. Highet seemed to find plenty to do. He spent long hours closeted with Mr. Rand and his own estate steward, or sat alone studying numerous books and monographs on agriculture. Occasionally Anne volunteered to read one of these last, so that they might discuss it together. Mr. Highet always welcomed these offers, listening closely to her opinions; but Anne could not make him understand, somehow, that she quite enjoyed exercising her mind in this way. He imagined she did it only to oblige him and persisted in thanking her elaborately, and rather formally—"As if," Anne sometimes muttered to herself, climbing the stairs after one of these demonstrations, "he were nothing to me, nor Fevermere any affair of mine—as if we were strangers!"

But though his manner towards her seemed unduly strained and courtesy-laden, she could not think how to bring it up without perhaps offending him, or risking embarrassment to herself. After all, it was no part of their marriage bargain to become intimates. Mr. Highet owed her no affection; so, if he seemed constrained, she must bear it quietly and consider that perhaps he believed this the best way to go on. Business-like relations were more stable, she could not deny, than tender ones.

Still, it made her unhappy, particularly after he had spoke so warmly on New Year's Eve. She felt superfluous at Fevermere, and lonely. Maria and Mr. Mallinger had one another, and Mr. Highet had (lowering reflection!) his mother. Altogether she was not sorry to find Sunday the nineteenth soon at hand.

It was a happy day, and the sight of Maria's radiant face across from her in the carriage on the way to church did much to buoy Anne's heart. But when she sat in the pew next to Mr. Highet and heard the banns read out by Mr. Samuels—just as she had heard her own—she could not help feeling pain as well as joy. Had it not been for Ensley, would she ever have agreed to a marriage so solitary and strange? Even to escape from Linfield? But it was done. She stole a glance up at her husband. He seemed absorbed by the service. With a small sigh, Anne likewise returned her attention there.

Leaving the church, she kissed Maria soundly, and Mr. Mallinger almost tearfully (for really, how she would regret Maria!) and swore by every thing that was holy to be in Cheshire for the wedding. The lovers strolled away together on another of their endless walks, while the party that had come from Fevermere four in the carriage drove home only three. Anne kept unusually quiet and, as soon as they were home, threw herself furiously into her packing. It was a relief to think she would be off to London the next afternoon.

That night, at her last supper at Fevermere, her mother-in-law (in spirits, of course, thought Anne) teased her about eating frogs, and catching the shocking morals and manners of the French. "How the champagne will flow!" the old lady chaffed her amiably. "And how elegant the ladies will dress! 'Another glass of burgundy, ma'am?' Lord Wellington will ask you—for I don't doubt you'll dine with the commander-in-chief himself. 'Oh, yes, if you please,' you'll say, 'and another frog leg, if you don't mind.' Oh, my dear!" And she went off into a wild gush of laughter in which Anne had no trouble recognising the ancestor of Henry Highet's explosions.

Since she fully expected, in fact, to meet Lord Wellington often in Paris, Anne did not know how to answer this sally and so sat uncomfortably silent. After a minute,

"Perhaps while you are there you can persuade the French to raise their limits on imported British goods," Mr. Highet said, so soberly that for the first time Anne wondered if he disapproved of her going to Paris. But it was not as if she meant to emigrate, as so many wealthy Britons had since the end of the war opened the city to them and left England in a growing shambles. She intended to stay only a month or two, till the start of the Season.

She answered, smiling, "I doubt whether my influence extends to any circle in control of such a thing, but I shall certainly remember the point if I meet the appropriate Minister."

Mr. Highet did not return her smile but sat in dour silence. Then, "I hear of nothing but plots against the government there," he said. "Be careful."

This time there was no mistaking the disapprobation in his tone. Was it a question of money? But he had said himself the estate was flourishing. No; she thought he disapproved of France. Nettled—for surely part of their arrangement was complete freedom to do as they liked?— she rather coolly replied, "Pray have no fears for me, Mr.

Highet. I have a head on my shoulders—and mean to keep it there."

Though she did not depart till the next afternoon, he took his leave of her the following morning, before he rode out to a farm some miles distant. The awkwardness of the previous evening hung over their adieux, even as Anne (at least) wished it violently away. They were alone, but Mr. Highet was at his most reserved, as if all the warmth of the holydays, the games, the skating, New Year's, had never happened. Anne was confused, but she governed herself, bade him good-bye with as much heat as the chilly spell that had come over him, or them, would allow (which was not much), received his wishes for a pleasant journey, and watched him go. A few hours later, Maria stood by her carriage to see her off. Their parting, at least, was more natural. They embraced, they wept, Maria begged Anne to stay, or if not, to come back as soon as she might; Anne wept harder, would not give a date to her return, shook Mrs. Archibald Highet's hand, and climbed into the carriage.

She had a week in London to pack and prepare. Brief as the time was, she passed it anxiously, fearful lest she blunder into Ensley some where. She had substantially recovered, she felt, from the pain of parting with him; indeed, the month in Cheshire had had the welcome effect of making him seem a part of a much more distant past than was really the case. Still, she did not care to see him yet if she could help it. Fate, and extreme preoccupation, combined to grant her wish: London was behind her in a whirl, then she was rattling in a coach towards Dover, then crossing the water, then in France.

She had never been to the Continent before. Every thing interested her—the hard eyes of the *concierges*, the fantastically rapid French of even the smallest children, the food (so different from England's), the endless flow of wine. They were through the wintry country between Calais and Paris in a day and a half. Then came the heady excitements of the city itself. Lord Quaffbottle sprang to life again: Each afternoon, Anne scribbled furiously his adventures on a jaunt in Paris. She sent the results back to London weekly in the diplomatic pouch (a favour easily won from officials at the Embassy). She accompanied Celia to dressmakers and milliners, glove-makers and mantua-makers, and suddenly, fashionable Mesdames began to cross Lord Quaffbottle's path. With nearly thirty thousand Englishmen in Paris, it was not long before Sir John Pudding, the English emigré, was born (at age forty-six, and weighing nearly sixteen stone). Soon the world of "A."'s letters was teeming with Sir John Pudding's wife, their numerous offspring, the great commander Lord Illington, Mademoiselle Pelisse, le Comte de De, and a host of other characters who made those English people still in England to read of their exploits in the *Times* laugh very heartily indeed.

Anne laughed also, and felt more like herself than she had in some while. Though she missed Maria, she could not imagine a better antidote for the losses she had sustained this winter than the company of Charles and Celia Grypphon. She and Celia often came in from the Opera or a ball and sat up till five in the morning gaily annihilating the reputations of the people they had met that night, or avidly speculating on the safety of the current government (it was true, as Mr. Highet had said, that rumours of a new revolution were heard everywhere), or planning a ball or supper of their own. When Anne came down in the morning Charles was always there, affable, kindly, ready to escort her to a shop or on a brief excursion into the country. She had made a clean breast of things to them—how and why she had broke off with Ensley—and it helped her that they seemed to understand, even to approve, her actions.

As for Mr. Highet, now that she was so far from him, the letters he sent her were (perversely) open and easy. Not tender, or intimate, but quite free of that removed formality she had seen in him those last weeks in Cheshire. It was a relief. Gladly, Anne replied as openly and easily. But she seldom spoke of him.

Celia, though she liked Mr. Highet, took Anne at her word when she maintained their marriage had never stepped outside the bounds agreed on when they contracted it. She introduced Anne as Mme. Highet, but gave a tiny shrug of pure dismissal when asked where M. Highet was. French gentlemen taking an absent husband very lightly, Anne soon had her admirers in Paris, was sent flowers and invited to dance quite as if she had been single. Celia, moreover, appeared to expect her to behave so—to flirt, to pay attention to her toilette (now much refined by Parisian purchases), to encourage this gentleman and deftly fend off this other. But Anne did not feel like flirting. Cheerful as she was, buoyed and exuberant as were her spirits since reaching Paris, she found no gentleman whom she cared to know more than another. When, after some weeks, Celia asked her about it, she replied that perhaps it was too soon after Ensley. Her feelings were not yet her own.

But then a letter came from Lady Bambrick, mentioning that Lady Ensley was expecting a happy event. Save a mild satisfaction that Ensley and Juliana should succeed in this desired object, Anne felt nothing. Not resentment, nor the painful throbs of a crushed (or even a mending) heart. They had their lives, she hers.

Why then was her heart not her own?

The answer to this question came to her, not in a blinding flash (as such things sometimes are said to do), but slowly, over days and weeks. First she suspected it dimly, then she thought of it clearly, at last she dared to write the possibility in her diary. Finally, one evening when the young Vicomte Langloît smiled brilliantly down at her and inquired (for lack of a better way to bring the conversation round to her pink, perfect ears) where she had got those lovely opal drops in them, Anne felt such a rush of pleasure in saying, "A dear friend; my husband, in fact," that she knew beyond any doubt that—however he might feel towards her—she loved Henry Highet.

The vicomte must also have heard something particular in her answer, for he soon recalled a pressing engagement elsewhere in the ball-room (they were at a soirée given by the Austrian Embassy) and vanished into the crush. Anne did not regret him, or even notice his desertion very much. She had turned her attention to a quandary that was to absorb her for the next several days:

"I love my husband," was the way she phrased it to herself. "Dear heavens! Now I'm properly dished!"

SIXTEEN

THERE COMES A MOMENT IN THE AFFAIRS OF EVEN the most polished wit when, facing a crisis, he (or she) does what any dullard would do: obeys his common sense. In the affairs of Anne Guilfoyle Highet, this moment had come. She loved her husband. He did not know it. She would tell him.

Oh, she did not reach this idea all at once! No, she first entertained many other schemes. She considered never telling him, asking someone else to tell him, going away and staying away till one or the other of them should be dead. She considered elaborate stratagems to test (before telling him) how the news would affect him. She thought of feints to bring him to Paris, to London; excuses to go, herself, to Cheshire. All these ideas and many more, requiring every kind of analysis, special knowledge, Machiavellian insight, occurred to her. And yet, when she had sifted and pondered, and muttered aloud to herself, and written the possibilities in her diary, and obliquely (she thought) sounded Celia and Charles out for their opinions, and mulled and reflected and puzzled till she nearly forgot the question—at the end of all this, it came to her, that she must go to him and frankly tell him the truth—that the minimum she owed to herself, to the possibility of her own happiness, was to let him know.

The idea of writing the news in a letter she discarded after some ten seconds' meditation. No, this sort of intelligence did not travel well. It must be she herself who travelled. And so, one wet morning late in March, she kissed Celia and Charles good-bye in the high hall of their Paris house and embarked (escorted by Lizzie) upon the long journey. She stopped at the house in Mount Street only long enough to write that she was coming—nothing else. Then she was off again, travelling somewhat arduously through cold, early spring rains and the resulting mud. She arrived about four in the afternoon on the third day after leaving London.

All this way she had been planning her actions, considering how she would say to Mr. Highet what she had to say. The more she thought of it, the more convinced she became that what she was doing was necessary and right; at the same time, however, the closer she got, the more difficult, even dangerous, her task seemed. Suppose her announcement horrified him! Or disgusted him! And yet, the more she reflected, the more she had an idea . . .

Never mind. She would not concern herself with consequences. Never in her life had she felt so wholly in the grip of an emotion. Frightened as she was, she could no more hide her feelings from Mr. Highet than—well, than Mr. Mallinger had been able to hide his from Maria.

Trigg admitted her, politely ignoring how travel-stained, crumpled, and weary she was (though not half so much so as when she first crossed the threshold of Fevermere). Holding his hands out for her bedraggled cape, "Very good to see you back, if I may say so, madam," he told her, his red face beaming.

"You may certainly say so," Anne replied with a smile. She turned to permit him to remove the cape. "And if I may say so, it is very good to be back. Mrs. Trigg's rheumatism—?"

"Better, thank you for asking, ma'am."

"Ah, that is well. And is—er—is Mrs. Archibald Highet at home?"

"Mrs. Archibald is at the rectory, taking tea with Mrs. Samuels."

Well, that was good luck. Untying her bonnet, "And—ah, Mrs. Insel?"

"With Mrs. Archibald, ma'am."

This was a disappointment; but Anne sternly told herself it was just as well. She drew a deep breath and asked finally, "And is Mr. Highet at home?"

"In the library, ma'am."

Oh heaven! So near as that! Her heart at once began to thump. "Will you tell him, please, that I shall look for him there at five?" she said, handing over the bonnet. "And ask Joan if she will kindly fetch some tea and a basin of hot water to my room."

"Very good, madam." Trigg bowed his round head and vanished on his errand. Anne climbed the stairs muttering to herself, "I must not be afraid, I must not be afraid . . ." Once in her bed-chamber, she bathed her temples, swallowed some lavender drops, changed her shoes, and tried to compose her thoughts. Her very spirit seemed to tremble inside her, but she would not lose her courage. "I must be brave, I must be brave," she mumbled to herself while (tea drunk, toilette freshened as well as could be) she made her way back down. A ship's clock on the mantel of the library struck five exactly as she knocked on the door, then entered. Mr. Highet was alone.

He looked up from the depths of a leather-covered armchair, letting the volume he had been studying fall to his lap. He seemed enormous—impossibly broad-shouldered, impossibly long of leg. Even his features were overlarge, the soft, brown, sleepy-lidded eyes, the red mouth, the dark spill of curls. Anne's jade eyes widened unconsciously as she looked at him, and the expression on her face made it appear that *he* had somehow startled *her* by being where he was.

After a moment he stood, smiled, and came across the room to shake her hand. His dark eyes scanned hers as if searching for something—the reason of her sudden return, no doubt—then turned away as he offered her a seat on the leather sofa, a glass of negus or a cup of tea.

"I have had tea, thank you, sir," she said, striving to appear calm in spite of an ungovernable quaver in her voice.

He sat beside her on the sofa, gazing down on her golden head. "Paris has done you good, I think," he said, still smiling. "How glad I am to see you. But—"

"Why am I come home?" she filled in as he hesitated, then coloured and amended, "Why am I come back to England?"

"No. I was going to remark," he said, with his customary slowness, "that you seem nervous. Is any thing amiss?" Impulsively, he took her hand, which was shaking (and shook the more after he took it, for she had felt again that shock of pleasure he sometimes inspired in her). "You are trembling," he observed, kindly concern in his voice.

"Mr. Highet, I shall speak bluntly and quickly, for I do not know how else to tell you what I have come to say. I apologize in advance, for I fear I must take you by surprise. Indeed, as you once said to me, you may dislike what I have to say very much. You may deplore it. In that case—as you also said to me—I can only beg you to remember I would not have spoke except for"—she faltered, looked confused, went on—"expect for the very sincere admiration and—"

Again she faltered. Mr. Highet's face had gone from looking rather alarmed to an expression of complete absorption in her words.

"And esteem . . ." Her voice broke off. She was pale, and gave (though she did not know it) an appearance of being very fragile and small. She glanced down at the hand that still held hers, steeled herself to one last push and said, "In brief, sir, I know it is no part of our agreement—in fact quite the opposite—and I am very sorry for it; but I have come in the last months to like you so well, to esteem you so much, to enjoy your company so greatly, that I can only conclude— Can only conclude—"

Here the words stuck in her throat. As in a nightmare, she could not go on. She looked wildly about. When she heard the following words, she could not at first locate their source:

"I love you."

Had she said it? She swallowed. Her mouth and throat

were dry as dust. She did not think— Anyhow, the voice had not seemed to be her voice— But Mr. Highet was turning towards her, taking his hand from hers and using it to hold her shoulders, to hold her so she faced him. His large eyes were looking intently into hers and— Good God, it must have been he who said it! Listen, he was saying it again!

"I love you, Anne. If that is what you have come to say to me, if that is what you apologize for feeling, pray tell me so at once," he entreated her. Tears—she quite thought tears stood in his eyes.

She could only peep, "Yes," gaze up at him, and be suddenly crushed in his embrace. And here, in his arms, her face covered with kisses, she came as close to fainting as she did on that long-ago day—years and years ago, it seemed—when Mr. Dent had told her her fortune was sunk under the sea.

However, she recovered, and in due course regained her composure to such a degree that (mind, this took half an hour or so) she could sit back and ask, "But my dear— Henry—if you felt all this for me, why did you . . . ? When did you . . . ?"

"Begin to love you? Before we married." Mr. Highet also sat back, folded his hands, and gave a smile that was unmistakably sly. "You see, long before you came into Cheshire, I knew of you. Not only through Herbert, but because—contrary to your prejudices—we are not quite so sleepy here as you imagine. I am perfectly aware of the identities of a whole host of London personalities. I read the papers (as I hope you are aware by now, at least). Moreover, I correspond with any number of people who go—as I do not go—up to town now and then. I knew your reputation as a wit, and as a beauty. When you came,

I found both reputations richly earned. But you see, to me wit and beauty are all very well—very enjoyable, most gratifying—but they are neither of them attributes that make a person admirable or worthy. They are attractive, but hardly sustaining."

Mr. Highet paused here to stroke his wife's face, then tenderly kiss her forehead. Only her impatient, "Yes, and then what?" recalled him to the fact that he had broke his story off at the middle.

"Ah, yes." Carefully, he folded his hands together and placed them firmly in his lap, as if bidding them to stay there. "I confess, then, that when you first arrived here, I viewed you with a good deal of—well, scepticism. Your contempt—at the very least, your condescension," he put in, seeing she was about to protest, "towards me and, indeed, every aspect of farm life, I observed directly and without surprise. I must admit, I had quite a bit of fun at your expense in those early days—when you no doubt imagined you were having fun at mine."

Anne leaned forward to object. Then she remembered the first time the Highets had come to dine with her at Linfield, recalled Mr. Highet's (as it seemed to her) extreme, blundering obtuseness, his unwanted pity for her, and a flood of other details—and sat back in silence.

"Yes," said Henry, seeing in her face that his point had been made. "And yet I found as time wore on that you were a deal more spirited than I had expected. Behind your wit lay, not only contempt, but real intelligence and—occasionally—sincere good humour. Behind your beautiful face was a thinking mind: and not only thinking, but generous, as I saw from your behaviour towards Mrs. Insel, towards the staff of servants left to you there, and even, eventually, to me. I began to suspect, as was indeed the case, that you had no choice but to stay here. I admired the cheerfulness with which you confronted what must have been a dreadful change. In brief, I came by slow degrees first to admire, then to love you.

"And yet," Mr. Highet went on, "there was the problem of Lord Ensley. For although I know you did not think it, I was perfectly aware all the while of your—" Now it was Mr. Highet's turn to stumble in his words, and to change colour a little. Darkening, "Your *liaison* with him," he presently resumed. "What was I to make of that? I knew your removal to Cheshire must have unsettled things greatly between you. When I met him—I make no secret of it—I did not like him. But finally I read in the *Gazette* the announcement of his betrothal. Cheerful reading for me, I assure you," he continued. "I made up my mind to offer for you as near to the very hour of his marriage as I could manage."

"You did not! You deliberately—?"

With a smile, "Naturally," he said. "I suppose you thought it coincidence?"

She nodded, staggered to learn Henry Highet could have been so calculating.

Smoothly he went on, "It was quite the opposite of coincidence, I assure you. I could not imagine a moment you would be more likely to accept the idea. For I knew then, you see, that you still did not love me. I believed—or hoped—that I had earned your good opinion, and even to some extent a mild affection. I suspected that, in time, if I played carefully upon your—well, let us call it a streak of delightful perversity in your nature—if I kept myself distant enough, you might eventually come to me. But I offered knowing full well I might be letting myself in for a life of the extremest frustration. Still, at the least I could be your friend, and do you a service, and then—" Finally, he shrugged. "Life is long. I suppose I had my hopes," he concluded. "And indeed, when I saw you in London; when I heard you say you had broke with Ensley—I fancy I saw you do it, in fact, at your dinner party?" he interrupted himself.

Anne nodded again.

"Yes. My hopes began to rise. I asked you to Cheshire on the pretext of helping Mrs. Insel, but if she had not needed help, I should have thought of another reason. And when you came, and seemed to enjoy yourself so well—when I saw you play with my nephews, and even laugh at yourself—well, I confess it was all I could do to keep from seizing you and carrying you off to— Ah, er-umph," Mr. Highet broke into a short fit of coughing and lamely concluded, "Ah . . . seizing you."

"But if you felt all that," Anne objected, still rather stunned by this recitation, "why were you so awkward and distant with me my last weeks here? You were, you know. It hurt me."

With a long sigh, "I know," he said. "It was the only way I could keep myself from—from doing—the other . . ." He looked so uncomfortable that she laughed and said,

"You mean, the ah, er-umph! seizing thing? I see. But even so—why *did* you not make a clean breast of it? Tell me every thing, as I told you today?" she asked, in real perplexity.

Gently, "I wanted you to come to me," he said. "If I had told you . . ."

He fell silent and Anne realized that, indeed, if he had told her, until very recently she would have been at best confused, at worst repelled.

"It was too soon, at Christmas, any how," he took up presently. "I suppose I would have told you, one day— but first I hoped you would come to me."

"As I have," she said, reaching her hands to him and slowly submitting to be drawn again into his embrace. "What a story!" she said, after an interval. "How could I ever have imagined? I feel rather like a fly who has been strolling—whistling and thinking of nothing in particular—round and round on a spider's web! And you, sir, are the spider!"

But this he would not endure. "You are something of a spider yourself, Miss Innocence," he objected. "Do you suppose I am ignorant of the identity of 'A.'?"

Aghast, she drew back from him. "You do not—"

"Oh, but I do! All the while you were here, and were writing of Lord Quaffbottle in the country, I was reading of Mr. Mutton Slowtop, the idiot sheep farmer," he informed her. "And his giantess mother! Merciless, you are! Do not deny it. Lord Quaffbottle, like you, has gone recently to France—and now how astonished I will be if he does not find something to take him away. Oh, you are 'A.' right enough. In the flesh!"

"Then you knew all the while?" Her chagrin, her horrified remorse, were such that she could say no more, but only sat with her mouth agape, staring at him while she recollected how many insults she had heaped upon the cloddish Mr. Slowtop and his monstrous parent. "You never told your mother?" she demanded, as this new, awful possibility dawned on her.

Mr. Highet shook his head. "She will have enough to perplex her when she learns our marriage of convenience is to become one of great inconvenience to her," he said. Then, observing the relief on Anne's formerly stricken countenance, he threw his large head back. He opened his mouth, was silent, then whipped forward with a terrific whoop and exploded into as hearty and prolonged a fit of laughter as any his wife had heard from him. But this time, instead of remaining aloof, or settling into a freezing silence, or even sitting apart with a polite smile pasted on her lips—this time Anne joined in.